DUNGEON MADNESS

Book Two of
THE DIVINE DUNGEON Series
Written by DAKOTA KROUT

MOUNTAINDALE
—— PRESS ——

TABLE OF CONTENTS

ACKNOWLEDGMENTS

There are many people who have made this book possible. Chiefly among them is my *amazing* wife, who always encourages me to do the best at any task I set my mind to. She somehow finds time in her already-overwhelming schedule to help me be the best author, produce the best work, and be the best version of myself I possibly can be. Thank you, my love!

Last but certainly not least, a great thank-you to all of my friends who made their way through the awful early editions of my epic fantasy in order to give me advice and suggestions on storyline and descriptive writing. A special thanks to my friends Dylan S. and Hans M., who helped revise this book. And then revise this book. Then... revise again. Thanks to both of you for your careful reading and comments! Friends like you are rare and wonderful.

PROLOGUE

ROUGHLY TWENTY-THREE DAYS AGO

A sibilant-yet-melodious voice sounded in the predawn darkness.

"Prepare, my acolytes. It is time to begin. For too long, we have suffered injustices at the hands of the children of light. Each time we have worked to better the world for those like ourselves, we have been forced once more into obscurity and degradation. This is truth, yes? Our time has finally come!"

As one, hundreds of men and women of multiple races stood to attention, then briskly and properly genuflected toward their dark leader.

"Hail, Master! It is as you say!"

Their timing—beat into them—was perfect. Their voices were synchronized. *Necromancers* were bowing to another being! The entire fighting force showed a discipline and level of training that had not been seen in a military since before cultivation became widespread so many millennia ago.

Black eyes flicked between the bent forms, studying posture and ensuring proper respect was given. Slowly, a smile appeared on the face of the Master. It would have made any sane man shudder. "*Lovely.* And well done. It is far past time to give you all your orders. Rise."

The people straightened their posture as one, trying to never show a hint of discomfiture in their Master's pernicious presence.

"As I am sure you remember—those of you who survived—the last time we tried a plan of this magnitude, we were stopped. We were rushed, unprepared for our true opponents in the world. We were defeated... because of one simple fact. We stepped into the scorching light before we were ready. We allowed ourselves to be goaded, to react to the fear and hate, the propaganda spread against us." The voice paused, savoring the moment. "Now, we are ready. We prepared the caverns and the altar. Our brother sacrificed himself to *become* our arsenal, and all he now needs in order to provide us with an unending stream of weapons and minions—all we need—*are sacrifices!*"

Monstrous creatures stepped forward, falling into ranks behind the rigid horde of Necromancers. "Go. Take your creatures, your minions, your slaves. Take them, and do what no army of the undead has done before. Return with *captives.*"

The Master gave a minuscule nod to his troops, and they began to cheer fanatically. The undead moaning and clattering joined the noise, and soon, the terrifying laugh of demons and abominations joined in as well.

The hordes marched into the night. They would bring captives as ordered... after they had their fun.

CHAPTER ONE

Dale's group wearily began ascending the stairs that led to the surface. Covered in dust, blood, and other foul substances, their main goal at this point was to clean themselves up and go to bed. They began moving upward, but Dale nearly missed a step when a voice sounded in his mind.

<Can you still hear me?>

"Son of a–" Dale whispered as his eyes darted around.

The others in his group took no notice of his odd behavior; in their minds, there were plenty of reasons that Dale might be talking to himself. He had just died, after all.

<I ll take that as a yes. Try something real quick. Instead of speaking aloud, try *thinking* your words at me,> I eagerly directed him.

Dale's mind spun as he tried to think of something to say before finally landing on the obvious. "*What are you?*" he thought as hard as he could.

<Dani, I'm not getting anything from him. What should we do? I think talking aloud will make people think he is mentally damaged, so... Oh. Is that it? Yeah, I'll tell him. Dale! Hi. My name is Cal. I am the dungeon, so kind of 'aim' your words at me.>

Dale again tried to use his thoughts, pretending he was talking to this 'Cal', "*Hello?*"

I responded in a very excited tone, <There we go! Listen, Dale, I don't really think you should tell other people about this. We don't have time for explanations since you are about to meet up with a bunch of powerful people, but we *will* talk later.>

"Hey! You can't just suddenly pop into my head and then not give me any infor–" Dale began thinking indignantly at the voice. At that very moment, they reached the top of the stairwell and opened the door to find a sea of cheering people... sprinkled with a handful of furious faces.

"You irresponsible little shit!" Madame Chandra stepped forward and started aiming a slap at Hans, who had the highest cultivation rank of Dale's group and was their de facto advisor.

Rose smoothly stepped in and blocked the blow, shock on her face. "Grandma! What is *wrong* with you?"

"We just saw you fight a *Beast*, Rose!" Chandra hissed at the young Half-Elf. "He was supposed to *protect* and *guide* you all! Not lead you directly into a death-trap!"

Rose stayed firm in the face of the High Mage. "He did everything he could! That Beast was something none of us could have expected, and it broke almost every bone in Hans's body when he attacked it, giving the rest of us a chance!" Rose was flushed and furious. "We would all be dead *right now* if he hadn't been able to inject poison with the daggers he found! That Cat was moving too fast for us to land a single hit until Hans basically *sacrificed* himself for us!"

Several healers voluntarily stepped forward and offered their services to the weary group as Rose tried to calm Madame Chandra down. Most of the healers subtly avoided Dale; he was covered in a foul, waxy substance that stunk like rotting meat dipped in a latrine. Rose slapped away a few hands that got a bit too liberal with their 'examinations', while the hulking barbarian of their group—Tom—allowed the hands of blushing ladies to roam freely.

Hans chose that moment to collapse into unconsciousness, quickly followed by Adam, their cleric. Adam had used a large portion of his cultivation base to create a powerful incantation during the fight with the magnificent Beast, a Distortion Cat. Using his Essence in such a manner had permanently dropped him a full rank, reducing him to D-rank four. If his cultivation rate continued as it had in the past, it would normally take him a year or more to attain his former power. Luckily for him, he was near a high-density source of Essence and should be able to rank up much more quickly.

Hans's issue was more basic; he had recently had many of his major bones broken as well as suffered major internal damage to his organs. The intervention of the Glitterflit type Bashers in the dungeon had healed him enough to escape the dungeon, but after a cursory examination from a healer, he was rushed off to surgery. Several of his bones had been shattered, and when they were repaired inexpertly down below, they hadn't aligned properly. Hans would need to be shaped by a flesh Mage to fix all the damage correctly and would be out of commission for at least a week.

The other members were also properly examined after that announcement. Luckily, all of them were deemed healthy. Dale was given several odd looks, likely because he was far healthier than the others and *he* had recently died. Although, obviously, he *had* gotten better. Several people tried to grab his attention, but immediately upon catching a whiff of his rank self, they all made appointments to meet him later. As soon as he was deemed healthy, Dale rushed to the river to get cleaned up. Frank had sent a runner to get him soap and clean clothes, refusing to allow Dale to walk through highly populated areas.

Dale pulled off his armor at the edge of the river, diving in as the last bit of clothing fell to the ground. He surfaced with a gasp, the ice-cold mountain water shocking his system. He looked around as the water darkened and quickly began scrubbing himself as hard as he could with some sand to break up the crusty mess on his body. The slow current carried the foulness away; a fish bobbed to the surface a few yards downstream, stunned by the high concentration of toxins dripping from Dale's body. He had never seen a fish gag before...

The young man shuddered as he remembered the sadistic Beast that had skewered his heart, how it had stared into his eyes practically laughing as the light faded. He tried to remember what had happened next, but there was a blank between that and waking up again—a *very* unexpected outcome. He was shaken from his dark thoughts when a young man ran up with a basket containing a robe and toiletries. Dale thanked him and promised a tip when he got back to his tent. The freckle-faced boy grinned and ran off to his next task. Dale had a reputation as a good tipper.

After scrubbing at himself for nearly ten minutes, Dale realized that no matter how much effort he used, he couldn't seem to get rid of the odor. With a start, he realized his mistake. He quickly found a toothbrush and crushed-mint paste in the basket. While he enjoyed the feeling of his teeth returning to a normal taste and coloration, a small crowd of people gathered at the edge of the river. These people were his current council: Father Richard to represent the Church and its interests, Guild Master Frank of the Adventurers' Guild, High-Magous Amber of the Mages' Guild—specifically the smaller subset of the portal guild, Madame Chandra to represent the... well, her own interests, Dale supposed. To round out the group, there were a few people that came with these esteemed individuals to take down notes.

"What," Dale croaked around the toothbrush, letting some foam drip down his chin, "never seen a dead man take a bath?"

One of the note takers gagged.

Father Richard's eyes flickered with some dark memories. "Hmm. Of all the things I have seen dead people do, I have to admit that bathing is a first for me."

Dale snorted, sending tears to his eyes as the mint in his tooth cleanser burned his nostrils, though he welcomed the pain. It was the first time he had smelled something new since he woke up.

"No, Dale. We are here to make sure that you are... okay," Madame Chandra spoke gently.

Dale snorted again. "Am I okay?" He pondered a few moments. "Yup. Just dandy." He spat out the toothpaste and dunked under the water again, rinsing himself off one last time. He walked to the shore, tired enough that he was willing to ignore the fact of his nudity as he came out of the water to collect his armor. He grabbed it and unceremoniously began scrubbing the accumulated filth off his breastplate.

Amber gasped at him.

"Dale! Your body! Oh my..." Tears sprang to her eyes as she looked at the previously husky man. His body looked emaciated, the flesh sagging around muscles that no longer pulled his skin taut. All fat had been burned away, leaving a very thin man with haunted, blazing blue eyes.

"Your eyes used to be brown, didn't they...?" Richard muttered under his breath.

Madame Chandra took a more direct approach. "Dale, what happened down there? We saw only the last bit of the fight when the darkness cleared away. We saw you get killed... but then you got up for some reason. How? Actually, no. Leave the armor here, and I will have it cleaned professionally. You are just swirling that goop around. Put on that robe, and we will go to the *Pleasure House*. You *obviously* need some food with high nutritional density. As much as you can eat—on the house as usual. Come with us, Dale." Her speech ended on a pleading note.

Dale nodded, dropping the armor and stumbling toward her. His stomach more screamed than growled as it was reminded that food did—in fact—exist somewhere nearby. Frank wrapped him in a robe and led him toward the restaurant with the others following behind.

CAL

I had tried communicating with Dale again several times after he had left my dungeon, but as soon as he stepped fully out, either he could no longer hear me or was simply not responding. Well, *fine*! I had more important things to do than keeping tabs on a low-level adventurer anyway.

<I'm having some trouble here, Dani,> I told my faithful Wisp.

"Anything like the Cat that nearly killed us?" Dani chuckled sardonically.

I thought for a moment, just long enough to make her grow nervous. <Um. No, nothing like that...>

Dani nodded fiercely. "Good! Because you promised me that you would take a week off experimenting, right?"

<Well, a few days... would a few hours be sufficient?> Doing my best to ignore her glare, I quickly continued, <Let me explain the problem? When Dale's new group came through here, I threw everything we had at them. *Everything.* There are no living Mobs in here except a few *Shroomish*, and with the barrier over the entrance, we are not getting any influx of Essence from outside.>

She began to look a bit concerned. "Oh, I hadn't thought of that... ""

I tried to ease her stress, <I don t know if it will be too much of an issue. After all, they will most likely open the door in a few days. The Essence gathering Runescript in here is pulling in every drop from the dungeon and *keeping* it here while I work to absorb it. What I wanted you to consider is adding a new floor and possibly changing how I do a few things.>

She looked at me querulously. "Change a few things? Like what? I like the idea of adding a new floor, but will you have the Essence to do that *and* make changes *and* respawn every Mob in here?" Every time she said 'and' like that, it made me a bit more nervous that I was giving myself too much to do, but I felt that these things *all* needed to be done.

<Well, I might not get it all done right away, but I will over time. Shall we go over the changes I want to make?>

She acquiesced to my request a bit grumpily, but I didn't hold it against her. We had spent the last day being closer to death than we had ever come before.

<Let's start with the first floor. The mining area is annoying to me, but it brings in a lot of rather weak people every day. I want to expand that room so more people can work at once and widen the entryway so that a full contingent of miners and tools can come through if need be. Right now, two people can squeeze through the archway at a time, and I want to make it wide enough for at least five.>

Dani thought for a moment and nodded. "That'll be fine if you are going to add another floor anyway. Can we get rid of Shroomish and other weak things on that floor? Oh! Can we add a flower room there? Maybe grow some herbs in a more concentrated spot? I want a garden!"

I laughed at her sudden enthusiasm. <Sure! I know you have been bored recently, so how about I give you total control over what goes where in there? In there, you say 'do this', and I will follow all your orders!>

"About time!" She playfully frowned at me. "Thanks! It'll be the prettiest room in here..." She turned misty-eyed at the thought.

I looked at her form. <Wow, you can shape your body? You literally look like a human eye that is tearing up.>

Dani haughtily informed me, "There are many things that I can do that you've never bothered to ask about!"

<Oh? Like what?>

She scoffed. "I can't tell you. How would I be able to remain aloof and mysterious?"

<...>

"What?"

<This sort of response is why I never ask...>

She squeaked with outrage, flashing crimson.

<Anyway, I was thinking that we leave the Bashers on that floor with a squad of enhanced Bashers as the floor Boss. We leave the Shroomish—they are our only ranged attackers—sorry about that. On the next floor, we have only enhanced Bashers with the old Alpha squad's upgrades, keeping Raile as the floor's Boss. Good so far?>

"Yes, but I feel like you are about to make me mad again for some reason," she muttered her dark premonition.

<Good guess!> I chuckled at her glowering. <I want to make the third floor a mix of Distortion Cats and advanced Bashers, with a Cat as a Boss if I can manage it.>

"Cal! We just got the Distortion Cat killed, and you want to make more of them?! Aren't you going to have bad memories, seeing them all the time?" Dani demanded. If she had feet, she would be stomping around throwing a tantrum.

I tried to soothe her, <No, I think that making them our guards will help us get over it quicker. Plus, we survived just fine, didn t we?>

"Not the point!" She sighed loudly, "Fi-ii-ne. What else?"

I smiled, knowing she was as interested in these changes as I was, even if she pretended otherwise. <Well, you know how I sometimes get distracted when battles are going?>

Dani snorted. "What? *You*? Distracted?"

<You think that you are *sooo* funny. Back to my point, sometimes people don't get the loot that they should because I forget to drop it for them. What would you say if I wanted to instead have a place in the room for loot? A place where all the loot goes that they *should* be getting? That way, I can just refill it when a group empties it. Oh! Better yet, I can set one of these Essence collectors to a seed pattern! Then it will automatically refill!> I was nearly shouting in excitement by the time I finished.

"Hmm. I thought you liked giving personalized loot?" Dani reminded me of the fun I had messing with people.

<Well, I still can, right? If I see something *really* spectacular or learn about a glaring weakness, I ll reward them for it,> I promised her. <I'm thinking a box? Maybe a hole in the ground?>

Dani rejected those options, "No, it needs to be something obvious. How about we make a treasure chest?"

<A what?>

"It is essentially what you are describing—a really fancy box that swings open on hinges. We can put it at the exit to the room, so groups will have to survive and travel all the way across the room to collect their rewards." Dani was getting excited that she could use her experience from before she bonded to Cal.

"Kantor did something similar, but I never knew why—so I never brought it up. Now it makes perfect sense!"

<Great! You will help me with the design, right? I've never seen a 'chest' before.> I was excited to start, but there was more to discuss. <Now, since we are getting larger again, I was thinking that instead of only allowing the people on the second floor to leave the dungeon on the stairwell,> I paused for dramatic effect, <I could arrange the Boss Rooms so that after every Boss they could choose to leave! That way people will be more confident in fighting the Boss immediately.>

"I don't understand what you mean. Do people *not* feel confident when going into the Boss Rooms?" Dani queried with a frown. "Why do they bother to come in here then?"

I explained my reasoning as succinctly as possible, <I should hope they are worried every time they fight! What I mean though is that some people will turn around and leave instead of fighting the Boss because they are worried that they will be too injured afterward to get out of here. If there is an option every level to make a quick escape, the Bosses will get a lot of kills, much faster than they normally do. If they get enough kills, they may be able to evolve naturally without my help. That is my hope at least.>

"Smart!" Dani exclaimed. "That's a good plan. Where should we start?"

<Let's change up the first floor, then populate it. After that, we will make the small but necessary changes to the second floor and finally add on the third level. If I work hard, I think I will be able to get everything done before they unblock me.> I chuckled at the thought that I would soon be able to fight again.

CHAPTER TWO

Dale woke up flailing, reaching for a weapon to throw off the shadowy figure stabbing his...

He sat up, shaking off the nightmare. Grimacing, he attributed the night of tossing and turning to eating like a pig right before bed. Certainly, it couldn't have been because he was stabbed through the heart the week before. He almost started drooling at the memory of the huge steak and sides of vegetables, although they had barely satisfied him. With all his meridians opening at the same time, his body had used all available resources to purify himself and supply Essence to the tissue throughout. A week to heal and recuperate wasn't enough, but it would have to do for now.

Thinking back to how no one had an explanation for how it happened without his knowledge, he felt a little better. If no one else knew what had happened, maybe it actually *was* the dungeon who had fixed his body. Maybe he wasn't going insane and hearing voices that weren't there... He shook himself, refocusing on his body.

His Essence was pouring along the open meridians, constantly infusing his flesh with health, strength, and resilience. His body looked ruined, emaciated to a skeletal frame. He looked down; his ribs were prominent enough to be countable, and his waist looked positively nonexistent. Despite his outward appearance, he had never been stronger. His muscles were permanently infused with the Essence that now flowed through them, strengthening him beyond what his body had been capable of before. Dale could arm-wrestle a small bear and easily win right now, and his new body was at its *weakest* point currently.

While he would be able to put flesh on again, he would never need to worry about gaining fat. His body now processed food very quickly, burning through all the calories and protein he could take in. When he was again well fed, his muscles would be like steel and his skin like hardened leather! His stomach chose that moment to remind him to go eat, so he reached for his armor... only to find it missing.

He looked around wildly, then shook his head as he remembered how Madame Chandra had told him that she would have it cleaned and he could pick it up today. This also reminded him that he could eat at the restaurant for free for the next week, since he had saved Rose. He perked up; the *Pleasure House* served breakfast! He got to his feet expecting stiffness or pain, but his body moved as smoothly as if he had just had a light workout. Must be a side benefit of all the Essence sloshing around in him.

Before stepping out of his tent, Dale started cycling Essence to his eyes so he could see the flow of power in all things. With this enhanced vision, he could see blots of color moving around outside, denoting moving people. Seeing no one near his door, he cautiously stepped outside, feeling naked without his armor.

"Boo!" a harsh voice shouted next to him.

"AHH!" Dale whipped around, raising his fists, only to see his friend Hans laughing at his terror.

"Ha-ha-ha!" Hans laughed, slapping his knees as he doubled over. "You sounded like a little girl! Oh, man! Whew! I needed that. Thanks, buddy!"

Dale glowered at him. "Hans! You should be resting! Also, don't you think that you should be a bit nicer to me? I died last week!"

"What? Nah, that isn't something to get worked up about. Happens to all of us. You are fine now, right?" Hans stopped laughing once he saw the serious look on Dale's face.

"Dale," Hans sounded deadly serious now, almost angry, "you can't let this affect you so much. Yeah, that sucked, but are you going to give up on cultivating? Are you going to stop fighting in the dungeon? Should *I*? I owe over six hundred gold to a flesh Mage for all the re-sculpting of my body. Should I just tell him 'too bad, I'm done fighting because it is dangerous'?"

Dale looked like he had been slapped. "I... I don't..." he stammered.

"The correct answer is *abyss no*!" Hans shouted, getting angry now. "Dale! Look at you! Sure, you look like shit, you smell, and it is likely you won't get a woman until your eighties, but what else is new? How do you feel? Do you feel like a warrior, a champion that slew a monster *way* above his cultivation rank, or are you going to allow yourself to feel like giving up so you can keep acting like a *victim*?!"

Dale flushed, "I'm not acting like–"

"Oh really? Then why have you been all weepy and pouty this whole week and so far this morning? Yeah, I heard how you were acting, and I've been watching you for almost a whole day to see if the information was accurate! *I* was embarrassed for you! You are acting like a spoiled little brat that has a bunch of people to run his life for him. Did you even realize that the *entire council* was there last night? Why do you think that was? You think *just maybe* they might be getting together to see if you are mentally fit to continue owning this land? You think they *might* be plotting to petition the king for a writ that will allow them to take the land from you if that is the case?"

Dale's face paled; he hadn't realized that was even a possibility.

"You need to *start* going to council sessions and *stop* letting people you *barely know* make all of your major life decisions for you! Now, tell me that you were acting stupid because you were tired, and you will be the strong, assertive Dale I know you to be!" Hans nearly shouted in his face.

"I... I'm sorry, Hans, I have been acting stupid because," Dale swallowed, "because I was so tired out. I'm good now. I'm all ready to get back to the team."

Hans's demeanor changed like a whiplash. "Oh great! Good morning, Dale. How are you today?" He went in for a hug, acting like he hadn't been about to start slapping the man.

"I'm... good?" Dale licked his lips nervously.

Hans shoved him away, spitting.

"Gah! I know I was standing close, but you didn't need to lick my lips! What the heck?!" Hans spit to the side. "You need to brush your teeth."

"Well, your morning breath isn't fresh and minty *either*!" Dale shouted back. They both stopped for a second and looked at the other. The tension lasted only a moment as they both started laughing hard enough that their sides started to hurt.

"Ugh... C'mon, Chandra owes us breakfast. I'd rather not go back to the mess hall. I hear the head cook has been on a rampage because no one is bringing him herbs anymore."

"Free food at the *Pleasure House?* I'm so there!"

They started walking toward the towering restaurant that had savory smells wafting from it, collecting their teammates Adam and Tom on their way. They exchanged pleasantries as they made a bee-line for the food; that is, they took many unnecessary turns and side routes in order to avoid the early morning traffic. By the time they reached the doors, Adam looked ready to faint from hunger and Tom was getting loud.

Tom boomed at the now-nervous host, "Hello, tiny person. We need a table as presently as can be arranged. As a boon from the owner, Madam, we have been offered a place to eat as often as we are able to find the room in our stomach. I have found the room, have you yet found a table that can seat us?"

The stammering host tried to get in a few words, but as soon as Tom stopped speaking, a side door slammed open, revealing Rose in a set of comfortable robes. "Tom! Keep it down. It is barely light out, and if you keep the noise going you are going to wake up Grandma! She will *literally* slice your face off!"

"I highly doubt that she would..." Tom began loudly, just before Hans slapped him lightly across the face.

Hans whispered, wide-eyed, "I've seen it happen. She is strong enough that she replaces it and heals you, but you really don't want that to happen. It is *rather* unpleasant."

Tom flushed, then went pale. Mutely, he nodded

They were led to a table as far from the ground floor as possible, into a room where the highest quality food was served. Quickly, a server appeared with a selection of exotic fruits and fried meats for an appetizer. More courses were laid upon the table each time one was finished, so there was no point in time when they did not have food readily available. Finally, groaning, they had to beg the server not to feed them anything else. He smiled and bowed, vanishing into the kitchen as they prepared to leave.

"Well, what should we do today?" Adam polled the group with a loud burp. "Oh, more room!" He finished a small scrap of meat on his plate.

Dale shrugged noncommittally. "No idea. The dungeon is going to be closed until they finish the walls and stuff around it. They don't want to take any chances that the Mobs will escape and attack unprepared people again."

"Just when I was finally able to start cultivating..." Rose sighed in frustration.

As a chaos cultivator—a person who had dual affinities in celestial and infernal Essence—she had never been able to properly cultivate before going into the dungeon. Even after the trauma of the last few days, she was eager to get back into the dark depths.

Hans looked around, seemingly offended. "Ugh...? What do you all mean by 'we'? I thought that we had decided that we were a temporary party?" When everyone looked at him in shock, he chuckled, "I'm just playing! There are some things we should do today though. Tom, you need to come with me to the main Guild tent. I'll sponsor your entrance to the Guild and make our team official."

Hans glanced at Adam next. "Adam, you should get with Father Richard about the best way to strengthen yourself and learn to use your staff to its best effect. Rose, you should get your bow checked out and get ready for this evening. Dale, you know what you need to do today." He gave him a significant look, which made Dale nod and look away in shame.

Rose looked at Hans with a raised eyebrow. "What is happening this evening?"

Hans grinned lecherously. "Our second date, of course!" He waggled his eyebrows.

"In your dreams, old man." Rose crushed him without a second thought, walking away. "I have my own plans for the day. See you all later!"

Adam hadn't said anything, but his face was pale. Dale nudged him, "What? You okay there, buddy?"

Adam nodded slowly. "You want me to train with Father Richard? Is this *Richard Demonbane*? The man trained by Cardinal *Kere Nolsen the Slayer of Shades*?" His voice was frantic and rose in pitch to an uncomfortable level as he spoke.

"I've never heard that title before, but I only know one Father Richard, so... most likely?" Dale smiled at his pale friend. "Don't worry, he is really nice. He does sometimes take over conversations, but otherwise, he's a really good person to be around."

Hans joined in smoothly, "Well, I mean he would have to be, but meeting your childhood hero isn't often an easy task." He grinned slyly at the now blushing Adam. "Is it, Adam? Eh? Is it?"

"Leave the cleric be, my mentor! Allow us to tarry here no longer. My heart races at the thought of joining the Guild! A childhood dream is what thee wishes to acknowledge? The Guild and being one of its members has always been my dream. I have held this dream dearly for years and..." Tom's voice faded in the distance as a sour-faced Hans was pulled along toward the Guild tent.

"Heh. C'mon, Adam. I will introduce you to Father Richard. I have to meet with him anyway." Dale started leading his friend away when the host for the restaurant yelled for him. He turned back. "Yes?"

Chapter Three

"Dale?" the host asked to make sure of his identity.

"Yes...?" Dale leadingly prodded.

The man nodded. "I have some gear that was left for you by the *Sword Polishers*."

Dale did a double take at the name. "Uhhh. What? I'm not sure I should be associated with... oh! My gear! They are the professional cleaners, then?"

"Yes, please gather this up. I can't lift the morningstar more than..." The host trailed off and blushed as he realized that he had said more than he intended.

"No problem!" Dale stepped into a small side room and put on his armor, smiling at the familiar weight. For the first time since he had purchased it, the armor didn't stink, have any blood on it, and was rust-free. It also didn't fit quite right, but seeing as his body was several sizes smaller than it had been the last time he wore it, this made sense. Leaning over, he picked up his bound morningstar. The massively oversized weapon weighed almost forty pounds. Without the Runes on it that allowed for it to be nearly weightless in his hands, he could have never used it in combat.

When he supplied a bit of Essence and activated the Rune, he could swing it as easily as a thin stick—without losing any of the destructive force its weight afforded. Truly, it was a potent weapon. He stopped admiring himself and looked around for the shield, not seeing it. He stepped outside and asked the host where it was.

The man uncomfortably informed him that the shield had been destroyed in the dungeon, and the scraps that he had brought back were unable to be salvaged. Dale nodded; he had expected this but had been hoping it was not damaged so extensively. It was a rental, after all...

He met up with Adam outside, and they moved toward the only other permanent building currently in the area, the church. Walking into the coliseum-style area where Father Richard gave his sermons, they admired the solid quartz floor that normally allowed people to see into the dungeon's Boss Room. To their shock, instead of the Boss floor below them, all they could see at the bottom was a purplish rock that Dale recognized from previous encounters.

"Cursed earth?" Dale gasped, dumbfounded at the sight.

A morose voice sounded from across the open area, "It appears so... It seems the dungeon has blocked the view until we open the front door again. Why dungeon? Why do you do this to me?"

Dale looked up and saw Father Richard standing from his morning prayers. "Oh, just who I was looking for! Father Richard, this is Adam. He is a cleric that joined my group recently, and we were hoping that he could come to you for training in the celestial arts."

Richard sighed, eyeing a blushing Adam. "Why not? It isn't like anyone comes here for a sermon unless they can see the fighting going on below... I suppose I could use an acolyte or two. Come along. We will start immediately." He turned away, Adam hastily following, but he stopped when Dale cleared his throat. "Yes?"

"I'm going to be calling a council meeting today, and I was wondering if you have a room that we could use to stay away from prying eyes and ears?" Dale delicately informed him, looking around at the empty building.

"I'm sure we could manage that for the right price. Let's-" Father Richard began earnestly.

Dale cut him off before he could finish, a bit of steel in his voice. "Surely in this *very large* church, you could find a room the council could *occasionally* use?"

Father Richard looked confused for a moment, then began to sweat as he realized what Dale meant. When he had built the building, he had only been given one lot of land to build on, but the final construction took up three full lots. The price for using the land had yet to be... negotiated.

"Oh, yes! Of course, anything you need, Dale! Let me say how good it is to see you taking an interest in the work going on in the area! Come along, young Adam. Let's go see what you can do and where we can start your training!"

Dale chuckled under his breath as a nonplussed Adam was whisked away. He turned around to look for the other members of the group that he needed to talk to. Hopefully, they would all be as willing to participate as the priest. He thought about the order he'd go talk to them. Dale eventually decided to find Chandra at lunch, Frank right away, and Amber just after Frank. Amber was likely a morning person, right? He would have to find out. Dale walked to the Guild tent, entering directly into Frank's office—past an indignant secretary that tried to make him wait his turn.

"Some of *us* have been *waiting* for a meeting!" a voice called out. Dale looked over his shoulder to see Hans tapping his foot with arms folded in front of his chest. Dale grinned, made a rude gesture, and pulled a rope to close the cloth they used for a door.

"Good morning, Dale," Frank cordially greeted him. "Can... whatever this is... wait? I have meetings all morning."

"It'll be just a moment, sir," Dale promised him with a dismissive hand wave. "I'm just letting you know that I am calling a meeting tonight. We will be holding a council meeting at the church."

Frank looked up from the invoice for defenses he was reading. "Hum? A meeting for what?"

Dale nodded; this was a new thing for him, so he could deal with a bit of confusion. "A council meeting—we have things to discuss. I've let things run on their own for too long, and I need to remind everyone that this is still *my* land. Dinner will be provided. Please be there at five o'clock." He turned on his heel and walked away without waiting for a reply.

Frank frowned and looked back at his invoice.

CHAPTER FOUR

Dale walked directly across the well-worn path in front of the Guild tent, stopping in front of a light purple tent that was roughly half the size of the one he had just vacated. There was a post driven into the ground in front of it that had a wooden plank attached. He rapped on it—assuming it was a knocking post—in an attempt to call out a representative of the portal guild. When no one appeared, he started knocking louder and faster, not stopping until he heard shouting. His new cultivation rank allowed him to hit the post impressively hard.

"*What?*! *Why?*!Is the sun even out? Why are you bothering us this early? If there is still someone out there when I get there, I am going to turn you into a newt..." The tent flap was thrown open, but the angry face of the inhabitant quickly settled into a neutral expression. "Oh. Good morning, Dale. What?"

"Good morning, James. Is Amber available?" Dale replied, making James pull in a breath with a hiss as he looked around.

"Dale, it is very important to follow protocol when talking about people in public," James noted severely. "You need to call her 'High Magous Amber'. Also, no. She is not some floozy available to you whenever you feel like having a chat."

"Fair enough. I will try to remember the titles. Please tell *High Magous* Amber that I am holding a council meeting tonight at five o'clock in the church. Dinner will be provided, and anyone not in attendance will lose their *temporary* seat on the council. Have a pleasant day, good sir." Dale nodded at the demanding man, walking away whistling as James fumed.

Having nowhere else to be until lunch, Dale walked into the area that had been set aside for shopping and began browsing the shop kiosks that were beginning to open for the day. Pleasantly surprised at the variety of goods available, Dale weighed the thought of spending his coin against the thought of needing something and not having it. He had just decided to look at the potions available from the apothecary when the sounds of a scuffle reached his Essence-enhanced ears.

"Please! This cost me thousands of gold! I'll be ruined! Please, just take my money!" a voice begged from the shadows of a tent that connected to a kiosk. Obviously, the merchant that was here had rented a small plot of land and set up shop. The sign out front showed a pair of the crossed pickaxes that miners used in the dungeon.

"Well, then it'll be worth taking, won't it? We'll take you up on the gold as well. Thanks for the idea!" A couple of voices chuckled at that comment, which was followed by a meaty thud, a small grunt of pain, and a sob of frustration. Soon after, the tent flap was thrown open, and three hairy men walked out of the tent laughing darkly. They froze momentarily when they noticed Dale looking at them, but then tried to nonchalantly walk away.

"Stop right there, criminal scum!" Dale called harshly. He immediately felt like a moron for his word choice, but what were you supposed to say in these situations?

They stopped, but not for the reasons Dale wanted. "What did you just call us?" They rounded on Dale, the biggest one gripping the shaft of a familiar pickaxe.

"You heard me," Dale announced boldly, walking toward them slowly. "Drop the pick and the stolen money. Do so, and I will let you leave the mountain gently, after you gather your gear and supplies. If you don't... I won't be so gentle."

"What are you gonna do? Pass out on us? Bleed all over me? You look more than half-starved! Where did you get that armor? Your dad give it to ya? It's three sizes too big!"

The big, hairy man swung the pick a few times as though he were warming up. Dale was watching him and saw him pass Essence into the pick to activate it, unwittingly binding it to himself.

Dale's eyes narrowed. "*That* was a mistake. You just bound that pick to yourself!"

The man looked at Dale in surprise. "So? It's *my* pick." He let the pick swing into the ground, blasting away a huge shower of dirt and small stones as the force enhancement Rune activated. "Leave off, or that'll be you, pipsqueak."

"Well, now you have two options. You are going to have to either pay for the pick, or we will have to unbind that pick from you. There is precedent for people to *die* to make that happen—please make the smart decision." Dale looked at the others, reaching for the hilt of his morningstar which peeked over his shoulder. "And you two?"

"Shoo, brat!"

One of the muggers was clearly getting nervous. "Hey... I'm really not looking for trouble. I didn't know what they were planning to do in there..."

The big one growled at him. "Shut it. You're in this with *us!*"

Dale nodded at the reluctant man. "Please lie down and put your hands on your head." The man did so, while the others jeered at him.

Dale grasped his weapon and swung it to the side to bring it in front of him. The men's eyes widened in shock as he held the massive weapon in front of him with one hand, pointing it at them. "Last chance."

One scoffed, while the other spat, "Fat chance! That's obviously not real, so how about you fu–"

Dale moved forward, taking an aggressive combat stance. The thieves sputtered and moved to attack before he could take the initiative. The largest brute swung his pick with a grunt, forcing Dale to dodge. The weapon hit the ground, spraying up another shower of dirt and gravel.

The second attacker pulled out a short sword, truly little better than a long dagger. It was rusted from having blood left on it after battles. The blade was serrated by hand—it was likely he had taken a file to it. That would cause nasty wounds and lots of bleeding if Dale was cut, so he gave the weapon as much respect as the Inscribed pickaxe. The blade licked out at Dale, but he dodged backward, turning the maneuver into a tumble as the pick came at him again.

The two took turns attacking, working together in a way that spoke of long familiarity. They should have been able to *easily* overpower the smaller man, but... there was a factor in Dale's favor that the two men didn't understand. Dale had been fighting to the death daily for *months*. These slow, broadcasted attacks were fairly easy for him to avoid so long as he didn't panic. He was also trying to incapacitate them without killing them since he had no wish to become a known murderer. The blade of the short sword came at him, but Dale stepped past it, closing with the surprised killer. He lashed out with his fist, and his newly strengthened muscles allowed him to break the arm at the elbow, twisting the bones into an unnatural shape.

Thinking the man was out of the fight, Dale dodged another slow attack from the pick-wielding man. A scream that didn't sound like pain behind him made him duck. He dodged a wild blow just in time. The man with the twisted arm was swinging his sword with his off hand. His broken limb flailed around, obviously causing him pain. He didn't seem to care and continued slashing wildly at Dale.

Dale rebutted by finally bringing his weapon to bear. He swung and impacted the man in the leg, the force behind the spiked head causing the unprotected flesh to burst like an overfilled waterskin. He swung again, catching the man in the head as he dived at him. The dying man was able to tackle Dale to the ground before fully expiring, leaving him exposed to the man with the pickaxe.

With a strange look on his face—a cross between the sick elation of an impending kill and the loss of a longtime friend—the brawny miner stepped forward and reared back with the pick for a powerful attack. Dale braced his weapon on the ground and activated the Rune, sending the head of the weapon flying forward. The oversized spiked ball tore through the side of the man, leaving a gushing, gaping hole. The miner caught his breath, gagging and vomiting before collapsing. The blood poured from him unabated for a few moments before slowing to a crimson trickle.

Dale shakily deactivated the Rune and the head of his weapon *whooshed* back to settle on its hilt. He felt stunned; he had never killed a human in combat before.

It... it was too easy. The overgrown rabbits in the dungeon were harder to kill than this! Sure, they didn't have the sheer strength of these two, but they were harder to hit and avoid.

Dale had to fight to hold down his gorge.

"Oh god. Oh man. Pl-please, sir... d-don't kill me!" The man lying prone begged, half gasping, half gagging as a puddle of blood sloshed over him.

Dale looked away from the sight, almost in shock. It was disturbing how this man thought that Dale would kill him as he had the aggressive thieves. "I'm not going to. Do you have any money that you haven't stolen?"

"Not much... sir!" the man belatedly added, fearful that Dale would take offense.

Dale sighed, swinging his weapon sharply through the air to get the gore off it, frustrated that it had just been cleaned and was now filthy again! "Keep ten silver for the portal fee, and go somewhere else. You have an hour to gather your non-stolen items and go to the portal. If you try to take anything else that you stole, you are to leave my mountain immediately. If you take more than an hour, walk off my mountain and travel without the use of a portal."

"Y-you. You're him. I'm s-sorry, I'll go!" The man scrambled to his feet and ran, leaving Dale wondering what the ex-thief meant by that last comment.

CHAPTER FIVE

Dale grunted and gathered the stolen pick and money the men had on them, then went over to the shop and knocked on the wooden kiosk. Soft sounds of weeping reached his ears, quickly cut off as the man heard the knock.

"I'm closed," a miserable little voice floated out to him. "Permanently."

Dale had a grim little smile appear on his face. "You may want to come out anyway."

"Dale?" The man shocked him by recognizing his voice. He scrambled out of his tent as Dale waited. Noticing the pick, the man fell to his knees and tried not to cry in front of the man who had given him a plot of land for so cheap. "You got it back! Thank you, Dale, thank you!"

The man was familiar to Dale, but he couldn't place him. "Here you are. I think this is your money as well. I'm sorry to say I cannot remember your name. It has been a while, and we only met briefly...?"

Accepting the proffered goods, the now smiling man waved away Dale's concerns. "My name is Tyler. I am a merchant that currently specializes in general goods and pickaxes for miners. I used to be an antique dealer, but rare coins and decanters are a very niche market. I also dabbled in identifying unknown items such as Runes, but the Spotters' guild is far more knowledgeable than I."

Dale smiled as well. "I'm just glad I was able to help. You bought this pick then? When?"

"Just this morning!" A small glint showed in Tyler's eyes. "Are you interested in getting into the mining business?"

"Not so much—my team was the one that sold it! I was just thinking that I may have some spare income for once." Dale laughed at the crestfallen look on the merchant. "Don't worry. I am sure someone else will want it as soon as the dungeon is open again."

"I certainly hope so!" Tyler fervently agreed. He looked just a bit past Dale and went a pale. "Oh. I see how you were able to... reacquire... my lost goods."

Dale looked back at the bodies behind him. "Yeah, I'll go get someone to take care of those. Who oversees security around here? I'll have to report this to someone, I'm sure. Hopefully you will testify that this wasn't murder?"

Dale's question got him a strange look, and Tyler told him something he hadn't considered. "No one does security here. Since this is essentially a campsite right now, no one has bothered to put that kind of infrastructure in place. Also, no one can get the materials for constructing *permanent* buildings since there are no trees here, so instant justice is the norm; we have no prison of any type. Well, there are trees at the bottom of the mountain that we could use... but hauling those would take way too much effort for most people to bother. Since the portal is open, most people that can afford it are going home at night. Hence, this stays a campsite." Tyler was babbling a bit, but to be fair, he had had a very trying morning.

Dale's brow furrowed; he apparently had more items to add to the agenda for that night's meeting. "I take it that since the main population that is staying is only merchants and people too poor to afford to leave, the crime rate is beginning to increase?"

Tyler nodded sadly, glancing at the bodies again.

"Why haven't I heard anything about this?"

Tyler grimaced. "The people that are too poor to leave are also not strong enough to fight past the first floor in the dungeon. Look how easily you dealt with those men." He pointed at the dead thieves. "Now, if you spend most of your time with the Guild—strong men and women—you should have realized that this sort of thing is far beneath their notice. The philosophy of the Guild is that the *strong* prosper. If you lose your property, it is your own fault—for being weak."

Dale was disgusted by this fact, a side of the Guild he had never seen before. "They just let it happen?"

Tyler nodded again.

"Okay, Tyler, you seem like you have a good head on your shoulders. You also seem business savvy, and you are the first person I've talked to that doesn't seem to have a grudge against me. Would you do me a favor?"

"For you? Anything!" Tyler exclaimed proudly, reaching into the secret compartment where he stored the majority of his money, obviously thinking that Dale wanted a reward. He was very glad the thieves hadn't found this drawer.

Dale grinned. "Great! I am having a council meeting this evening to discuss the problems in the area. I would like you to take a position on the council. You would be there to represent the miners and low cultivation-ranked people in the area. Would you accept such a position on the council, as a favor to me?"

Tyler slowly dropped the fistful of gold coins back into the storage chest. To his credit, he did not answer right away. He carefully weighed his options and thought about the responsibilities and paperwork a job like that would entail. Eventually though, he winced, mumbled under his breath, and agreed to join.

"Wonderful! We meet tonight at the church, five o'clock sharp, please." Dale waved and went on his way, returning to the

Guild to find someone to dispose of the bodies. After a few coins changed hands, two men ran off to collect the bodies and place them in a small wagon near the dungeon entrance. Apparently, dumping bodies into the dungeon was a convenient way to get rid of them. No one wanted to go out of their way to bury them after all. Dale was disturbed by how easily their murder was accepted, as well as how easily they would vanish without a trace.

When it got closer to noon, Dale hurried over to the *Pleasure House* and met up with Madame Chandra, quickly explaining about the plans for the evening before meeting his friends for lunch. Chandra agreed to bring the food if Dale paid for it, which was fine with him. At lunch, he talked with his party and ironed out a few strategies for what he should say tonight; they gave him a few good ideas and conversation topics to discuss with the group.

After lunch, Dale went to his daily training with Craig. His mentor had him practice his combat forms with Josh to get used to using his new and oversized weapon in combat. Luckily for Dale, the Rune on it that allowed for him to lift it didn't reduce the power it had when it struck an opponent. The increased size did make it a bit more unwieldy but also increased the range he could strike his foes with. At the end of the session, he was very happy with his new morningstar as well as very grateful for the tips his instructors gave him. He went to towel off when he noticed that he hadn't broken a sweat.

He thought for a moment and realized that he was also not sore or tired from the full-speed fighting; he also realized that the benefits of opening all his meridians were beginning to show.

Craig nodded in approval when Dale mentioned this and informed him that over the next few days, he would only get stronger. When his body finally got used to the changes, he would only need two hours of sleep a night, be much stronger and tougher, and even his capability for learning would increase.

Dale took this all in stride, having heard this explanation before. He moved on to the next phase of his daily training, sitting down to cultivate. He opened himself to the Essence of the heavens and the earth and began drawing it in.

At least, he tried to. When he tried cultivating from the earth around him, instead of Essence, a thick corruption began to flow into him, forcing him to stop cultivating immediately. Worried that he had just damaged his Center, he looked within himself... and was shocked by what he saw.

He had traced the flows of Essence through his meridians since coming back to life but hadn't *really* looked at his Center-well, not beyond a cursory check to feel his ranking. Now looking closely, he found that his Center was contained entirely in a Beast Core! Inspecting it mentally, he found Runes delicately carved in the gemstone which allowed his Essence to flawlessly integrate with his body, sending and receiving Essence to and from his meridians. He searched for an explanation, but the only solution that came to mind was that the dungeon truly *had* messed with his body. He needed to find answers, but with a start, he remembered why he was inspecting himself in the first place.

He searched for any hint of the corruption that he had absorbed but did not see anything in his meridians, Center, or Core to show that he had absorbed any of the taint. Frowning, he opened himself up and began cultivating again—and again, only received corruption for his efforts. Quickly stopping, he tracked the corruption as it raced to his Center, but right before it entered... the taint vanished.

Frowning, he focused harder on his meditation and realized that there were several tiny Beast Cores around his

Center! One of them had a soft, brown glow, and he realized that this tiny gem had absorbed all of the corruption he had taken in. For a moment, he was tempted to run and ask Craig about this development but ultimately decided to keep it to himself. He tried a slightly subtler question first, just to test the waters.

"Craig, why couldn't Rose cultivate before going into the dungeon?" Dale asked his mentor, explaining about Rose's dual affinity channels when Craig asked who she was.

"Oh, that explains it." Craig nodded sagely. "To cultivate with multiple affinities, you need to draw Essence from a source containing *both* of them at the same time, else you will only draw in corruption. If she had tried to cultivate before, she would have shortened her lifespan a good deal. Let me amend that a bit—I say 'same source' which could mean getting fire and earth from molten metal or lava, but a high enough concentration of both in an area *would* allow for cultivation."

"I see. So, if someone somehow opens an affinity channel, they would need to cultivate both types at the same time. Therefore, if it were earth and fire, they'd *need* to be around burning earth such as lava or melted metal? There isn't a way around it?" Dale was drawing on his recollection of a half-forgotten conversation that took place months ago.

"Correct, but opening a second channel is unwise as it can ruin people. Increase your rank too fast, and it can lead to health issues or an unstable Center. Also, increasing your rank can hurt you if you do it too fast. If you keep smashing through your limits without giving your body a chance to acclimate to the new power, your flesh may not be strong enough to contain it," Craig informed him ominously, making Dale remember his rapid—forced—advancement to the D-ranks.

"That is why Nobles—with their cultivation techniques that draw in so much more Essence than the average person—need to constantly train their bodies at the same time. Typically, the young ones spend ten hours a day exercising or fighting and have healers on hand to fix torn muscles and damaged flesh when they overdo it. They actually only cultivate an hour each day but can absorb as much Essence in that time as most can in a month. Also, they are the only cultivators that bother with the E-ranking."

Dale was dumbfounded at the effort that Nobles had to put into their cultivation. "How old are they when they get into the B-ranks? Wait, E-rank? I haven't seen anyone in that rank that I know of..."

"Ah yes. The 'echo' rank. The E-rank—obviously between the F and D ranks—is the process where a strong cultivator—usually their parent—'echoes' their cultivation technique into the target person. This 'attunes' the new cultivator's body to Essence and allows for more rapid growth since there are fewer impurities for the body to purge as a cultivator increases their rank. Of course, this process has its own risks. As for the rest... hmmm."

Well," Craig thought a moment, "ascending into the B-ranks is not as easy as breaking into the D or C-ranks. Just absorbing Essence is not enough; you need to make a connection to a fundamental law of the universe. That is, you need to learn the true name of a concept to channel your Essence through and bind your aura and cultivation base to it. This binding has to be compatible with the Essences that you use so that you can exchange your varied Essences for Mana."

"Let me guess," Dale muttered dryly, "it really hurts."

Craig looked at him admonishingly, then grunted and nodded slowly. "Nothing in our world worth having is gained without pain and effort. This process, in particular, is quite punishing, which is why there are so few Mages ascending each year. The connection allows Mana to flow through you, replacing all bonds of Essence with bonds of Mana. The Mage ascendant is literally ripped apart at the smallest level and rebuilt with Mana. I'm told there is nothing more painful known."

"Naturally." Dale shook his head. "Back to my point then—how long does it take them to reach the peak of the C-ranks?"

"They begin training their bodies at age five. They are shown how to cultivate very pure Essence at six, just so they don't become corrupted as they grow. At fifteen, they are tested to see if their bodies can survive the harsh conditions needed. Most fail and are tested again at age twenty," Craig began his lecture, settling into a familiar cadence as he talked.

"From fifteen to twenty, they begin to open their meridians, and their physical training is doubled. Twenty hours a day. When they are tested at twenty years old, those who are deemed acceptable are given their family's cultivation techniques. Those who fail... well. They are given what are known as 'branch family' techniques. These techniques are intentionally, deliberately not as powerful as the main family's technique. It is meant to keep them subservient to the main branch. By twenty-two, they are expected to reach the D-Ranks. By the age of twenty-five, the C-ranks, at which point they are considered adults in their families. By thirty, they are usually almost ready to ascend into the B-rankings."

"Considered children until twenty-five?" Dale was aghast. In the mountains, the average lifespan was forty years. By twenty-five, most couples had several children. He was considered odd back in his old village for not going out to find a wife, but he had been too busy—and that was before finding the dungeon. Now he was busy for other reasons.

Craig nodded. "Not quite. They are considered children until they reach the C-ranks, but some geniuses have been known to do this in their early teens. What is wrong with being considered a child, though? When you are going to live for several hundred years and you don't need to worry about income, food, or health issues... why not?"

"Wow. I cannot even imagine that kind of life! I had always seen royals as pampered, spoiled brats," Dale muttered a bit too loud, making Craig wince and look around, muttering worriedly under his breath about treason. Dale looked up and noted the position of the sun, realizing that he needed to leave if he wanted to make it to his meeting on time. "Thank you, Craig. See you tomorrow then."

"So long." Craig waved. "Careful with the almost-treason..."

Dale made his way to the church, avoiding stumbling drunks that seemed to be everywhere. The Guild was providing free beer and ale while they built defenses around the dungeon entrance, and people were certainly enjoying and taking advantage of this benefit. Walking on to the stairs, Dale was greeted by a pale, sweaty, and exhausted looking Adam.

"Adam! Are you alright?" Dale asked his friend, concern evident in his voice.

"Yeah... just... exhausted..." Adam panted. "This... way..." He led Dale into the church, stopping at a door and waving him through. He seemed to fold in half as his head sank down, trying to catch his breath.

"Um. Thank you, Adam. Don't die." Dale walked into the room, ignoring the glare sent his way. The other members of the council were there, including Tyler–who looked very nervous around these powerful individuals.

"Thank you all for coming. We are here to discuss the growing population around the Dungeon and what steps we need to take in order to make this a successful settlement and not just a work camp," Dale announced, taking the chair pointed at by Madame Chandra. "Dinner should be on the–" He looked over as the door swung open to reveal covered platters. "Ah. Dinner is here. Thank you, Madame. Let's eat, and then we will start our discussions."

After the last plate had been cleared and everyone was sufficiently stuffed, Dale asked all non-council members to leave before resuming the conversation. "I have been failing myself and my people by foisting the responsibility of running the city on to other people. Today, I was reminded that allowing others to run my life could only lead me to ruin. Not that I think my counselors don't have my best intentions in mind, of course," he qualified his statement as a few frowns appeared on the faces around him. "I simply think that it is time to start making this into a safe, secure settlement."

"Dale, I hate to have to be the one to bring this up," Frank cleared his throat, "but you are hardly qualified to run the area as a camp, let alone a city. If, on the other hand, you were willing to sign a few of the landowner rights over to me, I–" Frank was cut off as the others jumped in loudly, denouncing Frank and trying to explain how they were the most qualified to run the place.

Father Richard was almost shouting, "This place needs the moral guidance only I can provi–"

"I can plan the organization easier than anyone! My access to logistical–" Amber hissed.

"I am stronger than all of you–" Chandra smirked belligerently.

"STOP!" Dale released a roaring growl. He continued speaking to the room full of surprised faces, "I will not be ceding my rights to *any* of you! Or to anyone else! This is *my* land, and I'll fight to the god-blasted death to keep it!" He stared them down until they looked away, blushing at their behavior. "I have already taken steps to correct my deficiencies as an administrator. Madame Chandra, I have recently come into enough money to purchase the memory stones, so please order what we discussed."

"What?" Frank began, then coughed as he realized his constant interruptions were starting to make him look bad, as though he had ulterior motives. "I mean, didn't we discuss that I would provide any teachers you needed?"

"You did," Dale agreed, "but I need more than just fighting instructors. Madame Chandra is taking care of the details for me, so please don't worry that I am going to pass the cost on to you. Now, if all personal concerns can be set to the side, there is some business to discuss."

"Go ahead, Dale. I'm fairly certain you have our full attention," Amber chimed in ruefully.

Dale nodded. "Good. I have had some major issues come to light today. Walking around, not looking for trouble at all," Father Richard snorted softly at these words, "I came across a merchant being robbed. Tyler, our newest counselor, can attest to this firsthand. I took care of the bodies after I stopped the thieves, but it never should have been allowed to get to that point." Dale looked around at faces that were rapidly turning to boredom.

"Also, I have been noticing large piles of garbage and waste. The paths, such as they are, turn to mud if there is so much as a hint of rain. Living quarters are erected haphazardly, and there is almost no organization. I need to find a new path to breakfast almost every day!"

The others shrugged a bit; most of this had no effect on their lives. No one would dare try to rob them, and a simple cycle of Essence made mud fall away from their feet. Sure, breakfast was important, but they all had it delivered to them in the morning. To top it off, they were nearly immune to disease due to their power. Dale looked around, shocked that the entire council—except Tyler, who was nodding along—seemed not to care at all.

Dale powered onward, "We need a guard force that protects the people here, someone that knows about sanitation to take care of our issues, and a city planner that can lay the groundwork for buildings and roads. Also, we need to designate areas for bathing and cooking. Drinking fouled water again really isn't *particularly* high on my to-do list."

Frank started talking a bit condescendingly, "Dale, I think you are putting too much thought into this without really thinking at all. For one thing, finding people to do those mundane jobs will be rather difficult around here. Also, how are you going to pay for this? Your personal wealth may be rather high for someone your age, but it isn't enough to fund a city."

"I may be able to allay your concerns, Guild leader," came a voice that sprang from the shadows of the room. The Dark Elf Brianna stepped into the light, pulling a chair out and seating herself. Only the shock of not noticing her until this point kept the others from attacking her.

Frank's eyes narrowed. "Oh? Who are you, and why should I not kill you and throw your corpse in the dungeon to rot for interrupting us, Dark Elf?"

A nimbus of Mana-powered light had appeared around each of the Mages in the room as soon as Brianna's presence was known. Dark Elves had bad reputations after all.

"To answer your questions in order, I am Princess Brianna of the Huine nation, the ambassador charged with securing good relations with the person in control of the land a Silverwood tree is growing upon. Also, a full member of the council." Shocked faces looked at Dale, who nodded. "As for the second question," her eyes flashed, and Frank found himself blind while a blade tickled his neck; Brianna breathed softly into his ear, "because you can't."

Vision returning, Frank looked at the Elf who had not seemed to move from her relaxed position on the chair. "You're a god's-blasted Moon Elf." He spat on the floor.

"Hmm," was her uncaring reply. "Sorry I'm late, Dale. No one told me about the meeting. I just happened to find out about it."

Dale nodded, trying desperately not to show that he had forgotten she existed. "Thank you for finding out and attending. Since I had been unable to get notice to you, I wouldn't have held it against you. You mentioned you may have some solutions to our problems?"

"I do indeed. I would be more than happy to provide a guarding force—one that will patrol the grounds unseen. That way, there will be no interruption to business and crime will be handled... quietly. I already have several contacts on the way to fill the positions of city administrator and sanitation officer." Her slouched, relaxed position never changed during this speech.

"Pah! And what will this cost us?" Frank barged into the conversation again.

Brianna eyed him like a tasty morsel. "Oh? Now it is 'us'? I do believe that you were attempting to drop the entire

cost on Dale a moment ago just so you could ignore the issues."
Frank paled a bit without looking at Dale. Brianna continued,
"No, we care little for gold and such nonsense. We will need a
small area to set up a barracks, an administration office, and an
embassy if it won't be too much trouble." This last phrase was
directed at Dale.

"You will have it. Let's allow the city planner to plot the
best locations for that," Dale agreed, speaking slowly in an
attempt to appear as if he were actually considering the offer. "I
don't want a haphazard layout like I saw in the capital a while
ago. I want clear line-of-sight down streets and easily defensible
areas. To that point: defenses. We need walls, stone roads if
possible and maybe areas where people will be able to take
shelter if caught in the weather. Winter is fast approaching."

Dale cut off Frank as soon as he started blustering again,
"Yes, I *know* it will cost money, Guild leader. Anyone have an
idea about how to raise the funds?"

There was silence for a moment; then Chandra spoke
up, "Well, I have been wondering why you have not been
collecting a fee from people living here. That, and you have not
been taxing those who enter the dungeon. The Guild is charging
their members, but there is a huge amount of money leaving–
without any going into your coffers."

Dale almost knocked himself out slapping himself in the
forehead. "Seriously?! Why has that not been...?" He took a
deep breath. "Well, I seem to recall being told that the council
was formed to protect the area and that it would have my best
interests in mind. That has been proven false on yet *another*
issue. Thank you for bringing it up *now*, at least."

The other members winced, fearing that they were about
to lose their chance to influence the area. Or worse, be told to
leave. Instead, Dale surprised them. "From now on, council

meetings are going to be an open discussion, as we've always done in the mountains. Anyone with an issue—anyone who has a stake in this future city's success—will be allowed to speak to the council without retribution."

Dale sighed as the people around him made faces. "This means landowners, merchants, and people who *live* in the area and enter the dungeon. People who only show up to challenge the dungeon get no say and will pay a heavier tax on goods taken from the dungeon. My council will hear the complaints of the people living here and bring a plan of action to the city administrator to try and fix as many issues as possible. Never forget—please—that the final say will always be *mine*, and I hold the right to revoke any decision."

"I know it is not possible to please everyone, and that is not my intent. If there are *real* issues that have an impact on people, we need to address them. That is my focus. Start collecting a fee from anyone who exits the dungeon, and make sure they sign a simple contract before they enter that will compel them to pay a fair amount. Unless there are other items to discuss, we are done here for the evening." Dale looked around, but everyone else was shaking their heads. "Anyone want off the council after hearing this new information?"

More fervent headshakes and a few people murmured 'no'.

"Great! Chandra, Brianna, may I speak with you in private, please?" Dale shooed the others out. "Madame, I need those stones as fast as possible. Brianna, I need to hash out the details of our agreement with you and have us sign a Mana sealed contract. Just words between us will not be enough."

Brianna snapped her fingers with a grin. "Drat."

CHAPTER SIX

The restructuring of the floors had taken a couple full days; moving them into the positions I wanted was Essence-intensive. Adding a very basic third floor took another day on top of that. The third floor had been interesting to design because I found an underground stream that was icy cold and flowing dangerously quickly. Originally, I had planned to use the water for traps, but Dani had come up with a better idea.

"Cal, what we are looking at there is a generator for water Essence! The faster it moves, the greater the amount of Essence that will be released by it as it flows! If you can constantly add a bit of dungeon soil to it as it flows downstream, animals and magical Beasts can potentially get addicted to the Essence if they drink enough! Over time, that will draw them in from hundreds of miles away!" Dani bubbled as cheerfully as the stream.

<Wow! I didn't know that was possible! ...Obviously. So, moving water generates Essence?> I threw a question her way as I began to change the course of the water a bit.

"Yeah... kind of. There is a bit more to it than that. I've never really taken the time to explain that to you, have I? There are two kinds of Essence around you: 'loose' Essence and 'bound' Essence. I started calling the Essence in the air 'loose' and you just kinda went with it." She giggled.

<I can't be curious about everything; I would never get any work done! So, what is it?> I playfully admonished her.

"Fair enough, yup. So 'bound' is what you can pull directly from the element that contains the Essence you are after. It requires a lot of cultivation to become refined enough to move into a being's Center. You remember how it is pretty difficult to pull Essence from stone, right?" she bounced a question back to me.

<Yes, and I would rather not have to do it ever again, if that is okay. I really like my new Runes.> I looked fondly at the Runes that pulled in Essence and condensed it for me. <Automating tedious tasks is awesome.>

She laughed. "Actually, that's a really good lead-in. The second type—'loose' Essence—is released from its 'bound' state by interacting with another type of element. For instance, steam Essence is not really its own type; it is intermingled air, water, and fire Essence that are all tightly woven together." She paused for a moment to let me think about her words. "Since the water here is flowing so fast, it is interacting with the rock around it and releasing lots of mud Essence. That loose Essence is what is being collected and purified by your Runes!"

<So I don't need my door unblocked to gain more Essence right now?> I thought about how best to use this new information. <What if I use just a *little* for traps? If I draw some water into an enclosed space and heat it up a lot. The interaction would accumulate loose earth, water, and fire Essence, right?>

"Hmm. Well, yes, I suppose—" she started.

I cut her off to finish my thought, <When the trap goes off, it would blast steam outward, adding air to the Essences!> I finished gleefully.

"Interesting! I wonder what type of Essence that might produce? Air, fire, water, and earth. Hmm. I like it, though. Solid plan, Cal." She paused a moment. "Oh! Instead of a trap that only goes off when someone sets it off, why not make steam vents that blast as soon as the pressure gets to a certain point? That would add a puzzle-like area to the dungeon since anyone passing through would need to find the pattern that steam shoots out of the vents!"

<I like the way you think, pretty lady. How about a tunnel for that, which groups will have to go through? Or,> I paused, thinking as she blushed, <we haven't set up the third floor yet, just cleared some of the area. How about we make the third floor one huge puzzle? Instead of tunnels every which way, then individual rooms, why not one big room made of twisty, turn-y paths?>

"Like a labyrinth?" Dani offered a word that I hadn't heard before.

<... A what?>

"Labyrinth. It is a big, dangerous maze. I don't know, Cal. That seems like a huge undertaking. Not only do you need to decide on a pattern for the room, but you would need to connect the walls to the ceiling and floor and make them so hard and dense that people couldn't just smash their way through." She considered it, then turned on me suspiciously.

"This isn't... you aren't... you are, aren't you?"

<I have no idea, but would love to be a participant in this conversation,> I stated blandly.

"You are trying to turn the floor into a giant Rune, aren't you?"

<... I had considered it.> I sheepishly muttered, somewhat upset that my master plan had been caught out so early.

"You are gonna get us killed," she groaned. "Fine, but under no circumstances will you activate it until we both agree to do so. Deal?"

<You got it, pink sugar!>

"Mm. No. Just no," she shot down another attempt at a nickname.

<Ahem,> I pseudo-coughed. <So have you decided on a pattern for the chests? I'd like to make those and place them as

soon as possible.> I was already starting to shape the stone on the third floor into a rough estimate of the Rune I was after. After I had it correct, I planned to raise the stone to meet the ceiling, but for the moment, I left it an inch high as a marker for expansion at a later date.

"I think I have finally settled on a design, but I reserve the right to change it at any time." She sent an image along our mental link, and I quickly made a small version for her to examine.

<That look about right?>

She seemed happy with the result. "Yes! Also, I think we should show which ones hold special gear. The low-level, average chest should be dark stone. As they become more difficult to find or the monsters guarding them get stronger, we make the chest out of better material and put better stuff in them."

<So like the coin system humans use? Make the second-tier copper coated, then silver, gold, and... on the super rare ones, how about I make it gold and splash some of that potion on it that makes things glow?> I ticked my ideas off on my mental fingers.

"Perfect! I also particularly like the idea of hidden chests. Let's make them waste a bunch of time looking around if they are greedy. More chances to kill them. Maybe we put chests in the walls that only miners will find as well as increase the danger? Maybe if they hit the wall in the wrong spot, it'll open a steam vent?" she offered, already planning out where to place them. "Or maybe an acid vent? I'm imaginative too!"

<Oh, that's good,> I agreed maliciously. <We can decide on the loot to put in them later. Are you about ready to start creating the Dungeon Cats?> I had decided to call them that

instead of Distortion Cats in the hopes that Dani would like them better. It didn't really help.

"You know, do we really need them? I feel like some of your Bashers could use Beast Cores at this point..."

She was trying to forego the Cats again!

<Dani, we have been over this,> I gently prodded her. <The Bashers are only... less than decent... fighters. They came from prey animals, so I basically need to *force* them to fight. Predatory animals are ideal; they have natural weapons and the instincts to go with them. The Cats are even better! They are Beasts! They are intelligent! I can set them up with a Beast Core! Even if they die, they will be able to have memories transferred to new Cores, and I can push their spirals into a new Core instead of absorbing them, allowing them to return to full strength as soon as I respawn them.>

"I know." Dani sighed heavily. "You *are* right. You've told me all this before... just do it, and let's get it over with."

That was all the permission I required, so I set about creating a new Cat right away. Pulling the pattern of its aura from memory, I energized it with the subtle combinations of Essence it needed in order to produce flesh, veins, nerves, tendons, bones, and, after a few minutes, fur. In just a few minutes, standing six inches tall, a white-coated Dungeon Kitten stood on shaking legs before us.

Mew!

Dani screamed, breaking my concentration, "AHHH! I love it! Hi, kitty! You. Are. So. Fluffy!" She zoomed around it so fast that it couldn't keep its eyes on her. It tried to bat at her a few times but, after a moment, flopped to the floor and curled up. It was only thirty seconds old, so I felt it was acceptable that he was a bit tired.

"Cal, this has to be the third-floor Boss. We'll evolve the others first—let me play with the kitty!" she begged. "I name you Snowball, and all who face you shall feel your wrath!" she told the kitten seriously.

It tiredly purred back at her.

<Snowball? C'mon. Imagine this place in two weeks,> I pleaded. <'Look out, it's... Snowball! Yeah, ol' Johnny got mauled by... Snowball.' Heh. That... that's actually hilarious. I'm in. Snowball it is.> I created a few more kittens, being careful to keep the fluffiness to a minimum. I did not want a repeat of Snowball. I was happy that Dani seemed to have gotten over her fear of cats, though.

I inspected these new kittens and decided to try something slightly different than my norm. First order of business was to move them into another room, since, well... let's just say I didn't want to hear about it for days if they, um... exploded.

The Cats should be strong enough to accept multiple types of Essence, by my calculations. And, well... I was going to find out if they were, anyway. Instead of pulling Essence from my own Core, I redirected the dense Essence in my room into the Cat. Mainly just to see if I could. I added one part water, one part air, and three parts pure Essence. The test subject, ah, *kitten* tensed up at first, trying to escape the intrusive injection of power, but as it started to grow, it relaxed and laid down. Pulling Essence from the surroundings worked, which made me very happy since I did not have to deplete my Chi spiral, which creating things always had before. This had the added benefit of not depleting my store of corruption either.

The Cat stopped growing when it reached D-rank two. It was sixty-five pounds and four and a half feet long from nose to its haunches, ignoring the tail. Waiting for a disaster, I watched as it stood and stretched, testing out its body. It suddenly shimmered, becoming almost insubstantial and leaping into the air. It floated along, slowly descending to the ground thirty-six feet away. That was a leap from a standstill! If it were running, how far could it go? I decided to call it a Cloud Cat after its mixed Essences. I let it walk around, quickly spawning some rabbits for it to hunt. Not Bashers, of course, I didn't want to start bad habits. It hunted them by pouncing and silently gliding toward them, then lashing out from above with quick, efficient strikes. I grinned. Silent but deadly.

Next, I tried fire and earth. I wanted a Magma Cat! I would have called it a Lava Cat, but we *were* underground. Therefore, magma! I directed the combination of Essence into it, but soon after, the Cat started hissing and burst into flame. Within moments, it was ash. I was glad Dani was otherwise occupied since that was originally the combination I had wanted to try on Snowball... I digress. Maybe I just needed to alter what I added a bit? I directed fire and earth Essence into my next attempt but with earth Essence outweighing fire by a factor of two to one. The Cat's body seemed to accept this combination, and it began growing. At its full size, it was two hundred and ninety pounds, five feet long from nose to haunch.

I looked closely at it, not seeing what advancements might have been made until it decided to stretch. Its claws appeared to be solid steel, and they gouged huge chunks of stone out of the ground with casual ease. It yawned, showing that its teeth had also gained this enhancement. It spotted a rabbit bounding across the ground and got ready to pounce. It launched itself like its spine was a coiled spring, shooting across the distance in a blink of the eye. That concept struck me, and so I named it a Coiled Cat. I was *very* pleased with the outcome of this experiment.

Now that I had realized that varying the ratios of Essence could produce different effects even with the same elements, I felt more prepared to create variations. The next, um, *successful* creation I made was a combination of water and earth with water just a *tiny* bit more prevalent than earth. The one before, I had used... just *way* too much water. I glanced at the puddle of ooze and fur off to the side and shuddered. This new successful model grew to full size but then started losing all its fur. It glared into the darkness around it. Totally hairless, the Cat certainly looked harrowing.

I sent a rabbit its way, and the Cat *hissed* and swiped at it. Six inches before touching its victim, the rabbit's fur and skin split as if the claws were deeply embedded, eviscerating the small animal with contemptuous ease.

<Celestial feces!> I exclaimed, half in disgust and half in anticipation of using this against heavily armored foes.

It cuddled up to the other Cats, and I was very happy to see that it had a sweet disposition despite its disturbing appearance. It started feeding the kittens with the shredded meat, and I decided on its name.

<You, my not-so-pretty kitty, are a Flesh Cat.>

I wanted more! I kept going, failing over and over until I finally found another viable combination. I poured infernal and water Essence into this Cat, happily watching it grow. Its body took on a mangy look, the fur falling off it in clumps; its coloration shifted to black speckled with unhealthy-looking white, and when it meowed, it was more of a yowl. The other Cats still seemed to have no issue with its appearance and accepted it quickly. I made a rabbit for it to hunt, but it ignored it in favor of a nap. Guess I would need to see it in combat to see what it could do. Based on how it looked, I named it a Wither Cat.

Dani had been trying to catch my attention for a few minutes, so I finally focused on her. "Look, Cal! Snowball is dancing!"

Dani was hovering just out of the kitten's reach, and it was on its hind legs slightly jumping as it tried to swat her.

I burst out laughing. The mental shift from creating deadly monsters to watching a kitty dance was just too much for me.

<Oh my goodness, Dani!> I laughed and laughed. <You can just keep him if you want. I don't need to upgrade him. I could keep him a kitten... basically forever.>

Dani smiled but refused, "No, he needs to be a big strong Boss Mob." Then she sank toward the kitten and continued, "Yes, you do! Who's gonna be a big kitty? You are!"

<...Right then.> I focused on the Cat and started pushing in fire and air Essence. I had barely begun when it started to hiss and shake.

Dani's voice was dangerously calm. "Cal? Did you... *test* this combination yet?"

<...> I was frantically adjusting the levels of Essence.

"*Do not kill my kitten*," she hissed venomously.

I tried to find a solution as quickly as possible and struck on an idea. I already knew that I could combine more than two types of Essence, so I quickly added one more. Water Essence flowed into the mix, balancing the other two as the Cat settled down, breathing heavily. The Essence flowed into it, though I was careful to leave it a rank below me so I could still fully control it. At D-rank four, the Cat was as large as its progenitor and twice as fluffy. Its size was deceptive; it weighed only two hundred and ten pounds, though it was eight feet long. The tail brought his total length up to fourteen feet.

It started exploring the room, luminous white fur bouncing as it explored its new body. Dani watched it to see if it would display any unique abilities, but it seemed content to frolic around the room. After a few minutes of watching it in admiration, Dani asked, "What type of Essence does it have?"

<I think it is 'steam' type,> I answered uneasily. Try to calm down, Cal; it survived, Dani won't shatter me.

"Really? Open up a steam vent in here. Let's see what happens," she directed me.

I quickly obeyed, glad she had seemingly forgotten that I nearly made the Cat pop. In moments, a steam vent allowed a dense fog to roll across the ground, the superheated vapor settling on every surface. Snowball looked at the steam, head cocked to the side as it took in this new phenomenon. It reached its paw into the fog as if it were playing with a new toy. Where the fog landed against Snowball, he blended perfectly and vanished, his hair moving in the same waves as the vapor. A perfect camouflage! I could not tell where he was without looking for the disturbance in the air and Essence around him.

Snowball stepped fully into the steam, and within seconds, only his three eyes were still visible. Even then, I could only see them because I knew where to look. He went over to the vent and stood directly in the hottest part of the steam. After a moment of staring at it, he started *licking* it like a salt block. I made a few rabbits in the room, and Snowball eyed them hungrily. Running across the room, Snowball had no need to attempt to remain stealthy. His charge made no noise or disturbance as long as the Cat stayed in the steam. He pounced on a rabbit, and where his claws penetrated... the flesh cooked.

Snowball hissed at the dying rabbit, releasing a narrow stream of superheated vapor. The rabbit cooked, dying instantly as its flesh boiled and popped. Snowball ate the tender corpse, blood marring his white coat only until he reentered the fog, at which point the red stains either vanished or were bleached into invisibility.

<I have enjoyed my day today,> I mentioned to Dani.

"Ha! I wonder why." She chortled. "Come on, let's go work on my plant room. I want to see if we can whip up some kind of catnip."

While she fussed over her flower arrangements and herb placement, I slowly built walls in the third floor and populated it with Cats and advanced Bashers, then sprinkled traps and treasure chests throughout the gigantic labyrinth. We were deep enough that I could take as much horizontal room as I wanted, allowing me to make the floor fully half a square mile.

My Boss area was at the direct center of the maze. I had sunk my Runed area and the Silverwood tree downward slowly, then formed a clear layer of quartz over it that would magnify the view from above. Adventurers looking in from above would not be able to tell that the tree and I were lower in the Dungeon until someone made the trip. Also, this way, the people in the area above would be able to see *two* Boss fights without fear of dying themselves, and the tree would still get sunlight and moonlight.

The chests were ready, the dungeon was populated, and the aesthetics were pleasing. The walls in the maze weren't quite ready, but they were growing.

When a light breeze laden with Essence suddenly moved in my depths, I realized the door was open!

We would see how far people were willing to go for their greed...

CHAPTER SEVEN

Dale's team was working hard under Craig's tutelage, practicing moving as a unit without interfering in one another's attacks. After a little more than an hour, Tom was gasping for air—although his oversized warhammer was feather light. Though the amount of Essence he had to constantly supply to the weapon was minuscule, the strain wore him out quickly. The others in the group were in the D-ranks, and several of them had multiple open meridians. Dale—a rarity—had *all* of his open, making his endurance and control of Essence much more refined.

"You need to break into the D-ranks, Tom," Craig informed him. He mercilessly continued, "Look at those around you, still working hard while you gasp and pant, holding your knees. Are all of those muscles for show?"

"I—*pant*—apologize for my weakness," Tom gasped. "I shall work harder on my cultivation. I shall not rest peacefully until I am able to stand beside my team through all of our trials."

Craig nodded while the others rolled their eyes. "Good! In that case, I *do* think that you are ready to open a meridian."

Tom looked up hopefully. "I have heard this term several times and have seen the effects of opening several at a time with Dale. Will it shrink and collapse my body as it has with him? What does this process involve?"

Craig snorted, the first time Dale had heard anything approximating a laugh from him that day. "No, that was a result of his Essence suddenly blasting every impurity out of him at the same time. If he had been conscious, it would have shattered his mind and permanently ruined his body."

Dale choked on his laughter a bit at this revelation.

"I want you to strip as much as you feel comfortable with, whatever you keep on will need a professional clean... or to be burned," Craig warned.

Tom stripped so fast that the others didn't even have a chance to think about looking away before they saw dangling bits. Barbarians clearly did not have the same social norms of decency, and he had no issue being nude, even in combat.

Craig chuckled. "I should have been clearer. This is fine, but... next time perhaps you keep on your smallclothes?"

"Nothing small there," Rose muttered, blushing at the shocked look the comment earned from Hans.

Craig directed him to open his heart meridian—the same one Dale had started with. After several minutes of intense concentration, Tom gasped and became pale as Essence rushed through him. He clutched his chest as the wave of Essence wrapped his heart, spitting up blood and filth as his Essence met his lungs. Black sweat collected over his body, and the air took on a tang of foulness. When he finally looked at his friends, his eyes were a deep red from broken capillaries. The blood was filling one of the sclera, giving him a frightening visage, especially with the other gore and filth on him.

"That felt horrible," was Tom's understatement of the day. "The worst kind of heartburn imaginable, then as if I were breathing dry, overheated air from a forge."

"You are a fire cultivator, yes?" Craig inspected Tom for damage as he talked. Tom nodded, so Craig continued, "You need to work on the purity of your Essence. For the next month, cultivate nowhere but in the dungeon. The purity of the loose Essence in there will dilute the taint you have absorbed. If you keep pulling in the amount of corruption you have been, there will be serious issues when you try to break into the D-ranks, not to mention the C-rankings."

Tom stepped over to the river to clean himself, and a Dark Elf appeared to Dale's right. He bowed, ignoring Dale's startled yelp.

"Your Grace, I have come with a daily report for you, as per instructions. Would you like to hear it now or in private? There are no matters of particular sensitivity."

Dale cleared his throat and ignored Hans's pantomime of him squealing. "Here is fine, good sir. If you are going to be bringing the report regularly, might I get your name and ask that you reveal your presence at least five feet—maybe ten feet—away from me? Also, why are you calling me 'Grace'?"

The bow deepened. "This one thanks you for your kind regard! My name in the human language will likely be easier for you to pronounce—it is Jason. I am calling you 'Grace' because your dealings with the Lady Brianna—as well as your holding of land—have allowed you to be granted a title from our Queen, and you have been named a Duke."

Jason hesitated in order to choose his next words carefully. "Understand, please, that you hold no rights to inheritance, but we acknowledge that you have quite a significant influence on our future. You control the land upon which a Silverwood tree grows, after all. Hence the title, as an offer of goodwill and a form of diplomatic immunity from other kingdoms. Although, to that end, I believe you also now hold the honorary title of Baron with both the Lion and Phoenix Kingdoms."

Dale was nonplussed as Hans's face clouded, looking like a storm was about to break forth from him.

"And now he is a Noble too," Hans grumbled. "Of course. His head is going to swell to the size of a–"

"And... what are the benefits of this position?" Dale apprehensively questioned the bowing Elf.

"To ensure that there are no misunderstandings when dealing with our culture, I have been given a memory stone that will grant you our language, political knowledge of our courts, and the customs of our people. This alone would be worth several hundred gold, but our Queen feels it is necessary for future dealings... as your life has been in jeopardy sixteen times while conversing with our Princess. Since you have been unaware of some... cultural differences," Jason clarified for him, voice never varying from an even cadence since he had begun speaking, even when discussing the near-executions.

Dale started sweating a bit now, a feat that over an hour of constant combat training had been unable to replicate. "I would like that stone *very* much," he rushed to say. The Elf grinned slightly and held up a small stone. There were motes of light moving in it, not unlike a Chi spiral's, but they obviously held a specific thought pattern.

"Your discretion regarding our politics will of course be... appreciated," Jason muttered in a slightly threat-promising tone.

Dale nodded and pressed the stone to his head. The light from the stone shot into his skull, creating pathways and memories in his brain that may as well have been there from birth since they melded with his own so well. The stone shattered to glitter, and Dale stood still for several minutes while the information became a part of him.

Finally, he shook himself and looked at Jason, who was still bowing. "My deepest apologies! Please stand, Lord Jason. I am sure you realize that I did not understand that you were waiting upon my command to rise."

Rose took this moment to close her hanging mouth with an audible click. "Dark Elves? Here? And Princess Brianna is here as well?"

Jason looked over at her, and in a barely civil tone, he nodded at her and responded, "Yes, she is here, half-breed."

The others looked shocked, but Rose—and now Dale—understood how poorly Elves viewed mixing of the races.

Dale didn't want to give him a chance to further offend anyone or have someone attack him. "Report."

The Elf launched into his report, detailing several crimes that had been stopped and how fights had nearly started when the Elves moved on to their new land and evicted those living in tents from the area. They had redirected many people along the riverbanks so that cooking water was pulled from upriver, clothes cleaning was farther downriver, and bathing was done at an even greater distance downstream. Sanitation was still an issue, but the position of sanitation officer had been filled. Garbage and refuse were being collected. The current plan was to begin dumping it into the dungeon as soon as it was open, as it would all vanish shortly afterward. Perfect solution!

Dale nodded as the Elf spoke, asking what had been done with the people committing crimes. He was informed that they had been delivered to Protectorate Cole, who had been appointed by the council to give judgement to criminals. Originally, Magistrate Acman—a Dark Elf—had been offered to fill the position, but it turned out he was obstinate and hard to work with. Even Jason had to admit—internally of course—that even such an illustrious Elf as Magistrate Acman may not have been the best for this position. Even in the short amount of time he had been there, Protectorate Cole had proven his worth repeatedly. Cole had worked at honing his abilities in aura reading to the point where he was able to discern between truth and lies at a glance. Therefore trials were short and efficient and justice meted out quickly.

Tom came back, dripping from the quick scrub in the river. As he dressed, he curiously eyed the Elf.

Jason glanced at him in return—noting his sodden state—and grimaced. "Apologies, Your Grace, it seems we missed a bather."

Craig smoothly joined the conversation, "My fault, I had not heard about the new rules and sent him to bathe after opening a meridian."

Jason bowed again. "I should go and warn any who were collecting water. I shall return on the morrow."

He vanished and—Dale assumed—left. Dale's team went to lunch, eating with their usual calorie-desperate gusto to the slight—yet poorly hidden—disgust of their server. After finishing, they stepped outside, where they were met with both excited and angry shouting.

"What's going on?" Adam wondered aloud, his mind clouded with exhaustion. Father Richard had begun training him in earnest, and the mental fatigue of the training was horrendous.

Dale squinted at the milling crowd. "I don't know. I haven't heard noise like this since they first opened the portal. Shall we look into it?"

They walked at a fast-yet-measured pace, staying in formation as best as possible. Craig had drilled into them that if they made combat tactics a part of every daily routine, it would be easier to keep their bearing and formation while in battle.

They waved down a man who was running toward the Guild tent. "What is going on?"

A happy grin flashed across his face. "The dungeon is open!"

A sour-faced man near them overheard and growled, "Yeah, but they are charging everyone fifteen percent of their earnings if they want to go in. Fracking council put it out this morning. So long, single-run retirements!"

Dale looked at Hans as the complaining man walked off. "What did that mean?"

"Most people who live in the middle of nowhere—like you used to—can earn enough by going through the dungeon a single time to retire, either from the coins they collect or by selling other things they bring out. Those whiners will still get wealthy; they just don't want to give up any money for the greater good of the people living here."

Hans shook his head. For the first time, Dale fully understood the political ramifications of what he had been doing, and the conversation devolved into the pros and cons of several nuances of the situation, much to Hans's delight.

They chatted for a few minutes until Hans asked a very pertinent question, "Did you get all of this political savvy from that memory stone?"

Dale considered. "I must have. I mean, I have been trying to learn faster, but I had been getting better at it only very slowly. Now it feels as natural as breathing to have an in-depth conversation concerning the taxation benefits of a high-yield resource center such as a low-corruption dungeon."

Hans laughed. Never had he imagined that Dale would become a true contender in political and economic debates. It normally took years of study to be able to hit the finer points of the conversation they were having! Dale wouldn't have understood half the *words* they were using even that very morning. They walked to the entrance to the dungeon, noting the queue of people waiting in front of the new fortifications.

The walls were hardened stone, seamless even if they *had* been put up in haste. There were many kill slots in the stone; these were places for weapons, arrows, or magical effects to pass through to kill any monsters that tried to escape the dungeon. The doors were stone banded with metal—obviously made by Mages as there were no seams or welds in the work. Unlike normal fortifications, these were built to keep things *in* and *kill* them, not keep things *out* while defending the location.

There was at least one spectacular benefit to owning the land; Dale's group bypassed the line waiting to get in and went directly to the clerk.

She looked up, bored. "Guild or standard?"

Dale looked at her as a troubling idea crossed his mind. He hoped he was wrong about what she was about to say. "What is the difference?"

She released a long-suffering sigh. "Oh my *gawwd*... Non-Guild need to pay a fifteen percent tax to the landowner so he can throw a party or something. Guild rate is the standard flat twenty-five percent."

"Throw... a... *party?*" A vein on Dale's temple began to throb. "No, there is a fifteen percent tax on *everyone*, and the Guild takes twenty-five percent of the gross amount *after that.* Also, the tax is in place to build this campsite into a city so you won't have to wade through *feces* on your morning commute. Who sent these orders?" Dale was trying *very* hard not to yell.

She made a very unladylike noise. "You have a problem? This came straight from GL *Frank.*" She finished her sentence like he was an idiot, and with that, the conversation was over.

"How... interesting." Dale had a maniacal grin on his face. "Oh Hans!" he said in a sing-song tone. "Be a dear and send a runner for the Guild Leader, please. Or GL Frank, as *she* calls him."

"...Dale," Hans began worriedly.

"*Now,* please."

Hans sighed and motioned to one of the messengers who were near the entrance. He sent him off with a sad look.

"Who do you think you are?" The clerk looked pissed off. "You don't summon the Guild Master like he is a common thug." Her face looked troubled when Frank appeared next to Dale moments later. He had moved so fast that he was invisible until he stopped.

"What?" Frank barked at the clerk. Then he noticed Dale. "Oh. I thought there was an issue with the dungeon. What is the matter, Dale?"

Dale explained about the tax rate, and to his credit, Frank looked confused.

"I sent the orders about the tax rate this morning." He looked at the clerk, who gulped. "Where is the memo?"

"S-s-sir, it was just a misunders–" she began but was quickly cut off by Frank.

"I didn't ask for you to talk, I *asked* where the memo was," he growled. "Hurry up. I ran out of a meeting for this. Literally."

She rummaged around in her papers, obviously stalling. Frank made a noise and stepped in, pulling out a paper hidden under her logbook. He showed Dale the proclamation, then held it close to the clerk. "Are you trying to make the Guild look like a bunch of greedy, self-serving shakedown artists? Or can you just not follow *orders*?" He tore into the despondent clerk.

"Sir, I just thought that–"

Cutting her off again, "Obviously, you *didn't* think. This is the *second* time you have been caught disregarding orders. I shudder to think about all the times you must have gotten away with things if you have only been caught for these *gross* infractions! I know that you aren't technically part of the Adventurers' Guild, but do you think you will keep your job if I go talk to your master at the Scribes' Guild? Your job isn't exactly *labor intensive,* and it pays well. I'm sure we could find someone *trustworthy* to fill it if you do something like this again! Give me a count of the reported incomes of the Guild members who've entered—by the end of the day."

Frank turned back to Dale. "I'm sorry about this, Dale. The Guild will cover the differences in reported incomes today. We can't charge the people who already went in, after all. They didn't agree to the rate."

Dale smiled. "Frank, my real worry was that you had a hand in this. Seeing that you've so quickly resolved the issue renews my confidence in you. I am very glad that my choice of you for the council was the correct decision."

Frank nodded but wondered if Dale understood that what he had just said was as much a compliment as a warning. Probably not. He knew Dale didn't have the understanding of political subtleties to make that kind of remark, so he took it at face value. "I certainly hope *my* loyalties are never again called into question and that I keep your confidence for a very long time." He glared at the quailing clerk and removed himself at high speed, returning to his meeting.

Dale looked around at his nonplussed team and the suddenly silent line of people waiting to enter. The clerk was nearly in tears at her public admonition. Her newfound realization that professionalism was the only thing allowing her to keep her job forced her to hold back the waterworks.

"Well. Shall we enter?"

CHAPTER EIGHT

Dale's group walked into the much larger entrance and looked around, whistling at the bustling mining activity. Whereas before, the door had entered into a shallow cave entrance and only eight or nine people had been able to mine at a time without injuring their neighbor, now it seemed like half the population of the camp was chipping away at the stone.

"Excuse me, could I get by you there?" a man asked them politely.

Turning to let him pass, Dale exclaimed in wonder—he was meeting a nonhuman half-breed for the first time in his life.

"Of course! Hello, my name is Dale. It is a pleasure to meet you, sir. Can I ask your name?" Dale almost stammered in his excitement.

The man was built like a Dwarf, having the beard and the height, but his features were distinctly Orcish. He was also in full plate armor and wore it with an ease that spoke of constant use. The man eyed Dale for a moment, looking for disgust or pity, then broke into a wide grin, revealing disturbingly pointed teeth.

"Well, some of the asshats around here call me 'Gnorc Gnorc' like I have damn gnome blood, but I am a Dwork—and *proud of it.*" He roared at a couple of miners nearby who had been making rude comments about him. He held out his hand and shook Dale's in a powerful grip. "The name's Evan."

"A dork named Evan?" Hans failed to hide his mirth at the subtle taunt. "A Half-Dwarf, Half-Orc... with a human name."

"It's pronounced *Dwork.*" Evan eyed Hans. "I don't know if we will get along well, you and I. It has been a pleasure to meet *you* though, Dale. I need to get to work. I have a month to make my first payment on this beauty." He hoisted his pickaxe, the same one that Dale had rescued from thieves recently. Evan stepped over to an unoccupied area along the wall and put on a helmet.

"That is an odd piece of gear to wear," Tom commented. "Matter of fact, I have not seen any other miners wearing *any* armor, let alone full plate." His curiosity was sated moments later when Evan gave a mighty swing of his pick and the wall in front of him shattered with a thunderous roar. Splintered rock bounced off the Dwork's armor, sending him staggering back a few steps. Instead of moving forward again for another blow, he waited a few moments. The fallen rock in front of him started to vanish, leaving behind chunks of pure iron ore.

Evan collected the ore into a large bucket and smiled. "Best job I've ever had." He swung his pick again with a mighty grunt.

Dale's group had had enough of the noise and so started walking into the dungeon's depths. After the first turn, most of the natural light vanished, leaving them in a blue-tinted gloom. The groups allowed in the dungeon were spaced a minimum of twenty minutes apart, which would allow for Mobs—dungeon monsters—to respawn and Essence to re-accumulate in the air.

Dale felt the Essence around him with his enhanced senses, remarking that it was a little less concentrated than usual for the first floor. He asked Hans for his opinion but was told that since they were usually the first to enter the dungeon each morning, the Essence had usually been able to build up. Also, the Mana barrier over the door had likely blocked Essence production, lowering Essence in the dungeon further. They moved quickly through the area, overtaking an F-ranked group that glared at Dale's smiling group as they returned to the surface. The people in that group were sweaty and dirty.

Obviously, they had worked hard and decided to cut their losses and leave before dying.

In the second room, they found things greatly changed. Dale's first impression was that they had stepped outside; there was lush greenery all around, and the room was brightly lit. They had to squint as they looked around, unaccustomed to the brightness after walking through the tunnel. Feeling relatively secure, Dale looked up and saw that the ceiling had a thin layer of glass over it which held glowing fluid between it and the rock, accounting for the bright light. There was no path. The room was completely overgrown in what could almost be called a beautiful arrangement of flowers and herbs.

"Wow. It is *beautiful*," Rose breathed in deeply, smelling the combination of herbs and flowers.

<She said it is beautiful!>

Dale heard my smug voice in his mind; he looked around for the source and swore softly.

"*So, you are real then, Cal? Not a figment of my imagination brought on by stress and trauma?*" Dale thought hopefully at the dungeon.

"None of these flowers compare to you, sweet Rose," Hans poetically promised the uninterested female.

Rose glared at him. "You are old enough to be my *grandpa*." There was no response from Hans, just a pained look.

<Yes, I am real. Sorry about this. I have no idea *why* you can hear me. You really shouldn't be able to... It must be a side effect of my experiment. I can kill you if that would help?>

"*Experiment? What do you mean?*" Dale ignored the offer of death for some unknown reason.

I thought about how much I wanted to tell him. <Well, I wanted to see if I could fix a human, and then you conveniently

died after helping me out. So, I figured, you know, might as well try to see if I can do it.>

"*There is no other reason? You didn't want an ally, a slave, or anything like that?*" Dale thought heatedly.

<Nope, just wanted to test myself. Plus, you did help me out, so I feel it was justified if you survived. It won't happen again. Nothing personal, but you humans are fairly tasty. Can you try and invite some different races in? I haven't tried Elf yet, but a few have poked their heads in here so, you know, I am getting excited,> I assured him.

Dale shook his head. "What the hell is going on?" he muttered. Then a Basher slammed into the side of his leg, leaving him no more time for questions. "Ow!"

They tightened their formation, protecting their less well-armored members in the center. Tom stated the obvious, "I cannot see a thing through this underbrush. Where are they?"

Hans nodded at the question. "The Essence in the plants makes them too dense to see through, and so I can't tell where the Mobs are based on their auras alone. Look out; I am going to open up some space. Otherwise, look for moving plants!"

The knives in his hands took on a soft shine, and he swung them in a slow arc. The plants in front and to the side of him fell over, clean cuts separating their stalks. Several Bashers were also torn in half, adding thick, red blood to the runny sap dripping to the floor. With a clear kill zone, they made short work of the weak Bashers in the area.

"No loot dropped," Adam noted after waiting for the familiar clink of coins.

Rose's keen eyes spotted something. "What is that?" She pointed at a rock-like formation that was tinted green to blend in with the plants.

Hans's eyes gleamed. "That, my dear, is a treasure chest!" He rushed over and caressed its surface, rubbed his face on it, and then lifted the lid. Inside laid several thick copper coins and a potion containing a syrupy light source. "Score! I can pour this on myself and pretend I'm a ghost tonight!"

"Are these typical in here?" Rose looked around for danger as she awaited an answer. She had only been in the dungeon once before, and that traumatic experience had her on edge now.

"Nay, 'tis a new occurrence," Tom informed her gravely. "Though I must say, I prefer collecting from a single area instead of scrambling along the floor on all fours chasing a rolling copper."

<Heh. I do miss that aspect of things. It was always fun to put them just far enough away from each other that people would have to bend over and reach like twenty times. Remember that handsome book writer who tagged along with a group for 'inspiration'—what was his name? Dakota? When his team was distracted, I kept making slow, chubby Bashers attack him. He started swearing and sweating at the same time! He squealed every time a Basher came close! I don't think I've ever laughed so hard before.>

Dale steadfastly worked to ignore the voice talking in his head.

They debated stopping to cultivate but decided that it would be better to get to an area where the Essence in the air was denser. They continued onward, now on the lookout for treasure chests as well as monsters and traps. Dale was directing his friends around what his enhanced vision saw as thin stone in the wall—when he heard a giggle in his mind. His eyes narrowed, and instead of bypassing the section, he smashed the wall, revealing a bright silver chest.

<Aww, how did you know?>

Dale opened the chest, finding several shining bars of silver and a few healing potions. He distributed the potions, keeping one for himself and ignoring Hans as he was the least likely to get hurt. The others looked at him oddly so Dale tried to justify his actions without letting the dungeon know how he actually figured it out.

"The size of that space was a lot smaller than the traps normally are, as well as being shaped differently."

The others nodded, cheerful at their good fortune. Those bars of silver would bring in a good chunk of money, roughly twenty silver coins per bar. They continued past some obvious traps and into the third room.

This room was similar to how it had been arranged in the past with a few blatant differences. The very large open space had lots of Bashers, but they were mainly clustered in large groups with only a few wandering the areas between them. As they studied the room, the rationale became obvious. The thicker clusters of Bashers were around small chests of various colors. The rarer the coloration, the higher the population of Mobs. At a few points they normally would not explore in the room—such as midway and far to the right—there were even advanced Bashers that they only normally saw in the Boss Room and on the lower floor.

Hans whistled when he saw why they were there. "Look! They are kind of hiding that chest, and it is *glowing*! Can we go open it? Pretty please?" He batted his eyelashes at Dale as if he were trying to be seductive. "I'm greedy and owe a flesh Mage a *lot* of money."

Dale chuckled; he was glad that Hans had asked and didn't try to undermine him as the leader of the team. "Really hard to report what we don't know about, right?"

That was the phrase they had always used to make Craig give in when they wanted to explore.

"Aww, yeah." Hans maliciously unsheathed his daggers, and the team got ready to fight.

They moved forward, killing the Bashers in their way and taking no hits from the—fairly—predictable attacks.

They learned to fight monsters in the order they came across them after Rose loosed an arrow at one a good distance away. The arrow struck its target, a Basher, who squealed and limped toward them. The group it was in—as well as every group they passed—joined in the charge, until a wave of bounding fur was sprinting toward them.

"Oops," Rose muttered as the team glared at her. Tom stepped forward, swinging his hammer down to lightly graze the stone floor and then continuing toward the Bashers. The weapon impacted the floor at an angle and sent shards of broken stone flying forward at high speeds. These shards shredded the small bodies like crossbow bolts. Easily a half dozen were killed, while others were badly wounded, bleeding out in moments in a few cases. The rest continued onward, ignoring their fallen comrades.

Rose began releasing arrows while Dale stepped forward to attack. Since there was still some distance between them, he activated the enchantment on his weapon and started swinging. The spiked head of the weapon stayed in perfect alignment with the shaft, which meant that it moved far faster at a distance than the shaft of his weapon. Physics.

At its maximum range, he could swing the shaft of the weapon slowly and the ball would blur through the air, greatly increasing the amount of force applied to whatever it hit. Any of the Bashers that were struck lost flesh in chunks and usually died, but they were small and nimble while the weapon was unwieldy at range. He missed far more than he hit when he was trying to mash the scurrying creatures at any greater range than he was used to.

Still, they were able to finish off the Bashers with little issue, though Hans groaned as a bit of blood landed on his otherwise immaculate clothes. They certainly planned on collecting the contents of the chest the group had been guarding, but first, they attacked the advanced Bashers to get to the *glowing* chest. Hans stepped forward, then suddenly appeared behind them, stabbing two Mobs through the brainstem before they could react. One heavily armored Smasher bounded toward the main group of humans, but Adam braced himself and thrust the pointed end of his staff toward it in a panic, skewering the Basher through the eye and into its brain with a lucky attack.

They stopped, breathing heavily due to their pumping adrenaline, and started chuckling. They were so excited! The group hadn't taken any injuries, and it was obvious their practice of formations and teamwork were starting to pay dividends. They opened the chest, revealing two Runed holy symbols and an Inscribed dagger. Working exuberantly to clear the room and open all the chests, they moved on to attack the Boss Room.

CAL

Dale's group seemed to be doing fine. Ugh. Too well, as per usual. Some of the other groups in here were doing less than perfect, and Dani and I decided to watch them for a bit. Specifically, we focused on a group that I had taken a personal dislike to. They called themselves 'The Collective' and had stolen a live Glitterflit a few weeks back. I had no idea how it was doing; after it was taken out of the dungeon, I could no longer sense it. I assumed the poor bunny had either died or was dying since most of the Mobs in here needed the Essence rich environment to survive for long periods of time. I thought for a moment; maybe the Shroomish would be fine in the wild... but who knows?

'The Collective' had just defeated Raile and were opening the chest in the room. As per usual, they complained about the amount of money as well as the quality of items. To be fair, I had started intentionally creating weapons with flaws so they would break after enough uses. I had learned my lesson after giving Tom what basically amounted to an unbreakable warhammer that he swung around all the time. Now, Runes were typically hard to break after Essence had gone through them at least once. Therefore, I introduced *intentional* flaws. Plus—hee-hee—Dani told me that if a Rune broke while Essence was moving through it, 'interesting' things could happen.

This group of six finished collecting their loot and looked downward, where they could see the Silverwood tree through the glass at their feet. After a brief argument, they found the stairs, one set leading up and connecting to the surface and another leading down into unknown danger. The argument they had was simple; it was based on whether or not to smash the glass and jump down. Eventually, they made a decision and walked toward the stairs; this wasn't because they wanted to do things in the proper order, ohhh no! The reason they deigned to find the stairs was that they *tried* to smash the floor. Heh. Good luck with that. I had reinforced it with Runes and powered it with earth corruption. To smash through, they would need to supply at least an equal amount of wind Essence—and enough force to *break* the hardened, glassy surface.

They walked down the stairs, and I started to get excited. Soon, I would get to test my new creatures in combat! The stairs continued at a forty-five-degree angle downward to the north, which meant they would have to come into the labyrinth very far away from the center of the room—which they would need to *find* in order to fight the Boss. They paused in the small, six-by-five-foot room I had created at the bottom of the descent, looking around critically. There were four doors in the room, excluding the stairs back out. Above each of the doors, I had carved small pictures: a drop of water, a flame, a stone, and a whorl to represent wind.

They stared at these, then determined that they were representative of the trials they would face down each hallway. Heh. They actually had *no* meaning! I put them there to confuse people and make them think there was a pattern to things. They stepped boldly through the 'stone' doorway and started walking down the narrow hall. Unlike the tunnels above, there was not even a soft glow to see by. Also unlike the floors above, these halls were straight and had many, *many* branching paths. After they were a few turns in, I sealed the door they had entered through by quietly lowering a slab of stone. Unless you had seen it happen, it would look like just one of the many dead ends.

The majority of this group were D-ranked, with the leader a bold C-rank. They walked along without light, using their Essence enhanced vision to see. This allowed them to see and navigate using the Essence in the air, but they did not count on how *thick* the Essence actually was in this room. Using the loose Essence to see by on this floor was like holding a bright lantern in fog. You could see directly around you but not *through* it. The cost of their arrogance came due quickly—and with compounded interest.

As they passed an open connection in the tunnel, a Flesh Cat silently lashed out at the member in the rear. The highly armored man started squealing—unaccustomed to pain as he was—and the Cat retreated a few feet, readying itself to pounce. The other members of the group quickly formed a perimeter around the fallen man, and their healer tried to diagnose him.

"He... It is like a sword ignored his armor and laid open his gut! I need a potion, now!" the healer barked. The man guarding the doorway reached into his bag and started fishing for a potion. The Flesh Cat took advantage of his inattention, pouncing forward and furiously mauling him, swiping back and forth almost a dozen times.

The man's screaming died off quickly, and he fell to the ground, dead with no obvious marks on him, but blood flooded out of the joints in his armor. The leader of the group flashed forward, skewering the Cat and concurrently landing a blow that snapped its neck.

"What in the abyss is that? Pull a potion from his pack; I need to finish the healing! ...Ugh. Too late." The healer shook blood off his fingers with a grimace.

The leader gave a grim smile. "It's an unexpected windfall! The Guild pays *very* well for new Mob corpses to study." He pulled out a small sack and started stuffing the corpse into it. Somehow, he fit the eighty-ish pound, four-foot-long Cat into it and put the small bag back in his pocket. Callously, they rummaged through the corpses' pockets and took their expensive armor, then left the dead men on the floor and continued exploring. The remaining men—bizarrely—seemed *happy* with the outcome, as it meant they would have a larger cut of the profits.

<What in the heck?> I turned my mental attention to Dani. <Did you see that?>

"Yeah... I can't believe they just *left* their friends like that!" Dani commiserated with me.

<Huh? No, that's fine. They stuffed a whole Beast into a tiny little bag!>

"Oh. Sure, I'm fairly certain that is a dimensional bag. They are made from heavily enchanted and inscribed standard Beast Cores."

<What kind of Beast Core? What do you mean by 'standard'?> I was always happy to learn new things.

"So, you know how I told you about the different ranks of cultivation?" Dani prodded. She continued after I mentioned that I did, "At the different cultivation levels, Cores gain different properties. There are flawed, weak, standard, strong, beastly, immaculate, luminous, and radiant Beast Cores. Essentially the Beast's diet, age, and strength of cultivation affect the quality of their stone. Immaculate Cores are usually only found in B-ranked or higher Beasts and are extremely receptive to enchantments."

<What kind of a Core am I?> I plaintively wondered. Not because I wanted to be the best kind, certainly not. It wasn't like I worked at being the best, most beautiful, or most dangerous dungeon that exists.>

"I am fairly certain that you started out as a 'beastly' Core. Your configuration is categorically different though, so now it is hard to tell where you fall in the rankings. Remember, you were altered with—what I can only assume—was Spiritual energy, and it shifted around what makes you a cohesive whole."

<You mean my molecules were shifted into a non-standard configuration?>

"...Sure." She looked at me like I had started spewing Orcish. "An-n-yway that is why you were able to make a soul stone to house Dale's Center. While the configuration had been set by Spiritual energy, the pattern was easily replicable as it was a physical change. It all comes back to the fact that you are a *very* different type of Core. I'd say one of a kind, but, well, Dale."

<Right. Well I'm just going to go ahead and call myself 'radiant'.> I preened a bit.

"Knew you would," Dani muttered, grinning as I huffed at her.

CHAPTER NINE

Dale smiled happily at how his bag clinked as he walked along. "Today has been a good day."

The others agreed, as they had each made exceedingly good money. After finding several chests, both standard and hidden, they had to slow down and adjust their pouches so they would stop banging against their sides. They were just coming to the end of the fifth main room on the expanded second floor. Sitting down, they began cultivating with as much focus as possible.

Tom was drawing in as much at a time as he dared, his open meridian helping by drawing off a good portion of his Essence and keeping it circulating. This allowed him to pull more into his Center without worrying about damaging himself. Remembering Craig's orders to not cultivate outside of the dungeon, he pushed himself even harder.

"HA!" Adam shouted, making the group collectively reach for their weapons. "Did it!" He looked around with his grin slowly fading as he saw the sour faces looking at him. "Oh, uh... Sorry. I just regained my D-rank five." He had dropped a rank by using too much Essence in an incantation during the fight with the Distortion Cat a week ago.

"That was *way* faster than expected!" Hans clapped him on the arm. "Great! Easier to get to a rank when you've been there before, isn't it? Don't worry, it happens sometimes."

Adam looked at him curiously. "You have lost a rank in the past?"

"Yeah... everyone wants to try enchanting at least once, ya know?" Hans ruefully sighed. "Let's just say there is a reason you should *buy* them and not *make* them."

The others fell silent as they thought about his words; they had all considered enchanting in the past.

Rose shook off the sudden melancholy first. "Well! Are we ready to hit the Boss Room? Raile is waiting for us, and I promised Grandma Chandra that I'd bring her some fresh Raile steak since we are eating it so often. She's losing money."

They all jumped to their feet and got into formation, cheering themselves on and getting mentally prepared to fight the massive Basher. They cautiously marched into the final room of the floor, noticing differences immediately.

Adam informed them of the most obvious one. "The Silverwood tree is gone!" he called in a shocked tone.

Dale started sweating with unadulterated fear; if the tree was damaged, the Dark Elves would most likely kill everyone in the area—after torturing them for a few weeks. He looked around the open, flat room for any sign of its whereabouts, noticing the new, glassy floor just as Raile charged them.

"Here we go!" Hans whooped as they tensed their knees, throwing themselves out of the way and scattering. "Our first real Boss fight as a team!"

Rose responded as she began launching arrows at the presumed weak points in Raile's armor, "What, the Cat didn't count?"

"Nope!" Hans did a cartwheel over Raile, avoiding getting trampled by inches. "That was some kind of wild monster that got in here. This is a real test from the dungeon."

"A *test?* Hardly!" Tom roared. "This rabbit should be cooked well and served to me, not disgracing this dungeon with its weakness!"

This statement shocked the others so much that they paused a moment too long, and Dale paid for his inattention by taking a light blow to the edge of his breastplate, heavily denting it as he was thrown aside. Ignoring Dale, Raile turned slowly and stared directly at Tom, pawing at the ground just before charging. Tom stood still in defiance, not moving until Raile was almost in striking range. Then he swung his mighty warhammer back and around, bringing it down on Raile's head with enough force to shatter the protective armor and send shards of stone into the soft brain below.

Raile's momentum was transferred downward as his head stopped moving, and his body flipped. It began coming down on Tom, but he braced himself and dodged almost entirely out of the way, losing only a bit of skin as the rough armor met his unprotected flesh.

"Ha! I was certain of my ability to defeat this foe alone; this validation of my increasing skill pleases me greatly." Tom looked at his teammates with a huge smile on his face, bleeding from small cuts where razor-sharp stone shards had sliced him.

"Did you just ... *taunt* Raile?" Hans unbelievingly exclaimed.

"Just so!" Tom nodded. "I was under the impression that he was an intelligent foe, and it was a pleasure and honor to defeat him. My insults do taint my victory, but I felt a great need to know my progression for certain."

<See if I fall for *that* again.> Dale ignored my quiet voice by force of will.

"This was way more fun than fighting that demon Cat was!" Rose was flushed with victory, already spending the rewards in her mind. "Is there another chest in here somewhere?"

"There it is!" Dale shouted exuberantly, jumping in the air and whooping. The others turned in excitement, ready for treasure but were disappointed to see Dale looking downward.

Adam raised an eyebrow. "The treasure is under the floor?"

Dale shook his head. "No! The tree! There is another floor, and the tree is below us! We're gonna live!" This comment earned him a few odd looks.

"Oh. Well." Rose spotted the treasure chest tucked away on the far side of the room, its exterior a bright but not glowing golden color. "There is the chest!"

All of them moved to collect their rewards, and even a highly relieved Dale peeled himself away from his view. They pulled open the chest, finding it filled with silver coins and potions. There was another pickaxe in the chest that appeared to be inscribed as well as a set of arrows that glowed with bright enchantments to their enhanced vision.

"Dibs!" Rose called, pointing at the dangerously barbed arrows. She lifted them out and let Hans scoop the coins into a bag he had with him. "Shall we sell the pick, or is one of you feeling like taking up mining as a hobby?"

"Let's sell it. I know a guy who would be happy to get us the best price for it," Dale said, thinking of his new friend Tyler.

Hans eyed him. "Don't forget that the Guild still gets a cut, no matter who you sell it through."

"Of course! I was just thinking we could bypass the listing fee that they make you pay at the Guild auction house. If we go directly to a merchant, we'll get more," Dale assured his friend.

Tom was eying the stairs leading down into darkness. "Dale, how would you feel challenging the next floor? After such a fast fight with the glorious Raile, my blood screams out for battle."

Dale went silent. "Well... we have no idea what is down there. Should we wait for a report?"

Hans nodded. "That would be a *wise* plan."

"I'm up for it," Rose offered as she tested the balance and flexibility of her new arrows, ruffling the fletching to inspect the craftsmanship.

Adam made a noncommittal noise when the others looked at him.

"Perhaps... just a peek to see what awaits us?" Tom pleaded, edging toward the stairwell.

Dale looked around; each of them nodded, and Hans shrugged. "We can at least see what the next floor looks like, I suppose."

They walked down the stairs for several minutes, the angle making them seem to walk a far longer distance than it actually was. At the bottom, there was a small room with three doorways spaced oddly far apart.

"What do those symbols mean, do you think?" Adam pointed to the carvings above the doors.

Hans grunted. "No idea, but unless I miss my guess, this is also a doorway but closed." He pointed at the square stone-like symbol. "Maybe it is the exit? It opens from the other side, you think?"

"Well, let's take a look. Which one do you want to go in?" Dale put the matter to a vote.

There were three votes for the 'fire' door, hardly surprising as two members of the team were fire cultivators.

Hans clapped Tom on the arm. "Go team hot stuff!"

"Hot stuff?" Tom considered the words. "If you mean the fire of battle with which we temper our souls, I agree to this team name."

Hans blew out a lungful of air slowly. "You know... you just... let's just go, Dale."

They all stepped into the darkness and took a few steps when Hans stopped them. "Wait. Do you see that?"

They looked about them, but Adam was the one who answered, "I see nothing. The Essence is very dense on this floor though."

"Exactly. Too dense. Stay here." He walked forward a few feet and vanished to their enhanced vision. "Where did I go?"

"Didst thou... find a tunnel, perhaps?" Tom called uncertainly into the darkness.

"Nope!" Hans was in front of them again. "Stop enhancing your sight. Watch and learn." He reached into his pack and produced a light potion. He shook the vial without opening it, and it began glowing brightly. Within moments, they were able to see as far as the tunnel extended, at least until it took a sharp turn. "Now, enhance your vision again."

They did as instructed, and their range of vision suddenly dropped to a few feet.

Rose broke the silence, "How strange."

"Agreed, this will make it much harder to watch for traps." Dale mentioned as an afterthought, "And monsters."

"On the plus side," Rose smiled as she suddenly plopped to the ground, "our vision is being impaired by free-floating Essence." She began cultivating, causing a small competition as they all attempted to clear the air in the tunnel.

CAL

<Huh. That was unexpected,> I muttered to Dani.

"What's that? Sorry, I was looking at my garden; another group chopped all the plants down," Dani told me sourly.

<Oh? Let's do something about that tonight.> I directed her attention to the adventurers on our level. <Look, they just... sat down! They normally try to clear the rooms first, don't they?>

"Yes, but to be fair, they aren't being attacked, and they are getting a *lot* of Essence. It makes sense to me." Dani looked at the other group in the area. "At least *they* aren't getting a chance to relax."

I had been haranguing 'The Collective' since they first reached this floor. Luckily for them, I didn't have fine enough control of the Essence in the room to make and control large groups of Cats. I could either make a few and control them well or make a swarm and let them run rampant in the dungeon. Since I didn't want a large group of uncontrollable Cats in the area.... Whoops! Back on topic. I had intermittently been sending squads of Advanced Bashers or individual Cats at the group, and they had slowly begun falling to my war of attrition.

I had just had a successful sneak attack! While they had been focused on the Bashers, a Cloud Cat had gracefully drifted down the long, straight hallway behind them and savagely torn into their healer. The screams of the healer had only lasted a moment, but it was long enough to distract the other members. They had each taken a few wounds from the Bashers, including one nasty burn from the hellfire on the horn of an Impaler—not enough to take them down but more than they were prepared to deal with without a healer.

Soon, their leader was gritting his teeth to steel himself against the others' complaints. So far, he was the only one mostly undamaged, and he had resolutely stuffed the body of the Cloud Cat in his bag and marched onward. Now it was obvious they were looking for an exit, and they retraced their steps as well as they could. They even had found where they entered but thought they were wrong since the door was closed and seamlessly blended with the stone around it. They had been wandering for nearly an hour when I noticed they were approaching Dale's group and the open doorway behind them.

The leader of the group cocked his head and motioned for his minions to be silent. He looked around the corner carefully, drew a blade, and motioned for his team to get ready to attack. A tap on his shoulder made him wave his hand in a shooing motion as he gripped his sword.

"Ah-hem!"

The leader furiously started to turn, glaring at the offender who had made the noise, only to find a gleaming dagger pressed to his Adam's apple.

"Well hello there, sunshine." Hans smiled blithely at the quickly paling man. "You weren't really going to attack a group from the Guild in here... were you?" He fluttered his eyelashes sweetly.

The man began to bluster, "What? No, of course not! I was just... preparing in case this turned out to be another trap! This dungeon is devious, and we have lost two... *three* of our group! These two have taken serious injuries." He waved at his underlings, who helped his case by looking extra pathetic.

"Hmm. Well, you are always welcome to leave *peacefully*." Hans stressed the last word and stepped to the side, narrowly missing a Wither Cat as it lunged at the group. It swiped its claws deeply into the arm of one of the members of "The Collective" before running to a safe distance, hissing and retreating back into the concealing darkness.

"What in the abyss was that?" Hans shouted as he watched the retreating feline figure.

The leader looked away from his bleeding subordinate. "That's one of the new Mobs. They are on an entirely different level than the ones above. The Essence in the air... I can't even tell their ranking. They die a lot faster than the armored Bashers, but the wounds they inflict..." He waved at the downed man.

Hans moved in for a closer look. He frowned at the man who was writhing on the ground and beginning to scream, "Cut it off! Oh, gods, cut it off!"

"It looks like a shallow cut... Is it poison?" Hans spoke over the screams.

"The name is Nick, by the way—headman of 'The Collective'," the leader said with a worried look at his downed man. "I don't think so, but I can't tell for certain. We lost our healer earlier on this cursed floor."

Dale's group had come closer when the noise became audible, so Adam was quickly motioned over. He immediately sent healing light into the wound and gasped, sweat forming as he waged an intense battle. The screams died down, and the man began thanking Adam profusely.

"No, this is not over. I merely delayed the infection until a more powerful healer can fix it," the cleric informed his now nervous patient.

"What happened? What did it do?" Dale quizzed his friend.

<Yes, what *did* it do?> I asked with a quiet chuckle, making Dale look around in quiet fury at the surrounding— seemingly empty—dungeon. I had a few Mobs turn their heads so light bounced off their eyes at him, just to freak him out a bit.

Adam turned serious eyes on his group leader. "Whatever that *thing* was injected infernal Essence into the wound. The corruption wrapped the meridian, pulling it closed. Then it started forcing its way in, attempting to climb the meridian through a non-infernal affinity channel. I had to wrap the whole thing in a layer of Celestial Essence, and... I slowed it and eased the pressure, but it will gain strength again soon. It is already dismantling my barrier. He needs a powerful cleric if he wants to *live*, let alone regain use of his arm."

They lifted the man and exited the labyrinth with Hans and Nick providing rear security. Quickly climbing the stairs, they exited my awareness only a few minutes later.

<Dang. I did not realize it would be so effective!> I turned my joyful thoughts and attention fully to Dani, who hovered in the air with a line of worry coming across our link.

"Cal, I think that maybe this floor is too powerful for the majority of the people that typically come into the dungeon... Do you think that we should tone it down a bit?"

She seemed a bit nervous.

I certainly considered her words but ultimately decided that I disagreed with her. <I... think that this is the best course of action. Having a new floor should warn the adventurers that it will be far more dangerous, and I know for a fact that the loot on this floor is far better than what is on the other two.>

"You think they will agree that the rewards justify the risk then?" Dani queried me seriously.

<I do. Also, I never liked the fact that so many people were able to get right next to us. I seem to remember you telling me a long time ago that it should be *insanely* hard to get into the heart chamber.> I wondered where this was coming from; she had always been the biggest proponent of eating as many people as possible.

"Hmm. Okay, that is fair... I just worry about drawing in people that you can't handle. For instance, that powerful Mage that walks in every morning, avoids everything except Raile and then tears his armor off and butchers him. Do they eat him up there?" Dani curiously wondered.

<I assume so. He is just a glorified rabbit after all. Plus I have absorbed some jerky people dropped that contained a bit

of his Essence.> Dani shuddered when I mentioned this, so I tried to change the topic. <So, you were getting upset earlier when people cut down all of the plants in the garden room?>

Dani took the bait. "Yes! Not only that, but I have come up with a way to solve the problem."

<Do tell.> She sounded vicious and furious, making me get all excited!

"A Mini-Boss."

My enthusiasm waned a bit. <A what? Are you making up words again?>

She laughed. "You are going to like this! There is no real reason to cut down all the plants, right? So, we punish them for doing it! If they cut down a certain amount—let's say more than half—we allow a Boss to spawn in the room."

<I'm in. Did you have something in mind, or should I try and make something?>

She was silent a moment before answering shyly, "This is the part you... might not like."

<Go on. I said you had total control of that room, right? I won't go back on my word,> I assured her.

"I want you to put Banes in there," she informed me to my great disgruntlement.

<Dani. I thought we were finally done with those,> I whined.

"Hear me out! That wasn't the part you won't like. I want you to upgrade them... and use the tentacles from the Distortion Cat," Dani directed me.

I looked at her in great surprise. <Dani! Those made the Cat go insane! They are *horrible* parasites!>

"Right, right, right. But they made the Cats insane because the Cats were moderately intelligent. On the Banes, they should just be an appendage. Then the Bane will have a long, medium, *and* short-range attack! They might actually be useful! Think about it, revamping an old Boss that never got a kill..." She trailed off tantalizingly, watching for my reaction.

I was almost salivating at the thought of amending what I saw as a failed experiment. <Not fair. You know all of my weaknesses! I will try, but it is a moot point unless the patterns will mesh.>

"Just promise to give it your best shot, okay?" she muttered with concern. She knew how much I hated the mind-altering effects those tentacles used.

<Offensive! I always do my best for you!> I focused on the patterns in my mind, pulling them together and hoping that they wouldn't... I sighed. I tried the tentacle pattern with a different creature, then another...

"Well?" Dani demanded.

<Oh yes. They work with the Bane. Actually, the tentacles work with almost everything. Every different type of living creature I have ever made. I tried rocks and swords, but no luck there.> This garnered me a strange look. <What?>

"You tried on rocks...? You know what, never mind. Can you tie them to the room so that they spawn when plants are killed off?" she exasperatedly pushed the conversation forward.

<Yes... There we go! So, I redirected the Essence in that room into spawn 'seeds'. When about twenty-five percent of the plants are cut or destroyed, their Essence will spawn a new-style Bane. Basically, up to four can spawn in the room at a time. Now we just need to increase their rank and give them a new name,> I informed her, much to her delight.

I had kept my hidden 'failure room' on the second floor and was excited that I would get to play—erm—experiment again so soon after a large upgrade to my dungeon. I had made some upgrades to the room, basically what amounted to an acid waterfall that I could pour on to whatever was in the room. Then I could light it on fire—a very beneficial upgrade which allowed me to absorb my new creations right away.

I grew the small 'Bane plus tentacle' in the room and studied the G-rank nine creature. I was looking for signs of insanity or incompatibility and heaved a small sigh when there were no apparent negative effects.

<If this is what you were thinking, do you want me to use pure Essence or add in some combination of corruption?> I prodded Dani who was enraptured by the small Bane with a waving, probing tentacle.

"Oh! Um. If I have been correctly understanding what you've been doing recently, a combination would be best. Now, this has earth and water Essence, a bit more earth than water, creating a 'plant' Essence combination. With the tentacle, it has a large portion of infernal as well, so how about you try adding a mix of those three, keeping the ratios roughly the same?"

I looked at her in amazement; I had not realized she was paying that much attention when I babbled on about what I was doing! I needed to return the favor more frequently.

<On it. What Rank do you want it to be?>

She dithered a bit. "Well... the typical Mob on the first floor is an F-rank two or three, but this is a Boss... though there might be four of them..."

<Let's set them to be about the same rank as the first-floor Boss Squad. Most likely, they won't have all four show up at the same time, right? I say F-rank five or six, really *punish* them for damaging your herbs and flowers!> I got thoroughly enthusiastic about this idea.

"You just want more Essence," she grumbled with a chuckle in her voice.

<Well, yeah! If someone dies, I get all their refined Essence in one go! Otherwise, I need to cultivate just like the unwashed masses.>

I started directing Essence and corruption into the Bane, and it rapidly began to grow. At F-rank zero, a second tentacle sprouted; at F-rank four, a third appeared! I stopped it at F-rank six as promised and watched as it probed the air with the newly grown tentacles.

Remembering how the Distortion Cat attacked, I released a rabbit into the room. The tentacles went still, then the maws on the ends opened and tried to release a howl that would stun the small creature. They did roar, but there was no Essence in this howl. The wiggling weapons hissed in frustration. The rabbit tried to run away but didn't get far as the main body of the Bane released a thorn that killed the terrified creature from a dozen paces away.

<I've seen enough. I think it will work out just fine on the first floor.> I poured my favorite acid—etching solution—on to the Bane. It roared, coated in burning fluid, and slapped the tentacles on to the ground, uprooting the plant and throwing it out of the acid.

<Wow!> Luckily, the damage was done. After allowing a few moments for the acid to do its job, a new pattern flowed into my mind. Over the next few minutes, Dani and I worked out a plan to set up the Mini-Boss in the garden. Night was fast receding by this point, so there were no auras in the area to interfere with my work. Even the majority of the miners had left by this point, but there was one in full armor still banging away at the walls.

<All set, Dani. That'll be a nasty surprise for people tomorrow.>

CHAPTER TEN

Dale woke up and stretched, still amazed by his new body. He had only been asleep for three hours or so but was so well-rested that he had no choice but to get up and *do* something! He walked around until he grew bored, then he peered around the darkness and called out softly, "Any Elves nearby?"

"Right here, Your Grace." A form stepped out of the shadows. Dale hadn't met this one.

"Oh. Wonderful. I was wondering if you had... well first, what is the guard group here called?" Dale altered his tone and position to match the stance of a Noble talking to a respected elder. He assumed that almost any Elf was going to be older and wiser than him, so it should be a politically savvy move.

The Elf seemed to smile at him somehow, without his mouth moving. "We liked the title of your appointed judge, so we are currently going by 'The Protectorate' so *human* mouths can form the syllables of our position correctly."

Dale nodded. Though it seemed a bit derogatory, that was just how Elves acted. "Thank you for thinking about the people you are protecting. I need to speak with Princess Brianna. Do you by chance know if she is available?"

"She is. We require even less sleep than your people, so we have extended working hours. If you make your way to the Grove, I will go ahead of you to inform her of your impending meeting."

"That would be fine. Dismissed," Dale gave a ritualistic order, and the Elf vanished. "That wasn't too bad." He started walking toward the Elvish embassy—or 'Grove' as they called it—

when a distinctly non-Elvish form stepped from the lee of a large tent in front of him.

"Really, you shouldn't be out and about at this time of night, *Your Grace*," a rusty voice sneered condescendingly as Dale drew his oversized morningstar. "Haven't you heard that night air is bad for your health?"

Dale opened his mouth to demand answers—specifically why he was being stopped by this man—when a club hit him in the side of the face, knocking out teeth and breaking his jaw.

A dark chuckle came from the man in front of him. "Can't have you ordering us to leave, now can we?"

Delirious with pain, Dale still held to his training and began fighting the men that had appeared from behind buildings. He whipped his morningstar around him in tight arcs, blocking weapons and breaking bones. In moments, two attackers were dead, but the remaining men attacked without hesitation, beating Dale until his limbs were broken and he lay on the ground unable to fight back.

"Whew! Had a bit of fight in you, huh?" The first man laughed, grabbing Dale by his ankle and dragging him toward the entrance to the dungeon while the few other surviving men gathered the dead.

"Whhhhuuuu?" Dale moaned, face bouncing against a few rocks.

"What's that, dead man? *Why?* Well, it just so happens that you pissed off the wrong person. She's gonna waive the "tax" you put in place, and we get a bit of revenge. Ya see," he stopped and kicked Dale in the side, grinding broken ribs against each other, "fifteen percent tax means we haveta go in the dungeon almost ten times more than we should if we want. To. Retire." He finished the sentence calmly, kicking Dale at each pause. "You die, we get a bit on the side, and no taxes! Win-win-win for us, not so much for you."

The dragging continued, and Dale had a spark of hope as they approached the clerk checkpoint. The spark turned cold as the clerk that had gotten yelled at earlier stepped forward, grinning.

She looked up at the men. "Any trouble? Anyone see you?"

"Nope, all set here. Lost a few, but that was expected. More money for us if we don't have to split it, right?" The man grinned lecherously back at her. "I'll be back to take the other reward you offered later. Don't worry about the Guild. We will be able to honestly say that *we* didn't kill 'im." They started down the ramp—luckily for Dale's face, it was no longer a staircase—and quickly entered the dungeon.

They were just getting to the far side of the room when a miner stepped out from behind a corner, freezing as he saw what was happening. "What the abyss is going on here?"

"Don't you worry about it, half-breed. This don't concern your type."

The miner lifted the visor on his helm, revealing Evan the Dwork. "This be murder most foul, and I'll go to the abyss before I stand aside." He raised his pick and prepared to fight. It didn't go well for him. The other men were better armed and outnumbered the Dwork. They quickly rendered him unconscious and took his inscribed pick.

Laughing, the men went all the way to the first Boss Room, stripping Dale's armor before tossing him in alone. They debated a moment on whether or not to keep his weapon but ultimately decided that it was too easily recognizable. They threw his morningstar across the room, where it swiftly vanished

be gear or items beyond your capability to reach since you need to stay near me. Also, I want to see if my experimental weapon works how I think it should,> I assured her my intentions were good. Well. Beneficial. To us at least. <Oh! Also, Dale, if you would be so kind, kill them in the dungeon. Otherwise, it is just a big ol' waste all around.>

"Okay... Who are you talking to?" Dale looked around nervously at the sitting Bashers.

<Don't worry about it.> I turned to Dani, who was trying to get my attention. <Yes?>

Turns out she was just curious. "What is the weapon you are going to make?"

<Well... I know about a dozen Runes, twice that with their inverse. I need to expand my capabilities and see if I can weaponize some of the Runes that seem to be more... utility? Non-weapon?> She stared at me patiently as my tangent came to an end. <Right. Well, I have been thinking that the 'fluid repulsion' Rune that I have could be useful as a weapon, but it doesn't seem to affect living tissue. It is my belief that this is because of the aura that surrounds living things.>

She sighed. "Get to the point, Cal."

<Well,> I paused dramatically, <I think that if the Rune were to bypass the aura, it would affect them!>

She stared at me, nonplussed.

<Trust me. If it works, it will be an amazing weapon. So, I'm going to make a cloth wrapping for his hand. It has high-steel threading in it like chainmail. At the knuckles are small, spiked metal plates. The plate has a force enhancement Rune on it so he can hit a lot harder, and the spikes have the fluid repulsion Rune.> I thought a moment. <You think it needs anything else?>

"He does keep losing his gear. Is there a way to make it harder to lose?" Dani chuckled quietly, laughing at her joke.

I gave it serious thought, though. <Maybe... oh... this is a delicious idea.> I gave a wicked 'grin'.

She stopped laughing abruptly. "Oh no. What?"

<Wow! How about a little faith in my abilities?> I pretended to be hurt. She didn't buy it.

"Yeah, sure. What?" Dani demanded, tapping her non-existent toe.

<Fine, ruin the surprise. Humans have no use for corruption, right? What if it drew their corruption out of them and fed it to the weapon? It would make it harder to break, and if my door was any indication, no one could move or replicate it! Then when they die, I don't need to clean up all their taint!>

I was raring to go, the schematics in my head swirling into a cohesive whole. This... would be fun.

<Let's experiment.>

DALE

Nearly a half hour later, Dale climbed the stairs from the Boss Room, ascending into the predawn light. He clenched his fist, feeling the cloth tighten around his hand. He was wearing the new weapon—which doubled as the only piece of armor he had on—but Dale didn't trust it one bit. The dungeon, Cal, had called it an 'experiment', and looking at it made Dale a bit queasy. The armor was wrapped cloth, and had an almost slimy, oily texture.

Dale had been assured that activating the weapon would give him greater protection than plate armor, but the dungeon-creature—Cal—warned that there may be 'side effects'. Dale shivered, whether from the chill morning air against his almost-nude body or the dark thoughts, he was unsure.

The weapon that Dale had been given worried him. Would he really use this on another human? He thought for a moment. Yes. Not alone and certainly not without any other armor on. Dale started walking toward the Elven embassy, his original destination of the morning. He had not yet been there, and the amount of construction surprised him. Dale had thought that Elves would grow buildings or something—there were a lot of trees in this area now—but instead, it looked like workmen were constructing around the clock.

The buildings were masterfully created and were obviously built with defense in mind. Dale stopped in front of the only completed building, the sight forcing him to draw in a breath. The entire building was covered in Runes! He carefully looked at each individual Rune, trying to determine its purpose, but was stymied as he had never seen them before. He looked at more and realized in puzzlement that all the Runes were *exactly* the same. He thought about what this could mean as he was ushered in the door by the dangerous looking guard.

"Well! I didn't realize this was *that* kind of visit." Brianna stepped into the center of the room, looking at him oddly.

"What?" Dale was thinking about the Runes on the building. Maybe Cal would take a sample as payment?

"You are... um... in a state of undress, Dale." Brianna chuckled as Dale made the connection and flushed a bright red color. "Well, that blush goes *deep*! Did you need something?"

"Yes... I have forgotten why I was originally coming here, but I need a contingent of guards to come with me. A group of non-Guild affiliated adventurers and a clerk tried to kill me. That is why it took so long to get here. I need to round them up," Dale flatly informed her, ignoring his embarrassment.

"What?!" Her eyes scanned him, noting again the lack of armor and lingering on his hand. "You seem fine, so they clearly failed. Did they rob you?"

Dale shook his head. "No, they broke all of my bones and my jaw so I couldn't order them to leave my land. Then they dragged me into the dungeon and threw me into the first-floor Boss Room after tossing away my armor and weapon."

Fury colored her cheeks. "They will not survive the morning, but... how did you?"

Dale had agreed not to reveal that the dungeon was sentient. "I forced my Essence to flow and constrict quickly, allowing me to move myself like a puppet. I killed the monsters and found a healing fountain. I drank... almost the whole thing, re-aligning my bones with twists of Essence as they started to heal. There is *no way* I could do that again; I'm not really sure how I did it in the first place."

The words shock-and-awe did not adequately describe the look on Brianna's face as she paled. "Dale..." she began to question him.

"How about those guards?" Dale demanded loudly, ignoring protocol.

Brianna nodded, called in some guards, and personally joined them as they exited, intent on finding the failed assassins. As they left, a soft robe was wrapped around Dale, who nodded his thanks. He ignored the fact that it was bright pink.

They walked stealthily toward the clerk barracks, a large tent pitched between the Guild tent and the dungeon. There were rotating shifts for the clerks, so they usually had plenty of free space when off duty. As luck would have it, the majority of the men that attacked Dale were standing near the tent, softly chuckling at the sounds coming from inside. Looks like their leader was in the process of getting his 'extra bonus'. Dale pointed at the men and nodded; the guards around him blurred and there were suddenly several unconscious forms on the ground.

Without the noise, the sounds from inside were louder. A moan drifted out, making Dale blush a bit. The Guards lined up outside the tent flap and charged inside to a roar and a scream. In moments, the man and woman were led out with only a thin blanket covering them. The man blustered while the clerk cried, both of them pretending innocence. They saw Dale standing in front of them and went nearly silent.

"Oh shi–" the man spoke before being knocked unconscious.

"Wait! Wait, wait, *wait*" the hysterical woman screamed. "How are you here? If you are alive, we did nothing–" She was placed on the ground as well, after a light clubbing to the head.

"I assume they are why I was woken up so rudely?" a wry voice spoke. Dale turned and noticed Protectorate Cole—his appointed magistrate—walking toward him, escorted by guards and shivering. "It is starting to get pretty cold up here."

"Your honor," Dale nodded at the man, "these people attacked me with no provocation, removed all of my Inscribed armor and weapons, broke my bones, and left me for dead in the dungeon."

The Judge studied his face, nodding after a moment. "I see no lies in your aura, and yet, here you stand, seemingly unharmed. Explain?" he politely demanded.

"I made my way out of the dungeon without dying after the ordeal," Dale hedged, refusing to say more.

Cole stared at him and nodded slowly. "Fair enough, though we will talk more on this later. Wake them up. I will question them and give my sentence."

Soon, there was a groaning, pleading, and self-righteous mass of people on their knees. One by one, Cole asked them questions and seemed unsatisfied with their answers. Grimly, he walked back to Dale.

"Well. Before I make an unalterable decision, what was the total worth of your armor and weapons?" Cole quizzed Dale.

"I purchased the armor for several hundred gold at a Guild discount but never had the weapon appraised. I would place its worth around three thousand gold, as it had two powerful Inscriptions on it," Dale morosely informed him, trying to be professional.

Cole winced and patted him on the back. "Ouch. Well, that certainly decides it. They do not have enough money *combined* to repay that amount, but everything in their Guild accounts is yours as well as all personal items—which will be sold off. The attempted murder and placing of bounties against a Noble is enough for them to be skinned, salted, drawn and quartered, then burned."

The group started wailing, all but the woman. Cole looked at her and shuddered. "There was more wrong in her than just this would account for. I think being caught has broken her mind."

She looked up and gave a twisted grin. "Cole! Judgey! Let me speak!"

He stared at her and slowly nodded. "If you have something to say, out with it."

"Well your judgey-ness, all I have to say is this." She started laughing very creepily. "If you are what you eat, I am an innocent man! Haahah!"

Cole froze and looked coolly at the guard behind her. "She is *not* lying. Silence her. She will die first. Though I'd keep my hands away from her mouth if at all possible if I were you."

The guard being spoken to jerked his hands back.

Cole turned to Dale. "Is there a specific way you want this carried out, or should we use the standard I described?"

All eyes suddenly on him, Dale looked over the group with hard eyes. "We will give them the same chance they gave to me. Bring them to the dungeon."

CHAPTER ELEVEN

<It is a little early for most people to be coming in here, but there is a large group approaching,> I told Dani, concerned that a small army might be planning to attack me at once.

Before she could respond, I noticed Dale walk inside wearing a fluffy pink robe. Dani started laughing for some reason.

<Dale? I don't know what kind of fabric that is, so if you give it to me, I will give you a month to get me that bag that is bigger on the inside.>

Dale gave a subtle nod and loosened the robe as more people walked in behind him. There were a few men and a woman. After a moment, I recognized them as the people that had dragged Dale in here this morning.

<See, Dani? I told you he would keep his bargain.>

The men and the woman were stripped of all gear and pushed into the mouth of the tunnel. They started pleading—a few tried to run, but sharp swords blocked their paths. The leader of the men went red in the face and charged at Dale, who used this excuse to toss his robe to the side and take up a fighting stance. I quickly ate the fluttering robe, of course.

The man swung his beefy arms in an attempt to batter Dale to the floor but gasped in surprise as Dale easily blocked his arms. Dale reached back, then swung a wild yet powerful blow into the man's chest, activating his—I called it a battle gauntlet—for the first time.

The spikes on the knuckles penetrated the unprotected flesh while the force enhancement helped drive them in powerfully. As soon as the spikes had broken the skin and driven in a bit, the liquid repulsion Rune activated perfectly—as I *knew* it would! The fluid in the man—water, fatty tissue, blood—was driven away from the impact site. Suddenly, there was no blood for the heart to pump, and the organ went into shock and quickly died. The pain must have been terrible. His muscles were no longer hydrated, which would have felt like a muscle cramp in every affected portion. Luckily for the man, the pain was as short-lived as he was.

The dying man had broken blood vessels and arteries along his entire body as the liquid was forced back against its normal flow. He slumped in Dale's arms and fell to the floor unmoving. A rush of Essence assured me he had died. Seeing their leader mutilated so, the remaining men stopped trying to get past the ring of guards and slowly walked down the tunnel. The woman skipped.

A small groan startled both Dale and me as a form stood up a few feet to the side, hidden by shadows. "Ugh. Dale? Izzat you? You're alive? You 'scaped?"

"Evan!" Dale cried, grabbing the Dwork and pulling him into a hug. "You survived?!"

"Obviously," the blushing armored man muttered. "They sure knocked me out good, though. I am *so* surprised I woke up. May as well not have, though. I'm thousands of gold in debt now... and my pick is gone. Should just throw myself to the Bashers."

Dale laughed and slapped him on the back, unfortunately using his right hand. The Dwork was thrown forward while releasing a startled shout. He stood up and glared, brushing off his dented armor.

Stupid aura protecting his fluids.

"Oops," Dale muttered, deactivating his battle gauntlet. "I have your pick outside! You will be just fine, my friend."

The Dwork broke into a sunny, toothy grin. "Oh yeah? Well, thank you. Friend, huh?"

"Of course. Anyone who tries to save my life while not standing a snowflake's chance could be nothing less," Dale assured him.

"In that case," Evan grinned, "I hear your friends eat at that fancy-shmancy restaurant out there. Got room for one more?"

"Anytime you'd like, my treat! Forever." Dale led them out, leaving a few guards to watch for the convicts.

They needn't have worried.

The unarmored group had stopped in Dani's garden, forming a few crude weapons out of some wood they tore off of small saplings.

<Four percent,> I muttered. They continued, pulling fruit and vegetables for a light breakfast, unconcernedly swinging their sticks at the grass and herbs to get to the crop-bearing plants. <Twelve percent.>

They sat in a half ring, their backs to the wall. The woman ignored them, dancing around and gathering flowers while humming and singing nonsensically. Forgetting that they had no way to start one, they built a small fire pit and gathered plants to burn.

<Twenty-four percent,> I muttered in frustration. A small argument broke out; then one of the men with fire Essence grimaced and released a burst of Essence into the pile. Soon, they were sitting around a fragrant fire, watching for Bashers.

"Ohh! Pretty!" The woman reached out and plucked a heavy rose.

<Twenty-*five* percent,> I said with malicious glee.

The room went still, the Bashers no longer moving in the underbrush. A lump of earth began to bulge up from the ground, dirt cascading away from it as tentacles burst from the cracked soil. The men began to notice the lack of sound and reached for their makeshift clubs, and—in one case, someone brandished a burning log.

"What?"

"What do you mean, 'what'? Can't you sense the room? Something just changed."

"La-la-la."

"Someone shut that crazy broad up!"

"Ahh! Something got my leg!"

Yup. A *tentacle*, good sir. The man was yanked from his feet and dragged into the underbrush as his friends yelled and leaped to his aid. They crashed through the plants, only to stop in terror as a human-sized Shroomish with waving tentacles opened a massive maw in its stalk and bit the struggling man in half. Intestines and gore splashed to the ground. The remaining tentacles were petting the Shroomish like a human praising a small animal with a treat.

"What in the *abyss*?" one of the men gasped.

The tentacles suddenly stiffened, orienting themselves toward the new sound and lunging forward. One of the men was skewered by an undulating tentacle and pulled in, but the other dodged and began to run. The maw on the tentacle that had missed roared and stabbed the ground, uprooting the main body and throwing the entire plant at the fleeing man. The combined weight of the Shroomish and two dead bodies crashed into the man, driving him to the floor where he died quickly from thorns and poison.

The woman had ignored all of the commotion, continuing to gather flowers and singing broken melodies. A tentacle reached out and almost gently drew her toward the main body. An infernal maw crooned, and the Shroomish paused in its feast and appeared to consider the woman. It shook itself suddenly, releasing a cloud of spores which settled on her before the tentacle pushed her away—deeper into the dungeon.

<What in the crap just happened there?> I watched as the giant mushroom came to the end of its lifespan. I had designed it so that it would die five minutes after reaching full size; I didn't want swarms of Mini-Bosses running the place.

"Obviously, it is more effective in combat than we thought it would be," Dani murmured. "Keep an eye on the woman, see what happens."

<Oh! We never named that Boss. What do you want to call it?>

Dani looked at me like I was crazy. "Now? That is what you are thinking about?"

<...Yes?>

"Fine. How about... Glade?" she suggested after a moment's hesitation.

<Um. Okay. Why?>

"Well," she blushed a bit, "my other suggestions have been cute or pretty, but this one is more to do with its... existence. A glade is an open space in a forest, and these spawn when a space is opened due to chopping plants down. An 'open space' or 'glade' as it were."

I radiated approval. *<Awesome! A play on words! Two things I love, words and puns. Nice work. I hereby name them 'Dire Shroom: Glade' or Glade for short.>*

"Now, back to business?" Dani prodded me firmly.

<Yeah, yeah, I've been watching her. She is just sort of stumbling around... oh. There. She fell. She is in a tunnel though and... not dead. Nope. Just lying there with mushrooms sprouting all over her body. They aren't pushing through the skin, but they are certainly mushrooms.> I noticed her starting to

panic—Dani that is—<No, they don't have tentacles, but her aura is hiding the details enough that I can't tell what they do to humans. We are just going to have to wait and see. I don't think they are the reason she collapsed. She is just exhausted from the night I think.>

"Tell me right away if she does anything. I'll want to take action."

<I will. I promise.>

DALE

Dale got to know Evan a bit better over breakfast, and they made plans to meet up again soon. Unfortunately, they didn't have too much in common. While they enjoyed their conversation and parted friends, there was no real impetus to prolong their meal. Evan had his Inscribed pick back and wanted to get some sleep before re-entering the mining area of the dungeon, while Dale had several people to talk to about the events of the evening. Talking to the Guild and telling the Elves the full story took until lunch—when he had planned to meet his group.

"Oh look! The emperor deigns to speak to the *little people!*" Hans called as Dale walked into the room. They were at the *Pleasure House* of course.

"Oh, whine more. Pff. At least you entertain us by varying what you complain about," Rose chastised him.

Tom nodded seriously. "Verily, I have heard that the events of this early morning provide sufficient cause for Dale to receive lenient treatment from us."

"You doing all right, Dale?" Adam looked at his unarmored friend.

That Dale was out of his armor was strange enough, but coupled with his fiercely burning blue eyes and emaciated form, Dale looked downright frightening.

Trying not to scowl, Dale sat down and angrily cut into his steak. "Yeah, this morning sucked. Let's hurry up and get to the dungeon. I feel the need to kill something."

"About that..." Hans had all eyes locked on him as soon as he finished these words.

"Yes?" Dale drew the word out warningly.

Hans raised his eyebrow at the tone. "We can go in and fight, but I think that the third floor is going to have to wait a good long time. The team that we rescued had all D-ranked members, and three were killed while one was severely injured."

"How is he, by the way?" Adam interjected.

Once a patient, always a patient.

Hans tossed his hands in the air and made a noncommittal gesture. "He is stable, but they took too long to figure out how to fix the damage. I don't think he will ever get full use of that arm back."

"I thought they were just unprepared?" Rose contritely confessed.

"Just let me finish!" Hans ordered. "The Spotter report on the new Mobs was released this morning, and they were found to be D-rank two. They also obviously have some nasty abilities, and... they have Beast cores." The final comment made everyone wince.

"What? So what?" Dale looked at the faces around him.

Rose took pity on him. "It means that they are intelligent. We are talking at least near-human levels of intelligence. They have accumulated enough Essence that it began to crystallize and formed a central area for their Essence to accumulate. They are now Magical Beasts and far more dangerous than simple animals."

"There is that much of a difference?" Dale was unconvinced.

Hans took over the conversation, "Let me offer an example. You got ambushed this morning, yes? I read the report—when they were caught and sentenced, one of the men attacked you, and you easily stopped him although he was much larger than you... correct?"

Dale nodded, unsure of where this was going.

"Well, that man was in the upper F-ranks and had only one of his meridians open. The Boss on the second floor, Raile? That big bunny is F-rank nine and is already hard for us to beat unless *I* were to take it out and didn't bother to let you fight at all. Those men were *weaker* than Raile and were still able to beat you. Yes, it was because they snuck up on you, but well, they did. Not a criticism, but you really need to learn to control your Essence so you can better protect yourself. As it stands, I— that is, *just* me—could go to the third floor and likely be okay, but you would all probably die if you tried it." Hans finished his ominous speech by eating a scoop of iced cream.

Dale considered his options but finally agreed that Hans was correct. "Fine, what do we need to do?"

"There are several things to do, thanks for asking!" Hans exclaimed joyously, obviously uncaring of the somber mood. "Firstly, we need to get Tom into the D-ranks. Second, you should go collect the Essence techniques you were promised by the Elves. Third, you all need to learn to control your Essence. Finally, we need to get into the dungeon and cultivate until we go mad with boredom."

Dale's eyes bulged a bit as he remembered the memory stones the Dark Elves had promised him. "Dang it. Right, I'll go get them. How do we learn to use our Essence better?"

"You have a tutor show you. You have Craig. Adam has Father Richard,"

Adam shuddered at those words.

"Rose has Chandra, and Tom... I'll teach Tom." Hans sighed at the thought of long hours with the overly formal young barbarian.

"Huzzah! I had hoped that you would take me under thine tutelage but had thought the dream was only that. I am ready to begin my training forthwith, Master." Tom stood from his seat and bowed at Hans.

"No. Sit," Hans barked at the man towering above him. Tom complied, making Hans laugh. "See? He takes well to training."

This prompted a round of chuckles from the group and a blush from Tom.

The meal ended, and Dale made his way to the Elven embassy. He arrived in front of the highly Runed building and asked to see Princess Brianna. After a short wait, he was ushered inside to find her lounging at her desk with a box in front of her.

"Finally remembered these, I assume?" Brianna laughed at Dale's reddening face. "We had a bet going to see when you would. I had said tomorrow, dang it. I'm down ten silver! All is well, though. Ready to learn some of the most highly kept secrets of earthen Essence?"

Dale nodded again, not trusting himself to speak without his excitement breaking his voice. Brianna pointed out the stone that contained the Royal cultivation technique, and he reached for that first. A better technique would allow him to gain ranks much faster. He touched the stone, and the cloth wrapping on his hand suddenly parted, grabbing the stone and binding it tight.

"Hey!" Dale yelled at his offending armor. "Give me that!"

Obviously, the gauntlet didn't respond. The cloth wrapped bulge remained perfectly still.

Brianna looked at his gauntlet seriously for the first time. "What in the world? Dale, can I see that gauntlet?"

"Sure." He held up his hand for her to look at his new... weapon? Armor? He realized he didn't really know what to call it.

She arched her brow at him and asked him to take it off and hand it to her. He *tried* to do so, but as soon as he started unwrapping the layers, they tightened enough to stop the flow of blood in his arm.

"Ow!" He retracted his hand, and the wraps loosened to their normal tightness. "That hasn't happened before..." he muttered worriedly.

"You were able to take it off before?"

"Yes, I had tried it on my left hand, but it didn't fit. Then I took it off when I was wearing the robe..."

"When did you activate it? Before or after you took it off?"

With dawning horror, Dale realized what she meant. "I took it off *before* I activated it..."

Brianna nodded slowly, face far more pale than usual. "Dale, you are wearing a piece of cursed armor. I'll send a report to the Spotters, but you should be careful with that. While *very* powerful, they tend to damage the person using them."

"Of course they do." Dale sighed, waving away her concerns. "So, I am down one stone already. Any way to take this off?"

Brianna reluctantly nodded. "A strong enough flesh Mage could remove it by... well. They basically need to skin your arm. They take the top layer of skin and draw the whole construction off you. Very painful and very expensive. Also, with those wraps... I am uncertain that would work. They may just wrap themselves higher up your arm."

"Destroying it maybe...?" Dale tried to sound hopeful, yet was very unconvincing.

"That carries a high risk of taking the arm but is possible. You could also cut it off," Brianna reassured him.

"...Yay. Let's just do the other stones?" Dale reached for a memory stone—very intentionally using his *left* hand—and pulled out one that had an earthy look to it.

He placed the stone against his head and was mesmerized as the memories of a powerful earth Essence user flowed into his mind. He watched as the Elf discovered how to use his own Essence and how he pushed it out and looped it, forming the needed pattern in the earth and reabsorbing the Essence used, forming a continuous loop until the process was finished.

Dale knew with certainty that if he forgot to loop the Essence back to himself, it would be gone forever, and he would need to re-cultivate it. This particular memory was only meant to teach him how to use a movement technique, but it did so much *more* since Dale had never used his earth Essence for anything but activating a weapon before. The memory taught him about affinity channels, the pathways that were open to allow a specific type of Essence to move along them. The Elf had the earthen affinity channel open fully and fire open only part way.

Dale came out of the momentary trance he had fallen into and did what anyone else would have. He tried to use the technique, looping out his Essence and allowing the earth itself to propel him along. Instead, his Essence rebounded against his aura, lashing back into his body and making his muscles spasm before—vindictively?—pushing the muscle aside and flowing into his meridians. Dale fell flat on his face while emitting a rather rude stream of expletives.

"Dale!" Brianna tried to admonish him while also trying very hard not to laugh. "Just because you know *how* to do it doesn't mean you *can*. You need to practice that slowly! The Elf this came from was a master of earthen Essence and had mastered this technique over years of *experience*."

Dale groaned miserably. "I thought the whole point of memory stones was to be able to bypass that whole process..."

"No, they allow you to bypass the years of trial and error that go into *creating* the technique. You still need to practice it! There will be many failed attempts before you are able to use it at even a fraction of its strength." Brianna looked at Dale's nonplussed face.

"Look, if you picked up a sword, it would take years to create a sword form, build muscle to wield it, and practice enough to use it casually—not to mention using it in combat. If you got a sword art memory stone, you could bypass *learning* the forms and stances, but you would still need to build your own way of using it, muscle, and muscle memory. Get it?"

"I do. You are saying that this was not a pointless deal and I should be grateful that I don't need to spend years twisting my Essence in the dirt to see if something happens." Dale chuckled. "Fair enough, but... dang. I really wanted to try moving that fast."

Brianna raised her eyebrow with a grin. "You know, if you had *actually* succeeded in using that technique, it likely would have broken the bones of whatever limb you had touching the ground. You weren't properly braced, and your *legs* would have flown forward while the rest of you stayed still for a moment. If you think about it, you got off rather lucky."

"...I see," Dale stammered as he tried to think of something intelligent to say. "How about I just use the next one? I think we are planning on going into the dungeon soon."

He reached for the third stone and placed it carefully against his forehead. Memories of decade-long research flashed by. Dale saw—was—the Elf who created this stone. He remembered practicing by moving stones one at a time, moving on to making earth crumble at a touch, until finally learning and using the technique mastered in his old age... as he smashed Dwarven defenses from a distance, collapsing a mountain during a war.

Dale looked up finally, tears shining in his eyes. "Brianna," he gasped, "there has never been emotion in a memory stone before this! Why? The Elf felt nothing but horror for the technique he had made! *Why* would you give me this without warning?! Why would you *ever* use this technique again?"

Brianna patted him on the arm. "Most people that make memory stones work hard to send along only the dry information. The Elf who mastered this technique was one of the greatest stone Mages in our history, and he thought that there should never be knowledge of how to destroy. At least, not without a deep insight into the horror that came with it."

"Is there a reason I was given this stone?" Dale demanded, trying to shake off the feeling of killing a city—not an easy feat. They were now *his* memories; he may as well have actually been there doing the deed himself.

Brianna gave a weak grin. "Well... it is well known that this Elf makes stones that pass along his emotional state, so..."

"No one else wanted it, did they?" Dale cut her off.

"Pretty much. It is very powerful, though and should have given you techniques to use to build up strength until you can use the mastered version," Brianna informed him.

"It did, but I can see why no one wanted to use it. Very sneaky of you. Look, I need to get going, but we will talk later?" Dale started marching out of the room.

"Hold a moment? You have no armor and a new weapon that you have not trained with. Are you sure jumping into the dungeon is a great idea?" Brianna questioned him.

"Nah, it is a *terrible* idea. I'm doing it anyway. I'll see you later."

Chapter Twelve

Dani groaned as the mad woman covered in mushrooms threw herself at yet *another* Basher. It seemed that the lady was filled with an unhealthy rage; anytime she saw movement, she ran at it screaming, attacking with her bare hands or anything else that she could find. After she killed whatever she attacked, she seemed to get her mind back, at least partly. She would alternate weeping and searching through small treasure chests. Already, she had found a sharp dagger and armor for her legs, which was all she needed to fight successfully against the waves of Bashers.

"It just doesn't make sense! She is, what, F-rank five? There is no way she should be fighting all of those herself and surviving!" Dani despairingly groaned *again*.

<Dani, that is the fifth time you said that. I get it, I *really* do. I think that those mushrooms on her are driving her to attack. Look, she has serious wounds but is ignoring them. Anytime she sees something, she just *has* to kill it. Remind you of anything?> I queried her, trying to lead her to my own conclusion.

"The Distortion Cat?" She spoke after a few moments, "You think those are parasites like the tentacles were?"

<I do, and sooner or later, she will get killed, and I will know for certain. No worries,> I assured her.

Dani tried to focus on other things, but I could hear her muttering every few minutes. Finally, something changed. "Look! A group is coming closer to her! Okay... they see her. She is just crying right now. They look concerned...oh, dear."

They had gotten close to the near-nude woman and touched her bare shoulder. The woman gave a bestial snarl, turning and plunging her dagger into the neck of the man beside her. Howling, she ran at the other shocked members and was able to stab one to death before the others stopped seeing her as a human and began to see her as a monster. She was cut down in moments, and I waited to examine her pattern.

<Huh. Nothing,> I muttered.

"What do you mean, 'nothing'? Obviously, *something* happened there," Dani responded angrily.

I was very confused. <It must be an effect of the mushrooms. If they had left her body, I would be able to break it down and see the physical component of things. As it is, all I can see is a way to recreate her original body, and they just put her *current* body into one of those bigger-on-the-inside bags. I can't examine the changes if they aren't here, and it looks like that group is turning around and leaving. I'm not getting a chance here, Dani. Right, first thing to do is alter the pattern of the Mini-Bosses so they don't have spores anymore. I don't want an unknown factor in here.>

"Smart. How about–"

<Then later we will get some Bashers infected with the spores to see what happens,> I stated gleefully.

"O-o-of course we will," Dani muttered. "I rescind my 'smart' comment."

<What? Why?>

Dani gave a short 'haw' of laughter, but I cut her off before she could respond.

<Hey! Dale is here! No armor today. Hmm. He seems a bit peaked. Feeling alright there, Dale?>

"*You gave me a cursed weapon! No, I am not doing alright!*" Dale thought at me furiously.

<What's your point?> I watched as he ran forward and punched a Basher, the force of the blow coupled with the

gauntlet's Runes blasting most of the poor animal's blood out of its body. The small corpse looked very different emptied of fluids.

"My point *is that it is apparently killing me slowly and stealing my stuff."*

He definitely seemed a bit out of sorts. <What? Nah, there is no point for me to give you something that kills you outside of here. That battle gauntlet is tethered to the corruption in your Core. It will help purify the Essence in your Core as well... I'm not sure why you are upset, really. You're acting like a spoiled child.>

Dale paused in his rampage, the massacre of small furry animals slowing for a moment. *"Wait, you actually gave me something helpful? Did you* intend *for it to steal from me?"*

I had no idea what he was talking about, so I looked closer at his arm. There was indeed a bulge in the armor that hadn't been there before.

<Well, to be fair... while it *may* be helpful for you, it helps me out to not have to refine all the Essence you are going to give me when you die in here. Less corruption is good for me as well.>

"Oh, gee, thanks," Dale thought at me wryly, but now his face wasn't a mask of fury. Instead, he seemed contemplative.

I wanted to know what his armor had hidden, so when he gave a particularly wild swing, I gave a mental command to the wrap to release. To my surprise, it did! A shining Core flew across the room, shattering against a stony crenellation. I felt a small burst of Essence release, though it felt... different. It reached me, and my mind expanded.

I watched in silent awe—through eyes that were not my own—as hundreds of Elves sat in an ancient dungeon, meditating. I saw them all change the way they drew in Essence.

Hundreds of patterns of fractals changed from one moment to the next as every feasible possibility was attempted. The memory sped up, and a time period of decades passed in mere moments. I felt the frustration of the stones creator as he worked day after day with no noticeable improvement in cultivation technique.

In disgust, the Elf pushed away his fractal, and to his amazement, Essence suddenly flooded him. Another decade passed as he toyed with this new concept, altering the flow one tiny bit at a time. The final pattern, the fractal he found to be the very best, stayed in his mind as he ran off to explain his new cultivation technique. Slowly, the memory faded away.

<That's it? That is the secret? The product of almost a hundred years?> I laughed aloud, startling Dani and freaking out Dale. He looked around in terror for a moment.

"What is it, Cal?" Dani tore her thoughts away from another group gathering herbs in the garden room.

<It seems I have a new cultivation technique. I'm going to try it out.>

"*You have* what*?! You thieving bast–*"

<Sorry, Dale! I'm rather busy right now! I have... a... thing to do.> I turned to Dani. <It looks like I'll need to focus on this for a bit, kinda like when I first made my fractal? Keep an eye out for me!> I didn't wait for her to reply, although I am sure she understood.

I focused inward, taking the fractal within my Core and slowing it. As the flow of Essence lessened, I *pushed* with my willpower. The fractal rolled and split into damaged Chi threads. I grasped each of the threads and pushed, over and over. Soon, instead of a flat fractal that spanned my Core, I had an intricate *sphere* of fractals. The detail of it was mind-boggling, the quantity of fractals as numerous as the grains of sand in my walls.

When I was certain that I could hold the pattern without too much effort, it was nighttime and most of the population had retired for sleep or other assorted activities. The third floor was absolutely *stuffed* full of loose Essence; I had not used any nor cultivated for nearly half a day.

<Dani,> I mentally prodded her. <Dale is gone, right?>

"Hmm? Yeah, welcome back. Everything working out for you?" Dani sleepily murmured at me.

<Yes... I'm going to try to cultivate right now. Watch and see if you can tell a difference?>

When she acquiesced, I opened myself up to the Essence of the heavens and the earth. Like lightning had struck, the air in the room shifted and vibrated violently. I screamed as Essence was *ripped* out of the air and forced into me. Only the billions of pathways that the Essence needed to traverse kept me from exploding from the massive overdose. I stopped pulling, rather cheerful with the test run and feeling a bit full for the first time in days.

"What. The. Abyss," Dani gasped. "*If* I notice a difference?! What the heck *was* that? It sounded like the mountain was collapsing!"

<I think it is called a 'master level' cultivation technique. It looks like it took about a century to create and a decade or so to refine into its current form,> I told her cheerfully.

"You set it up in only a few *hours*? How?" Dani demanded in excitement.

<Here is the cool part, Dani. I've made this pattern *before* now. All I had to do was apply the fractal of Essence to myself with slight alterations.> I was keeping the key bit of information from her, and she started grumbling hard enough that I finally relented with a laugh, <Dani, look at the pattern. Recognize it at all?>

She stared for nearly ten minutes—almost giving up—when she had a breakthrough. "Cal! Is that... the same...? That is the same pattern as a Wisp!" She gasped in fear and amazement.

<All but the parts that make it living and thinking!> I crowed. If I had feet, I would have been dancing right then. <Do you know what this means? I knew Wisps were pure Essence, but now it makes sense how you can survive without a body! Wisps are incredibly Essence efficient. All you need is a *little* bit, and it keeps you going! You are a thought form surrounded by a cultivation technique, like how I am a thought form surrounded by crystal!>

Dani seemed dazed, the information a huge shock. The history of Wisps and how they came to be was one of their race's greatest sought-after secrets. This information was a huge leap forward to her knowledge, and she felt like she could be the first of her kind to learn *why* they existed and how they came to be.

"Cal... this is huge. You have no idea."

<Right?! I've been sitting on the edge of D-rank five. Is this the kind of knowledge I needed to reach D-six?> I plagued her with questions, not catching her mood.

"Uh... well, I suppose. Usually, moving into D-six requires you to learn how to store your Essence in your aura—further strengthening your body and such—but this will work just as well. You will certainly need to know by the time you break into the C-rankings, but I think that you can probably break through your barriers to advancement right now. Cultivate away!"

<Will do!> The air tremored again as I drew hard on the dense Essence in the air, while Dani stared contemplatively into the distance.

DALE

Dale awoke to the sound of rolling thunder and stepped out of his tent expecting to be soaked in rain within a few moments. He looked up to check the cloud cover but was instead able to see a clear, beautiful morning. He frowned. Normally a clear day helped to cheer him up, but now, he was only suspicious. By the time he had eaten and gotten ready for the day, the intermittent sounds had faded to nothing.

"Anyone know what's going on?" Dale asked his friends quizzically.

Adam looked up from a dauntingly huge plate of eggs. "Hmm? Well, I hear that a group of Nobles is going to be showing up today. I don't really have the details on that."

"Not what I meant, but that is certainly good to know. I was thinking more about that thunder." Dale gave a half-smile at his friend.

"Most likely no reason to worry." Hans popped a Basher-sausage into his mouth.

Rose snorted. "*Everything* worries our fearless leader." The dichotomy of the statement got a chuckle from the group. A knock at the door cut their merriment short.

Brianna opened the door and stepped inside. "Dale, have you heard that thunder? We were worried that–" Her mouth fell open as she saw Rose at the table. "Rosey? Little Sapling-Rose?"

Rose flushed and muttered, "Hello, Aunt Ironbark. Good to see you again."

"Rose!" Brianna rushed to hug the uncomfortable young woman. "Why didn't you tell me that you were here?! You look so well! Of *course,* you would be here, you can cultivate here!"

"You are babbling again."

Brianna snorted. "I tend to do that when surprised! To my point, why didn't you come see me?"

Rose blushed and looked down, mumbling.

"They did *what?*" Brianna roared.

Everyone jumped, and Hans looked around in confusion. "You could hear that? I couldn't hear that. You?"

Adam shook his head, eyes wide.

"She said that she tried to come see me and the guard told her in no uncertain terms that a *half-breed* was unwelcome anywhere near me!" Essence was flashing in her eyes, and a buildup of unreleased Mana was tearing a hole in the visual world around her, distorting her visage. She growled, "Who were they? Heads will *roll!*"

Chandra bustled in at a sprint. "You! Stop that at once. Losing control of yourself like this... Oh. Hello, my niece. Calm yourself."

"Pff." Brianna seemed to drain of anger. "Just because your daughter married my brother does not make *me* your niece."

A pounding on the stairs announced a new presence. "Hey! Whoever is throwing around highly concentrated Mana like that had better *stop*. You made my portal flicker. If someone had been in there at that time, they would have been sliced clean in half!" High Magous Amber burst into the room and glared at the occupants. "Who did this? Who woke me up at this ungodly hour?"

"Heh." Hans whispered to Dale, "Look at that! We have Amber, Brianna, Chandra, and Dakota all in the same room! Go talk with them. It'll be a conversation between A, B, C, and D!"

"Who is Dakota?" Dale whispered back.

"What?"

"You said 'and Dakota'." Dale narrowed his eyes. "Did you just... You just got my name wrong! Hans!"

"You must have misheard." Hans brushed him away. "You better go. It looks like we are about to have some bloodshed otherwise."

Dale glowered at his friend still but stood and addressed the deadly women glaring at each other, "The situation is over and done with. Please act like the adults, business leaders, or heads of state that you are. Thanks."

Hans gaped at Dale as he sat back down and started eating. "Very political. Smooth even."

Dale shrugged. "They aren't fighting each other anymore, right? Acting professional again?" Dale was facing away from them as they stalked closer, ready to start yelling again. "After all, I would hate to order them to leave. We can't have people that could single-handedly destroy a city acting like spoiled brats. People would get nervous."

The ladies paused, passed a considering look around, and straightened themselves. Dale turned around to see them starting to make polite conversation.

"By the way, High Magous, I hear we are going to have some Noble visitors arriving soon? Do you have any information about that?"

She looked for a moment like she was not going to say anything. "Ah well, they will be here soon, and everyone will know anyway. Yes, there is a full entourage of Nobles arriving. There will be a Prince and Princess, but mostly, there will be... how to say, non-main branch family members?"

"Ah. I see." Dale paused. "Non-main because they were born into those families or because they failed to achieve 'greatness' in a fast enough time?"

Amber looked surprised while Brianna smirked. Amber responded slowly, "I would say *born* into the family. I would also remind you not to ask *them* that question if you meet them. Most are in their mid-twenties and therefore not at the end of their trials as it is, and it would be considered the height of rudeness. Actually, since you are here, I was hoping to go over some land issues and building areas for the Nobles' contingent. Obviously, they won't want to stay in tents, but..."

Dale waved her down as his team gave low groans. "No, sorry, no city business right now! Get it approved by the council, then the city planner, and *then* me. We talked about this. We are just about to head into the dungeon. The team is getting a bit anxious to go."

His group looked very relieved upon hearing this.

Brianna piped up, "Still no other armor, Dale?"

"It is rather expensive to–" Dale began when Tom cut him off.

"Ha! As if he needs armor! Not a full day previous, he stood amidst the foes in the dungeon and battered them down with his bare hands. The carnage he blissfully brought down upon his foes was glorious to behold, and he stood like a true warrior! Barely armored, he weathered the storm. In my culture, he is at *last* considered a man!" Tom boasted on behalf of his leader. A shocked silence followed his words.

Brianna recovered first, "Well, I am sure he appreciates that. Moving on–quickly–does this mean you are planning on changing your entire fighting style?"

Dale nodded. "All of that armor weighed me down, and I *still* needed to dodge almost everything or I got seriously hurt. Don't get me wrong, I am glad I wore it in the past–I have muscles I never expected–but without it, I can slip past most of the attacks that come my way and counter them much easier."

"Hmm. Well, talk to Craig, your mentor," Chandra joined the conversation out of the blue. "He is a master of hand-to-hand fighting techniques, and I am sure he would be able to teach you."

"I plan on it. We have a training session after lunch and–"

Brianna broke in, "He is a master of *human* hand-to-hand fighting, but if you want a true martial *art...* I know a guy. You could be the first ever human to learn the Moon Elf style. You *are* entitled to it as an Elven Noble after all." She ended tantalizingly.

Stunned silence met her words. Hans broke it with a drawl, "*Yeee*ah, I would go with that one. The Moon Elves are considered the deadliest fighters without weapons in the world. More deadly *with* weapons, of course, but you know."

"What is the catch, Aunt Ironbark?" Rose rejoined the conversation with evident suspicion.

"Not so much a catch... as a commitment. Once you start training, you *cannot stop* for five years, and you will not master it for at least a decade. You must promise not to teach another the style unless given permission," Brianna spoke seriously.

"I would need to go there for five years? I can't do that," Dale reminded her. "I have too many commitments as it is!"

"You would not need to leave, but you would need to commit two consecutive hours to training per day, seven days a week, for at least five years. The only cost would be the standard fee for a memory stone," Brianna promised with a half-smile.

"So, *with* a memory stone, it would take a decade?" Adam spoke for the first time. He looked exhausted. Apparently, the training he was receiving from Father Richard was intense.

Brianna nodded yes. "I explained to Dale yesterday, just because you know *how* to do something does not mean that you *can* do it. The flexibility training alone takes a year, but it is worth it—if you know what I mean." She winked at Hans as she said this.

"I don't. It is good for you? Allows you to dodge easier?" Dale muttered. "Doesn't matter. The important thing is that I have been working hard on long-term investments into myself, my team, and this area. If this is just another thing that is a big payoff *eventually,* then it is worth it to do."

"It is *very* worth it. I will set up the training." Brianna gave Rose a kiss on the cheek and a promise to catch up, then walked off briskly.

"I have a kitchen to run. Have a good day!" Chandra turned to leave but was stopped by Dale.

"Madame! Any word on those other tutors or information memory stones? I remember that the funds had been transferred to you, but have heard no word." Dale watched for her reaction carefully.

Chandra turned back. "They are on the way, but when they heard where they were going, the representatives insisted that the tutors deliver the stones personally. I am unsure why, but you can expect some visitors in the near future."

"I see. Thank you. High Magous Amber, before you run off, could I ask you *why* the Nobles are suddenly rushing here en masse?" Dale turned to the other member of his council. He tried to hurry as his team was starting to fidget.

"Why not? The rumors have started already." Amber gave a frustrated sigh. "There are rumblings of war, of an undead army overrunning the northern borders and killing small towns. There is no *proof* of this yet, but the Nobles near the border are sending their children to... shall we say, neutral locations? The High Nobles—the Princes and such—are coming here as a show of solidarity, as a temporary measure."

"Bleh. Nobles suck," Hans muttered not quite quietly enough.

Amber gave him a pitying look but ignored him. "As it stands, I need to go and oversee the portal. Have a pleasant day, and please try not to die." With those words of 'encouragement', she took her leave.

"Well, that was fun. Let's go kill some angry rabbits," Hans suggested shaking off the chill Amber's look had given him.

Rose chuckled. "Good plan, but I was hoping to stop by the job board first. I could use some extra coins."

"Job board?" Adam politely wondered. "I haven't heard of this?"

"Yes, it is fairly new. It is a simple concept—people who want something specific from the dungeon post their requests. That way they can get around the brokerage fee that the Guild takes by going directly to the supplier," Rose informed them all. There was a resounding round of nodding as the others agreed to take a look.

They walked toward the dungeon, and sure enough, there was a large board near the clerks' stand that had drawings and postings for equipment and materials. There were offers for weapons, armor, potions, fur, meat, and so much more.

"It appears that we have been rather inefficient with the usage of our time in this place. Look at the standing offers for unrefined Beast Cores! A dozen gold for the lowest quality!" Tom amazedly recited the offer.

"Have we seen anything with a Core?" Dale looked around, but the others shook their heads. "That makes me nervous. They must be in there... the Cats, maybe? I'm wondering more about the herbs, personally. Look at this! They are paying silver for a large enough amount... why so much, and who is offering it?" Dale looked at the requestor's name and where to deliver goods to, paling as he did.

"Dale? What? Who is it?" Hans poked him in the ribs.

"HE LOOKS LIKE THAT BECAUSE HE–" the booming voice startled them all, then softened after a moment, "because it used to be *his* job to bring good spices to my mess hall, and he suddenly *stopped* without so much as an 'I am done'."

They turned to see the massive cook from the mess hall glaring at them. "Oh, you are *so* lucky you haven't had to eat the gruel that I've been forced to serve recently! Now there is some issue in the dungeon that is stopping my *other* suppliers from gathering enough! Tell you what, fill my order and I *won't* start telling people that you are the reason they got food poisoning the other night."

"So good to see you a-again," Dale stammered. "Of course, I'll get some. It would be my pleasure to help you out."

"Mmhh hmm," grunted the cook, eying Dale critically. "See that you do *soon*, oh fearless Baron." He turned and walked off in the direction of his slacking kitchen help. They needed to learn how to *properly* make that porridge.

"Why is he so terrifying?" Dale muttered softly to Hans.

Hans patted him on the cheek, not very gently. "Yeah. Let's go." He started walking down to the dungeon entrance.

"That isn't an answer!" Dale shouted at his retreating friend.

CHAPTER THIRTEEN

<Hmm. Dani, correct me if I am wrong, but war is where humans and other races fight each other or their own race, yes?> I thought at my floating friend. She was playing with Snowball again.

"Yes... Why do you ask?" I was about to respond when she answered her own question, "Oh, you must have heard someone mention something."

<Mmhm. They are talking about how this place is about to go downhill because there are Nobles coming. I like my floors to be nice and flat. Do they know a way to make me sloped?> I was a bit nervous, though I was certain I could correct any damage they managed to do.

"When they say 'going downhill', I am almost *positive* they mean it as a colloquialism." A moment of silence passed. "As a figure of speech, Cal. Not a literal reshaping of you. If there are Nobles coming, there will also be a lot of other people tagging along, either taking care of them or trying to flatter them."

<So, what you are saying... is that there is a better chance for high-quality food.> I was already almost drooling.

Dani grinned. "Almost certainly. Along with that, Nobles have access to weapons, armor, and items that other people simply do not. This could work out well for–"

She had ignored Snowball during their play session, and he was able to land a blow for the first time ever. It was certainly a play attack, but Dani instantly vanished!

<*Dani!*> I screamed in horror. <Dani, are you alive? Did he kill you?>

Snowball was looking around in confusion, then peered at my location and cocked his head to the side. While I was frantically looking around for my beloved Wisp, Snowball took a few wobbly steps and fell. This caught my attention, and I peered closely at the gigantic Cat. His eyes were pink!

<Dani,> I whispered. <Are you *in Snowball*?>

The Cat nodded, a distinctly non-catlike movement. He stood up and began circling the large open space, Dani obviously getting better at having limbs. Soon, the Cat was leaping into the air and spinning, then making complex motions and occasionally vanishing into the steam that permeated the room. After a time, the Cat came near the tree and fell, panting. He sat on his haunches and closed his eyes. Essence streamed out of its head, accumulating into Dani's normal form.

"Wow. That was intense," Dani slurred, flying toward me drunkenly. "Is that how *you* always feel?"

<You can possess Mobs now?> I assumed wonderingly. <That is amazing! It seems like it takes a lot of Essence, though. Let me fill you up. Did my reaching D-rank six allow this to happen?>

I directed Essence from the room into her, and she quickly perked up.

"Not sure, but that was so fun! Is that why you join in during battle?" she enquired excitedly, back to her old self after a bit of food. Did Wisps get something like low blood sugar when they were low on Essence?

<Well, that and I have a better chance of getting a kill if I don't leave it up to a rabbit. For obvious reasons. Dani! This is so fun! Let's make another Boss so that we can fight together!> I was so enthusiastic that she was reluctant to interrupt me, but she eventually did.

"I need a lot of practice, and right now, Snowball can use his body a lot more efficiently than I can. Let me practice for a few weeks while you think about a Mob that would work well in here. We already know that Glitterflits just get eaten, but maybe something along those lines?"

<I can try. Oh, look! Dale's group is gathering herbs. That is new. What a strange human! Seriously, why don't they get into a routine or something?> I snickered condescendingly.

"*You know I can hear you,*" Dale thought at me.

<Don't care,> I replied flippantly. <You are already at twenty-four percent. This should be... stimulating.>

"*I'm at what?*"

<Twenty-*five* percent,> I breathed smugly, watching a Glade form near the group of gatherers.

Dale was wary, but the others were unaware of the danger as the Mob reached its full growth. Rose turned around just in time to see a spiked tentacle flying at her. She dove to the side, crying out a warning. The Mini-Boss roared, furious that its prey had momentarily escaped. Barbed thorns began launching from its body, seeking to impale the adventurers.

I had to admit that without armor, Dale was far better at avoiding attacks, but I was excited for the first blow to land. Surely he would not last long once he started losing blood! The party attacked, throwing themselves at the Glade. The tentacles were far smarter than the main monster, and it showed in battle. Daggers and arrows penetrated the soft mushroom body but did no real damage. When Adam or Tom—especially Tom—swung, the tentacles would do their best to dodge the blow. Watching a tentacle contort at the last second to avoid the enhanced force Inscription on the warhammer was a thing of beauty.

The wild blows were having another effect, and I was cheerfully taunting Dale as it happened, <Forty-one, no, no, forty-*three* percent!> They were smashing plants left and right!

The Glade had large chunks torn out of it, and one of its tentacles was severed. It was still fighting strong; the mushroom didn't feel pain. Half of the plants in the room had now been destroyed as the group ducked, dived, swung, and fired at the man-sized mushroom. I giggled softly as a *new* Glade sprouted, quickly growing to full size and joining the battle. It fired a thorn, tearing a hole in Adam's unsuspecting arm and lodging deep into the muscle. Ouch! That barbed tip would be a real *pain* to pull out. If he got the chance, that was.

The group divided their attention between the two Mobs, trying to get into a cohesive formation. The tentacles continuously foiled their plans, and thorns forced them to stay defensive. The first Glade—beginning to reach the end of its life cycle—tore itself from its location and launched itself at the group. Well used to the tactics of Raile, the group easily dodged the large body. Adam swung his staff while the two remaining tentacles were engaged in combat and tore a huge chunk out of its side. The Mob stiffened and fell, its writhing appendages slowly coming to a halt.

The other Glade seemed to become angry, and the tentacles started cracking like whips. Since there was no one in Dale's group that was heavily armored, they had little choice but to dodge the flailing lashes. Hans began to get impatient and strode forward, activating some form of wind-based movement technique. He dodged each attack with barely a hair's breadth between them, swiping out with efficient cuts. Soon, all three of the tentacles were *much* shorter, and the main group was able to attack the body of the Mini-Boss. It quickly fell, though it valiantly attempted to pincushion them with thorns.

<I'm gonna have to warn you, Dale. If he does stuff like that often, I'll have no choice but to make you fight stronger opponents.>

"That was new," Hans glibly offered.

Adam was focusing intently on his arm, and with a concentrated loop of celestial Essence, he removed the barbed thorn from his arm and healed himself. I was suitably impressed; most of the people I had seen attempting to self-heal were unable to focus enough past their pain. He looked up at the group watching him and gave a weak smile. "Anyone know where those came from?"

Dale opened his mouth to speak, but Rose beat him to it, "They were guardians. When a certain portion of plants was damaged, they appeared. I say we cut down more and kill any that show up. There is *certain* to be a great reward for killing off such a mighty group of non-standard Mobs."

<...Crap. Dani, we need to make a treasure chest *really* quick.>

Dani and I decided what would appear in the chest and where it would be found. It would push up from the ground when all four Mobs were defeated, and the reward would vary based on how long it took to beat the Mobs, the ranking of the group, and if they planned to *use* the plants they destroyed or if they damaged them only for potential rewards. Dani came up with that last requirement.

Dale's group methodically started chopping, focusing on opening a space to fight in formation. They quickly hit the benchmark of major plants destroyed—I didn't count weeds like grass and whatnot—and a new Glade was formed. Prepared this time, they were able to efficiently cut down their foe without allowing this one to ambush them. The group rested a few minutes, replenishing their stamina and catching their breath.

When they were ready, they spawned and destroyed the final Glade.

Dale looked at the Mini-Boss as it rapidly wilted into mulch. "Let's make sure we gather all of this up. This amount of herbs should keep the cook happy for a long time, and I am sure we can find a use for all of these flowers as well."

"What? We're going to leave? We just got started!" Hans whined at Dale as his group leader resolutely gathered the herbs.

"Just for a few minutes! It isn't like we have gotten to the third floor. How would we carry all of this?" Dale grunted as he lifted a mound of herbs. "Every little bit helps, and this quantity of potent herbs will be worth some good silver."

Rose was thrashing around, kicking plants out of her path. "Where is it?! There *has* to be a chest around here *somewhere!*"

"Easy on the herbs!" Dale called angrily. "And who is gonna buy those flowers now?"

A soft sound of earth being pushed aside made Rose's head snap to the side. Her eyes locked on a slowly appearing treasure chest, and she threw her fist into the air. "Yes! I *knew* it!" She rushed to the chest and opened it, gazing intently at the contents. "Okay, looks like some poison, a few gems, one of those vials that might be either poison or a healing potion, and a couple... ohh! Gold coins!"

"Nice!" Adam cheered, walking over and taking a look. His brow furrowed as he looked at the loot. "Hans? Really quick, I don't think that these are gems... take a look?"

Hans stepped over excitedly and held one of the gems in his hand against the light, appraising it like a master jewelry maker. "This is certainly... not a gem...hmm." He was talking slowly as he examined every facet. "If I had to make a guess... I'd say it is a... half carat Beast Core with standard properties, possibly from a D-ranked Beast that had progressed with help from the dungeon. It may have been a metal-type as well."

Rose snorted. "A shot in the dark, huh? You probably knew what it was as soon as you saw it. You just wanted to be the center of attention for a while."

Hans looked hurt. "Rose, how can you say that? It is like you... know me better than anyone else, and we would be a perfect couple!"

"Keep dreaming. Why don't you go after Aunt Ironbark? You elderly folk should stick together."

Hans smiled salaciously. "Ah, but I knew that you were the woman of my dreams from the moment I laid my eyes upon you, and no other temptress could steal me away."

"Creepy old man, go get eaten by rabbits." Rose brushed him off irritably. "How much are these Cores worth?"

"Rebuffed again! Well then, I shall win you over by being a font of knowledge for you! The Core itself is likely worth a dozen gold or so according to the job board, but it has greater application as a power source for enchantments or Runes. If we brought this to an artificer, we could link it to Runes or create a dimensional bag for a fairly reduced price." Hans's voice turned contemplative at the end, turning the Cores over in his hand.

"Really? We can get that turned into a dimensional bag? At a reduced price, no less? In that case, I would really like one of those." Dale trotted over to the group, trailing leaves as he walked.

Hans asked if anyone else wanted one, and of course, the entire group did. He took himself out of the running as he already owned a specialized bag, as well as Tom since he could not power a bag even if he owned it. There were two stones, and after flipping a coin—two wins out of three needed—Rose and Adam walked away with a stone apiece. Dale seemed to feel a bit down about it but was promised that he would get the next one.

<Let's set off the explosion trap in there and bury them in rubble,> I growled at Dani.

She looked at me in confusion, but Dale quickly looked around in fear and ushered the group out to deliver the herbs and flowers. Hans and Tom worked together to carry out the body of one of the Glades.

"What was that about?" Dani was still confused as to why I talked about a non-existent trap.

<They were just standing around talking and being boring. I wanted to regrow the room so that the Glades will get another crack at groups going through. *Three* groups walked through there after the Mobs were defeated and didn't get attacked at *all*> I finished with a horrified shudder in my voice.

"Well then, let's fix that!"

DALE

Dale was walking away from the mess hall, cheerfully whistling about the morning's unexpected windfall. Not only had the huge bale of herbs been enough to get himself back into the cook's good graces, but there was a standing Guild reward of ten gold per new Mob found. Even splitting that, he was two gold— or two hundred silver—richer just from carrying a mushroom to the surface.

His good mood was quickly soured as he was making his way back to his friends.

"Look, this one has *hay* in his hair. Ugh, this place is disgusting."

"There is blood on him too! This whole place smells terrible, and everyone is unaccountably rude. Not a *single* person even bothers to bow properly, and they look directly into my eyes when they speak to me! You'd think that after I had the first one whipped word would have *spread!*"

Dale looked over and winced as the heavily shined jewelry the people were wearing dazzled him momentarily. There were two men around twenty-five years old that were looking around, loudly proclaiming their displeasure with everything that they saw. They were surrounded by a swarm of servants and steely-eyed guardsmen. Dale decided to let someone *else* deal with them and continued on his way. Or, that is, he tried to.

"You! You dare to just *stare* at us without speaking or begging our leave?" One of the men was flushed, walking toward Dale and shouting. "Were you looking at our armor? Finding weaknesses to try to exploit in the future? Don't you know how to respond to your *betters?* Speak, peasant!"

Hans had come looking for Dale and walked up just as the Nobleman was walking forward and shouting. When he heard the bit about 'betters', he cursed and ran off. Dale—who had been trying *really* hard to ignore the belligerent, entitled words—came to a perfect halt and turned around, fighting to keep his face emotionless.

"I am assuming that you have just arrived here, so I will try to explain how *very* misguided you are if you think that you are going to go around whipping people or insulting them." Dale's blue eyes were swirling with silvery Essence. He examined the Noble, noting that with the density and brightness of Essence, he was certainly in the mid C-rankings.

The Noble's face got even redder, and if he didn't have such an abundance of Essence, Dale would have worried about him bursting a blood vessel in his forehead.

"You *dare* to speak to me like this? Kneel before me and prepare to be whipped for your impertinence!"

Dale crossed his arms and raised an eyebrow. "No?"

The Noble looked entirely flabbergasted that Dale was not on his knees. "How are you able to resist a command from me? I am Baron Michael Adams, thirtieth in line for the throne!"

"How nice for you. Doesn't mean you aren't an arsehole," Dale ground out wryly, teeth clenched hard as he forced himself not to take a swing at the man.

Titters of laughter escaped a few of the onlookers. The Noble seemed about to begin frothing at the mouth.

"Easy, cousin! It is obvious that he must be from *my* land then, allow me! Kneel before me, Baron Thomas Adams, and present your hands to the guards. Your prison sentence will be short; I can guarantee you that," the other jewelry-bedecked man ordered ominously, coming forward to stand next to his cousin.

"So, you are threatening to kill me, I assume?" Dale hissed darkly. "No, I am fairly certain I am not going to do that either! Who the abyss do you think you are, acting like this? Is this Noble courtesy? Is this how you live up to your family's code of honor?"

Thomas took a step back, a flash of fear crossing his face. "Are you from another Kingdom? A peasant shouldn't even know what that means! How are you able to resist our orders?"

"None of your god-blasted business! I assume that you were sent here and are not particularly interested in *being* here, but I don't *particularly* give a damn! If this is the standard that you plan to keep, you will not be allowed to stay. Likely you are rather grumpy from your travels. I know that portal travel does not sit well with me." Dale tried to calm his temper, tried to speak as rationally as possible... but was having serious trouble. "If you plan to stay, I want you to pay reparations to the person you had whipped. If either of you 'imprisoned' someone, release them as well. You did so *illegally*."

"Pff! Not a chance. Obviously, you are an intruder in our lands, and we are well within our rights to have you arrested and summarily *executed*. Guards!" The man stood back with a self-satisfied smirk.

The guards near them took a few threatening steps forward, but Dale did not move. "Are you certain that *this* is how you want to begin your day? I get the feeling your parents will not be too happy if you ended up banished from here... or dead."

"We will add threatening a Nobleman to the charges," Michael pompously jeered.

"Interesting. My turn then." Dale grinned and roared, "*Guards!*" A full contingent of Dark Elf guards interspersed with the easily recognizable tabard of the Moon Elves appeared around the group. Even Dale was surprised; normally, there were only a few within speaking distance. The effect on the Nobles was quite profound.

"D-dark Elves?" Thomas stammered. "This entire place is crawling with *assassins*? Cousin, it was an ambush all along! They are going to wipe out a generation of the ruling class!"

Michael's anger seemed to have an unreachable peak, and his face was now turning purple. "You *coward!*" he screamed at Dale, voice breaking. He tried to run at Dale but, of course, was stopped by his guards.

Dale had allowed them to speak long enough. "Shut your food-hole! I am *Duke* Dale, owner of this mountain and liege-lord of this land! I also hold the title of Baron in *both* of your Kingdoms. Conversely, I am sure it is your *parents* who are Barons or Baronesses; therefore, you currently hold no influence in the Kingdom! Well, beyond what you apparently feel entitled to."

He turned toward the highest-ranking Elf he could see. "Captain, escort these... *children* to a holding cell. Ensure their guards and servants are given proper food, drink, and an area to rest. They are not to leave. There is a Prince or Princess coming from their Kingdoms, yes? When they do arrive, please have them escorted to the Elven Embassy where we will discuss the future of these criminals."

"*Criminals?*" Thomas shrieked. "What are you talking about? Based on what charges?"

Dale cocked his head and gave a half grin. "Why, threatening a ranking Noble. And insubordination, of course." He threw their own threats against them happily. The furious men were led away as Hans walked to stand beside him.

"They will never forgive this, you know," Hans murmured, appearing beside his friend.

Dale nodded. "I know, but it is better to stop this behavior before it can find a foothold in the area. I *certainly* won't let them stay here, but I can smooth things over with their leaders and hopefully ask them to command the Barons to leave me alone."

"Hmm. Seems like a dangerous gamble." Hans squinted at his friend. "What if they decide not to help?"

A real smile graced Dale's face. "That is why I am going to see the rulers *together*. That way they feel compelled to show off to each other and try to one-up the other in reparations."

"Subtle. I like subtle." Hans laughed. "When did you get so political? I remember blowing your mind with the idea of a capital city sewer. Did the memory stone give you *this much* political acumen?"

"The Dark Elves have been tutoring me a bit," Dale hedged.

"A bit? Well, I'll have to worry the next time we have a debate and you are *fully* trained." Hans clapped Dale on the back. "Let's go. The others are waiting."

Cal

"Dale's group just passed the first-floor Boss again," Dani warned me.

<I know, but I'm kind of sick of Dale,> I muttered, continuing to focus on my project.

"*Hey!*" I heard from him.

<Heh. Nah, I'm more interested in the group that just strolled in. There is a party of *fifteen* freaking people. Are they planning to start a war?>

I was looking at this odd group, noting that there was an odd discrepancy in their gear and cultivation rankings. The highly-adorned, well-armored people were in the C-rankings, while the guards with them varied through the D and C-rankings but wore a standardized uniform.

<What in the world? What are those people carrying?>

"It... it is some kind of water container?" Dani was looking at the same object as I was; it was a large square of glass that was full of water. It also seemed to have creatures floating in it.

<I'm going to look at that closer...> I focused my mind more intently on that area, listening in on the conversations happening.

"My Lord, *please!*" one of the men in a uniform was saying. "I just think that this is bizarre. A dungeon is a dangerous place, and you are forcing two of your guards to carry around an *aquarium*. What would happen if you needed protection?"

"Nonsense!" a haughty voice drawled. "The movements of the jellyfish amuse and relax me. Also, this is a *D-ranked* dungeon. With a hunting party of this size, what could happen? I could traipse through here alone and be fine, so don't question my orders again!"

This is about where I started losing my temper, but he did have a point. Every time a Basher or other minor threat appeared, it was wiped out without pause, never getting near the group. I focused my will on the treasure chests they were near, re-absorbing the treasures they contained. This huge, overpowered group would not be getting rewarded for their laziness.

Dani dreamily mentioned that the man had a point; the jellyfish *were* indeed fun to watch. That was enough for me to know that she wanted to keep a few as pets, so I started directing my Mobs at the tank. Soon, I was able to sneak a Basher past the vigilant guards, and he knocked the tank to the ground, where it shattered. The leader began screaming at his soaking wet men to save his precious fish, but the rush of Essence assured me that they were already dead. I inspected the patterns that flowed to me and found them to be incredibly basic, though they did have a natural paralytic poison.

<I don't know how useful these will be, Dani. They need to be in a certain type of water to survive, and they have no real intelligence. The *Shroomishes* are actually more intelligent...> I didn't want to tell her this because she had really liked the look of them, but facts are facts.

"Would it be difficult to make a few large fish tanks in the wall? Adding some scenery like that might be fun. Interesting to look at and not actually dangerous to people. Oh! I know! Make a few pillars that are glass tanks, fill them with water, and put the jellies in there!" She noted my hesitation and gave a frustrated growl. "Maybe make it have really high pressure, so if someone smashes the glass they get hurt badly?"

<Oh, yeah! That sounds like a plan. I bet the salt would hurt in the cut, too.>

She really knew how to get me to do what she wanted. Tonight, I would tear out some stone from the walls and make glass tanks that connected to each other. Then to make it look interesting, I would make small light potion pockets behind the tanks. Then the jellyfish would seem luminescent and pretty for Dani. Hmm. Actually...

<Dani?> I was comparing the jellyfish with another pattern in my mind and coming up with a match that made me nervous.

"Mmhm?" Dani was watching the huge, glittering group walk toward the first Boss Room.

<So, I did a thing...> *That* got her attention.

"What? You sound nervous. Is it loose in here?" She was looking around wildly, scanning the dungeon when nothing apparent appeared. "Where is it? What did you do?"

<I don't want to say it because Dale is in here, but can I make something and show you real quick?>

Dale perked up and looked around suspiciously when I said these words. People were going to start thinking he was paranoid.

Dani winced. "If you feel you need to…" Of course, that was all the permission I needed,

So an Essence 'seed' of the new Mob combination came into being. I did create it in the 'test' room, of course. I made a small tank of water before it was fully formed, and after a moment, a small jellyfish *plopped* into the water and began drifting about.

"Alright, I don't see the issue? You made a jellyfish." Dani looked at me like I was going insane.

<Heh, um. Look *closely*,> I pressured her.

She focused in on it, looking at its body and pattern. "Did you…? It is a cross between a jellyfish and a Wisp? It has a *Beast Core*? But… but it's in the F-ranks!"

<Yes, hence why I needed to talk to you first.>

"It is F-rank zero, I am not sure how this is useful. Plus, it is trapped in a tank." Dani looked ready to squash my plan before hearing the details, so I spoke quickly.

<While you are technically correct, I think you should let me test this.> I began directing a bit of concentrated Essence into the stingers hanging below the body, and two of them lit up. The Essence in the creature began building, its rank shooting higher, faster than I had ever been able to do without detonating a creature. At F-rank five, it began rising in the water and soon broke the surface. It slowly floated around the room, staying at a constant height.

Dani was impressed and yet had not seen the worth yet. "So it can float, but it is still…"

I began forcing Essence into the creature, and its rank kept getting higher and higher. I didn't use my personal Essence, instead opting to direct the unrefined and corrupted loose Essence in the dungeon into the creature.

"Cal! What are you doing?! It will explode or worse!"

It did *not* explode, so I stopped the flow of Essence when it had reached D-rank five, just at the edge of my ability to control the newly formed Magical Beast. It still had no intelligence and drifted slowly around. This is where I came into the picture! I imposed my will on the Mob that was full of every type of Essence and corruption and focused on the stingers hanging from the body.

Cr-r-ack! A huge section of the floor had grown into spikes, impacting the wall with enough force to shatter a large chunk to rubble. I focused on another stinger, and a massive gout of flame *whooshed* out, superheating the stone spikes. When they began to melt, I held two stingers close together and forced Essence and corruption through them. The air in front of the Mob shattered as the temperature dropped so fast that the minimal moisture in the air froze. The superheated stone spikes exploded, the temperature differential putting too much stress on the material.

I whooped in excitement; that last bit had been a happy accident!

Dani had stopped moving and asking questions, her body becoming a very pale light. "Cal... just... how?"

I waited to answer until I saw that Dale was distracted with a huge swarm of Mobs. I may have sent a few extra at them. A dozen or so. Hopefully, the terror would drown out my voice as I softly informed Dani, <The jellyfish portion allows me to control them absolutely with my influence. The Wisp in them allows me to just continuously channel Essence into them! Remember you told me a long time ago that Wisps can *never* take in too much Essence, as they *are* Essence?>

"Well, I suppose, but how are you able to use those incantations? The spells?" Dani desperately searched for answers, her world had just been turned on its side.

<Look at the endpoint of the stinger!>

Dani looked and gave a short laugh.

"Literally *only* you would think of this or be able to pull it off."

Instead of a claw-like end of the stinger, I had created a growth that was the *exact* pattern of the inversed Essence accumulation Rune, an Essence *release* Rune.

<I direct one type of Essence down each stinger, then power the Rune with *corruption*, forcing the Essence through the tainted pattern. I told you I would be able to weaponize non-lethal Runes!> I chuckled smugly.

"Yes, you did," Dani murmured. "How did you create an icy blast? Fire and water would make steam, correct?"

<Yes!> I crowed, proud that she had noticed the effect. <I used fire and *infernal* Essence! It pulls the movement—or 'life'—from the fire and allows me to essentially reverse the normal effect!>

She was almost as excited as I was, but her next words dampened the enthusiasm. "Oh. What is happening to the Mob now, though?"

I looked at the jelly, who was slowly drifting to the ground. <Hmm. Looks like it used all its Essence. It is back down to F-rank four, so it no longer has enough cloud Essence to float normally. I am going to give it more and see what happens.>

I started pouring Essence back into the jelly, and it quickly rose in ranking. It was soon able to float again. It drifted around the room, uncaring of obstacles or other creatures that I put in its way. This was not a creature that would attack others unless I was in control; it was simply too unintelligent. On the other hand, when the creatures saw the floating jelly, they seemed to become mesmerized. They followed the floating Mob in a daze.

"That is interesting. They seem to have retained the Wisp's natural defense mechanism," Dani observed softly.

I grabbed on to this piece of information. <How potent is that? Will it attract humans and other creatures? Can I use these to lure people into traps?>

"I am uncertain... looks like you will have to find out in your favorite way—human trials!" Dani laughed at my reaction, which was of course glee.

<Bwa-ha-ha! Oh, looks like Dale is not fighting anymore, better keep the information limited,> I reluctantly mumbled.

"*You are thoroughly insane, you know that, right?*" Dale thought at me angrily.

<Untrue. An insane person is unable to process events around them in a logical manner or react appropriately to situations. I am simply doing what is best for myself in order to protect what I care about. At worst, I am a sociopath,> I rebutted, causing Dale to pause in his negative assessment.

"*You kill people! What in the world are you protecting?*" Dale furiously demanded.

I gave him a harsh reminder of the past, <You know, the very first time you were in here, you killed a human as well. Since then, you have killed hundreds of my creatures and sent other people in here to die. If *I* am insane, you are well on your way to joining me.>

Dale didn't respond, but I did notice that he was attacking a bit more furiously.

CHAPTER FOURTEEN

<I really don't have a plan in place for this, Dani,> I muttered with trepidation as the massive group of people worked to crush Raile. As it turns out, you only need about six people with tower shields to hold Raile in place while others beat him to death. <They usually only come in here five at a time. This is just stupid.>

"Well, they look like they are going to continue down on to the third floor. Here is what I want you to do, start mass-producing the monsters down there. If they are going to try to overwhelm us with numbers, we will do the same! Also, get a few of those jellies out there," Dani angrily directed me.

<Yes, ma'am!> I joked with her to lighten the tense mood. <Also, we need to give them a name. 'Jelly' is too vague.>

"How about 'Assimilators'?" she offered after a few seconds.

I was startled out of my focus, creating mobs of Mobs. Heh. Wordplay.

<Assimilators? Why, what does that mean?> I tried to divide my thoughts so I could listen and create but accidentally exploded a kitten by adding the wrong ratio of Essences. Oops.

She gave me a *look,* showing she had noticed the kitten. "To assimilate means to absorb mentally, and since you force them to constantly absorb and reabsorb..."

<Sounds good, a fitting name. I need to focus for a moment; they are almost to the bottom of the stairs.> I created more Cats and a few Assimilators intermittently through the maze, keeping the Assimilators well away from each other. It was difficult enough to power one at a time; two would be *very* slow. To the point of uselessness even. I completed my goal just as

they reached the entrance, and I listened in on their conversations.

"What a useless dungeon," the shiniest man was complaining. "First, I lose my aquarium. Then we find bare *coppers* no matter the power of opponent we face. I thought others had said that potent weapons were found here almost daily. All that is here is *trash*!"

"My Lord, the information we were given states that the rewards are often much higher for small or low-ranked groups. Perhaps we should simply be split into smaller groups?" a man in uniform offered. The others around him perked up; getting away from their pompous charge would be a huge relief.

The haughty man pondered these words for a moment. "No. The information also noted that this floor was unexplored and the variety of monsters unknown. Let us clear this area, and then we can consider moving in smaller groups on future excursions."

They walked into the labyrinth, entering through the door with a drop of water carved over it. This hallway went forward for a short while before subtly curving to the right.

<They are almost to the first branching hallway. As soon as they are all out of sight of the entrance... now! Okay, the door is down, and they are sealed in!> I enjoyed my time by giving a play-by-play of the action to Dani; it got her all riled up and bloodthirsty.

"Woo! How are you doing on sealing the walls with cursed earth by the way?"

<Slower than I want, but it *is* coming along nicely, thanks for asking.> I was filling the walls with Runes, then powering them with corruption to enhance their durability. I did not keep Essence or corruption powering them at all times, but an activation as soon as it was ready would do two things.

One, it would ensure that the Rune was working properly. Two, it would allow me to activate it with a thought. Then if someone wanted to try smashing through the walls, I could easily make it a worthless endeavor. Unfortunately, Runes on that scale took quite a bit of time to perfect, even more so since I always rechecked and compared to Runes proven to work. I had certainly learned my lesson about activating hastily created Rune work.

<I have finished many of the walls surrounding the Boss Room, but it will be a few weeks until they are all complete,> I admitted to Dani. <It would be faster if I didn't need to hide them in the walls, but if I did that, the overall strength would be *much* lower.>

"That sounds good, Cal. How do you want to handle this? If you need to focus hard on the Assimilators, you will not be able to control any other Mobs, correct?" Dani was in full battle mode.

<Right, here is my plan. I can supply you with plenty of Essence so can you direct the Mobs? Take 'em over if you can. Then if you are defeated, just make a break for it invisibly. The Essence in the air is so thick that you should be able to blend in if they cannot see you with their eyes.> I trailed off as I noticed her staring at me.

"You want me to join in battle? What if I do exceptionally poorly? What if–"

I cut her off before she could scare herself, "Dani, there is no one that I trust more. Plus, you have been practicing, and I think you are ready. From here on, the only way to get better is to have actual combat experience. You ready? I believe in you."

She took an unnecessary breath—she had no lungs. "I'm ready. Let's go!" She flew off into the maze, just a streak in my senses. She latched on to a Cloud Cat, just like I knew she would. It had the most similar movements to her normal body.

I took control of an Assimilator and started slowly drifting toward a point in the maze the huge party would need to cross in order to reach the Boss Room. As I drifted, I continuously drew Essence of all types into the body and Core of the floating jellyfish. Now, this took a lot of my attention, but I was still aware of other things going on. I watched as Dani started her approach to the group, right as they were facing a massive swarm of Bashers. Dani leaped from wall to wall, pushing herself higher before the Cat became translucent and started drifting toward the unsuspecting group.

Dani passed over them, slashing with her claws and inflicting the first casualties to this group. Well. Other than their fish, but... anyway. Her first attack tore open the back of a neck as the man was looking down at the Bashers, exposing himself to the attack from above and behind. His arteries severed, the man dropped to the ground with a gurgle, splashing the Cat with a spray of blood. Her momentum continuing, she landed on the back of a uniformed man and leaped off him with a twist, snapping his neck and regaining altitude.

She was a beautiful specimen, landing on people and pushing off walls to maintain momentum and confuse her victims. She had just finished off her fourth target when a spear pierced the Cat's body, followed by a sword. I was nervous for a moment until I saw Dani floating merrily toward a small pride of Cats.

<Everything okay, Dani?> I worriedly inquired.

"*I am fine, but they killed Purrrrty. I want revenge,*" she growled back to me.

<Was... was that a pun?> I was watching her in amazement. She had never been more beautiful to me.

She chuckled. "*I knew you would like that.*"

The humans were bemoaning their losses and tightening their formation. A flicker of fear even crossed the leader's face when no one was looking. He directed two of his remaining guards in thick plate armor to stand near him, obviously hoping that their thick shields would protect them and—by extension—him.

Dani was about to take control of a Coiled Cat when I stopped her. <Dani, most of the remaining guys are in heavy armor. Try taking a Flesh Cat this time. That type can ignore some of the armor in the way.>

She agreed, and soon, a mangy looking Flesh Cat was slinking toward the group.

She never ceased to amaze me! Dani was able to switch roles *so* much more quickly than I was! If I tried to take over a Cat followed by another Mob with different abilities, I would often fail to use them to their best effect. On the other hand—not really my favorite colloquialism by the way, since I was a gem—Dani had to be physically present at the battles, which worried me. She seemed to be having the time of her life, though.

"Yeah! Take *that!*" she roared in my mind; an interesting side effect of our bond allowed us to communicate mind to mind when she was possessing a Mob. "Ha *ha*! Never saw me coming!" She had just taken down a heavily armored man, slashing at his unexposed leg. The armor quickly had blood pouring between the seams, and Dani took advantage of his distraction to open his chest entirely.

I was observing this and was able to see the total damage when the man died. The Flesh Cat's ability only opened... well, flesh. It didn't damage the bones or organs for some reason, except in weak points such as veins and arteries. I noticed this just before a huge mass of Essence impacted me, catching me completely off guard.

<*Oof!*> I grunted, distracting Dani enough that her ride was killed.

She rushed back to me, noting the glow of dense Essence surrounding me. "Cal, what is the matter? Did you break something?"

<I am... having trouble.> My mind was boiling as I fought to absorb the Essence.

She gasped in sudden understanding. "That last man was C-ranked! Oh crap, we aren't ready for this."

<Ready or not, here we go,> I grunted in reply. I had been under the misguided assumption that my new cultivation technique would allow me to hold a near-infinite amount of Essence but had not counted on my D-ranked Mobs being able to acquire the prolific, dense Essence contained in a C-ranked person.

"You can do this; it has happened before! Remember how I told you that dungeons can go from the F to the B-ranks in a matter of days with the right food? Well, you just got the right food to bring you into the C-rankings. This is going to be interesting!" Dani soothed me.

<I... like... interesting. You don't, though!> I wheezed a dry laugh. <Walk me through this, Dani. I'm starting to vibrate!>

Dani began directing me carefully, and through the pain of holding my atoms together, I tried to listen. "Cal, within every dungeon there is one thing that holds true. There is a space in you that is always hungry, always yearning for more. Where fleshy people hold their Essence in their bodies and use it to feed their life-force, you pour it into that tiny hole that can never seem to be filled."

Her words made sense—logically—but the meaning eluded me. <There is no hole in me, Dani! I'm perfectly formed!>

"Narcissism is going to be the death of you," she mumbled before speaking at full volume again. "Not your physical body, your aura! You need to go *deep,* Cal. Down to the exact center of your Essence where the Chi thread is vanishing."

I followed her words, then when I got to the center of my Core, I looked for a space. Not as a cultivator, not using Essence to enhance my senses, but as a *Dungeon,* looking at the patterns within my aura. Just as she had promised, there was a tiny void that an atom-sized thread was being *sucked* into.

<I found it! I think,> I jubilantly informed my partner. <Now what?>

"Start *forcing* Essence into the hole. Open it wider until there is a constant stream instead of an infinitesimal trickle."

<You want me to *open* a hole in my aura?> I exclaimed in shock.

She literally growled at me. "No, I want you to *widen* it!"

Her tone of voice more than anything else convinced me to follow her instructions. She had never sounded as angry and scared at the same time before. I grasped the hole with all my willpower, pulling at the edges and stuffing Essence in greater volume into it. Of course, it resisted at first, but in a short amount of time, I was able to create a wider channel.

Essence started flowing into the hole, and my aura began blazing brightly as the huge amount of Essence from the C-ranked adventurer found a place to settle. I was worriedly watching the hole in my aura, looking for where the Essence was accruing. No matter how desperately I looked, there was no extra Essence in me or the air around me.

<Dani, where did it go?>

"Follow it!" Her voice had a playful tone that surprised me; her mood had been vastly different not moments ago.

I latched my consciousness on to the Chi thread spinning into the unknown and found myself surrounded by darkness. The only light came from a small orb of rapidly spinning Essence where the Chi thread was accumulating. I looked on in wonder, then looked around, trying to determine how large this space was. I could see no walls or barriers and, therefore, had no way to determine the scale of this space.

From a seemingly vast distance, Dani's voice came to me, "Impose your cultivation technique on it!"

Again? Really? More of the same, just make it spin? Wow, what a great secret to the C-rankings. Almost grumpily, I reviewed my cultivation technique and began pulling at the orb of Essence before me. Unlike my Chi spiral outside of this place, this orb reacted faster than my mind could follow. Light arced away from me, the entirety of the orb vanishing into the distance as it opened into a galaxy of light around me. Each point of light looked as distant as the stars in the sky, and the threads connecting them were so thin as to be almost imperceptible.

Since the majority of the Essence had recently belonged to a human, I had as of yet been unable to remove the corruption. I *almost* did not want to. The corruption flowed along the strands creating a beautiful, shimmering kaleidoscope of colors. The final effect was like looking into a nebula, and it was undeniably beautiful. With reluctance, I moved upstream of my Essence, my mind refocusing on Dani and the dungeon.

<That was unbelievable.> I didn't have words to describe everything I had just seen.

"You have a beautiful soul, Cal. Congratulations on breaking into the C-ranks!" Dani applauded me.

I 'smiled' at her. <Thanks! Now, what do I have to do to break into the B-rankings?>

"..." She just stared at me for a few moments. "You are unbelievable, you know that? No time celebrating, no time seeing what you are capable of, having just jumped *four* cultivation ranks..."

I waited a moment to see if any more information was forthcoming. <What are you getting at?>

"Gah! Cal... ugh. Fine. To break into the B-ranks... are you ready?"

She tempted me with hidden knowledge.

<Yes! What?>

"You know that place you just were? That mental construct that is actually a small hole into the void, basically a pocket dimension for your soul?" she began, slowing her words and turning the conversation into a hidden whisper.

<Is that what it was? A pocket dimension in my soul?>

"Shh! That place, basically a giant empty space? Fill it with Essence!" she told me in a very anti-climactic way.

<That's it?>

"No! That is not *it*, but it *is* what you have to start with!" Dani glared at me. "As you approach filling it, you need to find a concept—a universal truth that meshes with your Essence. That will be the hardest part because your Essence is completely pure when you are done refining it. Your goal in life right now is to find a *pure* universal truth. It will likely be so profound that knowing the entirety of it at this point would break your mind and drive you mad! Don't rush this."

<Sorry,> I apologized sheepishly. <What happens if a B-ranked person dies in here? Something similar?>

"Not something you need to worry about really. Unless you had meshed your Essence with a concept, you would only get the Essence they had stored. I think. Usually, Mages don't bother with Essence after they are able to accumulate Mana." Dani thought for a moment. "Nah, don't worry about it. Oh! Look, that group is almost to the last fork in the maze!"

I looked over, and sure enough, the much filthier group of people were close to solving the labyrinth. <Oh, good timing. Breaking into a new rank, *and* I get to try out my new Mob? Yes, *please*!>

I returned my attention to the Assimilator and prepared to take direct control. Much to my surprise, instead of requiring the huge amount of focus I had needed previously, a line of intent seemed to impact the floating jelly, and it followed my commands smoothly, like the Bashers above us. Able to ignore the movement and positioning of the Mob, I quickly began funneling tainted Essence into its being.

My new ranking showed its worth yet again, allowing me to funnel enough Essence into the Mob for it to reach D-rank nine—*significantly* stronger than the last time I had controlled an Assimilator. I felt confident that this would be a spectacular event. The party rounded the corner, ignoring the swirling Essence in their haste or arrogance. They walked down the narrow hallway, blinded by the Essence in the air but not realizing how beneficial a simple light would have been.

The entire group was sweaty, dirty, and covered in gore of some kind. The ten remaining people were arguing furiously about the next bend they should take and whether or not to try turning around and retracing their steps.

I found their conversation annoying; they had already tried going back and found only a dead-end. Now it was time to form another 'dead-end'. Shameless pun! The only question now was what kinds of Essence to use... I wanted to try another combination but had no idea what would happen. Selecting earth and wind—two types that were opposites—struck me as a good idea. Either they would cancel each other out or something fun might happen.

I began building the Essence in the Runes attached to the hanging stingers, allowing it to reach *almost* critical mass before interlacing them and adding just a *touch* more Essence. The results shocked me, but not *nearly* as much as it shocked them.

Z-z-zap! A huge bolt of plasma—commonly referred to as lightning—shattered the air, flying uncontrollably toward the first metal object in its path. The sword that it first touched was instantly white-hot, glowing and slightly melted. The man holding it was dead before he even began to fall, but the lightning was still traveling. It flew into a heavily armored man, the personal guard of the little Noble.

I expected the lightning to bounce again, but it instead arched back and forth between his armor, fusing it into a solid mass of metal whilst cooking the man inside. The rest of the party stood in shock—get it? I am hilarious—for a long moment, which I used to examine my Assimilator. I had brought him up to D-rank nine, but after that bolt of energy, he had been reduced to D-rank three. Yikes. That was a *huge* amount of power for an underwhelming effect. I could do that one more time before the Assimilator began running too low to sustain flight, or I could use other, more effective, abilities.

I started funneling more Essence into the Mob, hoping to re-empower him before the humans attacked. I had just begun when they launched their counter-attack. As a unit, they rushed forward, grouping tightly together so they could protect the person next to them. Too easy. I just *couldn't* pass up this chance! I funneled infernal and fire Essences down the stingers, layering them on top of each other and releasing it just before the humans reached my Mob.

A blast of air as cold as the void snapped outward, the water in the air crystallizing and falling as shattered ice.

The three people closest to my Mob died very quickly as the blood in their brains froze, sending shards of ice deep into the gray matter. The people not caught directly in the blast began exhibiting signs of hypothermia but were able to reach the floating Mob before I could release more Essence. Blunt weapons impacted my Assimilator, but if they did any damage, it didn't show. Not having a brain to rattle was a definite boon in this case. Just as I was getting cocky, a sword lashed out and left a gaping wound. The Noble zipped forward, his hand entering and exiting the wound with blinding speed. He was clutching something, and my Mob dropped to the ground with a wet splat.

"It had a Beast Core." The Noble showed the glimmering gem to the few surviving members. "We were *not* told that there were Cored Beasts in here. When we get out, heads will roll!" He was shaking in fury, clutching the Core hard enough that I was surprised it didn't shatter.

<Dani, look! They are down to a regular sized party finally. Five people, better rewards. Not *great* rewards, these guys are all C-ranked, but you know. Better.>

I was watching the Noble throw a tantrum, kicking his charred, dead guard and ordering him to return to work. The others exchanged cautious looks when the Noble was not looking their way. An unhinged, powerful person was not who they wanted to be near.

"Fine! You lazy..." The Noble let out a tiny shriek of frustration. "Let's finish this stupid dungeon."

<Rude. I am quite intelligent, I think,> I muttered, making Dani laugh at me quietly.

"A bit biased though, aren't you?" Dani whispered to me as the humans made it into the final Boss Room.

"Great, even *less* visibility." The furious Noble looked around the steam filled room, sweating as the heat and humidity began to take its toll.

A low growl began to reverberate around the room, the tones rising and falling. The primal portion of the humans' brains took hold; they scooted together, goosebumps raising on their skin while fear flashed across their faces. Their eyes were darting around, trying to pierce the wall of steam around them.

"No. I'm done with this." The Noble raised his hands, chanting a few words as he moved Essence through the air. He *pulled* his hands, and the water in the air condensed into droplets. A hot rain fell to the ground with a loud pattering, revealing a now-furious, wet Cat.

One of the men shook slightly. "That is a *big* Cat."

The Noble looked at the speaker coldly. "Kill it." The group raced across the sodden ground, weapons at the ready.

Snowball took a deep breath, exhaling a fast-moving cloud of superheated steam as a tremendous roar! Able to see clearly for the first time since entering the third floor, the humans easily dodged the attack. Snowball moved in a whirl of motion, claws flashing out and trailing light-distorting waves of heat. A shield caught the blow, throwing the person holding it back and on to the floor. The shield had five glowing points on it where the claws had touched.

A staff came at Snowball, scoring a direct hit. Most of the damage was mitigated by the thick layers of fur covering his body, but he still yelped like a struck dog and flinched.

"Poor Snowball!" Dani whimpered, watching the Cat intently.

The Cat counterattacked, landing a blow on the offending staff. The metal-shod quarterstaff superheated where the claws touched, making the iron banding glow cherry-red and igniting the wood. The staff was thrown away, but the focus was on the greatsword the Noble was swinging haphazardly with a wild shout. Snowball ducked under the horizontal slash, losing a few tufts of fur to the razor-sharp blade. He reared up, head-butting the wild man and tossing him away like a ragdoll.

Another man stabbed from behind, driving a dagger deep into the muscle on the Cat's left-side back, eliciting a yowl. Snowball whirled around, landing a solid blow to his attacker and dragging him to the floor. He latched on to the arm the man threw up to protect his neck, savaging the armor-clad limb. Another stab from behind made the Cat run forward, each of his paws landing on the prone man as he did so. The multi-hundred-pound Cat, along with the force of his bounding, snapped many bones.

Snowball raced to a covered steam vent, arriving there just before his pursuers. He lashed out, and a blast of steam erupted into the room. The men behind him started screaming as the boiling air washed over them, cooking them in their armor like a lobster in a pot. They got out of the steam, blisters formed across almost every inch of skin. They stumbled around blindly, their eyes—from the sclera to the retina—solidified like hardboiled-eggs. Snowball struck out, slicing the neck of one of them. There was only a small amount of blood, the wound otherwise cauterized near instantly. Snowball tried for the second blind man, only to have a greatsword swing down, parting his head from his body in one clean swing.

The Noble shimmered into view; he had apparently been using a high-level ability, using a thin layer of reflective water to shield himself from Snowball's sight.

"Gotcha, you brute. Skin this Cat, and crack its skull open. I am nearly positive that this is also a Cored Beast, so find me the Core it is hiding."

"Skin it, my lord? How do you want us to do that?"

"What do you mean? Take its fur. I want this as a cloak! Do it the way you *normally* would."

The man looked confused; he was concussed quite badly. "But, my Lord... there is more than one way to skin a Cat."

The Noble sighed. "Just... lengthwise? Is that understandable in your limited mind?"

He walked over to the blinded man and used his Essence to form a thin layer of water over the destroyed eyes and exposed skin, keeping his body lubricated until they could get to a cleric. They quickly moved toward the exit, stopping as they noticed a golden, glowing chest.

"Likely not worth it." The Noble tried to continue onward.

Licking his lips, one of the men dared to go against the statement, throwing open the chest. Inside was a dagger, a sword, and a massive tower shield. I made that happen by extending the chest deep into the ground, only actually showing a portion of its size above ground. Each was well-made but had subtle flaws that would force them to break like a standard piece of equipment. I had promised Dani that I wouldn't give out unbreakable Runed items anymore, after all. Not recognizing that the items were Runed, the Noble scoffed and started guiding his blind subordinate up the stairs. The other two men grabbed the items and followed closely behind.

<What do you think, Dani? Do we need to worry about Mobs for a while or just focus on expanding?>

Dani laughed as a young version of Snowball appeared in the room and began growing quickly. "I think we are all set on Mobs for now, Cal. Let's hollow out the entire mountain range!"

CHAPTER FIFTEEN

"Dale!" A server who worked at the *Pleasure House* was running up to Dale. "Madame Chandra sent me to let you know that the High Royals have arrived and are waiting to talk to you."

"Thanks! This is pretty good timing actually. Would you let her know I will be there as soon as I bathe?" Dale asked the waiting server.

"Absolutely, m'lord." He didn't leave, seeming to be expecting something.

Dale raised a brow at him. "Yes?"

The man coughed lightly. "Well, this is really outside my normal duties..."

"Yes, thank you." Dale started to turn away, but Rose caught his arm.

"Dale," she whispered, "he wants a tip. Money."

"What? Why?" Dale returned in a normal tone, making her wince.

"Because he came here at a run when he could have dawdled and taken his time, making sure that you had no time to clean up or refresh yourself. The term 'tips' is an acronym for 'to insure proper service'. If you aren't a generous person, the people who can make your life easier will find ways to make it much *harder* instead," Rose explained in a hurried hiss.

"I see. Got it. I had just never heard of that before." Dale turned back to the waiting man. "Sorry for the wait, here, please take this as a token of my appreciation." He flipped him a silver coin, making the server's eyes go wide. The man caught it with a grin, running off the way he came.

Rose rolled her eyes. "Way to overpay, Dale." She sighed. "Ah well, at least you know *he* will always rush to you. You may have forgotten, but a silver is still about a week's worth of pay for people who don't risk their lives every day. A hundred copper? You remember, the little coins that you used to dive after in the dungeon?"

Dale rolled his eyes and broke off from the group, making his way over to the designated bathing area. He stripped down, quickly scrubbing himself and getting as clean as possible in the frigid water. Feeling much more awake and slightly shivering, he made his way to the restaurant. Along the way, he called for a small group of guards to shadow him, making sure there were no Nobles lurking nearby looking for revenge.

He walked to the doors of the restaurant, being stopped by guards with wicked-looking blades. "Halt, good sir. This building is closed for a private event. I apologize, but I must ask you to take your luncheon elsewhere."

Dale paused, surprised by the politeness shown to him. So far, all of the Nobles he had encountered—and their guards—had been exceedingly rude and pompous. "Thank you, but I was actually summoned to this event. My name is Dale. I am the owner of this land."

"Ah! Excellent." The guard smiled at him. "Well, come on in then. Be warned though that the guards in there are rather jumpy, so please don't make any threats or threatening motions. People have been accidentally skewered for *sneezing* too abruptly."

Dale watched him to see if he was making a joke, but the guard certainly *seemed* serious. "Duly noted. Thanks for the warning...?"

He stepped inside, walking into the main dining hall. There were only two people at a table with a smattering of guards around the room in various poses as they watched different angles. Normally, this room was bustling; people usually were here the *moment* the restaurant opened.

The man sitting at the table looked up. "Pardon me, may I ask why you are here?"

To Dale's surprise, though the man's body looked to be in his early twenties, his face was haggard and drawn. There were lines on his face and circles under his eyes that only came from extreme stress and lack of sleep, and the woman next to him had a similar visage.

"Pardon my intrusion." Dale tried to match the formality and suddenly realized that he had no idea what to call them. While he had amazing insight into the Dark Court of the Elves, he had little to no idea how much would translate to human politics. "Um. Your... Highness?"

The man sighed. "Please, I am really trying not to be discourteous, but if you are here to stare like the others were, I would *really* like you to leave. I want a nap so badly that..."

Dale rallied, slipping into his most politically professional mindset. "No, I am here to introduce myself and discuss matters that require our combined attention. My hesitation was due to not knowing the proper title to address you. My name is Dale, Duke of the Huine nation, Baron of the Lion and Phoenix realms. I am the owner of this land."

The man at the table blinked, a fast motion that turned slow, as though he were fighting to keep his eyes open. He opened his mouth to reply but was saved from answering by the other table occupant smoothly taking the reins of conversation.

"Hello and welcome. Please, be seated. I am Crown Princess Marie of the Phoenix Kingdom. This is Crown Prince Henry of the Lion Kingdom."

She continued, introductions complete, "Thank you for taking the time to offer your respects as soon as you were able, and please join us so that we may discuss the issues you bring. Also, please be aware that neither of us have slept since the rumors of war have begun, so our meeting must be a short one as we still need to find an area to sleep."

Dale sat down. "I can take care of that. I have quarters in the temple right now, and there is plenty of space available. A stone building, easily defensible," he nodded at the nearby guards as he mentioned this; they obviously appreciated the gesture, "which is well-appointed and spacious. I hope it will serve until we are able to find sleeping arrangements more befitting you."

Prince Henry waved away his concerns. "That will be wondrous; I have slept on nothing for long enough that anywhere is enough for me. I'd take a stable. Or the dungeon."

"Agreed," Marie intoned tiredly. "Thank you."

"Please, think nothing of it." Dale looked between these two. They were nothing like the other Nobles he had met thus far. He wondered if their politeness was simply the difference between main and branch families? "The first thing I need to bring to your attention is that I currently have the Barons Adams—one from each of your Kingdoms—under lock and key."

That woke them up, sharpening their gaze as they worked to keep their emotions in check.

Marie spoke first, "May I ask... *why* they are under arrest?"

"Currently just being held, pending your judgment of course. Their first actions upon entering this area were to accost anyone nearby that happened to look their way. They had someone—at least one person—whipped for not knowing how to address them properly. My guards are still looking for him, as they told me he was being held for some reason." Dale looked at the stony faces of the Royals.

"And?" Henry explosively sighed. "Until we come into our own inheritance, we cannot change the laws of the Kingdom. They have the *right* to act like the entitled snobs that they are. So their people will eventually revolt and potentially overthrow them. There is less a chance of that happening if these selfsame snobs reach the B-rankings, I suppose. Dale, every Noble is master of his own land until they break crown law."

"They also set their guards on me and threatened me with execution, if that means anything to you," Dale offered, aghast at the casual acceptance of random beatings.

Henry caught his breath and looked at Marie; she shrugged. "Well," Henry was glancing around, "what do you want to happen to them? Executing them, or even beating them, would start a war with the Baronies that we could ill afford right now."

Dale shook his head. "Nothing so drastic. I want permission to create my own charter, a set of laws that visiting nobility will need to follow, else I *can* punish them. I intend to build this area into a city, and I don't want people to think they can show up and attack *my* people! I would also like you to order them to follow my laws, on my land at *least*."

Marie chuckled ruefully. "*Your* people, huh? Well, Henry, we have been wanting to change the way peasants are treated, and he *is* offering this to us on a silver platter. If his area prospers, we can use him as a precedent for change."

Henry nodded. "I'm with you. Sounds interesting, Dale. Since you already have an honorary title, I can make it a *real* title and bind your authority to this land. Unless superseded by my Father's direct orders, I name you Baron Dale Phantom of the Barony Phantom."

"As do I, Crown Princess Marie, name you Baron Dale Phantom of the Barony Phantom." Marie laughed and looked at Henry, who was squinting at her. "It *is* contested land after all." She turned her attention back to Dale. "I would like to see the charter you propose and offer my services to help fill potential, ah, gaps in your laws that others may attempt to take advantage of."

"I offer my services as well!" Henry promised earnestly.

"Me too." Princess Brianna faded into view, sitting at the table. The guards did not appreciate this.

"Treachery!"

"Assassins! Defend the–"

Brianna yelled over them as the guards began to move, "Oh, calm down already!" The guards stopped moving, cold sweat trickling down their brow as knives glittered against their throats. "Everyone! Stand down." Dark Elves stepped away from the guards and vanished from sight. "Sorry, they were here to ensure there were no... *misunderstandings* as we met."

Henry replied surprisingly mildly, though his face was ashen, "As you did not assassinate us, I am rather pleased to meet you. It is not every day that a Royal meets a Moon-Elf, and the Princess at that if I am guessing correctly. More rare to survive the encounter..." He finished with a question in his voice.

The guards were not as pleased as the Prince pretended to be, closing ranks around the human Royals and glaring at the lounging Elf, who grinned and twiddled her fingers at them, trying to rile them up. From their prune-colored faces, she was succeeding.

Her demeanor shifting, she sat up and became serious. "I am very glad that you have granted Dale the powers of a landed Baron. He is a good man. You though," she eyed the Royals carefully, "from what I hear about you, you are working to downplay the power of Nobles, taking away their near-omnipotent power in their own lands. I hear that you are planning to give *peasants* similar rights to the Noble classes and plan to educate them on our cultivation techniques and abilities so they can live longer as well as do more than live their lives simply and peacefully. Is this *true*?"

Henry looked pained, so Marie again took the lead and nodded. "Yes," she said simply.

"Excellent. You are taking the same step that Elves took long ago." Brianna's lips twisted into a genuine smile. "There are risks and side effects to this plan of action. Once a critical mass of the population cultivates heavily, reproduction rates slow. When they realize this, they will cultivate more, trying to solve the issue. Eventually, your people will not be able to survive long without a constant influx of Essence, but they will be stronger, smarter, and healthier than ever before."

The known and well-explained consequences of their plans seemed to take the Royals by surprise, but they also seemed heartened by the cheerful outlook Brianna had painted for them.

"I will have my people draw up a charter with Dale's direction and present it to you in a few weeks for you to ratify or amend. Is this reasonable to all?" A few glances between the humans and a nod followed. "Lovely. Now, if you order the Barons to apologize and make amends, they must do so, yes?"

"That is so," Henry affirmed. "We can also order them to seek no revenge in any form. When we are done with them, they will only be able to sing your praises, no matter how it pains them."

Marie laughed tiredly. "I've been looking for a reason to put Adams on a short leash ever since he had a maid executed for refusing his bed."

Dale looked at her oddly. "Wait, people can refuse orders? The way they looked at me when I told them 'no' made me think that orders were unconditional."

"Only *legal* orders. Submitting to arrest or bowing when you have broken a law, even if it is a *stupid* law, is different. Rape is illegal no matter what Kingdom you reside in, and trying to use your position to force another into bed can be nothing else." Henry had to take a deep breath to calm his emotions. The others looking at him forced him to explain, "I hate seeing my people abused. It is my *duty* to protect and provide for them, and every failure to do so is another stain on my soul."

Dale nodded happily; he *liked* these people. "I feel that you would enjoy the company of my teammate, Tom. You have a similar manner of speech."

"I would be pleased to meet him! The only Tom I know that speaks like me is a northern barbarian, a giant, red-haired Prince." Henry chuckled at his memories. "Dale, while we are in town, I'll make sure to keep the other Nobles on a short leash. You likely won't even see them for a week or so."

Dale looked at Henry in horror; he had gotten caught on one part of the conversation. "Tom is a *prince*? Oh no... and I have him training with *Hans*. I need to leave. Please make your way to the temple. I will arrange accommodations on my way."

CAL

<Ah, night-time. When the majority of miners are gone for the day and people aren't picking medicinal herbs while dodging angry rabbits.> I sighed happily as I began refreshing the dungeon, removing scarring on the walls and floors from traps, missed attacks, and *successful* attacks. I glanced over at

Snowball, who was doing very non-catlike things. <Having fun, Dani?>

The Dani-possessed Cat stilled and looked at me. "*Very much so. How are things going up above? Is that Half-Dwarf still at it?*"

I looked; sure enough, the Half-Dwarf was merrily swinging his pick, blasting holes in the rock face. If he continued for another few minutes, he would be outside of the dungeon and into the mountain proper.

<Yup. On the plus side, he is helping me expand horizontally. Too bad for him, whatever he finds is likely going to be subpar. I can't really be expected to give him treasure outside of myself.>

The intrepid miner swung again, the force of his blow creating an opening outside of my influence and, therefore, my sight. He gasped, eyes going wide. He fell to his knees, and tears sprang to his eyes. He reached forward with one hand, dropping his pick. Apparently, there was a buildup of some sort of gas—yup, now that it was in my influence, I knew it to be methane. The pick hit the ground and threw sparks, creating a minor explosion. Really, it was just enough to throw the miner to the ground and shatter a few rocks.

He stood back up and stepped into the open area, outside of my vision. I watched for him for several moments, hearing his murmurs of glee and the pounding of his pick. He left within a half-hour or so, gleefully chuckling the whole time. I extended tendrils of influence into the area, widening my range as soon as was possible. I looked for anything that could have made him behave so out of character, but I found nothing. He must have done a very good job collecting whatever it was.

<Dani, what do you think was in there?> I was still frantically searching.

"*No clue, sorry. I am going to keep training. Snowball is a little harder to control than the other Cats.*"

<Fair enough.> After we had found out that Dani was *good* at fighting, she had been training constantly to get better. I didn't really have the knack for it; I was more of the idea man. I made things that could fight so I didn't need to.

I turned my attention to filling in the tunnel—where the Half Dwarf had been mining—with fairly porous stone that didn't shatter as easily as normal, which would reduce the efficiency of the blasting pick, making it far less effective.

While I was absorbing the rubble, a glint of metal caught my attention, and I looked at it closely. Aluminum? Was that what had excited him so much? There was so much aluminum in the stones and dirt that I had never bothered to give it out. Surely, it was exceedingly common, right?

I pondered on this all night whilst repairing and upgrading certain portions of the deeper levels.

When daylight started trickling down from above, and I felt the stirring of restless feet at the entrance. I turned my attention to the first group to step in. Dale and his people of course.

<Well, good morning there, sunshine. I hope you slept well and are ready for a fun-filled day of excitement and adventure,> I sent toward Dale.

He flinched, looking around for new or sudden traps. "*Can't you just leave me alone? I've been doing what you ask. Can I at least not get bothered by your incessant nattering?*"

<Fine mood *you* are in today. I think that you are getting a bit too much of an ego, been bossing people around recently?>

Dani had been spying for me recently, as well as mutterings from other dungeon divers mentioning Dale. <What are you anyway? People seem to have a bad opinion of you.>

Dale looked a bit hurt at these words. I think I may have struck a nerve. "*If you must know, I own the mountain. I was a sheep-herder when I found this place and was given enough money to purchase the land for a pittance. Now, people are magically forced to listen to me when I tell them to leave.*"

<Interesting, you own the mountain, and I own you. Funny how the world works,> I teased him.

"*You do not own me. I am a free man, and I will not–*" Whatever he would not do was interrupted as I shut down the nerves running to his legs, and he bonelessly toppled to the floor.

Nice, I hadn't been sure I could do that!

Returning control of Dale's legs, I waited for him to make an excuse to the others before continuing to talk.

<Since I enclosed your Center in a Soul Gem and essentially saved your life again, I have a *bit* of power over you. Also, since you opened yourself to me fully the other day...>

"Oh, right," I heard Dale mutter under his breath.

My connection to Dale *slammed* closed, only a tiny tendril of power remaining between us. If I had eyes, I would have blinked in surprise.

<Well.>

"*I can still hear you. Damn,*" Dale thought with deep overtones of exasperation.

<Can't really get around that—we are connected. Well fine, be that way. How did you do that?>

Dani was now listening in on our conversation through me. This was more exciting than making a Cat low crawl across a room with only its front paws apparently.

"*Why should I tell you? What do I get out of it?*"

Greedy little human.

<How about a trade? I'll ask you a question, and you can ask me something,> I offered generously.

"*No thanks.*"

What the...? <You don't have questions?> I was mind boggled at the lack of curiosity.

"*I have many, but I feel that giving you any information would be a bad deal for me.*"

Dale went back to trying to ignore me. That wouldn't do at all.

<How about we chat when you aren't busy, and I won't send every creature in here to overwhelm you?> I threatened. I think he could hear my bluff. Mind-speak can be annoying like that.

"*Oh, you are finally going to give up your pretense at being neutral? I bet Hans would survive, and the first time I felt you weren't playing fair, I would tell him. Then they would find a way to come and kill you permanently. My understanding is that dungeons who do stuff like that are destroyed quickly,*" Dale rebutted, making me almost growl in frustration. I could tell that *he* wasn't bluffing.

"Dale, look out!" Tom cried, making Dale spin around with his weapon at the ready. His team looked at him in confusion, and he blushed, murmuring something about hearing a noise.

"*Did you just fake Tom's voice in my mind?*" Dale thought at me.

<Mayyyybe.> I laughed at the swear words he thought at me. <What an angry person you are! Tell you what. I'll let you go first—ask a question. I'll choose to answer it or not. If I choose not to, I'll put better items in the next chest you are sure to find. Either way, I then ask you something.> I waited for a response, but none seemed forthcoming.

<If you don't answer because you don't know, fine, I wasted a turn. If you don't answer because you don't *want* to,

you will get worse loot. If you *do* answer, you get another turn, and so forth. You must answer as fully as you can.> I thought that was a fair deal, and Dani confirmed it for me when I glanced at her.

"*This is an agreeable compromise for now, I suppose. That is, as long as you swear to do nothing to distract me or create unfair situations for me or my team,*" Dale sent thoughtfully. "*This deal continues permanently, I assume.*"

<Yes it does! My turn!> I chuckled, feeling good about that trick.

"*Nope, if you think about that, I asked no question. You just supplied me with information.*"

Oh dear, it seems someone has been teaching Dale how to be crafty; now *I* was worried.

"*My first question is this: Do you actually have no control over me right now, or are you playing with my head to get answers?*"

<I really have no direct control; all I can do is try to influence you with my words and needs. My turn, *why* do I have no control? You did... something. What?>

"*Something that Dark Elves in political positions are taught early on in their career is that people can be controlled or influenced by others that are trained to do so. I tightened my aura, leaving less room for outside influences to penetrate.*"

Dale didn't make it sound easy, but I was still a bit worried about this. Is that the real reason I shouldn't create reasoning Mobs in here? Because if they worked out this method, I would lose control of them totally? Hmm. Something to think about.

"*I've heard you talking to someone else, who is it?*" was Dale's next question. I looked at Dani, who gave me a look that clearly suggested I answer in the negative.

<Can't tell you, sorry. You earn a boost to your next treasure chest,> I ignored his muttered frustration. <There is a Half-Dwarf that comes in here and mines. He left with something that made him happy enough to bring him to tears, but I don't know what it was. What was it?>

Dale seemed surprised but covered it well by punching an exceptionally fluffy bunny in the face as he contemplated his answer. "*Evan? I heard from him this morning—you really don't know? He had found some rare metal—he called it aluminum. It is worth more than platinum—per weight—and holds Essence so well that the metal itself becomes stronger. When enchanted, it becomes something that he calls 'Mithril'. My turn, how did you not know what he had taken?*"

<He was outside of the dungeon at that point. He tunneled in a straight line for so long that he was outside of my range. That area is now *inside* my influence,> I murmured while I thought over the implications of his last comment. <Okay, why is aluminum so rare? It is stupidly abundant. It is seriously everywhere. You have some on your boot right now.>

Dale paused, considering. "*I guess I don't know. My guess is that it accumulates in mineral deposits rarely, and there is no known method to extract it from everything else? If it is all around like you say, that is the only logical explanation that I can think of.*"

I grunted; he had answered as best he could so I had nothing to call him out on, dang rules. Why did I always set rules for myself?

"*I'm going to save my question for now. We are coming up on a Boss Room, and being distracted while fighting Raile is a bad idea. I hope you remember our non-interference agreement.*" He carefully phrased his words so that they weren't a question; Dale was getting clever.

DALE

The dungeon was getting to him. He had been distracted the entire time they were here, and the others were starting to catch on that he was not paying attention. A Basher had gotten past him and landed a damaging blow on Adam's leg when Dale was supposed to be watching out for him; even now, it was darkening into a deep bruise.

Hans was looking at him closely. "You back with us now?" he asked directly in the tactless way Hans was known for. "It looks like you've been arguing with yourself for the last hour, and if you aren't done, we should prolly just wait. You know, instead of fighting a bear-sized, armored rabbit that tends to squish people."

Dale flushed; he hadn't realized he was being so obvious. "Yeah, sorry, Hans. Sorry, Adam. I've been thinking about other things. I know we are suffering for it. I am now fully focused. Let's go kick this pig."

Tom cleared his throat. "Um. Art thou feeling proper? We go now to kill an overgrown rabbit, not a pig. If hallucinations or a fever are afflicting your person, we should seek a healer."

"He is fine, Tom," Adam interjected, "That was a saying, and it means that he is ready and willing to go."

"Ah. That does make more sense now."

They stepped into the room, and Raile wasted no time in making his attack. Sometimes he came from a hole hidden high in the wall, and sometimes he tried to hide, blending in with the wall. Today, Raile just seemed ready to kill and was dashing at them even as they stepped into his territory.

Raile ran at an angle to the wall, then jumped and pushed off it to maintain momentum whilst changing direction. Midair, he flipped just before landing, increasing his momentum and creating a much larger area of damage than Dale had previously seen. Stone shards went flying from the ground, chipped off and sent at high speeds from the impact site. Small slivers pinged off weapons, while others opened small cuts wherever they touched.

Tom roared and stepped forward, swinging his warhammer at Raile with deadly intent. This had worked the previous day, easily slaying the Boss, but today, Raile leaned back on his haunches and swung his paws like a boxer. The huge warhammer caught the blow just behind the head of the weapon, sending it flying across the room.

<Yes!> Dale heard in his head.

Expecting that the warhammer was gone, the rest of the group rushed to land their own attacks. The large Basher ducked and weaved, avoiding some blows and catching others on its armor. It threw a one-two punch that tossed Tom across the room, dealing damage—but not nearly as much as a charge would have. Rabbits are not built to be boxers, they are built to use their hind legs to supply power. The way it was acting right now was entirely out of the norm, making Dale wonder if Raile had gotten stronger or possibly higher ranked.

Rose landed a few arrows into the flesh around Raile's neck, prompting a Glitterflit to zip across the room and *boop* him with a powerful influx of healing Essence. Hans executed the Glitterflit with a cartwheel in midair, turning into a surprisingly effective whirling succession of blades.

Raile bounced, jumping straight up and coming down heavily, making the standing members of the group flinch, almost losing their footing. His armor fell off him as his ability—

Avenger—activated. His head suddenly had a crown of jagged granite, and Raile was *furious*. While the humans were off balance, he dropped to all fours and rushed Rose, as she stood in front of his real target—Hans. She easily dodged out of the way, and Tom was suddenly in front of Raile, swinging his warhammer in a fury. Raile dropped, head mangled beyond repair, and the others sat down to catch their breath.

"What was that?" Hans questioned the others. They shrugged, so he shook his head and skinned the Glitterflit.

"I heard he had an ability, but I've never seen him fight like that before." Rose considered the slowly melting form of Raile.

Adam looked at Tom who was shaking, trying to come down from his fury. "You okay over there, buddy?"

"I... I have too much of the rage of my ancestors. If I had... it would be easier if I had more to kill." Tom ground out through gritted teeth. His hands were white where he held his hammer in a too-tight grip.

Hans looked at the deeply breathing man and nodded. "That clears that up at least."

"What?" Dale looked between the two, and Tom seemed suddenly ashamed.

"I... there is something I must explain," Tom began. "I was born the crown prince of the Wolf Kingdom, but when it was found that the taste of blood sends me into a rage, I was disowned. The blood rage is an outdated remnant of a time in our history where those of us with the fire-infused blood were the only real defense against the ice giants. Now though... who would trust a man that can barely control his bloodthirst to be a leader of men? I was disinherited by my father, refused the cultivation techniques that were my birthright, and sent out to find my own way in life. Now... here I am."

"Is this why you took that extra swing at Raile that killed a member of your former team?" Hans's tone was laced with barely controlled anger.

"It is," Tom admitted shamefacedly. "I had taken a blow that tore my lip, and the fury raced through me. I could find nothing else to attack besides my friends, so I released my anger on Raile's corpse."

Hans barely waited for him to finish speaking before beginning to yell, "So you are telling us that a small injury to you may cost us our lives, and you never thought to *warn* us?!"

"Hans, maybe you should–" Dale tried to interject.

"No!" Hans shouted him down before turning back to Tom coldly. "I thought I was your mentor, a person that you trusted to teach you everything you needed to know. Why would you not tell me about something this important? If you can't control your body's reaction to fire Essence, we need to *fix* that. It isn't hard to do!"

"I am sorry." Tom was staring at the ground. "It is not so much a secret as a shameful... wait. What?" His head snapped up, eyes bulging with confusion and a touch of hope.

"I mean, it is a slow process, but it is just *tedious*, not difficult." Hans looked at the odd expression on Tom's face. "What?"

Tom swallowed, clenching his jaw as he tried to formulate a question, "There is a cure to the Blood Fire?"

Hans nodded. "Yup. It is such a rare condition that I suppose that it isn't widely known, but it is easy to learn."

"Hans, if you are jesting, I will be hurt beyond measure," Tom pleadingly informed his teacher.

"I am quite serious."

"I... can't believe it." Tom looked at the ceiling, his height and the angle hiding that his eyes were misty. "I could go home."

CHAPTER SIXTEEN

I watched Dale's team leaving the dungeon after cultivating for roughly half an hour. <Dale? Can you hear me?> There was no reply, and no feelings of frustration from his end, so I knew that he was out of range. He was a big, seething ball of brain chemicals churning with barely controlled emotions under that tough front he put forward. I turned my attention to Dani, who was practicing her fine control of the big Cats down here.

<Question for you, if you have a moment.> I waited for her full attention. <I had a chance to absorb that warhammer I gave away, but when I tried... nothing happened. Thoughts?>

She separated from Snowball, who sank down to the ground, exhausted. "Hmm, that is odd. You had it far enough away from him?"

<Yes, he had to run across the room to retrieve it. I had plenty of time to work on disintegrating it, but he was still able to get his weapon back intact. Trying to solve the issue in a logical manner made me hesitate. I would have warned you that he was coming at you otherwise. Sorry, Dani.>

She 'shrugged', more of a conceptual thing than an actual movement of body parts. "I had lost control of Raile by that point anyway. As soon as his ability triggered, he went into a blind rage and charged. I was just along for the ride."

We spent a little time thinking. I casually fixed a wall that had cracks along it before Dani spoke again, "Well, the warhammer was bound to him, correct?"

<Yes, I made that a built-in function... oh. You think that it being bound to Tom and making it circulate his Essence imparted a portion of his aura on to it, therefore blocking my influence from breaking down its pattern. That makes sense.

Dang it. So if I want it back, I need to get to it as soon as he dies and before someone else activates it. Hmm. Didn't seem to be a problem when getting Dale's weapon back...> I hadn't even thought that this would be a possibility; I had never even considered the effect that binding an Inscribed item may have.

"...Yeah. That is what I was going to say." Dani coughed. She looked over at Snowball, who was sound asleep. "Well, there goes practice."

<You could help me decide what to do. You may have been right a few days ago. I'm thinking that the third floor may be just a little too... what is the word? Overpowered? There was a group of fifteen people that I was unprepared for, and together, we killed off two-thirds of them, including a C-ranked guard.> I paused to see her reaction.

"Well, what did you have in mind, then?" Dani prodded me, obviously trying to get me to the point.

<We just found out that aluminum is rarer than gold. Why not change the way we do things a bit? We have gold right next to iron on the first level, and there are some miners up there that have been getting richer than people coming in to *fight.* That must be skewing the economy a bit. Let's put in a second mining area and move the current third floor down to create a fourth floor, then the third floor will be a mining area with monsters.>

"*Interesting.* That way, there will be a higher chance of growth for you. Currently, only about a third of the groups that enter the dungeon continues all the way to Raile. Usually, those are the people that are *sure* that they can fight Raile and win or, at least, survive." Dani pondered for a moment. "If only a third of the groups can make it down to the third floor, that means they will need to pull double duty, guarding and escorting as well as fighting. Then they are stuck until the miners are done and likely need to help haul ore outside."

I watched her in awe. <Wow, you came up with that on the fly? I've been thinking about this all day and night, and you still hit a few points I hadn't considered.>

"I am very intelligent," Dani noted breezily.

<And humble as well,> I replied dryly.

"I am afraid that virtue does not exist among my *many* talents."

Dani laughed at the strangled noise I made in response.

<At least you know your limits,> I muttered. <The question for me becomes: what Mobs do we put on that floor? Also, should it be a fairly open area, or should it be tunnels? And after it is going, do–>

Dani decided to cut off my thoughts at that point. "Why not worry about that *after* the floor is made? I know you have been extending downward with your influence, so let's take a week and lower the third floor far enough that you can grow that new mining floor quickly." She paused, gathering her arguments. "That way you can save on Essence by not using it in a big burst, and people may not notice for a while that there even *is* a new floor. No one has come to this one after that huge party got destroyed."

<Sounds like a plan to me. Then I can decide how to make the layout. Oh! What if we...>

Dani listened to me chatter for a few minutes about how I wanted to make the floor plan, oohing and ahhing in all the right places. She tended to be a really good audience. We had just decided on the ratio of gold to aluminum when I tensed up and focused on a point high above.

"What is the matter?" Dani was seriously concerned. After all, I almost never got this concerned; I was basically a laid-back people-eater.

<Three... Elves? Just entered. They are moving *really* fast. We are talking... I am only tracking them by the disruption in airflow. Already at the first Boss Room. Past. They haven't killed anything yet, which worries me. The Bashers haven't had time to react to anything,> I told her tensely.

"Do you want to drop the panic doors?" Dani was trying to keep a brave face, but when *I* was nervous, *Dani* always became even more so. The panic doors were her idea; after the Distortion Cat incident, she told me that I needed to put more direct defenses into high-traffic areas. The panic doors allowed me to drop five-ton cursed-earth granite doors, which should be sufficient to at least *slow* overly powerful people.

<I...> I hesitated; the doors took a huge amount of effort to reset, even for *me*. <They haven't done anything overtly hostile. I don't think I should just yet.>

Dani nodded, accepting my answer. Sometimes, I think she trusted me more than I deserved. "Where are they now?"

<Almost to Raile. Wow, watching their progress is ridiculous. They didn't even *bend* a blade of grass in the garden room. Oh...>

"What?"

<They bypassed Raile. He was still mid-air when they started down the stairs.> I strategically began moving the Assimilators around the third floor. Ugh, they move so *slowly!* Luckily, the third floor was not as straightforward as the others. The fast-moving Elves paused and began moving through the labyrinth, seemingly frustrated every time they hit a dead-end. Still, they were making good time through my tricks and traps, easily avoiding the attacks made by my Mobs.

They reached the final approach to the Boss Room and began moving down the straight corridor. My Assimilator raised two of its stingers to chest level on a human, and the air vibrated a bit as the Essence I was directing into my Mob passed through. The Elves never paused, actually *increasing* their speed forward. I had my Assimilator release as much Essence as it could channel, a huge burst of fire pushed through a focusing lens of celestial corruption.

The fire that poured outward was white tinged with gold, hot enough that a shock wave formed in front of it from air being burned and displaced. The rock walls in the fairly narrow hallway glowed cherry-red as the wave of fire moved past, some of it cracking or shattering from the huge temperature differential. Any shards of rock that fell off stuck to whatever they landed on, fused together.

This at least got the Elves' attention. Their eyes widened for a moment, then narrowed with intense focus. The first of them stepped forward, making a motion that displaced air but had no other noticeable effect. The second swept forward with her hands, forcing dirt and dust into a thick wall of particles in front of them. The third halted entirely, making motions that caused a band of—*infernal?!*—Essence forward, wrapping around the particle wall just before the wave of fire reached it.

I was watching the interplay of Essence as closely as possible to see what they had done—it was quite ingenious, really. The infernal Essence counteracted the celestial in the fire, and though the fire was still intense, it no longer burned like a bar of magnesium. The particle wall absorbed the force of the blast, and, apparently, the first of them had done something to the air that reduced the potency of the flame. The fire raged against their efforts for a moment, but when it subsided, a pane of clear glass stood in the hallway, allowing them to view the fiery landscape just beyond.

The first one punched the glass, shattering it and allowing a blast of heat to escape. The influx of oxygen made the hallway glow brighter for a few moments. Oh! That is what the first person did; the air must have had the oxygen removed from it in a small space. That would greatly reduce the potency of fire. I wonder if I could do something similar... oh damn, the people moved again.

They ran directly at the glowing area, right when I thought they would get third-degree burns on their tender feet. They began walking two inches above the floor. My Assimilator—completely wrung out—fell to the floor and cooked near instantly, cracking and spitting like bacon.

Oops. Forgot to replenish its Essence.

"Nice work on the air-boots, Minya. You do decent work for a *human*," one of the Elves offered a backhanded compliment.

"Thanks. Sure would be a shame if they suddenly failed over this molten floor, wouldn't it?" a raspy, distinctly human voice answered. I had heard similar voices on adventurers that smoked heavily.

The Elf in question looked at the bubbling floor, suddenly nervous. He swallowed. "It would at that."

The final Elf in the group spoke up, "Enough you two. Minya has a reputation as the best dungeoneer in the business, and *you*," she pointed at the condescending Elf, "have a reputation as a bigot. Who do you think Brianna would listen to if it came down to a complaint?"

"Whatever. I... where is the tree?"

They had turned the final corner and were now facing a thick wall of steam.

"I'd assume," Minya rasped, "that it is beyond the sauna."

"How helpful," the Elf sneered at the human's back.

"Stop it. This is a Boss Room. Be on your guard. Remember, *non-lethal.*" The mediator Elf barked.

Poor Snowball had no chance. As soon as he appeared from the fog the earth under him turned to sand, and he sank under his own weight into the now-rapidly solidifying stone.

"Done. To the tree."

They walked away from Snowball, who was snarling more furiously than I have ever heard. Walking into the next room, they blinked as the air was instantly clear of fog and steam. I had separated the Boss Room and *my* room after I noticed that the Silverwood tree was wilting in the high heat and humidity environment. Marching right up to the tree, they looked it over and *tisked.*

"Ugh, look at that. An *Enchantment.* How droll. It is weakening and *obviously High-*Elf workmanship," the male Elf muttered.

Minya appeared curious. "How can you tell?"

"Because it is hastily and poorly done but *artistic.*" The male chuckled, lost in his examination of the Enchantment around the tree. "Ah. Found it."

He reached forward and *plucked* with his fingers, and the pattern of the Enchantment started glowing, bleeding Essence into the air.

"Now we can put a better series of protections into place," the female Elf informed Minya in response to her arched brow. "What? This area is important to us."

"To me as well. We had an agreement, yes?" Minya folded her arms.

The female blushed while the male rolled his eyes. "Look, we can't just leave you in here by yourself, especially without the protections in place."

"So, you are *both* planning to ignore the agreement?" Minya began to glare, tensing her hands.

The male gave a cocky half grin. "Well, *I* am."

He had barely spoken the words when Minya was behind him, delivering a strike to the base of his neck. He choked a moment, then fell to the floor. Not dead, sadly. *This close* to taking a B-ranked amount of Essence!

"What about you?" Minya breezily questioned, gazing casually at her fingernails.

The female sighed and nodded. "I'll watch him in the other room." She collected her fallen teammate and dragged him away.

When the room was cleared of Elves, Minya turned her attention back to the tree.

"Dungeon," she called softly.

<Is she talking to me or making a statement?> I asked Dani, who just glared at me.

"Dungeon. Dungeon!" Minya got much louder on the second word. "Answer me! I *know* I'm not crazy!" She cackled a little after that, which led me to disbelieve her a *tiny* bit.

<I'm not talking to her,> I muttered to Dani. <She's freaking me out.>

"I just have some questions for you, Dungeon." Minya narrowed her eyes. Her next words were far rougher, nearly a snarl. "*Last* chance, Dungeon, or I'm going to reach in there and take your Core. I know you have a Wisp in there. I heard you talking to her. Feel like gambling with *her* safety?"

<Oh crap, she can hear me? How many people can hear me now? This is getting annoying!>

Minya blinked. "There are... others? Other people can help me prove my sanity?" Her expression had turned introspective.

<I take that as a yes. Um. Hello, Minya. Please don't kill me?> I began talking to her hopefully.

"What?" Minya refocused on me. Well, mostly. Her attention was seeming to wander a bit. "Oh. No, if you are talking to me, I won't hurt you. *Never ignore me!*" She snarled the last part.

<I will *not* ignore you,> I fervently promised.

"Good. I hear..." she swallowed, "I hear that the Essence in here is pure. That anyone can use it. But *upstairs,* it certainly had taint."

<It did? Dani?> My Wisp slowly moved into the open so Minya could see and hear her.

"Hi, human. Please don't kill me either." Dani was trembling a bit.

"What? Oh, no. I won't. I've seen what happens to dungeons that lose their Wisps. Hello, by the way." Minya's attention seemed variable. "Why isn't the Essence pure upstairs anymore?" she demanded with a demented stare.

"I would assume because we are slowly getting farther away from the surface," Dani soothingly told her. "Essence is flowing in from outside as well, and away from Cal, the pure Essence has a chance to mix with what is already there."

"Well, fix it! It is inside your influence. You are just getting lazy and fat with this Rune feeding you like a hedonistic emperor."

Minya spat to the side. I absorbed it from force of habit.

<Hey!> I looked at her and realized why she could hear me. <You have a broken aura!>

"She has a what?" Dani muttered, obviously not hearing me correctly.

I was examining Minya. She had a similar setup to Dale but poorly done and with a sub-standard Core. The Core wasn't even around her Center—it was in her stomach!

<Wow, that is a *lot* of corruption.>

Minya snarled and took a threatening step forward. "If I feel *anything* funny, I will destroy you."

"What is she talking about?" Dani whispered as she eyed the crazy lady.

I didn't keep my voice down, and Dani winced at my conversational tone. <I assume she is warning me away from messing with her anatomy, as she has only a very weak aural protection. I'm assuming she is here because she wants to make a deal, so,> I turned the conversation back to Minya, <out with it. What are you offering and what do you want?>

Minya looked downcast at losing her upper hand and took a seat on the floor. "I've never heard a low-level dungeon like this be so coherent. Usually, it is snarls and a few threats until they hit the upper C-ranks." She seemed to be talking to herself.

<I am *right* here. Thank you for the compliment, but get to the point please.>

Minya took a deep breath. "I need to give you a bit of background information. I've been a dungeon-diver for decades. A few years back, I got impatient. I wanted to break into the A-ranks and didn't want to do it the *right* way. The slow way. I found a dungeon that had four types of Essence in it, an elemental dungeon. That is, it had earth, air, fire, and water in near-equal amounts." She paused, tearing up a bit.

"I... I forced open two more affinity channels. I had always had strong affinities with air and fire, but I figured that if I could just *double* the amount of Essence I drew in, I could reach the A-ranks in half the time. Mere days after I had opened the channels, someone *killed* the dungeon. I could hear the screams in my mind as its Core shattered, and its thought patterns dissipated into its influence. A *huge* amount of corruption was released somehow. My raw meridians were forced open wider than I had wanted, allowing so much corruption into me that I would never have a chance to reach the next step in the B-ranks, let alone the A-rankings."

"Not only that, but the land is still poisoned and unlivable." She refocused on me. "That is where you come in! Ever since then, I can hear the voices in the dungeons. Others have called me insane, and I was starting to think they were right. You, though," she cackled, "you respond! You talk to me!"

<So you want me to... what now?> I cautiously asked.

"I want you to tell people that you are *alive*!" She cried out, "I want them to know that I was right all along!"

<So... you don't want me to fix you?>

"You can't *fix* me," she growled. "Someone already *tried* that. When I got free, the largest chunk of them that was ever seen again was a molar I somehow missed. Sure, I lost my place in the Guild, but they *deserved* it."

"Celestial crap! She's bonkers!" Dani mouthed at me while Minya was distracted.

<And they tried to fix you... how? Humans can't seem to work directly with corruption.> Uh-oh. My curiosity was piqued.

"Pff. And you can? Get real." She snorted, to my great offense. "They decided that what I needed was to swallow a Core and that they would just take it out after it had absorbed the taint."

<It seems that you *do* have a Core in you,> I noted, keeping the conversation going as I eased my influence into her brain.

She chuckled darkly. "I assume you have seen the process then? Where a person swallows a Core and then pukes it up a bit later? Sound accurate? Well, when a person does *not* take the Core willingly, there are... side effects. Like the Core sticking to them and draining them *slowly*. It is a bad way to die, Dungeon."

<The name is Cal,> I offered amiably, determined not to be caught working inside her organs during the conversation.

She nodded. "Well, *Cal,* the Core in me absorbs all the corruption all right. Also, any Essence that I try to cultivate. I've had to carve Runes to block the flow of Essence just to keep the Core from *exploding* and turning my abdomen into ground meat when it finally becomes too full." She lifted her shirt, exposing Runes carved directly into her skin that glowed with a malevolent light.

I memorized the pattern. I would experiment with it later. Heh. Thank *you,* Minya. <They seem a bit... shall we say, flawed?>

She agreed angrily, "Skin heals over time. The Rune is breaking up and will soon allow Essence into the Core. Then I will die. I want to prove my sanity before then. Also," a bit of Essence arched from the Rune, shocking her with a tiny bolt of lightning, "it hurts like a *mother.*"

<So that is all? You want your sanity proven and not to be fixed?> I clarified.

She folded her hands and tried not to be angry. "I would *love* to be fixed, but it isn't possible."

<Yes, it is.>

"Stop messing with my head!" she shrieked. "Just because I am desperate doesn't make me an idiot!"

<Well, what do you have to lose? Make a deal with me. What do I get for fixing you?> I remained calm, carefully attempting to hide my greed and excitement.

She looked at Dani. "Is he... serious? Also, is Cal a he?"

Dani smirked. "He is serious, and since he has no reproductive organs, he does not actually have a sex. I say 'he' because he has a masculine voice, and I think he was male before he got in that Core."

"Huh. I... I might live?"

<Depends on what you think your life is worth.> I was trying to rush her so I'd get a better deal.

"What do you want? I'm very wealthy. I could..." she started.

<No, I already have a guy for that. How about this? I want an agent. Someone who follows my orders and *willingly* gives me knowledge.> I watched for her reaction, ready now to open veins in her brain if she refused.

"You want me to... tell you about groups of adventurers?" she asked with an odd inflection.

<Not necessarily, but a warning about people that are after Dungeon Cores would be nice.>

She chuckled wetly; it seemed she was crying.

<I've found that memory stones are very useful to me. I want those.>

"How many?" She sniffled.

<What do you mean?>

"You want them a specific one? A set of Dwarven mathematics?"

<No, I want *all* of them. I want to know *everything* that anyone knows,> I replied dreamily. <The sum total of all knowledge.>

She looked crestfallen. "I'm not... *that* rich."

<You will be.> I chuckled, mentally rubbing my hands in greed. I had her, I just knew it. <Anything you need in order to get them, I will provide. Money? Done. Empty stones? I've got hundreds. You will also be well-paid for your services. I'll make you *fantastically* rich if you want it.>

"I just want to live," she softly muttered.

<Then that is even *easier* for me! Shall we get started?> I had already picked out the spot to start working. <Do we have a deal?>

She took a deep breath, eyes dilating a bit. "Yes."

<Let's get started!> I inflamed a tiny portion of her brain matter, and Minya slumped unconscious as I nudged a vein in her head softly.

Dani looked at me reproachfully. "Really?"

<Why do you think I wasn't worried about her threats? Dani, a human agent in the human world will be a huge benefit! Dale could have been the guy, but noooo. He had to be all whiny about how he got to survive. Ungrateful, I tell you.> I was looking at the interior of Minya's body at this point. <Woof. *Lots* of damage. I suppose if she hasn't been able to cultivate for a few years, her body must have been running off whatever she had stored. Look at this spot near her Center. I wonder if this is what happens when Mana doesn't have a layer of Essence as a buffer?>

"Oh, right. She was in the B-rankings. Yikes, I can't *believe* how much internal damage she has! How is she alive right now?" Dani seemed suddenly impressed by this person's tenacity.

<Force of will?> I created a molecule-thin barrier of Essence in her flesh, separating a few inches of tissue and spinal cord from her body. The Beast Core was too tightly bound to these areas to just take it out directly. I pulled out and tossed away the chunk of meat. At this point, I was holding her body together directly with Essence, replicating veins with hollow barriers. After I absorbed that chunk of tissue, I was able to perfectly reproduce it in place without the Core and hooks of Essence. I reattached nerves and blood vessels, regrew bone and muscle, and made sure it was all working together correctly.

I wondered why it was so easy to do. Mana users were exceedingly tough. I realized as I was working that without Mana being able to flow through her, the bonds had weakened. If she were unable to cultivate long enough, her body would have *literally* fallen apart chunk by chunk.

<All set. Now she will be able to cultivate again!> I looked at her ragged body. She deserved a bonus for being so willing to work for me. <Maybe a *few* more alterations?> I went through her body, fixing imperfections and damage like I would my tunnels. I smoothed her skin and replaced the areas that had Runes carved into them. Certainly not just to harvest more Runes—it was to help her! I, uh... promise!

I repaired the external signs of wear next, the lines of stress and pain, making her hair shiny and lustrous instead of lank and unwashed. I even trimmed her nails to a reasonable length. Her clothes were—well, needing to be burned doesn't quite cover it. Instead of trying to wash her or something of the like, I simply absorbed any foreign substance, then grew a new set of clothing on her.

Dani was fascinated by the process and offered a few other minor details that I wouldn't have ever thought about, like opening capillaries a tiny bit wider in her lips so they would be a brighter red or adjusting her eyebrow hair to be very thick, but only in a certain area. For some reason, she also had me remove the hair follicles anywhere that wasn't on her head. Dani had strange concepts of what 'fixing' meant.

It was now time to wake Minya up; hopefully, she wouldn't mind the changes. After all the fixes, there was nothing keeping her from getting up on her own, but it seemed that she was at the point of physical exhaustion. No wonder she had seemed insane. Even if she only needed a tiny bit of sleep, she still *needed* it. I washed her brain free of the buildup of toxins that lack of sleep allows to accumulate, and she opened her eyes.

She started moving slowly, obviously waiting for the pain that had been a constant presence in her life for years. I knew this because I had had to work on her frazzled nerves.

When she sat up and looked at herself in confusion, she had to ask, "How long was I out? I feel like I've slept for weeks. I feel... amazing."

"About thirty minutes," Dani informed her primly. "I hope you don't ever forget your part of the bargain. Cal really went out of his way to fix you. He could have created a *dozen* Boss Mobs with all the Essence he used on you."

Minya smoothly rose to her feet and began walking around. Her movements before had been jerky and rushed, like a person overdosing on stamina potions. She did a few flips and danced around, getting a feel for her body at the same time as showing her excitement. She whirled around and looked at where I was.

"I am yours forever, Cal. Anything you need, anything in my power to do, I will. Your whim is my order!"

A line of her aura suddenly raced to me and connected to my Core, then dispersed into the dungeon at large. Also known as *my* aura.

<Celestial crap, what was that?>

"That was an oath. At the B-ranks, when Mana is a part of our body, our word becomes our law. Words have *real* power, and a spoken oath is binding." Minya smiled, much more appealing now that I regrew a few teeth and straightened the rest. "I am yours unless you release me from my oath."

"Back off, hussy," Dani muttered *very* softly.

<Dani, the Elves are coming back. Go invisible.>

Dani vanished from sight with my warning, just before the Elves walked in.

"Who are you? Where is Minya?" the female Elf sharply demanded, drawing steel.

The male scoffed. "Who cares? The bitch knocked me out!"

"What did you just call me?" Minya turned toward them menacingly. They gasped as they saw the changes in her. Her voice sounded a bit strange to them, having been healed as well, but they recognized her quickly enough.

"Minya?" the female murmured in wonderment.

"Mmhmm." Minya allowed a smile to slowly spread on her face. "I'm going to sit and cultivate while you do your thing."

"You're going to *what?*" the male sputtered. "You're committing suicide?!"

"Oh be quiet," Minya muttered and moved to sit down.

<Minya?>

"Hmm?"

<Move over about a foot, there is a small hole there. Do you have a cup or empty vial? If so dip it in and collect the fluid,> I directed my new servant.

She dipped in a vial that she had hastily poured out, a potent stamina potion of some kind that decreased the feeling of tiredness. She dipped the vial into the hole and retrieved a shining fluid—condensed Essence.

<Do you think you can safely drink that? It is *absolutely* pure. You don't need to refine it, just add it to your Center,> I inquired of her.

She murmured softly, so the Elves wouldn't hear what she said, "Yes. I have the patterns in place for Essence up to the B-ranks. I am just depleted. This will help me get back on track, thank you."

I closed the hole as she put the vial to her flushed lips and drank. Her aura began to glow as her Center drank in the pure Essence. She didn't even show signs of discomfort—only relief—as her meridians began moving a torrent of energy versus the trickle it had been.

"Can I have more?" she asked a bit plaintively.

I tried to respond, but her aura had thickened and condensed, apparently blocking my words. She seemed to understand the problem after a few minutes of failed communication and subtly rearranged her aura so that the tendril of her aura that formed her oath to me had a clear path to her brain. Odd.

<Can you hear me now?> I prodded her again, earning a disgusted sound from Dani at the repeated question.

"Yes!" Minya cried in rapture, making the Elves whirl around, looking startled.

Dani chuckled. "That sounded overly sexual." Minya blushed and kept her face resolutely turned away from the Elves' view.

<Right, so. That amount of Essence takes quite a while to accumulate. I cannot just give it away constantly. Sorry,> I told her pseudo-sadly. I wasn't just hoarding it. Nope.

"No, *I* am sorry. You have done so much for me, and I keep asking for more." She paused a moment. "Can I help you at all?"

<You had said something about fixing the Essence upstairs? Something about me being lazy?>

Minya blushed. "Yeah, sorry..."

<What did you mean? Is there a way to fix that easily?>

Every little bit helps after all, and I planned on keeping her—essentially forever—as a researcher.

"I've seen dungeons collect the corruption into minerals. I've never seen any of them work directly with corruption like you seem to be able to do, so it should be something easy for you. They put veins of minerals along the air vents, sometimes with Beast Cores at the end. The Core draws in corruption along the mineral, leaving purer Essence overall. I have never seen Essence as pure as it is here, though," Minya thoroughly explained to me.

"What kind of minerals?" Dani inquired on my behalf. I had to be faster at asking questions apparently.

Minya thought a moment. "I've seen different things, but if I had to guess at the *best* mineral to use... every type of Essence seems to have a preference, so using topaz for celestial, emeralds for earth, ruby for fire..." She seemed hesitant to continue.

<Go on. What is the matter?>

"I am unsure of the next. I can only say what legend says, and I don't want to give you bad information." She grimaced and continued, "If legend holds true, opal is the only mineral that infernal really likes, but it travels through diamond fairly easily. Wind, for some reason, likes taaffeeite, and water is attracted to fluorite."

Dani looked entirely confused, but I knew *half* of the patterns to make those. <Okay, what would you need in order to find me taaffeeite, opal, and emeralds? I think emeralds are going to be the first priority because of all the earth Essence I collect.>

Minya bit her lip. "How much do you need?"

<A *tiny* amount. A sliver, really. Just enough to analyze.> Her reaction confused me. <What is it?>

"Oh! Um. Opals are treated like a controlled substance since they are allegedly 'known' to help Necromancers. Even a small one is going to be *really* hard for me to acquire." She looked around like I was about to start beating her.

<No real rush, infernal Essence isn't *particularly* abundant in here. Now I know why so many weapons and armor have gems stuck in them at least.>

I started growing veins of crystal and gems throughout the dungeon. It would take a few days, but if she was right, this could make me even *more* appealing to adventurers. <I think it is time for you to get going, the Elves are looking at ya funny.>

She glanced around, stood up, and bowed obsequiously at the Silverwood tree. Ha. That would throw off the Elves.

They walked to the stairwell, and before they left, she looked back and whispered, "Thank you."

<Don't mention it! Ever.>

DALE

"What now?" Dale sighed at the courier that ran up to him.

With a grin, the young man handed him a sheaf of papers. "Approvals that need your signature. New businesses and housing developments that need your signature, and yes, these are from the city planner."

Dale's eyes flicked around as he scanned the document. It wasn't a magical contract... but just like *any* legal document, it could still ruin his life for a long time if he signed it without knowing what it said. His Elven political tutor liked to slip in documents to test him. Sure enough, here was one saying he would wash dishes for a week in the Guild mess hall. He shuddered.

He signed what he needed to and threw the rest into the fire. The courier ran off with the documents and a shiny new silver coin as an unfamiliar couple of people walked up to him. They had on a *lot* of armor. How did they wear all of that? They were at least a foot shorter than Dale, and... oh. They must be Dwarves.

This was confirmed when the one on the left took off his helmet and squinted at Dale. "You Dale?"

"...Yes?" Dale answered cautiously, examining their auras.

"Are you sure? You don't sound sure."

Dale grinned. "I just don't know you is all. I'm Dale."

"Good! I'm Beor Moonshadow, this is my brother, Brick "Stonewall" Moonshadow. I have a proposition for you," Beor announced abruptly.

"Do tell." Dale grinned wider; he liked this brusque fellow.

"Walls!" Brick bellowed. Dale and Beor looked at his unsmiling face.

"Yes, thank you for your contribution." Beor chuckled as his brother's face flushed. "Well Dale, it seems you own this area. It is poorly defended, and you don't exactly look like you are swimming in gold." Beor looked meaningfully at

Dale's work clothes, torn and worn from daily bunny hunting. "I have a full contingent of Dwarves ready to step in and start building, and you seem to be without defensive walls around your... city?"

Dale nodded. "It'll get there."

"Right, well. You'll never see better stonework than Dwarven make, and as we have Mages along, it will be a fairly fast process. Whaddaya say, chief?"

Dale pondered for a moment. Walls certainly were going to be essential, and with winter fast approaching, they would help to cut down the wind a lot. "And in return for your expert services?"

"Flattery! I like it!" Beor chuckled. "We have a few requests, but nothing that will cost you more than a lease for a bit of land. We want to build a place to live, essentially a barracks." Brick made a noise. "And Brick here wants to build an orphanage. We'll even fix and maintain the walls for you. What the *abyss*–"

A Dark Elf had just stepped out of nowhere and muttered to Dale that he was needed near the dungeon. Dale nodded his assent and turned back to the pale Dwarves. "I think that sounds reasonable. If I may ask, why do you need a new place to live?"

"Well." Beor coughed; he was as pale as the Elf that had just vanished. "For one thing, it is obvious that you'll give *anyone* a chance." He looked meaningfully at the space the Dark Elf had recently occupied. "Next, we left our ancestral home after the King tried to have us killed off. Put us in a fight against overwhelming odds against an Orc horde."

"You are welcome here as long as you follow the law. Talk to my city planner about the details for the wall and your area." Dale patted the Dwarf on his arm. He still looked a bit sad. "I'm sorry. Anyone who would do that does not deserve your loyalty."

Brick snorted as they walked toward the building Dale directed them to. "Yeah, Dad's an asshat."

Dale started, looking back in shock. Great... more exiled Nobles.

CHAPTER SEVENTEEN

Dale hurried toward the dungeon and soon discovered the reason for the summons. There was an Elf blocking adventurers from entering, and the noise from the crowd of backlogged parties was inhibiting Dale from hearing *why* she was there. As he got closer and heard what she was saying, he sighed and *almost* left. Someone else could deal with the crazies for a while.

"No! I will *not* let you continue to murder helpless bunnies! They have done *nothing* to you, and their ruthless slaughter has gone on *long enough!*" the lovely Elven maid was shrieking at the grizzled man telling her to move.

"Get *out of the way!*" the man roared, attempting to shove her to the side.

She flipped him on to his back, promptly breaking his arm and two of his fingers.

"No! I am against violence, and all you want to do is get *money.* You will all promise to stop this madness, or I'll kill you all! I promise on my good name, Leporiday Lagomorpha!"

"Oh for..." Dale walked over to her. "Go *away.* This is a *dungeon.* Everything in there wants to kill us, and this is a livelihood. For a *lot* of people."

"They don't want to hurt anyone! I'll prove it!" She shoved Dale away, then ran into the dungeon, vanishing from sight.

The crowd went silent, shocked at her outburst. A few moments later, concerned people started talking about following the obviously unhinged Elf, but it wasn't long until everyone present could hear the drawn-out-then-suddenly-cut-off screams.

"What the hell is going on today?" Dale muttered as people looked around uncomfortably. "Has everyone lost their minds?"

He turned toward a tap on his arm, and seeing who was doing the tapping, simultaneously lost his breath and blushed.

Looking at him was a stunning beauty. She was smiling at *him*, wearing a set of clothes that could have been painted on.

"Are you Dale?"

Dale felt a bit crestfallen. "Oh gods, not another one."

"Excuse me?"

"Sorry, it has been an odd day." Dale rubbed his head violently for a moment and took a deep breath. Plastering on his most political smile, he said, "What can I do for you, ma'am?"

"Well," she looked him over, "I was hoping to talk to you about a mutual friend."

"Oh?" Dale tried to think of who she could be talking about. "Who would that be?"

"Come to my wagon in a few hours. We have *plenty* to discuss." She turned and started away, moving in a joyful way that—to the experienced—told a story about freedom from pain.

Dale saw it as flirting.

"Where can I find you?" Dale called after her retreating form.

"Just ask around for Minya. You'll find me." She tossed him a look and a wink over her shoulder.

Dale watched her go for a few seconds. "Damn. Now we have prostitutes here... at least Hans will be pleased. Is this something that will have to go in the charter?"

"Dale!"

"What *now*?" Dale growled as he turned to face a slightly deflated-looking shopkeeper.

"Oh. Um. I can come back later? Your Grace." Tyler started to hurry away from the irritable Duke.

"Don't go!" Dale grabbed his friend. "Sorry, Tyler, it has just been a long, strange day. What is going on?"

Tyler lit up when Dale started walking with him. "Well, rumors of royalty coming to live here for the foreseeable future is attracting people in droves! Business is booming!" Tyler cheered, covertly rubbing his hands together at the thought of new customers.

"Hmm. I'd better get with someone and discuss laws about moving. If the new people coming don't have skills and a way to provide for themselves, we are going to have a serious problem with crime soon," Dale muttered to himself.

"Say again?"

"Nothing, go on."

"Well," Tyler showed a toothy smile to his landlord, "I hear you have been looking for a dimensional bag? Just so happens I got in a new shipment this morning!"

Dale chuckled. He should have known Tyler was here on business. "I really do *need* at least one. How much are you charging?"

"For my savior and landlord?" Tyler pretended to think a moment. "A mere thirty gold."

Dale stopped and stared. "Good lord, man. How much would it be if you *didn't* like me?"

"Hmm. A platinum at least."

Dale choked a bit at the amount.

"Of course, if you were just a normal customer, I'd charge you about eighty-five gold." Tyler grinned at the look Dale gave him.

"You knew what I meant." Dale huffed, crossing his arms.

Tyler nodded sagely. "Yes, but you need to learn to be *specific,* my friend. Especially if your goal is to progress in cultivation. A misspoken promise or threat can *kill* you at that point. And do not worry, no charge for this information."

Dale squinted at Tyler. "Now you are just playing with me. Okay, what is the lowest quality bag you have? The cost I mean. Lowest *cost* bag," he amended quickly.

"You are learning! If slowly. That will cost you twenty-eight gold." He held up a hand. "That is the lowest I can go, even for you. I am taking a loss on it at the price I have quoted you."

Dale grumbled but agreed to the price. A short trip to the temple's bank later, he was the owner of a new, shoddy dimensional bag. He told Tyler he would return later for a better quality one and walked to the dungeon's entrance.

"*Cal? Dungeon?*" Dale called mentally.

I responded instantly, <Oh, hello, Dale. Anything interesting happen recently?>

"*No.*" Dale sounded suspicious. "Should *something have happened?*"

<Don't worry your pretty little head over it. Oh, wait. Yes, you should have met someone that would freak you out a lot. Looks like it is my turn to ask a question!>

"*Right. Well. Here is the bag you wanted.*" Dale tossed it into an empty part of the room, hiding his actions by pretending to urinate against the wall. "*I had forgotten about your question game.*"

<*I* didn't. Also, thanks, I look forward to seeing what you bring me next!>

Dale grunted and turned away.

"Dale!" The heavily armored Half-Dwarf walked up to Dale, grinning happily. "I had hoped to run into you soon. Maybe when you had cleaner hands, but now will do!"

"Hello, Evan!" Dale also seemed rather happy to see his friend. "How are things? I heard you found a deposit of aluminum?"

"Yeah, I did!" Evan's chest was puffed up proudly. "Though by this point, I am almost certain it has been converted to Mithril. Those Dwarves paid through the *nose* to get it." He laughed at a memory.

Dale was a bit nonplussed. "You sold it? I had thought you would hold on to it for a while, drive up the price. Also, for some reason, I would think you would give Dwarves a discount...?" He trailed off as Evan's grin vanished.

"You know what I am, yes?" Evan spoke seriously, more so than Dale had heard since he tried to rescue him.

Dale winced. "A Half-Orc, Half-Dwarf, yes?"

"Yes," Evan spoke slowly. "Do you know that it is not only Elves that hate mixing of the bloodlines? Do you know how one of my kind is made?"

"Well... I..." Dale hated conversations like this; he had no idea what to say.

"That is *correct*. Half-Orcs are almost *exclusively* products of, shall we call it, forced impregnation?" Evan shook his head and leaned back stretching a bit. "My case is a *bit* different, though. You see," he laughed bitterly, "my *father* is a Dwarf. He and a war-band got drunk on stone-piss, and he took a bet saying he could bed *any* woman. They got to choose who he would try to get with. That bet was made right before they attacked a small Orc camp, and guess who his friends chose? My mother. So, I have no love for Dwarves."

"That's... I don't..." Dale tried desperately.

Evan started laughing at Dale's face. "Don't worry too much, Dale. I had a good childhood. I just have a bit of a constant need to screw over any Dwarf around me. Orc women don't have children any other way—they are a very warlike race. I grew up a bit shorter than the full-blooded Orcs around me, but I had Dwarven stamina mixed with Orcish strength. I could have ruled the clan, but I wanted other things out of life than a small war band and constant fights for territory. Which brings me to my reason for seeing you."

"What can I do for you?" Dale asked with relief, happy the awkward conversation was over.

"I am in the mine easily *twice* as much as anyone else. They don't realize it yet, but the deposits of gold and silver are becoming more and more rare, as are reward chests and gems." Evan had lowered his voice quite a bit, looking around to make sure he wasn't overheard. "I think... I think a change is coming again, maybe a new area for mining. If it is deeper in the dungeon, I am going to need an escort to get there. I want to ask your team before anyone else does. I do the work of a full team by *myself,* so escorting just *me* would be much less work. Likely, it would pay better too. Interested?"

Dale pondered for a moment. "We have been spending a lot less time in here than we should since we can move through the first two levels fairly easily. I will talk to my team. If we see anything below, we will let you know, but I can't make any promises just yet. My vote is yes, if that helps."

Evan nodded. "That's all I can ask for right now." He clapped Dale on the back. "I'll look forward to seeing you soon." He stepped up to an unmarked wall and started slamming it with his pickaxe, the Runes on it allowing him to be lost from sight after only half a minute or so.

Dale made his way back to Tyler, collecting a much better dimensional storage bag from him. Tyler had assured him that this bag also reduced the weight of whatever went into it and that he had never found an upper limit on the amount of storage space it had. Basically, if Dale could carry it—and fit whatever it was into the bag—he could just keep loading things into the storage area. If the Runes on the bag were bound to him, he could say a word to bring out the item he was after. Of course, a bag of this quality went for a premium amount. Dale had hit the end of his funds, but he had good credit with Tyler, who agreed to let him pay it off in weekly installments.

He left Tyler's shop, excited about his new purchase, when he heard sobbing coming from a nearby tent. Remembering his last venture into the shop area alone, he *very* cautiously went to inspect the noise. He peeked around the corner, noticing a small group of people huddled near the source of the sobbing.

"They... they're all... they're *gone!*" She hiccupped, returning to sobbing immediately.

Dale moved in closer, recognizing the people as members of the Spotters, a group dedicated to the research and cataloging of all things mystical. "What's happening?" Dale softly asked the closest man.

The man, interrupted from his mourning, turned toward Dale full of fury. Seeing who it was, he deflated, almost going limp. "Spotterton was destroyed."

"I'm sorry, I've lived near here my whole life, where was this?" Dale pressed for a bit more information.

"Spotterton!" The man looked upset that Dale didn't recognize the name. "The training town for all aspiring Spotters, located several hundred miles due south of here? The pride of the Phoenix kingdom?" The man searched Dale's eyes, hoping for a spark of recognition. "It was destroyed, the people slaughtered in the streets and their homes like *animals…*and just left to rot."

"It had to be *necromancers!*" the crying lady screamed. "Who else would *hate* us so much?"

The others seemed to agree, but Dale was only a bit confused. "Why would necromancers hate you?"

A dirty look was sent his way in an attempt to chase him off, but Dale didn't budge. Ultimately, an owlish man deigned to offer an answer, "We—the Spotters' Guild—have been the source of almost all the new Runes for the last two centuries. If it weren't for us, this area would be crawling with the undead by now."

"But," this one word from Dale's mouth caused many fists in the group to clench simultaneously, "if it were Necromancers... why would they leave the dead?"

Anger turned to pondering, pondering turned to concern, and concern to fear.

"But," a small voice whispered, "who else would *dare?*"

"The only people who could tell for sure are you." Dale looked around the despondent group, "You are *Spotters!* The only people qualified to determine if this was magical in nature are *you.* I am so, *so* sorry for your loss, but you cannot let this hold you back. Even now, time passes and details are fading. You want to find out who killed your people? *Me too!* I am certain the *Kingdoms* want to know as well, but who else would be able to tell them?"

Faces around the group hardened, tears dried up. Several people nodded, and they set off to make preparations. Dale hurried back to the temple, making for his room. The night had quite a chill to it now.

CAL

<This is so... confusing.> I had just finished eating the dimensional bag, and the pattern it offered was so complex that even my analytical mind was having trouble understanding the nuances of what was happening.

"Why is that?" Dani was taking the day off from training and had settled on to a pillar of stone I grew just for her. It had a pillow on it made from the pink fabric I had gotten for Dale's discarded robe.

<The way this pattern moves together. It... imagine a person building a house. They know what they are doing, and they know *how* it should look when finished. Sadly, they only have a hammer and nails. With me so far?> I offhandedly tried to see if she was paying attention.

"Mmhm." Dani seemed less than impressed with my visualization technique.

<Okay. Now, again, say that person only has a hammer and nails. Instead of a saw, they beat the wood until it is broken *pretty* close to the way they want it. Then they just pound nails into the wood until a 'house' shape is made, and finally, they *slather* Mana on it to hold it together. Yes, they did the job... *technically*. Is the house garbage? Yes. And so is this bag,> I grouched, already trying to fix the errors in the pattern.

"I guess you should be more specific with Dale next time." Dani chuckled at my grumbling.

I paused. I hadn't considered that. *Dale,* you sneaky jerk! He is the bad carpenter that did the minimum amount of work to fulfill the order.

<Drat.>

"Pretty much." Dani laughed at my consternation.

<And the bag! The pattern is obviously enhanced with Mana to create the effect, but for the life of me, I cannot figure out *why*!> I was so angry that I dropped a two-hundred-pound rock on a Basher; it barely had time to squeak before being crushed. Sometimes you just had to kill something. Plus, the rush of Essence helped me calm down a bit.

Dani was now paying full attention. "Why do you say that?" She seemed to be holding back from saying something.

<It is like... how do I say this? I think I could replicate this without Mana. *Entirely* Essence based. The pattern has Mana encasing it though, and I am unsure if this is a safety feature or something else.> I was now focused on Dani. She was oddly quiet. <What?>

"Well," she finally just spit out what she had been thinking, "it... there has been a theory for a long time that almost anything done with Mana could be done with Essence."

<And it has... what? Never been tested?>

"It has but always unsuccessfully. People have worked together, tried to form things, spent *decades* doing research. The issue is basically that no one has fine control over *all* of the affinities, and even the people that are masters of one type have trouble meshing their Essence with others." She considered her next words. "You, though... hear me out. The biggest reason for getting into the B-rankings is so that you can *simulate* the effects of all the affinities."

<What does this mean, Dani?> I was getting excited about a new potential project. Dangerous times.

She took a deep breath. "I think that Mana users fill in the blanks of their creations with Mana because they cannot control all of the Essences. You *can*. I think that you may be the only being I have ever heard of that *could do it*. As a matter of fact, you have already come fairly close with the abilities your

Assimilators are using. Those are certainly outliers in terms of your pure power at the C-rankings."

<I could create things that currently only B-rankers are able to?> I felt a broad mental smile forming. <You are saying that this bag is only enhanced with Mana because the creator *had* to do it that way?>

"Yes."

<Ohhhh, yes. Ready to do some experimenting?> I was already setting up the testing room.

"Never," Dani whimpered, making me laugh.

The first step was to un-spaghetti the pattern. To clarify, there were loops and whorls in the pattern that had been erroneously placed. I assume they were included because the maker could not see the aura of inanimate objects. I wonder how people felt comfortable creating Runes? Did they just force the pattern on to an object and *hope* for the best? That must be a *terrifying* experience. I digress. So, I worked at untangling the pattern, properly refitting it to itself and adding connections in places that should help to increase the stability of the dimensional warping.

Yes, dimensional *warping*. Someone had to have done this for the first time in the past. I don't know who they were, but they must have had a pair on them bigger than my *dungeon* to be messing around with forces like these. Make no mistake, this stuff is *dangerous*, and this bag, in particular, was a disaster waiting to happen. How dangerous? Ask what remains of my test bunnies. I didn't use Bashers for this; they were too intelligent for me to feel comfortable using them like that anymore.

I kept thinking that I had the pattern correct, but a surge along an Essence stream would collapse the whole thing randomly, with rather... unrelated—I think that is a good word choice—*unrelated* effects. Like a patch of rock melting across the room or my rabbit transforming into a bird. That last one was really disturbing, all the extra mass peeled away in what *had* to be a painful way.

Dani asked why I insisted on having rabbits in the room while I worked, and after an arm appeared and pulled a rabbit in, I explained over the squelching noises drifting through the portal, <You see, I thought *that* pattern was correct. There was no indication that I had it wrong, and I would have started testing it. Something on the other side was waiting, something *hungry*. If the rabbit weren't there, and I made a full-sized version to test, what do you think would have happened?> Dani shuddered as she remembered a similar experience.

"Fair enough, do all your testing on rabbits!" She shuddered again. "Maybe add a few more in there just for, ya know, peace of mind?"

The experimenting continued, but after two days, I decided that it needed to wait while I added on the new mining area. The current third floor had been slowly descending over the course of a few days and now was deep enough down that I could add in the *new* third floor.

I started with a simple layer of stone for the floor, compressing it to become exceedingly dense. I had become very proficient with the creation of cursed earth, and it was only the work of a few hours to add the needed Runes to the flooring. The walls of the labyrinth had taken *weeks*. I felt proud of myself. Next, I—what the heck is that? Something was scratching at me. That is, at my dungeon. Not in the normal areas—for mining and such—but on the underside near the river I used to power my steam traps. I focused my awareness on the itchy area and almost screamed a little as a pick suddenly burst through the stone where my attention was gathered.

<Dani, someone just broke *into* the dungeon. I have no idea how to handle this situation,> I informed my friend and advisor.

"Where? Wait, what? Why would someone do that?" Dani laughed, trying to hide her nerves. "That is the same as writing a suicide note, right?"

<I guess. But who would come *up* into the dungeon? They would have had to be even further down in the mountain than we are, and we are... > I ran a quick calculation. Forty feet from the surface to the entrance, sixty feet down to the first-floor Boss, a spiral stair down to the second floor was roughly thirty feet. I had made the next descent into ramps so ore could be carted upward easier, another thirty feet or so. Last, there was a long, slanted staircase to the new fourth floor, but a straight drop would mean we were... <Two hundred and ten feet below the surface.>

"How did they break in?" Dani demanded, calling a Wither Cat into the area so she could go hunting. "Also, where?"

<They smashed through the floor using a pickaxe design I don't recognize. They came in through the wall near where the river exits the dungeon,> I directed her, proud of her quick reaction time and willingness to charge into battle.

"*I'm on my way,*" she told me grimly in the mind-speak way that she was only able to use when possessing a dungeon creature.

I refocused on the area where the pick had broken the stone. Why hadn't I taken the time to reinforce the floor down here? I mean, I knew *why*. I didn't think anything would be able to enter from below. The pick was still swinging, and another few were joining it. There were noises coming through as well, what *could* be conversation but in a language that I had never heard before.

Dani had arrived and was hiding out of sight in the pitch-black darkness. The hole was still growing and was about half the size of a grown human when the ringing noise stopped. A head poked through cautiously, and wide eyes adapted to the darkness looked around. They focused on Dani, who was crouched and ready to pounce. The creature spoke almost recognizable words at that point.

"Gdood Khitty. Nho fhood khhere."

Dani growled a low, threatening tone that made the hair on the small creature stand on end as it slowly backed away, deeper into the hole.

<Dani? Do you recognize what that is?>

"*I do.*" She growled again as another head poked into the hole. The terrified face vanished quickly after that. "*These are the reason the elder races are so against intermingling of the bloodlines. A cross between Gnomes, Orcs, Elves, and humans. The cross made a monster race that was enslaved by Orcs centuries ago. These are freaking Goblins.*"

DALE

Dale was having a rough day. Several of his requested teachers had shown up at the same time last night, but they were demanding payment up front. Having spent all his coinage on his new dimensional bag, he had to inform them that they would need to wait to be paid. He was able to set them up for room and board but not much else. If Dale didn't earn enough money to pay them—and soon—they were going to leave. He was going through his normal morning warm-ups when the beautiful woman he had met recently walked up to him.

"Are you ignoring me intentionally, or did you simply forget I existed?" Her first words chilled Dale more than the morning mountain air. "Please let me know so that I can decide how to respond appropriately."

Dale settled his form into a different stretch. "Good morning. Minya, is it?"

She nodded, crossing her arms.

"I am *exceedingly* busy. Please don't feel ignored. Every morning I start my day by preparing to enter the dungeon. I eat a small mountain of food, trying to regain my muscle mass. I had a small... sickness, let's say."

Dying counted as a sickness, right?

"That doesn't change–" she furiously tried to cut him off.

"Hold on." He tried to remain amiable. "Then I enter the dungeon in an attempt to get stronger as well as make enough money to replace the gear that was stolen from me when I was beaten, robbed, and left for dead in the dungeon. I also need money for my instructors."

He changed position to stretch his back. "After the dungeon run—which takes usually two to three hours—I go train with my Essence instructor, trying to harness my affinities into a useful skillset. Now after that, I have lessons in administration, mathematics, politics, logic, debate, tactics, and a few other things I am *sure* I have forgotten. I'll remember them in a nightmare, I'm sure." He shifted into a sideways bend that Chandra had suggested. "Around ten in the evening, I finish those classes."

Minya tried to speak again, but Dale cut her off.

"Then my *new* training begins! Hand-to-hand combat. My instructor for that seems to hate me; he straps weights to me and forces me to run and dodge things—that he throws at me— while he beats me with a staff." Dale paused, looking dreamily into the distance. "Soon, I might actually get to throw a *punch* during training. At something other than a wooden post, that is. Well. That ends around three in the morning. I get three whole hours to sleep if I don't want to bathe. Apparently, I only *need* two hours of sleep now, but a lazy morning sounds oh so nice."

Minya waited to see if anything else was forthcoming. "Is that why you are wearing that odd assortment of mismatched leather armor?"

Dale blushed a bit at the mention of his ill-fitted armor. "My team decided that going into the dungeon without any protection whatsoever was tantamount to suicide. They all got me something different as a present. No, they did not go shopping together, but it is the thought that counts. Is this really what you wanted to talk about? I am leaving in a moment."

Minya remembered that she was angry at being ignored. "I understand that you are busy, but we need to see each other. Why didn't you come to my wagon?"

"I..." Dale blushed. "Listen, you are certainly beautiful, but I have no time for romance. Not even a 'romantic evening'. Plus, I simply have no coin to spare right now."

"Coin?" Minya was confused for a bare moment before her temper flared even higher. "You think I am a *prostitute*?"

Dale stepped away slowly. "I am guessing by your reaction that I am wrong..."

"Damn right you are!" Minya growled. "If you were anyone else I'd scalp you! No, *Dale*, I am here to talk to you about our friend, *Cal.*"

Dale stopped moving, going totally still. "Where did you hear that name?" he whispered, hand unconsciously clenching into a fist.

"Where do you think?" She broke into a smug grin. "Looks like you aren't the only dungeon born around here anymore."

"What did you just call me?" Dale had never heard the term, though it sounded like it would make an amazing title for a book.

"It means that you are beholden to a dungeon for your life. It either created you, gave you back your life when it was lost, accepted an oath from you, or your parents were created by the dungeon. You don't even know what you are? You didn't bother to *ask*?"

"It's his turn," Dale muttered. He was looking down, deep in thought.

"What?"

"Nothing. Look, what do you want?" Dale demanded, angry that this skimpily dressed person was shoving things in his face that he'd rather avoid.

"I want you to make the dungeon strong. I want you to live and keep this area safe for Cal and his Wisp," Minya announced vehemently. "I want to advise you on the best course of action, should the need arise." She smiled and reached out to him.

Dale waited for her to stop talking. "No."

"No?! What do you mean *no*?" Her hand was frozen in the air.

"Exactly what it sounds like. I don't trust your judgment. The dungeon does its best to kill all of us *every day*, and I don't need another person whispering in my ear that is only working for their own agenda. You are always free to talk to me, *everyone* is, but I will not guarantee that I will listen to you. Actually, knowing that you are working for the dungeon *intentionally* means that I will likely *ignore* your advice, but you *are* free to give it. Good day." Dale walked away, leaving a sputtering, furious Minya behind.

Dale walked toward the dungeon; his talk had put him behind, so he had to miss a hot breakfast and instead eat dried rations. He was munching on some hard bread when the rest of his team appeared.

"Morning all," Dale muttered around a mouthful of crumbs.

"Good morning, Dale, we missed you at breakfast. Everything okay?" Adam was looking at Dale's pale skin and sunken eyes.

"Just swell." Dale swallowed the rest of his food. "You all ready? Anyone grab something from the job board?"

Rose spoke up, "I took a request for herbs and assorted plants from the garden room. It pays a few silver but is upgraded to gold if we can bring back an entire Glade Mob. Apparently, they are stuffed full of things that both the alchemist and apothecary want."

"I've got one for healing potions," Adam spoke up. "They are selling for a premium. Apparently, people are showing up all over the Kingdoms with mysterious wounds, and the healers can't keep up with what is being demanded of them. The downside to this job is that if it turns out the potions are poisoned, they will only pay a few copper. The poison isn't useful on weapons, apparently."

Dale nodded happily; this was a good chance at some cash. "I have a request from Evan—that we look for a new area that may be appearing. Apparently, precious metals and minerals are becoming rarer. He thinks it is a sign that a new mining area will be appearing. If so, we may have steady work as escorts."

The others seemed happy enough with this knowledge, so Dale sighed in relief. He really wanted to help out his friend.

"I've got one." Hans chuckled. "Oh look! It is snowing!"

The others looked around; it was indeed snowing, a light dusting that Dale knew was deceptively pretty. They would soon be digging tunnels through the snow if they wanted to enter the dungeon.

"Back to the request, it seems that the new residents are having trouble adjusting to the climate here." Hans chuckled again. He meant that the Nobles from warmer areas were nearly freezing to death. "There is a request for fur, specifically warm *rabbit* fur. Lots of it. Apparently, they want to not only clothe themselves, they want to carpet the floors, walls, and ceilings of their rooms. And they are going to pay pretty well for it."

"I have not heard of this request," Tom interjected indignantly. "I have been following the job boards carefully and have seen nothing of the sort. Where didst thou come by this information?"

"I hear things," Hans replied nonchalantly. "Also, there is a big demand for cloaks made from a single pelt, so if we can kill Raile without damaging his fur, we can start making some *serious* money."

"So, we know what our goal is today?" Dale looked around at the cheerful faces and felt his own spirit become a bit lighter.

"Money!" came the response.

"Then let's go!"

CHAPTER EIGHTEEN

<Goblins?> That's new. I wonder what they want. <Back off a little, Dani. We can always slaughter them if they start making threatening moves.>

"*Cal, they are* Goblins. *It doesn't matter what they want. We can't trust them.*" Dani snarled at me mentally.

<I think you are taking on a bit of the Cat's ferocity, Dani. Back away and let them in,> I ordered sternly. I almost never used a tone like that toward her, so the shock of it made her listen. She stepped away and sat down, still growling softly.

The Goblin standing nearest the entrance stepped cautiously into the room. His eyes kept flicking between the sitting Cat and the river next to him. Oh, right. Yeah, this was obviously a him. His clothing consisted of a few rags wrapped over his shoulders, a belt, and a wrap on his feet. It seemed his thirst overcame him because he squatted next to the river and took a deep drink. He shuddered in pleasure, then stood up with shining eyes and said something into the hole. More Goblins started filtering in, and all of them drank as soon as they could get close to the water without angering the massive Cat hovering nearby.

"*Why are they acting like this?*" Dani was no longer angry, just very puzzled. "*They should be terrified of me or trying to fight me.*"

<Maybe they are dehydrated?> I offered tenuously.

She snorted, causing one of the smaller Goblins to startle and trip, looking at her in terror.

"*These are Goblins, Cal!*" she informed me as if I hadn't heard her the first time. "*I think them being a bit thirsty is the least of our worries. Wait! They're addicted! Cal, they are* addicted *to the Essence-infused water! We did it!"*

Just then a wizened, old Goblin wearing furs of a higher quality waddled to the water. After drinking a hefty amount, he turned and looked at the Cat, grunting as his hands began to move. Soon he was dancing in place lightly, and I felt a buildup of Essence.

<Dani, look out. I think he is using an incantation!> I warned her.

She crouched and growled, but he didn't stop. There was a discharge of Essence after a moment, but there was no visible effect.

I was about to ask Dani what had happened when the Goblin started speaking again. This time, something was different; I could clearly understand what he was trying to say.

"Great spirit of the Dungeon, hear me!" the dancing Goblin sang/chanted. "We have felt your call and have tasted the power you have given freely to those who wish it. The water of strength has made us powerful enough to revolt against our former masters. They who had become reliant on our compliance. We offer ourselves and our children to you. All we ask in return is enough power to defend ourselves from those who would again attempt to destroy us or force us into servitude again! If this is acceptable, we offer our oaths to you freely!" the Goblin sang in a guttural voice.

Now, this is not what he said but what he *meant.* He was simply not able to shape his mouth enough to say the words, making me wonder if other races saw them as unintelligent simply because they were hard to understand.

The words that actually left his mouth were closer to this, "Big angry Spirit! You water make us strong! We kill lazy humans, let guard down! You let us live here, make us strong, all our clan kill only for you! You no let people hurt us! Deals?"

Dani couldn't hear the meaning—only the words—so she had no idea why I responded as I did.

<Many of you will die, day after day. I can make your clan large, strong, and numerous, but you will need to fight for survival almost every day. Do you still want to live here?> I questioned the Goblin Shaman. That is almost certainly what he had to be.

He seemed surprised to get a response, and a grin only a mother could love appeared on his face. "Abyss yes!"

"Did he just say 'hell yeah'? What is going on? What does that even mean?" Dani growled.

<Getting some ready-made Mobs, hold on,> I told her. <Well. What is your name?>

He responded with a name that was far too long to say quickly, so my response was, <Bob it is then. That is your new name, may you wear it well. Bob, I accept your oath and will do my best to honor it. I will do what I can to make you all strong for as long as you honor your end of the bargain.>

Bob nodded and motioned the others forward. Apparently, only a dozen or so Goblins had survived the journey to get here—let alone the uprising—and they were quite ragged. One by one, they sank to a knee and gave the same oath, and I responded in kind. Every one of them seemed surprised to get a response, but after their oath was given, a line of their aura mingled with mine, giving me direct access to their minds.

<Well, Dani, I think we found our third-floor Mobs,> I chattered happily.

"Cal... They stink, they are messy, and... don't you think they are a little too intelligent to be something you will willingly sacrifice?" Dani had flown back to me, and the Goblins were now setting up a small camp on the fourth floor while they waited for instructions.

<Nah, they made their choice in life. I won't use them for Runic experiments, but I did say I would make them stronger. Their average Ranking is mid-F, so a little boosting is in order.> If I had hands, I would have been rubbing them together in anticipation.

"...I never thought I would feel bad for Goblins," Dani muttered quietly.

I *almost* didn't hear her, but I still chose to ignore her barbed comment. I began working on the third floor. Now that I had an idea of what would be living there, I could add features and details instead of leaving the area as an empty room.

To begin, I grew a series of columns in the area, not all the way to the ceiling but about eight feet tall. I widened these until they were about four feet around and made what looked like worked stone grow between them. This gave an interior area of roughly four thousand square feet, which should be plenty of space for a dozen Goblins. The worked walls extended out from the dungeon wall, forming half of a hexagon. The walls of the dungeon behind the fortifications would have a higher quality of minerals in them waiting for miners.

I repeated this pattern several times, creating walled areas along this dungeon floor. There was roughly a minute's walk between each of them, allowing plenty of space for people to walk past and ignore the Mobs of this level. If they'd rather go straight for the Boss and ignore the mining operations, fine by me. I made a similar wall around the exit from this floor but far more elaborate and grand. This would be where the floor Boss lived, protecting the entrance to the next level.

It took several days to complete the basic layout, and I heard Dale try to question me a few times as well. I ignored him and only responded to Dani in grunts or short one to two word comments. I maintained the current stair system, bypassing this floor until I could make it a viable level. The final result looked like a spacious beehive from above, according to Dani. I turned my attention to where the Goblins were resting fitfully and studied what they were using for a sleeping system.

They were clustered together, several to a... let's graciously call it a tent. That wouldn't do at all for my dungeon; it did nothing to help them or intimidate adventurers. While I was studying them, I noticed what Dani had been talking about— they *stunk*. I was unsure if it was due to them not having access to bathing supplies or if it was personal preference, but that would not do. I resolved to wait until the shaman awoke to discuss how they wanted their homes to look. I needed to solve the stink.

Looking at one of the honeycomb fortifications above the river, I modified the layout a bit. I shrunk the walls, made stairs up them, and created terraces about two feet deep. These empty spaces I staggered, placing them a few feet lower than the one before it. I then worked to create a few Runes on the floor that would collect ambient heat and pour it into whatever medium I wished. Some warrior with more money than brains had fallen and dropped a flaming sword. A *flaming sword*. It was ridiculous! Holding a shining sword in front of his eyes— while in a dark dungeon—had destroyed his night vision. From there, he was easy pickings for my Bashers. I did appreciate the new Runes though.

To my point, I placed these Runes along the floor of the top level, activating them with just a *touch* of Essence. Then I diverted a bit of the river from its flow, allowing it to gently flow into the room. It hit the floor and turned to steam with a hiss.

Alrighty then, a bit less Essence in the fire Rune... I adjusted the heat and soon had a massive, multi-tiered bath.

The water that entered at the top was the hottest and flowed down into the next level. There it cooled a bit and eventually overflowed to the next level and so on. At the very bottom, it drained, returning to the river. I planted soapleaf bushes on the dividers. I was glad I finally had a use for these; even the greediest adventurers usually left them alone in the garden room.

What else, what else... food? Most likely, but what do Goblins eat? I looked back at their supplies and tried to find food, but I couldn't find anything that resembled edibles...Uh-oh.

<Dani, what have they been eating?> I was worried that I already knew the answer.

Dani scoffed at me. "Oh, now you are paying attention to me? I don't know, I've just been making sure they don't sneak in here and kill us."

<So they haven't been able to eat rabbits or *anything*?> My stressed tone alerted Dani that something was wrong.

"No, I haven't seen them eat... anything. Oh." Dani made the same realization that I had.

I woke up the shaman with a nudge to his mind. <Where are your food supplies?>

I didn't bother to let him talk; he simply connected with me through our bond and thought his answer at me.

"Great Spirit, we have continued our multi-week fast. We attempted to gather food, but your guardian made it clear that we were being tested on our resolve. We have eaten nothing since entering your depths and only what we could scrounge in the weeks prior." He seemed proud of this instead of horrified as I was.

<I... see. Good work so far, your endurance is astounding. Allow me to reward you for your efforts. What do you eat?>

"Anything we are allowed to," Shaman Bob informed me seriously, reminding me that their entire race was enslaved.

<Right. What do you like to eat? Meats, vegetables, is there anything dangerous for you to eat?>

"We prefer meat when we can get it, cooked, unlike what others think of us. We eat vegetables, though not many if we can avoid it. The Orc blood in us does not do well with green foods. While they reduce our hunger, our body does not process it, and there is no gain on our part unless we are in dire need of pooping."

<...Very informative, thanks. Listen, wake up your people and leave everything behind. I will direct you to your new home.>

A look equal parts glee and worry crossed his features as he moved to do my bidding. In a short time, the others were gathered and began walking, following a line of glow potion. They walked until they found the entrance I had made just for them and ascended into their new lair.

They looked around the dim room, which, to their large eyes, was as bright as daylight to humans. I had temporarily raised a small dais—a table—and covered it in steaming meats. Since I could make whole rabbits, I could make just portions of them as well. There was far more meat on the table than they could eat, though they certainly tried. Their mouths had mostly sharp teeth and no molars. The shape of them was wrong, a bit too wide for their heads, so they regularly spilled and dropped food while chewing.

This is a race hated and enslaved by almost all the others in the world, mainly because they are considered unintelligent and ill-mannered. I saw a race that tried to survive, even against all the odds stacked against them. When they had finished eating, most of them began to doze off, bellies full for the first time in—apparently—weeks. While I wanted them to sleep, I had something else to do first. Bob began prodding them, getting them moving to the area I had designated as the bath.

They grumpily climbed the stairs, but upon seeing the gargantuan area designed as a bathhouse, they all had the same reaction. They would pause, stare, look around for someone planning to beat them for disturbing the beautiful scene, then finally strip and charge into the water with a 'whoop'. I guess everyone likes hot baths. The soapleaf bushes were soon tested, as the Goblins scrubbed themselves thoroughly. I absorbed all of the ragged furs and makeshift weapons. It was even more low-quality than I had first assumed!

I had placed robes in piles nearby for when they all eventually left the bath—the last one an hour after entering. They dressed, feeling very comfortable for what may have been the first time in their lives. I wanted to make armor and weapons for them, but they needed to recover and become strong first. Anything I gave them now would be useless in a week since they were currently skeletally thin.

<Bob, I've been giving some thought on how to proceed,> I told him, waking him from a light doze.

He shook himself and sat in a meditative pose. "Yes, Great Spirit, what are your wishes?"

<First off, call me Cal. That is my name,> I demanded; this "Great Spirit" business was getting tedious.

"Yes... Cal," he murmured reverently.

<What do you know of memory stones?>

He had no idea what they were, so I talked with Dani and came up with a plan. We would attempt to store the entirety of the Goblins' memories in a memory stone before working on altering their bodies. When asked for someone to test the idea on, Bob cheerfully offered a Goblin to me that the others barely tolerated. Apparently, he was somewhat lazy and complained too often.

The Goblin in question was napping and had to be kicked several times by Bob before he could be considered awake enough to consent to the idea. I think that Bob was... less than truthful about some aspects of the upcoming process, but oh well. I had formed a memory stone that was roughly the same size as the one that had once contained the cultivation technique I stole from Dale. That one had stored roughly ten years' worth of deep thoughts and concepts, so I figured that it would be ideal for the less complex ideas and tedium that made up this Goblin's life.

I was a bit nervous; this was the first potentially working artifact that I had made which was originally made with Mana. If it worked as I hoped it would, it would be the proof of concept that I needed for other—stronger—workings. The lazy Goblin picked it up and made as to eat it; luckily, Bob slapped it out of his hand and yelled at him. Really, this stone was as big as his fist. I had no idea how he thought he could swallow it. He raised it to his head and held it there, face screwed up in concentration.

He didn't *need* to concentrate on anything in particular, but I think it made him feel better. The stone was designed to draw in memories, and this one was only set to stop drawing after it had everything that was coherent. No baby memories, but plenty of them from child to adult to now. I really expected the stone to leave him as a brain-dead lump of flesh, but the Goblin was only a bit dazed when it was finished. He handed the stone to Bob and wandered away to resume his nap.

<It worked, Dani!> I exulted in this small victory. This stone swirling with silvery light meant that I *could* reproduce Mana forged items without having Mana myself. I had examined the Goblin while the process was running, learning his aura and pattern. I began to remake the body when I had a thought and stopped. A ball of meat and blood plopped to the ground with a wet smack.

"Gross." Dani looked at the half-formed mass of tissue. "I am happy for you."

<Yeah, sorry about that. I figured that I should try and make improvements while I can. I'm not going to do that in here, though; that may freak them out a bit. To the experimentation room!>

My focus was instantly there, while Dani had to zip along the tunnels to join in the process. I always offered to share my thoughts, but she felt that seeing it for herself was important, like my thoughts were biased or something.

I was examining the pattern and making small noises of disgust as I did so. Dani grunted and told me, "Oh, just tell me what the problem is already!"

I 'waved' her down, <It's like this is the pattern from a brand-new dungeon just learning how to make things. If Goblins have a natural lifespan of thirty years I will be surprised.>

A quick conversation with the wizened old Goblin—Bob—convinced me I was correct. He was twenty-eight human years old. <It is all *wrong!* I can fix this bit here by reducing bone thickness a bit; that will allow them to open and close their jaws without issue. I'll increase bone density *here* in the spine, that had a similar structure to what I would assume an Elf would

have, and their feet are too narrow for their weight because of it. I bet they trip for just... just... no reason *whatsoever!*>

I continued further, decreasing thickness and length of the tongue a bit, increasing or decreasing bone density, and making the nerves and blood vessels intertwine and flow in a more natural fashion. I have no idea how these creatures managed to survive at all, let alone become a large race. Their entire lifecycle seemed designed around breeding and fighting, both of which they did inefficiently. Sure, they may have had lots of children, but from the looks of it, they only did the deed as a biological impetus. It was something that *had* to be done. They didn't even particularly *enjoy* it!

After all the reworking of the pattern, I began producing the Dungeon Goblin as an actual creature. The body formed easier than the original would have, the kinks and inefficient meridians replaced or smoothed. Essence would flow through his body at *least* as easily as it did through humans' bodies. The mindless Mob in front of me sat down, drooling a bit. Well then. I almost called Bob before remembering that I wanted to boost them, not just fix the wreck of their bodies.

How to begin, though? Goblins had as much affinity for Essence as the other intelligent races, but what would be the right one for... right, they should have an open affinity channel. I checked his open meridians and found that he had the makings of a powerful warrior. His body had open channels for earth and fire Essence, whereas those were blocked in the original. If I infused his body with Earth corruption subtly, his overall density and defense would be naturally higher. Thick skin and whatnot. I also allowed a bit more fire into his blood, which should allow for a short temper and plenty of battle rage. I only added a *little*; these guys would be armed, armored, and intelligent. They didn't need the same influx of corruption to make them into viable fighters as my Bashers did.

I put a simple set of clothes on him and directed Bob to the room with the memory stone. He came willingly but stopped in the entryway as he looked at the being in front of him with shock. "What *is* that?" he whispered. Well, what he *meant* to whisper anyway.

<That, good ol' Bob, is what Goblins *should* have been. A powerful, strong, intelligent, decent looking mix of the races. This is the opposite of what your bodies currently are. Right now, they are a mix of the races that has all the weaknesses of each and none of the strengths. This... this is the mix of races with all of the strengths and the weaknesses tossed away.> I was— I hoped understandably—proud of the result. <I'm not trying to be insensitive, but as you are now... you are pretty useless. Weak. Unbalanced. Essence inefficient. I've tried to fix that.>

Bob looked understandably disturbed and intrigued.

<The last step, Bob, is to place the stone against his head and give him memories. Otherwise, he is less than an hour old in an adult body.>

Bob nodded and stepped forward, transferring the stored memories into the new body. The eyes focused, the muscles twitched, and after a few moments, my new Dungeon Goblin looked at Bob and asked a question. He stopped mid-sentence, opening and closing his jaw a few times. His eyes opened wide, and he stood up, nearly falling over due to the new body's balance being different. It took a few minutes of practice, but he was soon running around, jumping and speaking almost non-stop. Gone was the previous slurring and hissing, and he strode around with proud, confident steps.

He now stood half again as tall as Bob, who was admittedly a shorter specimen. At five feet tall, my new warrior

Mob would easily be the tallest of the new Dungeon Goblin race. They made their way to the remaining Goblins, who reacted in a much different manner than Bob had. The females looked at the Goblin warrior with heat in their eyes, while the males looked at him with something akin to hero worship. He walked over to his progenitor, examining him from the outside. He didn't have nice things to say. Ah well, when you are suddenly far stronger, taller, more powerful, and have a greater capacity for intelligence than you used to, you may look back on your old self as a pathetic version. A bit harsh though.

I asked the others to undergo the same process, and soon, they were lined up so I could perfectly memorize their individual patterns. I made a memory stone for each of them and got to work. This time, the creation went faster as I had a template to work from. There were deviations to consider—such as gender—but overall, the bodies ended up fairly similar to each other. Then it was Bob's turn. The differences in his pattern were obvious as soon as I began examining him deeply. His cranium had more room in it, allowing his brain to develop more fully than the others had to this point. The new Goblins would be his current intellectual equivalent eventually, but he would have a head start in nearly every aspect but muscle density. I could fix that.

I increased his body mass, making him significantly larger and tougher than the others. He had a powerful connection to his wind affinity, and his new form also opened the way for an infernal affinity that would be nearly as strong.

What would that combination create? I was looking forward to finding out as he developed it! Bob walked up to his new form, pressing his memory stone against the newly formed flesh. The stone dulled for a moment, but just like the others, it retained a copy of the memories. I had them place the stones into a specially designed chest, which I then sank into the ground. I would keep it safe, just in case they all died simultaneously.

This was just the beginning for the group. Each of the half-hexagon areas would be a home for a copy of the group, as I planned to recreate the group multiple times. It may be strange for them to see copies of themselves running around, but that was just too dang bad. I waited until this group had full control of their muscles before opening the floor, letting them get used to their new and improved bodies for a few days. Then I had them restore their memories in a new stone. By pulling memories from that set of stones, I filled the new floor of the dungeon with a dozen groups of a dozen, one hundred forty-four new Goblins, to be precise.

There were still the originals, but I decided to keep them out of combat if possible, so I didn't count them toward the dungeon Mob total for the floor. I would let them live out their lives in as much peace and luxury as possible and add those memories to the stones so that I was never asked for vacation time.

Next up, I wanted a Boss for this floor, but none of them had the necessary build or willpower to be a strong Boss.

I turned to ask Dani her opinion when it struck me. Dani. She had been getting more vicious and bloodthirsty through her training with the Mobs in here. Why not see if she could pilot a meat puppet that had no will of its own?

<Hey, Dani?>

Dani looked at me with a critical eye. "Hmm. You only use that tone when you are about to do something I don't like... What is it this time?"

I 'grinned'. <Actually, I think you will like this. How would you like to be the third-floor Boss?>

"It sounds... interesting? Explain?"

I told her my plan, and she agreed on the condition that she got to help me design its body, weapons, and armor. Of course, I agreed. Why not? We started on the project, working out the kinks and having minor arguments. I wanted an agile fighter that could weave around attacks and counter easily, whereas she was adamant that that type of Boss already existed with Snowball on the third floor.

She wanted a huge, musclebound, heavily armored, female Goblin that used enchanted weapons. I argued for cursed items because the adventurers would be warier of using them if they took them from her. She agreed, albeit reluctantly. She seemed to think that the item would trap her in the body or attempt to draw her into the weapon. I assured her that at the first sign of trouble, I would turn the item to goop.

The new Boss was placed in the final half-hex—as I was now calling the Goblin encampments—on a throne. It was mindless, so it just sat there unmoving until Dani flew in and took control.

"Oh. Wow, this is so much easier than sharing a body!" Dani spoke with the Boss's mouth, the first time that she had not communicated with me mind-to-mind while inhabiting a Mob. She tested that functionality, and we found that we could still speak that way, which would make fighting easier. "Hmm. I want minions."

I snorted a quick chuckle. <Are you serious?>

"Yup."

<Wasn't the whole point of this floor to be easier than floor number four?> I carefully asked. She had an odd glint to her that spoke of a bit too much excitement.

"Well, then make the fourth floor *harder!*" she demanded with a laugh. "You did design it as the *third* floor after all."

Thinking about the situation carefully, I decided that she was correct. <Alright, I'll give you whatever you want, but I'm opening the third-floor tomorrow morning.>

"Perfect." Dani put me straight to work.

DALE

"You're looking good, Dale." Hans was looking at his friend and team leader with a critical eye. "I know you haven't been getting enough sleep, and you've been training like you think assassins are after you. What's different?"

Dale shrugged at him with a grin. "Hey. It isn't paranoia if they are *actually* out to get you. Nah, I guess the voices in my head just haven't been bothering me this week."

Hans laughed, and they walked toward the training ground. They were out today to see if Dale had learned anything from the Dark Elves since Hans was not just going to accept Dale's word on it.

They got to the arena and did a few warm-ups, stretching and preparing themselves in the pre-dawn light.

"I hear there is a lady after you these days," Hans coyly said. "You sly dog!"

"Ugh, I have no wish to see her again. She seems to deify the dungeon and has been making all sorts of wild claims." Dale shook his head and faced Hans. "You ready?"

Hans pondered a moment. "I don't think you should dismiss her so easily. She is known as the foremost expert of dungeon lore in the known world. Not only that, but she went for *years* without an influx of Essence. She has had to develop techniques and ways to be ultra-efficient with her Essence and Mana use. I bet she could teach you a thing or two." He ruined the seriousness of his words by waggling his eyebrows at the last words.

"You know that I thought she was a prostitute?" Dale asked his lecherous buddy.

Hans shrugged. "Happens to the best of us. Sometimes they seem far too amazing to be real, so you make a false assumption. At least you didn't *tell* her that you... you did, didn't you?" Dale nodded. Hans started laughing. "You had better go fix that relationship before she murders you."

"I'm not going to–" Dale leaned to the side, missing Hans's punch only by a scant inch. "Apparently, we're fighting now."

Hans didn't answer with more than a grin. He began attacking faster, slowly ramping up the difficulty until Dale actually broke out into a sweat. Dale tried to find an opening to attack, but Hans moved with a precision and economy of movement that left no noticeable opportunities. Soon, Dale was dodging with less and less space between his body and Hans's fists. Finally, it was all he could do not to cry out with pain as Hans pounded him into the dirt with well-placed blows.

"You are certainly learning, and frankly, you are doing well." Hans nodded and offered his hand to Dale. "You just need another decade of fighting experience or so. Also," he had pulled Dale halfway up, and now, Hans let him fall to the ground with an *oomph*, "you are too trusting. We are fighting, remember?"

"Rude." Dale rocked his body until he had enough momentum to stand. He was trying to learn a faster movement to regain his feet since his Dark Elf trainer beat him mercilessly with a stout staff whenever he was on the ground. "You about ready to head to the dungeon? Laying on the snow really isn't my favorite way to start the day. I could really go for some movement to warm me up."

Winter had arrived, at least the leading edge. A thin layer of snow was all that covered the ground, though not from lack of snowing. No, the wind had simply risen to new strength, blasting the snow off the mountain unless something blocked it. Less people were living here now, more and more were paying the fee to use the portal and live somewhere less intolerant of life. People said they hated it, it felt haunted, or it was the worst climate in the world. For Dale, it just felt like home.

"I'm ready, but do you think everyone will be there?" Hans gave Dale a significant look. "*I'm* not going to force her out into the cold again. That's your problem now, oh great team leader."

Rose had been rather resistant to venturing out into the cold air. To be fair, they had to be careful about how many layers they wore.

There was a person that had been too bundled up in loose robes and layers, to the point that the wind had caught on him like a sail and blown him off the mountain. They still hadn't found his body. Now, people were trying to see how few clothes they could wear and how tightly fit they could be before they started to succumb to the cold. Businessmen no longer hawked their wares, if you needed something, you came to them through their triple-layered tents.

"Hans, you're the one that is trying to win her over. If you can't deal with her at her coldest, you shouldn't get her at her–"

They came upon their meeting point just then, and the other members had obviously been there a few minutes.

"Oh, thank goodness, let's go!" A shivering Rose ran off toward the dungeon entrance.

Adam was shivering so hard in his robes that he couldn't speak, while Tom wore his sparse armor and looked completely normal. His nipples were unpleasantly puckered though, and Hans pretended he had to dodge them like a knife whenever Tom turned.

Tom grinned at Dale. "I see that you would do well in the Wolf Kingdom! This is a nice, warm day back home."

Dale replied in kind, "It's about time the temperature gets back to normal! I've been melting for months! Look at me, the heat reduced me to skin and bones! With this temperature, I'm finally able to start getting some muscle back!" The others, not invited to the bragging, groaned good-naturedly. The two laughing men had been having the same conversation every time they met up since the first snowfall.

"Hans," Rose was squinting at Tom against the wind, "can you teach me a good assassination technique?"

Tom had a small look of panic on his face. "Let us not be hasty! We will soon warm ourselves in the fiery blood of our foes!"

Adam ground out through his chattering teeth, "Maybe you stop bathing in blood and just take a normal bath?"

Winter had started to impact the hygiene of most people that stayed here full-time.

They got to the entrance of the dungeon and stepped inside, happy to be out of the worst of the wind.

Dale looked around. "Any new jobs?"

Hans grunted. "Eh. More requests for fur. No real surprise there.

The others sighed. While fur was moderately lucrative, it was smelly, messy, tedious work. It slowed them down to skin each animal they felled and so had taken to tossing the entire animal into their dimensional bags. This had the distinct disadvantage of weighing them down more but added a small benefit of being able to export meat easily. Basher was now considered a delicacy in the kingdoms as it retained quite a bit of Essence in the meat. If you had the correct meridian open, eating Basher meat allowed you to almost *passively* gain Essence. It was a great training aid.

"Anyone else? Please?" Dale had just a *touch* of desperation in his voice.

Adam spoke up, "Healing potions and herbs are on the rise again. There have been more attacks recently. From what I hear, entire villages in the south are vanishing overnight, while the same is happening in the north, just with the bodies being left where they fall."

Dale nodded; the gossip had been growing as more Nobles began appearing, coming to live semi-permanently. No longer was it just the second or third son of a branch family; now, firstborn and mainline Nobles had been arriving. Mountaindale—as his rapidly growing town had been laughingly dubbed—was the only place that was out of the way and remote while still being a viable training ground.

"So, let's start. I'll take point position. I want Tom on my left, Rose on my right. Adam, you are right behind me. Hans, take rear-guard, watch our backs.

They proceeded into the dungeon, doing their best to silently kill as many Bashers as they could. Recently, if they had been able to sneak up on them, they didn't swarm. People were taking that to mean they were getting stealthier, but Dale had a different idea. He was still hearing mutterings and words from Cal that meant nothing to him, like 'ossification'.

Dale knew that the dungeon was just distracted, and he assumed that without the dungeon guiding them, the Bashers were just less likely to attack people. He was fine with this; hopefully, it meant that he would have a more normal experience while fighting. They snuck up on a group of Bashers and began beating them quickly. Dale had found that grabbing one with his off hand and hitting it with his cursed battle gauntlet would almost always kill it.

He also didn't hurt himself when he did this, as apparently the Essence released into the gauntlet would just flow back into his Center if he struck his arm or hand. Luckily for him, since he had found this out by accidentally scratching himself in a sensitive area when he had been startled by a sneak attack from a Basher. The activated knuckles had left a scrape where he had moved his hand too quickly, but the blood hadn't been blasted away from that point.

"What the–" Hans had turned a corner and was shaking his head, half in disgust and half in laughter. "Someone has a sick sense of humor."

They took a look; there appeared to be a High-Elf made of stone on a marble altar surrounded by statues of bunnies playing in flowers.

Dale choked on a laugh. "Wow, I mean, yeah she was insane, but it is still sad that she just let herself die for no reason."

Hans glared at Dale. "If I die in here, and you find a statue of me, you'd better smash that shit. Especially if it is surrounded by bunnies and flowers."

"I'd rather take it to the capital and have it immortalized in their history museum." Dale started walking deeper into the dungeon as Hans let out a squawk of rage.

Rose looked back at the statue as they passed it. "I wonder who would do something like that?"

"Pay attention, Rose. There is a roving squad ahead," Dale quietly admonished her. Roving squads were groups of regular or advanced Bashers that didn't stay in a certain territory. They weren't usually too dangerous, but they sometimes came up behind groups as they were focused on killing a group ahead of them. Dale jumped forward, backhanding a Basher as it squeaked the alert.

Its head was almost torn off from the combination of the blow and pressurized blood at the impact point. Tom stepped forward, landing a blow with a small hammer. Hans had been training him and decided that the Essence he cultivated in a day didn't justify the use of his powerful warhammer. Since it took Essence constantly when in use, Tom had no argument to defend himself. Now that he was using a square ingot of iron on a stick, calling it a 'hammer' was really a bit misleading.

Tom was much slower with these ingot hammers, but they helped to train his muscles and aim. So what if he grunted every time he swung? They finished off the near helpless—at this to this group—Bashers and were putting the bodies in their bags when they heard a roar from ahead. Tom shook his head and limbered up his arms.

"It appears someone has spawned a Glade in the garden room. Shall we assist them?" A scream filtered down the tunnel to them.

"Let's hurry. It sounds like they aren't doing well." Dale started moving faster, rushing toward the sounds of scuffles ahead.

They burst into the garden room to see an armored man standing protectively over another man who was cowering on the floor. The group rushed in toward the Glade, and Dale started beating the overgrown mushroom in an almost rhythmic pattern.

Since they had found that this type of enemy took little direct damage from non-sharpened weapons, Dale was not hitting it squarely but rather near the edges so he could tear off chunks of the Mob. An arrow from Rose punched all the way through the Mob as it turned on them, leaving a rapidly closing hole in its wake. Hans began lopping off pieces of the monster, and soon, it was too damaged to remain upright. It collapsed to the ground, dead, and Dale turned toward the two people that they had rescued.

"Just two of you? Can either of you even *fight?* I've made sure that everyone that enters here knows the dangers of the known levels. Why the *abyss* would you be here?!" Dale roared at the two-person group.

CHAPTER NINETEEN

The armored figure raised his visor, revealing Evan. "Well, you know me, Dale. I see a person in trouble or someone doing something *incredibly* stupid," here he glared at the man he was protecting, "and I just need to try to save their dumb ass."

"Oh, hey, Evan. Good to see you. Wait, we heard a woman scream. Did you see what happened to her?" Dale was trying to look through the thick growth in the room.

Evan snorted, trying to cover a laugh. "Yup, that's him." He jerked a finger at the man who was now standing up.

"I am not a woman. Of *course,* I have read the warnings, but I expected them to be greatly exaggerated. The price of parts from Glade has *doubled* in the past few weeks!" The fussy man was worriedly looking at a new hole in his pants.

"Ah! You are the alchemist!" Adam remarked in an accusatory tone. Adam was the one who normally brought herbs and other items to the alchemist and apothecary. "Why in the world would you come down here?"

The alchemist took up a self-righteous pose. "Well, if you thought people were swindling you with product, wouldn't you want to see the production yourself?!"

Evan made a sound deep in his throat. "I walked in to see him kicking plants and throwing rocks at trees. He musta been at it awhile, cause it wasn't very effective." His comment made the fussy man blush.

"I take it you are satisfied?" Dale dryly drawled. "Or would you like to wake up another flesh-eating monster?"

"Well. I suppose I'll *have* to be satisfied, won't I?" The man turned and walked out of the room, somehow making even that motion into a study of pompousness.

"Ugh," Hans grunted. "Adam, how do you deal with that man? His face is just so *punchable!*"

Adam shrugged. "He gives us a lot of money."

Hans thought silently for a moment. "That would do it." He turned to Evan. "Now, as for you, do you need an escort out or something?"

Evan shuffled his feet. "I was actually hoping to follow you this morning. I don't know if Dale mentioned my offer..?"

Dale nodded at him. "I did, but we haven't seen anything different below. Why do you think there would be changes that you need to be present for?"

"Well, it's more like this... are any of you miners?" Head shakes were all around. "So you don't know what to look for. Here's the deal—last night I hit a critical point. The ore and material on this floor are not rare enough—or high enough quality—for me to be able to make my payment on time unless I work at least *twenty hours* a day. I have a hunch that I'll find what I need deeper inside. Also, I like sleep."

There was a brief conversation, but most of the team was fine with him coming along if he accepted that the risks were on his shoulders. Plus, Evan certainly had a likeable quality about him that resonated well with the group. He was a no-nonsense, hardworking, driven individual. Before continuing, they debated fighting the remaining Glade Mobs, but everyone was more interested in continuing downward and cultivating than wasting time on the upper levels. They skirted the majority of the Garden room, and after a few minutes of walking, they made it to the tunnel connecting to the next room.

So far, they were making good time, having only been in the dungeon for about fifteen minutes and already making it through the second room. They wandered through the tunnel, laughing at Evan as he cussed at traps that startled him, such as a rock fall. To be fair, he had more reason to fear collapsing tunnels than they did.

They started competing with each other to show off their knowledge of the dungeon, though Rose won when she leaned on to Evan... then reached out and punched the wall. A section crumbled away, revealing a shiny, gold-plated chest. Evan's eyes boggled at the small shower of coins they pulled out of the chest and thanked them when they loaded him up on healing potions.

Hans laughed, making Evan give him a questioning look. Hans ruined the mood a bit by informing him that the reason the healing potions to him... was that he was the most likely to get torn up and be in need of healing. After that point, they stopped showing off and returned to their usual formation with Evan standing near Adam. Now they were grim and serious again, which only served to make the Half-Dwarf more cautious.

Stepping into the third room was a new experience for Evan, the furthest he had ever traveled in. He looked around at the high ceiling, doing his best to see in the gloom and darkness. Without Essence enhanced vision, he would normally not be able to see at all, but his Dwarven ancestry allowed him limited vision. He yelped when the first attack came. There was a sudden rustling of armor and scratches of metal on leather as weapons were drawn and swung. High-pitched squeals came from dying Bashers, and a flash of hellfire blazed along a horn before the monster was slain.

"What the abyss is happening?!" Evan was crouched, pick held horizontally in front of him as he looked around wildly at the flashes of light, groans of pain, and shrieks of dying Mobs.

"Just," Rose fired off an arrow with a *thwap*, "another day in paradise."

The fighting quickly died off, and Evan was assaulted by the odor of animals being skinned. He had to fight not to vomit as the darkness and smells threatened to overwhelm his overwrought senses.

"You're all insane..." he muttered, making the others laugh. This didn't help with his assessment of their mental soundness.

A few minutes passed as they dressed the carcasses, storing them in their bags.

A glimmer in the distance caught Evan's eye. "What's over there?"

Adam glanced in the indicated direction. "Hey, good eye! Guys, there is a glowing chest over there!"

"Score." Hans started moving in that direction before Dale called him back.

Dale was looking at the chest, and something didn't feel right. It took him a moment to realize what the issue was. "Where are the Mobs? There's nothing guarding it."

This caught the group's collective attention and prompted Hans to move closer to inspect the chest. He stopped a few feet away,

"Trapped! I'm not really sure what this will do, so back up a bit!" He pulled out a heavy knife, throwing it at what he assumed was the activation for the trap. He flipped backward just as the knife impacted, and a blast of superheated vapor blasted from well-hidden holes in a ring around the chest. Anyone nearby would have been boiled in their armor like a lobster if they had been caught in the spray.

"That's a new one!" Hans chuckled, stepping forward to inspect the chest again. As he was setting his foot down, a spike shot upward, intent on skewering him. The spike shattered as it came into contact with his boot, and Hans chuckled. "Double trapped. This place is getting dangerous!"

Evan was a bit perplexed. "I'm glad you aren't hurt, but I am wondering... how did you do that?"

"Inscribed boot. I calculated how much force was coming up at me and passed Essence into the boot to enhance my downward force by that exact amount. The stone shattered, and luckily, my boot did not," Hans commented offhandedly as he threw open the chest. "Weapons!"

The others let out a soft cheer. They didn't want to be too loud. Sound attracted attention.

"Looks like... oh *yes*. I think we have a set of demon busters here!"

The cheer got a bit louder, and Adam danced a bit.

"Demon busters?" Evan quietly wondered, feeling like he was missing eighty percent of the conversation.

Tom replied this time, "'Tis what we have dubbed weapons that are specifically designed to destroy demons. The church pays *very* well for them, as the Inscriptions are very detailed and finicky. For a reproduction of this weapon style, near a year of work would be required. We also will need to assume that these weapons are single use, as they are intended to be stabbed into their target who will forthwith be returned to the abyss. A lot of work for this artifact, therefore a lot of money for us."

"Let's say three thousand, divided by the five of us... six hundred gold each?" Hans was calling out calculations.

"The *six* of us, Hans. We had already passed that point, only Evan noticing it brought us back to claim it," Dale admonished his friend.

"Nooo, come on! I have a Mage to pay off!" Hans whined.

Dale gave him a look. "And how many weapons are there?"

"...Three," Hans muttered sullenly.

Dale did a bit of math in his head. "Let's round that up to ten thousand gold. That means fifteen percent goes to the city, so we are at eighty-five hundred. Then a flat twenty-five percent to the Guild... so down another twelve hundred seventy-five. That leaves us seven thousand two hundred and twenty-five gold if we play our cards right. Divided by the six of us, twelve platinum, four gold, sixteen silver, and six copper. If we haggle it correctly, of course. And adjusting for the current rumors, we could boost the price a solid amount."

The others stared at him in shock. "What?"

Rose answered his question, "When did you start doing mathematics in your head like that? That was really impressive."

"Oh." Dale looked a bit embarrassed. "You all know that I am working to be a good little city Lord. I have been spending most of my money on memory stones that contain different concepts. I recently purchased the Dwarven mathematical system, and I guess it is kind of... I don't know, I just *need* to do math when it comes up like this."

"What's the cubed root of three hundred times thirty-two squared?" Hans looked at Dale excitedly.

"I... I'm not a jester, Hans. I don't perform tricks!"

This made the others laugh, while Hans muttered, "I'm never gonna figure that out."

Rose looked at Dale with a half-smile on her face. "I had wondered why you insisted on coming in here unarmored. You are welcome for the greaves, by the way. You're broke, aren't you?"

"*Oh* yes."

"Well, so are all of us! Just for different reasons. Don't feel bad. Back to work?" Rose prodded them.

They moved to the final room on this floor, killing off the Boss Squad and moving to the second floor.

CAL

"Dale's group is coming through the second floor right now. They're bringing along a miner," Dani informed me cheerfully.

<Now that is some good timing. We just finished up down there, and I want to get back to the *other* project I've been working on.> I heard Dale sigh as I started talking. <Yes, I still exist, Dale. Don't be rude.>

"Want me to let you know when they're getting near the third floor?" Dani offered. I gladly accepted. I really wanted to figure out the gate issue.

I returned my attention to the problem that the dimensional bag was becoming. I was using the principles it had allowed me to understand in an attempt to make portals that lead to each floor. I felt that the system I had in place to contain the energies and direct them *should* be working. Maybe there was simply an ephemeral quality to Mana that I simply couldn't replicate with Essence? Gah, no! I couldn't think like that! If I could just figure out why punching into a pocket dimension like this was making it so hard for me to... wait a second.

That explains my issue! I was trying to extrapolate the same pattern for an *extra*dimensional bag and use it to allow *intra*dimensional travel! I wasn't trying to break *out* of this dimension; I needed to connect two points so I could allow things to move *between* those points in the *same* dimension! I wrapped my mind around this concept and formulated a plan.

If I understood the issue correctly, what I needed to do was to set up a gate that matched another perfectly. Then I could connect those two by setting up a resonance pattern and forcing the Essence at the two termini to move at the same time with the same criteria. Essentially, I was planning on inscribing the *air* by moving Essence in a continuous cycle. Then something entering through one gate would find themselves exiting the other!

I had just started getting excited and was about to begin working on a model when I was interrupted by my lovely Wisp. "Cal, they're fighting Raile right... they beat Raile."

<Have they seen it yet?> I shook myself a bit, concentrating on breaking physics tended to leave me a bit dizzy. I wasn't sure how other people did it, but if my concept worked, it would be a bit paradoxical. It would be a gate that contained the other gate, which contained itself. The set of all sets that contains itself. It exists, I just needed to prove it!

"They haven't. I think it is only a matter of time now. They are looking at the chest. The miner is looking and scratching at the walls... and Dale is doing his customary double check of the Silverwood tree. Wave at Dale!" Dani laughed as Dale's face peeked into view high above.

Dale put on a strange expression, so I focused on his side of the conversation.

"I think there is another floor again." Dale saying this brought many more faces into view through my sunroof.

"Looks like! You think this floor will be as insanely difficult as that little maze?" Hans chipperly input.

<Little maze?> I snorted. <It's called a *labyrinth*, helloooo.>

"What is this made of?" Evan was trying unsuccessfully to scratch at the material they were looking through. "It's tough!" He looked at it closely, the natural light spilling in from above allowing him to look at it without impediment. "It seems like a pane of nearly perfectly clear emerald, but it's *huge*! I've never seen anything resist my pick either."

"It is likely a derivative of cursed earth. I'm betting that it *is* emerald but with a large amount of earth corruption in it," Rose postulated, gaining the attention of those around her.

"Why would it matter if it were emerald or not?" Dale asked her.

They dissolved into a discussion about mineral affinity as they made their way cautiously down the stairs.

<Here we go...> I was watching their faces as they stepped on to the third floor. Their shock was gratifyingly evident.

Dale

"Fortifications?!" Hans thundered. "What the crap kind of Mob hides behind *fortifications*?!"

Adam spoke up, concern in his voice, "Smart ones?"

His statement made everyone go quiet for a moment. "Shit."

"What do we do? Go up and knock? Hop over the walls? They aren't *that* high." Evan grumped a bit, pickaxe itching to be swinging.

"We do knock, but not with our hands. Nah, we use the door-knocker. Tom, pull out your hammer, you're up!" Hans directed with a sly grin. He glanced at Evan. "You're gonna like this part."

Tom placed his ingot hammers into his bag and pulled out his oversized warhammer. "I've missed you," he whispered to it, caressing it lightly.

He walked directly up to the large door, swinging his hammer with a roar. He had only ever used the full force of his weapon on a stationary object once before, and a member of his old team had died because of it. The weapon impacted the doors with the force of a localized earthquake, blasting the doors to splinters. Those shards flew into the Goblin warriors huddled behind the fortification, killing several of them instantly. The remaining warriors roared and charged from their breached fort, swinging deadly weapons with great speed and accuracy.

Dale's team joined the fight! Dale ran at an exceptionally large specimen that was wielding a warhammer and releasing saliva with every roar. Dodging its initial assault, Dale stepped forward, swinging a one-two punch. The first swing hurt Dale far more than the Mob, but the second blow shattered his victim's collarbone and interrupted the flow of blood traveling through its arteries for a moment. This caused the creature to collapse for an instant, almost unconscious. Dale pressed his attack, his next punch cracking the skull and scrambling brain tissue.

Dale let himself be too focused on inspecting his prone challenger, and an arrow sliced into his thigh. He dropped to a knee with a yell, hand clapping to the wound to try and slow the blood flow. Rose counter-sniped the archer, pinning it to a wall across the compound. Adam tripped a Mob that was running at Rose with his staff, then used the sharpened end to stab it through the heart.

Hans was playing with his foes; three of them were trying to land a blow while he moved scant inches at a time, learning their attack patterns. He decided that he had a good handle on how they moved and attacked, so he drew his own weapon and killed the three with a quick spin and a rapid stabbing. Taking a moment to survey the battle, he turned just in time to soak his front in a wave of blood and gore.

"Oh, come *on*! This is exactly why I didn't want you to be using that oversized killing machine in here!" Hans bellowed at Tom.

Tom looked at the clean-freak with an excited grin. "I had been under the impression that you wanted me not to use this for fear of draining my Essence. Now I understand why you were so adamant!"

"Did we get them all?" Dale ground out; trying to focus on his team was difficult when a foreign body was embedded in his flesh.

"We did. Hold on, Dale." Adam dropped into a crouched position next to his team leader, working feelers of Essence into the inflamed flesh around the arrow. When he had closed off the nerve endings, he carefully pulled the arrow. As he suspected, it had a barbed head. He started digging with a small dagger, increasing the flow of blood from the wound. "Drink a potion, Dale. I can't heal you at the same time as performing surgery."

"Evan, you mind?"

Evan stepped forward, uncorking a bottle and pressing it to Dale's lips. Dale gulped it down as Adam moved away, the pain suddenly returning as the Essence stopped flowing. Dale shot a bit of the potion out of his nose as he choked.

"What a nice place to sit and cultivate for, say, ten minutes?" Dale laughed a bit desperately.

The others chuckled, sitting down. Hans decided he would rather look around the area and began exploring the perimeter, taking Evan with him. Tom finished collecting the armor and weapons used by the Mobs and sat down to cultivate as well.

"What are these things?" Dale sniffed with disgust as the last of the bodies began turning to ooze.

"They look a little like Goblins, but they are so much bigger and well-balanced. If all Goblins looked like this, they would likely be accepted as a sentient race instead of a monster race," Rose told him with hope blooming in her words. She had a soft spot for creatures with multiple races in their heritage.

"Then what do regular Goblins look like?"

Hans came back just then. "Goblins look, sound, and smell like sickly children who drank too much and can't control their bowels. They are generally hated by all of the races and used as a warning against mixing the bloodlines."

"Oh, so that is why people act so poorly towards half-breeds? That's too bad." Dale didn't catch the look Rose sent his way. She couldn't tell if he was being serious or an asshole. "They can't choose their parents, after all."

"Pretty much." Hans nodded. "By the way, Evan found a likely spot for mining, so... mission accomplished?"

They could all hear Evan's pick swinging now as well as his cheerful chanting. A low layer of dust started rolling toward them after a few minutes, but it usually vanished before it got too close. There were benefits to mining in the dungeon.

"We simply sit and cultivate? No fighting, no real guarding?" Tom looked around at the nodding faces. "I... hmm. I will try not to be bored." He focused on the pattern he had been building in his Center and continued to cultivate.

They sat that way, working hard to build their internal Essences when a Dungeon Goblin poked its head in through the wreckage of the gate.

"It appears they are re-spawning."

There was another small battle; this time, the defenses worked in Dale's group's favor, as the attacking archer could not find a way to target them. The Goblins had to enter only a few at a time and were cut down quickly. Soon, the group was back to cultivating, doing their best to ignore the sounds of rock shattering behind them.

Hans spoke up, "It appears to be about a thirty-minute time frame for the Goblins to return. I don't know why it takes longer down here—maybe they are harder to create?"

They fought another two groups before Evan came back, smiling broadly and coated in debris. "I think I'm gonna like this floor a *lot.*" He was dragging a pack full of raw metal chunks, so bulky that he could hardly move.

"Eh. Maybe we can put that in our sacks for you?" Adam offered, looking at the hoard of metal. "I don't know how you're going to get that up the stairs otherwise."

After some good-natured arguing, Evan accepted the offer, and they split up the miner's goods. They attacked another fortification to see if it followed the same layout and ended up having a much harder time of it. These Goblins were prepared for the group and didn't bunch together behind the gate. When Tom smashed it open, they poured through the wreckage at him, ensuring he was hard-pressed for several moments until his team came to the rescue. There were additional archers who took up position on the walls, firing down at the group.

Dale had a hard time fighting while dodging arrows, but Hans weaved in and out of attacks as though he were out for a casual stroll. Rose focused on killing the ranged snipers, while Adam kept an eye out for anyone getting injured or enemies getting too close. Evan watched the team working together to take down the enemy, their bickering and friendly jibes put away for less dangerous times. He was impressed, and when the last

Goblin fell, he applauded them before running off to check for metals in the wall.

The team sat down to relax, breathing deeply and preparing their bodies for an influx of Essence. They were just at the twenty-five-minute mark when Tom suddenly looked up, gasped in pain and began sweating black filth. His eyes dripped tears of blood and blackness, and his breathing became ragged.

Dale leaped to his feet. "What's happening? Is it poison?!"

Tom couldn't answer, but Hans gripped Dale and pulled him back. "He's breaking into the D-ranks. This is going to be difficult. We can't expect him to be able to move himself. All of his mind is turned inward. Someone grab him and put him in a defensible location. What shit timing! Move!"

Dale figured that the others had been covered in filth from him before, and it was time to return the favor. He gripped Tom under the arms and dragged him toward the one-man mining operation. He had to adjust his grip several times; the black goop was slippery. There was a light trail of the substance leading to Tom when he was settled against the wall in a seated position.

"They're coming!" Hans shouted to the team. At the previous location, when the Goblins had tried to take back their fort, they came stealthily. Or tried to at least. Here, they were *sprinting* down the path, howling at the top of their lungs. "What? What is different?!"

Dale had a sneaking suspicion that there was a reason that this small Goblin horde was intent on their position. "*Cal, you are a cheating asshole!*"

CAL

<Hey, it wasn't *me* that made your teammate decide that an unmapped floor was the best place to go unconscious. How long does that last, by the way?> I chuckled at him.

"*Screw you!*"

<Ha! Yes! Thanks for not answering on my turn. Now I can throw harder Mobs at you! Such an *easy question* too!>

Dale was fuming as I opened the doors I had been hiding Mobs behind, and the now-imposing form of the Goblin Shaman stepped in to join the fight. He was mostly hidden behind the advancing warriors, but he started dancing and chanting almost instantly. I had found out that there was a good reason for the dancing, at least *outside* the dungeon. The movement pushed the shaman from areas of low concentrations of Essence to areas of slightly higher concentrations.

The dancing had a similar effect to what I did, which was to collect the unrefined Essence in an area and use *that* for incantations instead of personal Essence. I didn't know why humans, Elves, and the like didn't use this form of incantation. Either they didn't know about it, or they thought it was primitive. Either way, I was just glad they limited themselves.

The dancing and chanting grew in franticness, culminating in a wave of combined air and infernal Essence. A dark form congregated in front of him, then drifted toward the battle. Hans saw it first.

"Wraith!" he shouted in a light panic. "Enchanted or Inscribed weapons only! Adam, a celestial barrier on me, *now!*"

Adam began weaving his staff in front of himself, chanting a bit.

Huh, maybe they do use a similar technique... I looked at the Essence around him, but all of the Essence powering this working was coming from Adam. It seemed like a waste to me to just *ignore* all that loose Essence around yourself! Adam finished just as the wraith joined the battle. A glowing barrier sprang up around Hans, wrapping him in light. The wraith moved at the speed of darkness now that he was in attacking range. Insubstantial claws pinged off of the light, and Hans started retaliating just as fast.

Hans's daggers were slicing tiny slits into the fabric of darkness the wraith was made of, and blood-like blackness was dripping to the floor. Each time the claws of the wraith touched the light, a mind-bending amalgamation of celestial and infernal colors was released. The colors drew the eye to them, and the mind of the beholder turned toward insanity. This was the light of chaos.

Oddly—at least to the team of adventurers—the Goblins ran as the wraith died. A few stragglers were cut down, but the general consensus was that they didn't do too badly. The humans and half-human sank to the floor to recover. They were filthy, covered in blood and gore. They tried to figure out why the Goblins had run but decided that it was because the wraith died. They waited another thirty minutes, getting tense as they expected another attack. After an hour, they were getting concerned that something was different.

"Go tell Evan to stop attacking the wall. I'm done for today. That wraith took most of my willpower to defeat," Hans directed Adam.

"What would have happened if it had been free to attack you?" Dale wondered softly, not sure he wanted an answer.

Hans rolled his arms, stretching a bit as he stood. "They drain you with each attack. They latch on to your Center and *pull*. They suck in Essence to continue to exist. Even if they die, if they have landed a blow, there is now a hole in your Center that leaks Essence. *All* of their victims die, and usually fairly quickly. Luckily, Adam is a cleric that is a cut above the rest."

Adam came back at a run. "Tom's gone."

Heh. About time they noticed.

CHAPTER TWENTY

Dale's group scrambled to get into formation and follow the trail of the long-retreated Goblins. They had Evan filling Tom's position temporarily, mainly because he was well-armored. Quickly moving through the room, they were easily able to follow the trail of sludge that dripped from Tom. They came upon the large fortified area that was home to the floor Boss and stopped a good distance away.

The walls had patrolling Goblins armed with powerful-looking bows. The doors were wood banded with iron, a far cry from the simple wooden structure the others had at their entrances.

Evan grunted, "Now what?"

Dale shook his head. "I don't know. We need to get in there. We need to *help*–" Hans covered Dale's mouth; he had been getting a bit loud at the end.

"What we *need*," he stared into Dale's eyes, "is to *not panic*. If he is dead, charging inside in an act of vengeance isn't worth getting ourselves killed. If he is alive, we need to make sure he stays that way, and that means a *plan*."

"First off, how to get in. Now, we could try and scale the walls, being as sneaky as possible. If we can get in there without anyone noticing us, we might be able to..." Hans stopped talking as Dale was shaking his head.

"It won't work. I'm sorry to say but they already know we are here." At Dale's words, the Goblins on the wall stiffened, then gave up the pretense of watchful ignorance, focusing on their location.

"Well piss. Anyone else have a plan?" Hans griped.

Rose thought for a moment. "Why not do what we've been doing?"

Hans sighed. "In case you haven't noticed, we are currently missing our giant, ginger door-knocker."

"Forget the door." Rose grinned for the first time since discovering Tom was gone. "Let's go through the wall." She hitched her thumb at Evan.

CAL

Dang, these guys are good! I couldn't blow my cover of neutrality by telling the Goblins what the adventurers were up to, so I was relying on their training and willingness to die repeatedly. That would surely be enough to stop a few D-ranked and a C-ranked... I sighed. My Goblins were going to die.

I glared as the adventurers put their plan in motion. Rose fired an arrow, killing one of the archers on the wall. This drove the other archers into cover, and they began firing wildly at the location the arrow had come from. So much for training and willingness to die. While they were hidden from view, the humans basically *waltzed* up to the wall and began marking out their plans for a new door. Every time a Goblin tried to get a look, an arrow either impacted them or sailed by their oversized noses. When Evan reared back for a swing, there were three dead Goblins already!

The pickaxe came crashing against the thin wall, blasting open a Dwarf-sized hole. The Goblins started toward the breach in the wall but were driven back as a hail of arrows and throwing knives came through. Evan took the opportunity to smash another section, creating a large hole and actually collapsing the entire section of wall, killing a few Goblins as they either fell into

Hans's blades or as stones rained down. Evan took some damage from the falling rock, but his stout frame and heavy armor made the pain laughable. At least he would need to work some dents out. Nothing like creating a minor inconvenience for someone! Take that! ...Yeah!

Hans and Dale rushed into the compound like avenging angels, throwing themselves recklessly at the defenders. Dale had a new fighting style that was upsetting for me to watch. He dodged but so poorly that I was *sure* he was about to have his blood splatter on the floor. Instead, he clunkily avoided attacks and threw punches that were poorly placed. His blows would have been entirely ineffective if he didn't have his Inscribed battle gauntlet on. This allowed him to turn weak punches to non-lethal areas into deadly attacks.

Hans was a different story entirely. He was fighting with a rage and speed I had never seen him use before. Actually, he was screaming as he repeatedly stabbed a Goblin.

"Where is he?" *StabStabStab.* "Where is my student?" *StabStabStab.* Hans was furious, and when he attacked, his knife entered and exited a body three times so fast that it looked like just a single blow. It appeared that he was no longer holding back, no longer trying to teach the others anything. He never stopped marching toward the center of the fortification, though he was moving at a measured pace instead of sprinting.

An arrow flew at him, but he caught it and whipped it back, treating it like a throwing knife. It hit the bow of the Goblin who had fired it, shattering it and ricocheting into the Mob's neck.

Did he do that intentionally or was it luck? ...Either way, no more arrows at Hans. Mental note there. A warhammer-wielding warrior ran at him, and Hans shot forward and delivered a kick to it. The kick *chunked* the poor Goblin.

Let me explain, the kick was from his Inscribed boot and blasted the surprised Goblin into three separate chunks of flesh.

<I don't think we're gonna win this one,> I mentioned to Dani. She had a different opinion.

"Since he is going all out, way above the level of the Mobs, can I too?" She was hovering near the floor Boss.

<Oh... you want to use that? Go for it, but I'll warn Dale. It's only fair. He'll whine otherwise.>

Dale complained about my statement but was listening intently as he continued to fight. <Dale? Since your teammate is going all out, I'm adjusting the floor Boss accordingly. For future reference, if a huge party of people comes in, or a few overpowered people, I'm going to do my best to kill them. That means lots more Mobs or something like... this.>

Dani had full control of the Boss now and was standing up. At seven feet tall, this Goblin Amazon was at least three times as strong as the other Goblins and would usually carry a warhammer in each hand while wearing standard armor. Right now, we were moving quickly to get ready for a too-strong opponent. I activated a Rune on the throne that the Goblin normally sat on, and her armor crumbled away. A quite expensive way to undress. A stone slid aside, and a large chest shot up from the opening. She opened the chest and pulled on the body-hugging chainmail inside.

A double set of battle gauntlets finished her preparations. These were a bit different than the ones Dale wore, as these had large blades that reached to the massive Goblin's elbows and extended past her hands. Hans walked into her area right as she finished equipping her weapon, and a throwing dagger punched through her armor and into the muscle on the right side of her abdomen.

Dani roared in pain and turned to face the enraged Hans. She hissed at him in true Mob style, "Die worm!" With that, she activated the Inscriptions on her weapons and armor. The shiny but easy to damage armor—made of pure aluminum—had a column of Essence move through it. It glowed bright silver for a moment before darkening slightly to a silvery-purple. Her weapons did the same, but the right hand darkened further as infernal Essence raced along it. The left-handed blades sprouted fire-Essence-fueled-flames along their edges, and she charged.

Hans had a moment of surprise that almost cost him his life. He threw another dagger at such high speeds that it vibrated the air in its passing. This hit the armor above Dani's knee and bounced off without a scratch. She kicked her leg forward, adding a bit of a spin as she struck him in the face. His surprise kept him from dodging fully, but his attempt allowed him to keep the bones in his skull from fracturing as he sailed across the room.

Hans had barely regained his footing when Dani was over him, stabbing downward with her flame-coated weapon. Hans weaved away, but the intensity of the flame scorched his skin, causing blisters to form on his neck. He crouched and then pushed upward, lifting Dani off the ground and tossing her to the side with an ease that his size made questionable. While she scrambled to her feet, he attacked with his blades.

StabStabStab.

ClinkClinkClink.

His attacks did scratch her armor but failed to penetrate. She swung at him with her infernal blades, but he crossed his daggers in an 'X' and caught her blow with ease. He pushed, throwing her arm upward. Hans reared back and kicked her in the chest with his powerful boot, sending her into the wall. It shattered on impact, and she lay there stunned for a moment as Hans raced over.

"Too strong of armor, huh? Fine!" He stabbed his dagger down into her eye, and she spasmed.

He stood straight, then reached down and retrieved his blade. The fight was over...

<Nope. Made those modular this time.> As he pulled out his dagger, the eye came with it, trailing a severed bundle of nerves.

"Look out, Hans!" Dale screamed, saving his friend's life as a wave of heat blistered Hans's back. He had barely escaped by rolling away.

Hans came to his feet several feet away, ready to block, but Dani had crossed her blades and was several paces away. He started toward her when the Essence around her weapons surged. Hans was *very* skilled; he kicked off the ground and went straight up, driving his daggers into the ceiling and holding on as a wave of life-ending cold rolled in a path away from Dani. She needed a moment to collect herself—that attack took a *lot* of channeled Essence—a moment Hans didn't allow. He threw a dagger at the crossed blades, and this time, they were so cold that the impact shattered them.

Now, these blades had Essence moving through them, and as they broke, they momentarily created Runes that shouldn't have existed. Uncontrolled Essence rushed into them, creating a tiny gravity well that crushed the Goblin Amazon into a small orb. It only lasted a moment, but the ground in all directions had shattered, and the high-density ball of matter crashed to the ground and embedded itself there. I took the opportunity to begin absorbing it—just so the group didn't get a ball of condensed Mithril.

<Dani? Are you okay?> I hadn't seen what happened to her, but I wasn't too worried. She was essentially Essence, and a small thing like gravity shouldn't be harmful.

"I'm fine!" She was returning to my room. "That was *so* much fun! I have so much training to do, gah! I can't believe he won! I had him so far out-armored!"

I was exceedingly relieved, and I had a new Rune to research.

I looked back at the battle, well, at this point it was over, so *former* battle. Hans was stalking around looking for Tom, but Adam found him first.

"Get over here! It's *bad!*" Adam began shouting.

They rushed over to find Tom trussed to a pole over a vat, where the black sludge was still dripping off of him. The vat was collecting the anthracite liquid into a jug, and there were little pieces of material stuck in him that ensured the sludge would continue to come out of him as his Essence tried to purge foreign objects from his body.

"Oh... god." Rose looked sick. "His arm..."

His arm—or more accurately *stump*—was poorly tied off, blood draining from what remained. The Goblins had been trying to tear his warhammer away from him, but even with his attention inward, his body had refused to release it. After struggling with the unresisting form, they scratched their heads, shrugged, and used their rusty knives to chop Tom's arm off just below the shoulder. It was not a clean cut, and they had needed to saw for several minutes, but Tom was finally warhammer-less.

Adam was working on the bleeding stump. "I... I can't get the wound closed! He is losing too much blood. If I don't work to replace that, he will die either way!"

Hans grimaced. "I really hope you can't feel this." A layer of fire appeared around his hand, and he gripped the open wound. The smell of charring flesh filled the air, and Dale had to struggle not to gag.

Evan's stomach rumbled as the aroma reached him. He looked around sheepishly as the others glanced his way. "Right, yeah, well. I have Orc blood in me. It's not like I'm gonna go take a bite of him. Sheesh, bring me in front of the Protectorate."

"Is he stabilizing?" Hans's words were sharp, directed at Adam.

"Yes, though that is going to be an ugly scar," Adam muttered. He paused and looked around. "On the *other* hand, he is completely fine."

Rose fixed him with a look. "You are making a pun? Now? Really?"

"Right. Go find the treasure. Take anything not nailed down. Anything that we can sell." Hans had several odd looks sent his way. "What? Regrowing an arm is *stupid* expensive—it takes months to get the hand bones correct. He is going to need a lot of money as a down payment. We can do it though. He will be fine, I promise." Hans patted Tom on his unmoving back. "Welcome to the in-debt group. You're late to the party!"

With Hans's words, the group relaxed greatly. Adam released a weak chuckle. "Going to the University in the capital would cost more than an arm if I remember correctly."

"No joke! Higher education?" Rose responded, finally allowing herself to see the humor in the situation.

"They take an arm *and* a leg."

The group started to laugh while Evan looked on in horror.

"You people are pretty... dark." He wasn't making eye contact with anyone and was fidgeting with his pickaxe.

Dale responded since that comment had killed the moment. "He's gonna get his arm back, and he survived. That is the best outcome we could have ever hoped for, *far* better than we had hoped. We are just trying to mask our pain, Evan. Please don't think we are uncaring."

"Ah, I see. Gallows humor." Evan grinned. "Well, if you need quick money, take that jug. Breakthrough oil from a fire cultivator is explosively flammable and goes for a good price since it is so rare. That should help pay for the work he needs done, at least a bit. Bring it to the alchemist we rescued, and I bet you'll get an even higher price than normal."

"Good call!"

They began searching for a treasure chest, and sure enough, they found it in a slightly hidden alcove. The glow potion on it had them all excited, and for a moment after opening it, they were disappointed at the contents. Sure there was a handful of gold coins and a couple small, silvery ingots. But... potions in a chest of this rarity? They felt cheated until Evan took a look and nearly shat himself.

"That's not silver, you brain-damaged, monster-loving bunny punchers! That's aluminum!"

Evan was almost drooling as he saw the processed ingots. Then a sick look crossed his face. "For the love of god, don't sell that here or tell anyone where you got it! This floor will be *overrun* by Dwarves! They'll look for ingots like that one by smashing rocks with their pickaxe-density *erections* if they get wind of the dungeon releasing processed aluminum!"

Rose shuddered. "...Thanks for *that* visual."

"It was pretty vivid, wasn't it?" Hans laughed, picking Tom up and draping him around his neck like a scarf. "Let's get going—the sooner Tom gets to a safe location to heal, the better."

Just before they made it out, I whispered in Dale's ear, <Torture wasn't my intention. I told them to just kill him, but they wanted that oily stuff. I hope this doesn't ruin our fun.>

DALE

Dale's mind buzzed. *That* was what the dungeon was worried about? That Tom surviving was a reason to dislike the dungeon *more* than he already did? He shook his head. What an alien mind. He looked at his friend, not unconscious, but not aware of what was happening to him. Tom was pale from blood loss, but luckily, the healing center was right at the top of the stairs.

They stepped into the open and handed Tom over reluctantly. Adam went with him, but the rest were ordered away as the healers got to work. The group trudged through the mounting snow, hurrying toward the river.

There had been an unexpected benefit of the Dwarves setting up shop in town.

While the Dwarves had received space for the walls, a barracks, and an orphanage for free, they had purchased the rights to an area along the river. Now, normally, Dale refused any offers to purchase land next to the river, as it would be too easy for a business to cut off access to the only water source in the area. But the Dwarves... they set up a bathhouse! It was expensive to use but certainly worth it to stay clean. At least to Dale's group. Hygiene was becoming an issue, and Dale was thinking about providing funds from the city to buy the bathhouse and make it a public service.

They soaked in their respective areas, enjoying the feeling of warmth after the bitter cold. Their armor and clothes were being cleaned at the same time, for an additional fee, of course.

They were just finishing, pulling on their clothes when a courier ran up to them.

"Lord Dale?" the young man said questioningly.

Hans jumped in, "Careful there, youngster. Technically, you need to address him by his highest rank. In this case, it would be "Your Grace" as Dale is a Duke. He doesn't care, but other Nobles tend to be a bit jumpy about that sort of thing."

Dale glared at his friend. Conversely, the courier was nodding seriously.

"I'll spread the word. I'll ask the Messengers' Guild to give us some training in court etiquette. At least that explains what happened to poor Geoff." He looked at Dale. "Your Grace, I was asked to inform you that your friend is stable and still undergoing the breakthrough process. He will be there from three days to a week, depending on his willpower."

Dale nodded and flipped him a coin. The courier bowed slightly and started to leave, then saw that the coin was gold. His eyes widened, and he looked back, but Dale nodded and made a 'shush' motion, finger on lips. He got a *deep* bow in return before the man returned to work.

"You are going to spoil them." Hans poked his friend in the side.

Dale allowed a conniving look to cross his face. "Who will they go to first with important news—the generous and noble Dale or the spoiled Lord who makes unknowable things happen to their friend Geoff?"

Hans approvingly laughed. "You are getting good at this politics thing. What do you want to do for the next few days? Find a replacement teammate or take a vacation?"

"How about we sell the ingots and find a flesh Mage to fix Tom? Oh, and tell Father Richard about those weapons.

How much is it going to cost to fix up Tom, if you can estimate for me?"

"They always charge half up front, so somewhere between ten to fifteen platinum." Hans was fixated on the smell of roasted meat coming from the *Pleasure House*.

"*What?* A thousand to fifteen hundred gold is *half* of what they'll charge?" Dale was aghast.

Hans had an odd look on his face. "Dale, we made more than triple that on this *single* dungeon run. Before taxes of course. Stop thinking about money as a long-term... thing. You are going to be around long enough that you will eventually amass a *huge* amount of money."

"See, you say that," Dale rounded on his friend, "but aren't you in your sixties and in debt to a flesh Mage?"

"As soon as we sell off the stuff from this run, I won't be. Even after paying for Tom's arm," Hans countered easily. "To change the subject, what was the deal with that Boss? That thing nearly killed *me*."

"Hrumph." Dale thought about how to answer without giving away too much information. "I think it was a reaction to you going all out like that. Did you see how it tossed away its old armor and weapons as you went all furious and stabby?"

"A dungeon that scales its difficulty to the people fighting? Doubtful." Hans had a faraway look.

"I wouldn't go that far. For instance, we stay out of floor four because we'd die very painfully, but that was certainly a reaction to you," Dale promised. He glanced over his shoulder after hearing a noise, spotting Minya storming toward them. "Incoming."

"Why are you ignoring me, Dale?" Minya growled as she stomped toward them.

"Because I think that your ideas are insane?" Dale answered frankly.

Minya stopped, throwing up her arms. "Wow."

"Yeah, that was harsh, Dale," Hans admonished him. He turned toward Minya. "Hello, my name is Hans. Before you ask, yes, I *am* single."

"Not interested. Dale, you know as well as I do that this dungeon is different; it needs special care, or things are going to go very bad, very fast. You *need* to put me on the council," Minya demanded, daring him to argue.

Dale took the dare.

"It *isn't* going to happen. Also, if you don't stop asking people to let themselves be sacrificed to the dungeon, I'm going to bring you up on charges for attempted murder." Dale caught the flicker of shock on her face. "Yeah, I heard about that and the cult you're starting. If I hear about you starting trouble, I will either banish you or put you in jail. You could be the first person to make it to a cell that wasn't drunk!"

The others usually just died.

"You're making a *mistake*, Dale," Minya promised darkly. "It isn't me you are going to have to worry about. I won't do anything that could get me kicked out. You don't want to talk? Fine, but when this city starts burning, come to me. I'll happily save you all, no matter how crazy you think I am." She stormed off, the snow melting out of her way.

"What a woman," Hans and another voice breathed at the same time. Hans looked over at the other speaker, glaring. "Who are you?"

Dale looked over to see a ruggedly handsome man dressed in completely unsuitable, bright colored, fluttering clothes.

"My name, good sir, is Brakker." He swept his feathered hat off, bowing deeply. He righted himself, pulling the hat back on as a stiff breeze blew snow over the exposed area. "Good god, you are all insane living here."

"How can we be of service?" Dale asked to be polite, continuing his trek toward lunch.

"Since you ask..."

Dale groaned at these words from Brakker. "I am a humble Bard, seeking my fortune in these frozen wastes. More pressingly, I am looking for a place to survive the winter. I am told you two may hold some sway over the proprietor of this fine dining establishment?"

"Just... sure. Come on, we'll introduce you to Madam Chandra."

Dale was soon rid of the man, but as they started lunch, musical notes began floating into the room.

"More weirdos."

"Nah, Bards are cool," Hans told him around a full mouth. "Give it a month, and he'll be the most popular man in the city. Good job getting him on your good side. I'd advise you to keep him there. Unless you want unflattering songs about you to be drifting around."

Rose perked up; she had joined them recently. "Right, don't you have some songs out there?"

"No," Hans asserted firmly. "We're going to the capital for a few days, wanna join us?"

"Sure. Looking for a buyer?"

"Mmhm."

They left for the portal, planning on being back in three days, the earliest that Tom might wake up.

CHAPTER TWENTY-ONE

<I think it is ready.> I was looking at the dual gates in my test room. They were as similar as I could make them, actually grown as a single unit and then separated into two distinct items. There were esoteric Inscriptions spanning the entirety of the archways, mirrored perfectly from one to the other. Along these inscriptions were embedded Cores for storing Essence, behind which were hidden Runes for Essence gathering.

"Well don't keep me waiting! Do it!" Dani was watching raptly, ready to either cheer our success... or run like a maniac upon failure.

I activated the Runes at the base of each arch, allowing them to start accumulating Essence. Now it was a waiting game. I had designed these arches to power up slowly, filling the cores with a minimum amount of Essence before allowing the next Rune in the series to activate. This way, I could monitor the progress and halt it if there were an error in the Runescript. Also, it would allow the two arches to activate simultaneously, which I felt was important.

"Is it going?" Dani impatiently flew in a circle.

<Yes, but it'll take a while to gather Essence.> I paused a moment. <Didn't we talk about this earlier?>

"You mumbled a few things under your breath when I asked you questions about it. Does that count?" she replied on *just* this side of civility.

I felt a bit sheepish. <I get a bit... focused.>

"A bit? Okay, and a two-mile-wide meteor tends to kill off a 'bit' of life upon impact," she teased me.

<Right, wait, so a meteor is a chunk of stone or metal that drops out of the sky really fast, correct?>

"Just let me make fun of you without having to *explain* myself!"

<Ugh, fine. Don't satisfy my curiosity. Well, I've been pumping extra Essence into the room there, so it is being collected much faster than it normally would. If you want to watch, it is about to activate,> I informed my grouchy best friend.

She looked over at the arch as the final Rune activated, entranced by the interplay of Essence as it weaved together from the center of each Rune, traveling into the exact midpoint of the air in the archways. I should note, there were Cores on the frame that were specifically designed to absorb all of the corruption from the Essence as it was gathered. That meant that the Essence reaching outward now was as pure as I could possibly make it, so it looked like slow-moving lightning. It connected, branched, wove and unwove itself through all the other strands of Essence until an effect began to make itself noticeable.

A hole began forming, quickly and silently expanding. I was watching how Essence around the arches was reacting, preparing to stop the process if there was an adverse reaction. The portal was now open and looked like a flat soap-bubble. From one side I was able to look through the portal and see out the other, while from the back, there was only a slow-moving swirl of colors. The colors confused me until I realized that it was only the interplay of purified Essence with the loose Essence in the room. It didn't seem to be affecting the stability of the portal, so I saw no reason to try messing with it.

"It's beautiful, Cal. You create the coolest things. It is so quiet too! The one outside always hums and sounds vaguely threatening." Dani was debating on getting close or not. "Is it safe?"

<Let's find out.>

I created a rabbit in the room and directed it to walk through the light.

Splatter.

<...No.>

"What just happened?" Dani demanded, dodging falling chunks of rabbit meat.

<I'm hoping that the issue is that it entered from the rear of the arch. Let's try making it go through the front,> I muttered as I was creating another test bunny.

"You are a cruel being."

<Nah.>

The bunny hopped to the front of the arch, squirming a bit to avoid puddles of blood. It *really* didn't want to go into the light. I gave it a little mental push. It stepped in, vanishing a bit at a time, reappearing behind itself through the other arch. Success!!

"You actually did it!" Dani whooped!

<Yes! This is so—wait a second. What do you mean, 'actually'?>

"Is it still stable?" she skillfully avoided the question.

<Hmm. Yes, but it is sucking up Essence at a prodigious rate. I need to find a way to remedy that, or it won't be a useful portal. Also, I want to replace the stairwells with these wherever possible. Then people can teleport around the dungeon, and there is a small chance of them failing to use this correctly and exploding!> I liked portals!

"Always thinking ahead." Dani morphed into an eye and rolled herself. "How about this? Can you make portal 'keys'? As in, when they make it to a portal, they have to have a specific item in order to get to the next floor?"

<I could do that.> I paused. <Actually...>

"Yes?"

<I could take that a step further. What do you think the odds are of a group like Dale's dying on the first floor?> I rhetorically asked her.

"Pretty low? Unless they come in bound and gagged?" Dani remembered a situation Dale had been in recently.

<Right, so why make them go through that early area? If they can make it to a level once, it is pretty likely they can do it again. How about I make an attuned key that allows them to return to whatever level they like? That way there would be a better chance of them going to harder levels right away, which means a higher chance of them failing to survive?>

My argument made sense to Dani, so she agreed that I could do it. The hard part was going to be altering the structure of the portal so that it remained inactive and charging while accepting incoming key requests via proximity. I explained this to Dani, much to her disgust.

"Just make things happen and let me explain it away as 'magic', would you?" She was unbelievably uninterested in the technical details.

I made the adjustments, creating a single, long archway which I split into twenty arches. I wanted two arches per level—at the start and after the Boss. I kept a few as spares, in case of future expansion. I added all the Inscriptions and Cores to the arches and let them sit for a few hours to accumulate all of the Essence needed.

The keys were an interesting artifact. I decided to create them as a short, modular chain. At the end of the chain was a chunk of gemstone with a tiny Core buried in the center. When a gemstone was collected from a Boss in the dungeon, it could be added to the chain. This would grant access to that level directly when the correct gem was touched as the holder walked through the portal. To that end, I altered the first floor a little bit. It had a clear quartz 'window' in it that allowed viewing into the second floor Boss Room and was directly below the Inscribed celestial quartz. I replaced the clear quartz with a clear pane of fluorite and began filling it with water corruption after adding a few Runes.

Now, I wanted to make sure my previous efforts weren't wasted, so I made a clear keygem that would exit at the top of the stairwell and into the church area above. The first floor would be accessed via a topaz keygem—from inside the dungeon of course—the second floor via a gem of fluorite, the third floor with an emerald, and the fourth floor with a ruby. I made sure that the viewing panes reflected these changes, though it meant removing large sheets of minerals. I wanted to have my own stylistic theme, and no one could tell me 'no'! Okay, Dani could... but if she didn't know about it, she couldn't stop me.

Returning to the explanation of my portal setup, I only allowed incoming portals to connect to the start of each level; I wouldn't want someone taking a Boss by surprise. I thought about making the chain as a bound item but decided against it. After all, if someone too weak stole it and entered the dungeon, they would be almost assured to die. A too-strong person wouldn't be bothered by the first levels at all, so it felt like a logical wash to me. The next step was testing. I spaced the arches out and brought a Goblin in to test them for me. I'd have used rabbits, but they lack opposable thumbs.

I wondered if I could fix that...? No, no, focus!

I was glad that I had spaced them out; most of them worked just fine, but two had a slight variation in the Runescript.

One of them exploded, and I lost a Goblin. I cleaned up the room before bringing in a new one. When I found the next failure, I wasn't even aware of it for a moment because the Goblin simply never reappeared in the second portal. I waited, but it seemed that this arch had sent the Goblin... elsewhere. I didn't know where, and I decided not to try and find out. I let that one stay on after deactivating the Essence accumulators, and it eventually was just pretty stone again. I reabsorbed it, then began moving the arches throughout the dungeon.

I was sure that they would be a conversation starter in the morning.

DALE

"Thank you for coming on such short notice, sir," Dale respectfully said to the flesh Mage entering the bitter cold of Mountaindale. They had just stepped through the portal and were hurrying toward the church.

The flesh Mage nodded, a regal motion that caused a flutter of jealousy to race through Dale. The man had obviously worked on his own body and used himself as an advertisement. He was the most symmetrical person Dale had ever seen. He was almost disturbingly handsome, with chiseled muscles and a powerful frame. His voice was deep and mellow; Dale had no doubt that this was the most charismatic man that he had ever talked to. It was actually intimidating on a deep level.

"Thank *you* for your advance payment. I hope that you understand my reluctance to come here, and I thank you for allowing me to bring along a guard," the Mage uttered in a honeyed tone.

"Why not?" Hans tried to say brightly. "It only costs us an extra *gold* per week."

"Exactly." the Mage agreed, not noticing the sarcasm. "I assure you, Your Grace, Nez is worth every copper."

The black-haired, blue-eyed swordsman walking ahead of them didn't bother to join the conversation. His gaze was flickering between the people walking around.

He vanished suddenly, only a *zap* and flash of light allowing the group to follow his progress after a moment. He was next to a tent, sword against the throat of a Dark Elf. He uttered his first words since they had met him.

"Assassins. Instructions?"

"Hold!" Dale cried out before the Mage could speak. "The Dark Elves are here by my *request* and are acting as the policing force for this city. Hurting him would be a very bad idea."

Ru'Nez the Blade nodded, stepping away from the Elf and sheathing his sword. "My apologies. Normally, beings that are stereotypically assassins are something that a host would mention to others... before bringing them into his territory."

The Elf looked at the swordsman and nodded, vanishing from sight again.

Dale winced at the intended rebuke. "Sorry about that."

The Mage waved a hand to show that there was no harm done. "He is just proving his worth again. He does that. Where is the patient?"

"Ah. This way." They moved into the chapel, finding Tom propped up in a ring of intense fire.

The Mage looked at him critically. "He is currently undergoing breakthrough? I'm not going to work in that fire. We'll have to wait until he is aware. I do charge by the day..."

Dale agreed with the flesh sculptor, as it was hard to argue. They found an empty room for the Mage, and Dale decided to leave him there and walk around to see the improvements in the area. He was almost to the exit when two people carrying a litter with a bleeding man ran in. Dale almost ignored this but realized that injuries from the dungeon usually resulted in people coming up the stairs, directly into the church. He followed them, waiting for their explanation.

"Sir, we found him like this out on t'mountain." The speaker was a local, someone who had lived on the mountain their whole life. He took off his hat and was holding it in his hands—fidgeting—while he talked to Dale. "He tol' us that his horse 'ad died, and he were from some village down south." He paused, chewing on a fingernail. "They's been attacked, some kinda human-lookin' monsters. 'Parently, them same monsters been follerin' the river, killin' everone that's in they's way." A small coughing fit. "He's been trying to warn people, but he's been barely ahead of 'em this whole time. I think he lost 'em at the bottom o' t'mountain, where the river waterfalls down."

The other local simply nodded along, saying 'yup' every once in a while. Dale thanked them, told them to go get some food on his credit, and went off to gather the council. It took nearly an hour for the members to gather. Apparently, they took less notice of messengers coming to talk to them than they did Dale.

Go figure.

Dale wasted no time. As soon as they were gathered, he launched into an explanation of the situation. Unfortunately, they treated the problem with much less care than Dale desired.

"Dale," Amber countered soothingly, "you can't fly into a panic every time some random peasant thinks there are monsters after them. There are monsters all over the place in this world." She chuckled at the look Dale gave her. "What? If there weren't, don't you think the Bashers would have garnered more attention? Mutated, horned rabbits that attack people?"

"We don't know if this is real, and it is a second-hand account as it is. We need to wait until we have more information," Frank condescendingly stated. "Let's send out some trackers on horses. It'll be a few days before we know anything for certain."

They left, leaving Dale with a growing pit in his stomach. They were correct, but people living in the Phantom Mountains weren't prone to flights of fancy. He heard Madam Chandra talking about an unrelated topic as they walked away, proving that they were treating this far too lightly.

Chandra was discussing with Frank, "But if I buy enough of them, I can change the name to the *Chan*tom Mountains!"

"People would always spell or pronounce them wrong! They'd write it with an 'S' as the *Shan*tom..." Frank's voice faded into the distance.

Dale decided to go check on the fortifications. He walked to the quartz-flecked new walls, feeling relief as he got closer and they blocked the wind. The walls were not a ring around the city but simply walls that blocked the paths needed for travel. The Dwarves were relying quite a bit on the natural fortification of sheer cliff face to block unwanted travelers. A section of stone was rising slowly from the ground, doubling in height by the time he arrived.

"Hail the walls!" Dale shouted, feeling better after the exercise he had gotten from his short jog to the wall.

"Hello there!" Beor shouted back, pausing from overseeing the work. "What brings you all the way out here? There aren't any new ways into the dungeon since that first one."

"What? *What?*"

"Don't worry about it, we sealed it up."

"...Right. Well, we got a report about a gathering of monsters at the base of the mountain, and I just wanted to see how the walls were coming." Dale tried to ignore the previous comments.

"Monsters, eh?" He pulled on his beard. "This beauty'll stop just about anything, and we're working in Runes so that it'll ignore other earth Mages. We should have this last section done this evening if we hurry a bit. Now, we won't be staying here, so you need to post guards or things'll just swarm over it."

Dale tried to think about who would be willing to watch the walls. "Crap, there is *no* one."

"Eh?"

"Nothing, I just need to find a way to hire on guards..." Dale thanked the Dwarf and hurried back to the main areas.

He found the city administrator after asking directions a few times and worked out a plan of action with the harried man. They would have guards by tomorrow, but they would mainly be lookouts, not fighters that could actually *defend* the wall. That would take much longer to accomplish, but Dale was still relieved that they would at least have advanced warning if something were coming. He was walking back to the chapel when Adam came running out.

"There you are! Hurry, he's waking up!"

Adam turned back and ran, Dale hurrying behind him. They walked into the stiflingly hot room just as Tom gave a great shudder and took a deep breath. He opened his eyes, and a smile crossed his face. The smile turned to a frown and then a yell of pain and rage.

"Ye *gods!* I knew that breakthrough was painful, but this just seems *excessive!*" He groaned, trying to rub at his arm. He paused, a look of horror crossing his face. "My *arm?*" Tom roared. "What foul deeds have been done to me in my absence? Was I *neutered* as well?"

Rose had a startled look on her face. "We... didn't check?"

"I'm not being literal! Get thyself away from my smallclothes, you!" Tom barked at a cleric that was reaching a bit too low.

"Tom!" Dale exclaimed loudly, demanding attention. "This happened in the dungeon! The Goblins ambushed us and took you, cutting off your arm as they tried to get your warhammer."

Tom calmed down as Dale talked, a reaction to having to listen to orders on a daily basis. He looked down. "I cannot fight as I am. I am sitting, and my balance is off, nearly toppling me. The joy I felt at achieving my breakthrough has fled, and all I feel is shame."

"Oh relax, you tight-ass," Hans joined the conversation in his usual fashion. "All this means is that we need to do some specialized training. At the end of it you are still going to get your arm back, so don't start wallowing. Plus, you just extended your natural lifespan by a handful of decades, so even if you *weren't* getting your arm back, giving up wouldn't be an option."

Tom's face rose and fell and rose again, emotions playing across his features as Hans berated him into listening and thinking of the situation from a different standpoint. He stood and thanked Hans, moving to hug him.

"Back!" Hans dodged the clumsy attempt at an embrace. "I don't do half-hugs, sorry."

Tom looked stricken, then gave a wet chuckle. "You are *such* a terrible person."

"I know, but it works for me." Hans laughed and slapped Tom lightly on the face. "Let's go meet the Mage who is going to be giving you a new arm."

CHAPTER TWENTY-TWO

"Well, it *is* pretty. Sell it as a bauble?"

If I had hands, I would slap these stupid adventurers. They only saw the profit and never the usefulness or true beauty in an object.

The person asking the question scratched himself and sniffed his fingers, making Dani cringe.

"I mean, a jewel on a chain? It's not even a bracelet? Is it supposed to be earrings of some kind?"

"Nah. There's only one. Earrings come in pairs."

Did I need to make something blaze with Essence in order for people to treat it as anything other than a shiny stone? I released a frustrated noise; no one had used the portal system yet. A bunch of people had found the stones, and a few people had even found down to the third floor's keys! I noticed that someone was now wearing a bunch of them as a necklace. I had made them modular so you could connect them together, but I still had to sigh when I saw the topaz, fluorite, emerald pattern repeated over and over as simple jewelry.

The archways on the floors had been noticed, but after an initial assessment, they had been ignored. After it was found that the Cores couldn't be pried off, the arches were largely forgotten. It was *days* before Dale's group came back, and I was surprised at how much I had missed a semi-intelligent group of people being here regularly. They were talking about something, but I was looking at Tom. He had an odd chunk of armor on, and it took me a moment to realize that someone had strapped a buckler on to him where his arm had been. I snorted with laughter at the odd sight and listened to what they were saying.

"New jobs, anyone?" Dale was all business today.

"Yup, someone felt that Glitterflit pelt and decided that they *must* have an entire wardrobe of them. It is a *huge* offer of money. Apparently, they were told how difficult it is to get that type," Rose informed the group.

Hans shrugged. "I don't know. I kinda have a soft spot for those little guys."

"The Spotters are asking for an entire Goblin. They want to determine the differences between them and their non-dungeon counterpart," Adam announced. "Double pay if it is alive."

"Too much effort for a live one. We'll see how it goes otherwise."

"Evan wants us to escort him down to the third floor again."

Dale paused. "That triples how long we stay in here; does anyone have plans after?" A few shrugs were his answer. "Guard duty is a go then, make sure he visited either the alchemist or apothecary. If we learned anything last time, it is to not let him come down here without a night vision potion."

Tom made a noise and raised the shield a bit. "I think you and I learned different things during our last dungeon run."

This got a few laughs from the group.

"Right, well, here comes Evan. Now, everyone ready to go?"

After checking their supplies, the group of six walked deeper into the dungeon.

<It's been a few days, Dale. How're things?> I nonchalantly asked the team leader.

Dale's movements gave nothing away. His eyes stayed focused and roving, looking for danger. "*It is my turn to ask questions, and I am going to save it* forever *so that you can't screw me over again.*"

Hans suddenly laughed. "Look! Tom, you're in the statues!" I had replaced the statue of the crazy Elf and bunnies with one of dozens of small Goblin arms holding up a single, larger arm.

"That is *not* funny. Who takes the time to make these odd statues?" Tom grumbled, looking a bit sick as he wriggled his stump.

Their questions ended as combat began. They fought through the first floor with ease, finding six sets of the topaz keygems in the Boss Room's chest. Dale looked at the gem intently, muttering, "What the heck is this?"

<You know, I'm glad you asked, Dale.>

"Son of a shit."

Hans glanced at Dale. "You okay there?" Dale just nodded.

<That is what I call a 'keygem'. I created a stable portal system between the floors. You just walk up to the archway, touch the keygem, and the portal will activate for whoever has a keygem. If someone without a keygem walks into the portal, nothing happens... but I can't guarantee that it won't open as someone else walks in, which could be messy.> I paused to let him imagine things. <Messy, like they are suddenly very 'pieceful'. Piece of him over here, piece of him over there.>

"*You know what, Cal? I'm not even mad. That is actually really useful information,*" Dale thought at me, laughing as I squirmed. I preferred making him needlessly mad. He walked over to the archway, and it suddenly blazed with light. He looked through it and saw the startled faces of a few miners glancing his way. Dale waved and stepped back, explaining to his team what the item was.

Hans was nearly dancing. "The Portal Guild is going to be having *kittens* over this! They've had a monopoly on human portal travel for a century! Listen to how *quiet* this portal is too! And so stable!"

I felt like blushing from all the praise.

"The Runes on here, they look like they shouldn't work together at all—like they should just blow up and kill us all—but it is *actually* working! Miracle?"

<He'd better go back to the compliments; that sounds dangerously close to an insult...>

DALE

The group pressed on, eventually returning to the third floor. They each had two gems on their chains, signifying that they were able to move directly to the second floor. Now they were discussing their options. Should they press on to the Boss directly and get the floor keygem, or should they mine for a while first? They decided that the best option for them at this time was to attack, getting the third-floor keygem.

They followed the curving room, bypassing the honeycomb-like fortifications and the glaring archers therein, dodging arrows when they got a bit too close. The grand door of the Boss's area loomed in the distance. It was illuminated by the light pouring down through the huge pane of emerald set in the ceiling, creating a sinister environment. Adam shivered as he looked upon the gate, and the others clearly had mixed feelings. Tom glared at the area; he only knew what had happened from stories, but this was where he had lost his arm.

"You're sure that the reason the Goblin Boss was so powerful was that I was going all out?" Hans glanced at Dale, waiting for confirmation.

"Ninety-five percent," Dale responded agreeably.

"Does that mean 'yes'?" Hans raised his eyebrow.

Dale had forgotten that Dwarven mathematics was not common knowledge. "Err. Yeah, it means I am almost positive."

Tom nodded gravely. "It is good to be a positive person." The group went silent, Tom staring ahead and rubbing his chin. "How do we get in?"

Rose shrugged. "Go through the wall again?"

"No, we may not always have Evan with us. We should practice other tactics." Dale looked for structural weaknesses or obvious flaws.

Unsurprisingly, it was Hans, the ex-assassin, who came up with the plan.

"If we were to go to that portion of the wall where it connects near the natural curve of the cave, we could press our back to the cave and 'walk' up the wall," Hans announced thoughtfully.

"How would that even work?" Adam's eyes were filled with disbelief.

Hans walked over to the wall, casually dodging an arrow that sailed his way. Rose sniped the attacking Goblin while Hans demonstrated the technique.

"Put your back like this... and *push* with your legs." He started walking up the wall horizontally, much to the amazement of the others.

Adam watched, trying to memorize the movements. "I would never have dreamed that this was possible."

"Neither do most guards. Or the Nobles they are supposed to be guarding," Hans mentioned, halfway up the wall. He dropped back down to the ground, landing softly.

"I am certain that is harder than you made it look," Tom commented.

Evan nodded along with the statement.

"You want to try something *difficult?* Do this." Hans jumped from a standstill, pushing off the wall, then the cave, over and over until he was standing on the wall. "It's only about eight feet tall, so I guess it isn't *too* hard."

"You are ridiculous." Rose chuckled, reaching into her bag. "I thought ahead! I bought this rope and grapple yesterday."

Hans made a face at her. "Boo! Cheater!"

"Doing something in an intelligent manner is not 'cheating'," Rose blandly replied to Hans, swinging the rope and connecting it on the first throw.

Again, the wall was only eight feet tall; it wasn't too hard to launch it up to the top. They climbed the wall one at a time. Rose remained on the lookout for more archers and so went last.

Standing on top of the wall looking down, they could see the Goblins moving into defensive formations. The Goblin Boss... Queen? Amazon? Amazon. Was standing up and lifting twin warhammers to taunt the group in.

"Let's stay up here." Evan chuckled nervously.

Dale paused from his downward descent. "You know, why not? It's not like we need to have a knock-down, life-or-death battle every time, right? Rose, can you turn them into pincushions? Hans, what's the range for your throwing daggers?"

The whole group was a tiny bit thrown off, but Dale made perfect sense. Rose shrugged and started sniping the Goblins who were yelling obscenities and scrambling to avoid arrows. A knife thunked into the Goblin Boss's neck, severing the arteries. She roared, stumbling around for a minute before slumping to the ground. The group descended, killing the Goblins that had managed to survive the brief scuffle.

"This just seems... wrong somehow," Tom rumbled as he rammed a Goblin with his shield, finishing it with a hammer blow from his ingot hammer.

Dale patted him on the back. "I think that we have gotten so used to constantly fighting that we forgot our main goals. We are here to cultivate and gain money or items. We aren't actually here to fight, that is just usually, you know, how it goes."

They looked around for items, scavenging the weapons that hadn't vanished before they got to them. They found the treasure chest under a partially collapsed section of wall, pulling out coins, a few Inscribed items, and a keygem each for the floor.

"Looks like we got what we came for. Ready to test the portal system?" Dale looked around with a goofy grin.

"Are we sure we won't just explode when we go in it?" Adam questioned, making the grin drop from Dale's face.

"No... "

Evan stood forward. "I'll test it. You'd be coming here for my benefit anyway, else you'd just fight floor-by-floor as usual."

Before anyone could nay-say him, he stepped forward holding the topaz keygem. He entered the portal and exited on to the first floor, much to Dale's relief and a series of miners' amazement. The entire group tumbled through the portal, blinking owlishly in the sudden bright light.

"I'm gonna send a runner to explain this to the Guild, then we go back in?" Dale looked around to several nods of acknowledgment.

Rose coughed. "I'm going to run to the latrine..."

This spurred a whole host of other minor things they wanted to do before delving back in, so it took about half an hour before they all reconvened.

"You know," Dale thought aloud, stepping through the portal, "this isn't making me sick. Going through the big portal outside always makes me nauseous."

"Could be any number of reasons." Hans leaned against the wall. "A difference of perspective moving through, like going from facing south to east suddenly. Could be a fluctuation in gravity, going from a low to high-pressure zone. Or it could simply be that the portals aren't all that great out there. They found a design that worked and never tried to improve on it, maybe."

They moved into a honeycomb fort and killed the guards, ending the fight with only minimal injuries. Feeling quite pleased with themselves, they settled down and ate a picnic lunch that Adam pulled out of his bag while Evan began mining. They cultivated for hours, staying in the dungeon far longer than they normally did. A few groups had found them, to their great surprise. They would run in yelling war cries, only to be stopped by a lazy wave and a 'hey there' from Hans.

They finally left, exiting the portal at the entrance to the floor, not bothering with the Boss a second time. They were cheerfully selling their wares and ore to Tyler when a courier ran into the tent at breakneck speed.

"Mr. Tyler, the council... um. Your Grace, we have been looking for you as well." Dale nodded, motioning for the lad to continue. "The council is having an emergency meeting. They need you both as soon as possible."

"The church?" Dale asked, moving to the door.

A head shake. "The Guild tent, sir."

"Let's go, everyone. I'm sure you'll want to hear about whatever this is, and I hate re-telling stories." Dale motioned them all to follow; they took off at a jog.

Entering the Guild tent, they could hear concerned muttering coming from the war room. Dale threw open the flap, marching inside.

"What's happening?" He looked around, noting an absence. "Has Father Richard been informed of this meeting?"

Frank responded grimly, "He is the *reason* for the meeting. His quick reactions saved us, but he may well pay with his life."

"...Explain."

"There was a person brought in, the one who collapsed. He had been injured by whatever was coming this way. That man... he had some kind of disease. Soon after treatment, he collapsed into a death-like state. Growths appeared on his body, and then... he woke up. He went mad, attacking anyone nearby. It was horrible."

"A disease? That's what we are here for?" Amber interrupted, scoffing. "At the earliest stages of the B-ranks, we are *immune* to disease."

"Not. This. One," Frank ground out. "Listen, when that man woke up, he was not right in the mind. He flew into a mad rage, attacking anyone who came near. He used any weapon he could get his hands on but was not shy about using tooth and nail. Father Richard captured him, obviously suffering no physical injury. This did not go... well." Frank swallowed, voice hoarse. "When he no longer had a chance to escape, he... the sick man... he ruptured his Center."

"Oh god." Chandra's hands went to her throat.

"Father Richard placed the building under Celestial quarantine instantly. You see, he survived the after-effect, but the man seemed to release some kind of dust or possibly seeds of some kind. They settled on every surface, and many of the people still trapped in there are showing symptoms that the man came in with."

"Could it be necromancers?" Brianna interjected. "Who has the means to do this?"

"Wait, please back up. What do you mean that a man ruptured his Center?" Dale commanded the group's attention.

"It is a forbidden suicide attack. That is, it is forbidden to teach, but obviously, it is hard to punish those who use it." Hans growled grimly, the council showing surprise at his knowledge of secret lore.

"The person using it shatters their Chi spiral, and *all* the Essence contained in their body leaves in a single instant. It is an attack powered not only by the refined Essence but also by any corruption they have in them. Fire cultivator? Crack the Center, and you have a fireball powerful enough to melt Mithril. If a Mage were to use the technique, it would have an effect similar to a volcano erupting."

"Correct," Frank agreed, continuing his assessment. "We do not think this is related to the rumors of necromancers. The Spotters have their own theories."

A squirrely man stood up. "Thank you for the introduction. Father Richard brought an infected person close to his barrier so we could do our job. The growths forming on this man *have* been seen before, but at that time, they were a mere curiosity. We saw no reason for it to remain here, as the person the growths were found on was dead when she was brought to us. We... we sent the corpse via portal to... to Spotterton," he finished brokenly, stifling a sob.

He took a moment to regain his composure. "The symptoms described are the same as what was reported, and the growths are becoming more prominent and recognizable. There is no mistake. They are a variant of the mushrooms from the dungeon. Specifically, the Glade monster.

"No," Dale whispered in horror.

The Spotter nodded grimly. "It is the *only* explanation. We have been hearing reports of entire towns being killed off. Anyone dead was left where they landed, rotting away. We now think that anyone who survived was infected and joined the horde. It's madness. The victims are not rational—all they want to do is either kill or infect others."

"That can't be all! They have to have some goal, some destination!" Amber smacked her palm on the table, cracking it down the center.

The Spotter hesitated. "They *have* been following the river. The river exits from here, and lower down the mountain, it connects to another river that—we think—is coming out of the dungeon. It could be that they are attempting to re-enter the dungeon."

"Could we just... let them?" Brianna silenced the room with her question.

Tyler spoke up for one of the first times ever at a council meeting. "I don't think that would be wise. We'd need to let them into the town—the dungeon is almost at the center. If there were anyone around, I'm sure they would be attacked. Are we sure *that* is what they are after? If not, this place becomes inhabited by contagious creatures. If re-entering is their goal, what happens when the dungeon begins to create a copy of these things? I've heard stories of the Distortion Cat that broke in. Yes, it was defeated, but within days, there were Cat variant Mobs in the dungeon."

"Good god," Frank whispered. "I hadn't thought of that."

"It's already from the dungeon, isn't it?" Brianna scoffed. "It *knows* how to make the disease!"

The Spotter gave a half-hearted nod. "Yes, but... this version is mature, fully developed. It would—potentially—be a disaster if the dungeon began to replicate this."

"What do we do?" Tyler broke the silence that followed the Spotter's words.

"There may not be a problem coming our way, so we need to send messages to the Kingdom and the nearest towns. If they do come for us... we need to eradicate them," Dale grimly announced. "Close everything, all businesses and leisure activities. We need to gather everyone and make an announcement."

An hour later, Dale walked to a platform with the other members of the council. There was an agitated, muttering crowd that grew slowly larger as people exited the dungeon or filed in from other activities. Dale walked to the hastily erected podium and began to speak.

"Hello, everyone." As he spoke, the roughly three thousand people in the area quieted down to listen. There were only about seven hundred people who fought in the dungeon; the rest were traders, merchants, cooks, waiters, or any other number of support staff. "We have a serious problem."

"You're droppin' the tax? About time!" someone called out, making a low rumble of laughter roll through the crowd.

"No." Dale's frank answer and serious tone stopped the chuckles. "It is possible that we are going to be coming under attack within a few days." A rumble of a different sort sounded. "There are—what we are estimating to be—a few thousand infected people on their way here. Violent, vicious, extremely dangerous, and contagious people."

"What do they have? Plague?"

Dale answered this question since it was heard over all the others. "They have a disease of a mystical nature. It originated here, from this dungeon."

He paused, gathering air in his lungs to continue his proclamation.

"We are calling it '*Dungeon Madness*' until a better term is found."

"No!" Minya stepped forward, shaking her head. "*Dungeon Madness* is a different, *much* more dangerous problem. We don't want to confuse people."

"Whatever, Minya! We'll call it 'Mad Dungeon Disease' then!" Dale decided to get this over with. "Currently, there is no known cure. Unfortunately... it seems to be effective against everyone, even Mages."

This—more than anything else he had said—caused the icy touch of fear to affect the listeners. At the Mage rank, there was no more sickness, no more injuries from age or other human ailments.

"Then let's get the *abyss* out of here!"

This comment was generally accepted to be a good idea.

Dale shouted over the noise, quieting them with his words, "I won't stop you from leaving right now. I *will* say this, though. If you are here now, and you make your living fighting in the dungeon... if you leave us... if you leave the people who are going to be relying on you... I will *not* let you come back. You can make your living elsewhere. Someplace safer."

A roar of outrage sounded from nearly every voice. It took several minutes before order was restored.

Dale continued, trying to explain himself, "If you are not a fighter, it is understandable that you leave and actually *encouraged.* Those of you who fight for a living, let me ask you this. Where will you go? This dungeon will make you rich and powerful if it is not converted into a disease spewing disaster center! If you are not willing to fight for others, fight for your own future! Fight for your greed, your self-serving desires!"

"What do we get out of it?"

Dale's shoulders slumped. "A place to live, money, and power that is there for the taking? That isn't enough?"

"No!"

"...What about half taxes for six months?"

There was a pause as people took in his words, and faces lit up. A few people nodded, some clapped.

Then a voice rang out!

"...Death to the infected!" was the roar of bloodlust and greed following Dale's offer.

"For Mountaindale!"

CHAPTER TWENTY-THREE

The mostly-tented city was emptying out, hundreds of people leaving per hour. To their credit, most of the fighters remained, as did the Guild cook. The cook was having a grand ol' time, his favorite phrase being, "I knew you'd all come crawling back! Them pansy waiters won't stick around to feed ya, but ol' cook-ie will *always* be there for you!"

"I can't believe how empty it is out here," Dale murmured, looking around the near-empty plain. Where tents had been, there was grass or dirt showing, but those spots on the landscape were slowly being filled in as the wind carried drifts of snow around.

"This is awesome! When people come back, I can actually force them to set up in some kind of order!" The city administrator was staying, much to Dale's confusion.

"Well... I'm... happy for you?" Dale's face gained a crooked smile.

The administrator nodded, walking away. "I'm happy for all of us! Gonna have a nice looking city this year!"

"What a strange man." Adam was watching the administrator pull out a measuring rope and start outlining property boundaries.

"He gets the job done, and he loves his work." Dale smiled. "Good enough for me."

"The Dwarves have finished the wall, and unless I'm mistaken, that is the rider that was sent out to scout the other day." Hans pointed at a man on a horse that was lathered up, nearly dead with exhaustion. "I'll put fifty gold on him having bad news."

"No deal."

It was *bad* news. The horde had found the road up the mountain, having been stymied by their unsuccessful attempts at swimming up the waterfall. As soon as a few started going up the road, the rest had followed. They had been a bit off in their estimates as well. There were nearly ten thousand of the creatures that had once been human.

"*How?* How are there so many?" Dale demanded of the silent council.

Amber shook her head. "It shouldn't have been possible. There are maybe a thousand people in a good-sized village. Unless there was a near one hundred percent conversion rate from the disease..."

"I know what happened." Prince Henry walked into the room.

Everyone stood, murmuring, "Your Majesty."

Henry waved for them to sit while he paced. "This year we were holding a census in the kingdom. To ensure accurate records, we had made it mandatory that each town hold a post-harvest festival and bring in anyone within fifty miles." He stopped, looking close to tears. "That mass of infected represents nearly a sixth of our rural population."

"Good god above."

CAL

<Sure has been quiet the last few days. Even the miners are gone. Except Evan, of course. Do you think he ever sleeps?> I prodded Dani. I think I was driving her insane with my incessant talking, but I was so bored!

"He leaves for a few hours every day," Dani said the next part under her breath, "I'm starting to think he has the right idea."

<I'm not *that* bad. Maybe Minya will wanna chat.>

Dani bristled at my comment, though she didn't vocalize anything. So far, Minya was the only person that had a keygem that granted access directly to the room with me and the Silverwood tree. Dani was upset that I was showing so much favoritism to her, but Minya was already proving that she was a good investment. She was well-informed, intelligent, discreet, and brought me presents *all the time*.

Though she was waiting on the first shipment of memory stones, she brought me interesting trinkets daily. She had also walked into the dungeon and started discussing topics with people. That was an interesting way to learn things. I had particularly enjoyed when she had started talking to a smith who was buying ore from a miner. I learned so much about desirable metal purities and alloy creations that day!

Just that single conversation would have been worth the risks of keeping my pet human. There was more; she had talked to a bowyer, carpenters, and other tradesmen. Each of these conversations helped me understand concepts that would have taken years of trial and error to figure out otherwise. Something as simple as using larger bricks at the base of a wall to help strengthen it changed the way I looked at things. I had thought that using the same size throughout was the best way, so I had simply made them huge. Silly me!

As though our discussion had summoned her, Minya walked into the dungeon and started talking to me, "Cal, there is a serious problem."

<What is going on?>

"Did you release a parasitical virus into the wild?"

<What? Why would I? People dying outside of here doesn't benefit me at all.>

"Okay. Thank goodness. I had to ask. Well, they think it is your fault. Apparently, there is a multi-thousand person horde of infected people coming this way. When they die, they release spores like a mushroom would," Minya informed me with a hint of relief overshadowed with fear.

<...Uh.>

"Hmm?"

I mentally winced. <That actually may sound a bit... familiar?>

Minya paused, thinking through her verbal options. "Did you do it on purpose?"

<No, it was a side effect of creating a new Mob. The result was uncontrollable for me; it made the victim insane. I removed that in the next batch, but someone took her out of here. They wanted a reward for a new Mob, if that means anything to you,> I tried to explain myself.

She gained a considering look. "So it *was* the Spotters' Guild's fault. Thank you, Cal. If they get in here, would you make more of them?"

<No. Like I said, the result is uncontrollable, and they would kill me as well, given the chance.>

Minya nodded. "Then I'll go see how we can turn this to your benefit."

She stalked out of the dungeon with a look on her face that reminded me she was very dangerous. I wouldn't want to face her when she was this determined. I hoped she was going to go yell at Dale.

I turned to my Goblins, as they had been having some mental issues themselves. Each day, any survivors would add their memories to the memory stones that I had provided. This meant that they would lose, at worst, only a day of memory if they died. I had also made them into what I called *Delta* memory stones, as it would only take what was different from previous memories, not make a full copy. The problem was surprisingly not with the Goblins who died frequently; it was with the ones who lived every day.

They all made copies of their memory to the stones, but the survivors did it much more frequently. There were only twelve total stones. I had made them share in the hopes that the accumulated experiences would make them smarter and more dangerous. This worked... to a point. Then there was the worst-case scenario. The first Goblin to show problems was the massive Goblin that carried around a warhammer. His mind had snapped, and he reverted to a bestial mentality. He didn't attack the other Goblins unless they got in his way but was absolutely mad for combat. He would fly into a rage at the first hint of a fight, ignoring all attempts at defense as he threw himself at his opponent.

I had allowed that memory stone to continue and simply called them 'Goblin Berserkers' now, but the new Goblin Warriors I reverted to the old, original memories. He had to relearn a lot, but it was a good lesson for me. I made a memory stone for each encampment and would let them diverge as individuals from this point forward. No need to make sentient beings slip slowly into insanity.

The shaman had had a lot of fun with the Delta stones, having a dozen of himself trying new ways of doing things, then using the accumulated knowledge to push himself in new directions. Every two days gave him nearly a month of research, so he was progressing quickly. As a seeker of knowledge, he was the only one disappointed when I took away the Delta stones, so

I gave them back to him in secret when other Goblins weren't around.

Since the dungeon was approaching empty, I started experimenting with Essences. The combinations were so interesting, and I had barely scratched the surface of their potential. Slight variations in the corruption levels produced astoundingly different results. For instance, earth and water in equal amounts made 'mud' Essence. A bit more earth than water made 'plant' Essence, while a large amount more water Essence made 'blood' Essence. There were combinations that I was *sure* did something, but they didn't affect the things I could test them on, so it was hard to tell what kind of affinity they were.

What really interested me were the opposing affinities. Let's just discuss the *equal* amount of each. Earth and wind; water and fire. These, at first glance, seemed to simply cancel each other out or make something seemingly useless. Fire and water made steam, right? Wrong! Fire and water intermixed naturally also needed a third component, air! *That* made steam. When combined *without* air, it made an interesting fluid that super-compressed itself! This 'superfluid' when released or exposed to air would violently explode, decompressing itself straight to a gaseous form! Useful? Not a clue, outside of traps.

Earth and wind made freaking *lightning* when combined! I had really thought that would be an effect in the purview of fire, but I was pleased to be proven wrong. Chaos, the intermixing of celestial and infernal, had mind-altering properties that made it very difficult for me to work with, as I was a thought construct. I would suddenly start, having a feeling of a breakthrough, only to realize that I couldn't remember what I had been doing. It was *incredibly* frustrating.

"Hey, um Cal?" Dani was speaking in a horrified voice.

<Hmm? What is it? You okay?>

"Have... have you looked at the Mobs on the fourth floor recently?" Dani seemed to be going somewhere with this. I focused but sensed no life, well, beyond a few insects that had made their way in. Useless bugs, couldn't even evolve to a useful configuration.

<Where are they?> I couldn't find any of the Mobs!

"They're all dead, Cal. Look for bodies."

This time I changed what I was looking for, finding corpses littered around the floor.

<What? What happened? Who did this?> A horrible suspicion came over me. <Did I do that?>

"What? No, how would you forget killing five dozen Cats and double that in Bashers? Are you okay...?" Dani now had a *really* nervous look. She tried to shake it off. "No, Cal, we are pretty far underground. You and I don't notice—as we don't have lungs—but the air quality is so bad down here that it became polluted and poisonous. It happened quietly; everything just sort of laid down and died over about an hour."

I inspected the air, and sure enough, it was *bad.* There was an overwhelming amount of earth Essence and little air Essence at all, except around the Silverwood tree. I thought about how to fix this; should I open vents to the outside? That would take a while, but it was doable...

"So, if you could go ahead and grow some plants down here, that should take care of it," Dani interrupted my thoughts.

<Wait, that's it? No air ducts?>

"Yup. Plants will release breathable air, and at the rate you can grow them, the air should be breathable in an hour or so. No air ducts needed," Dani promised me while looking wistfully at Snowball. I started absorbing him so she would be able to move on a little faster.

<Sorry, Dani. I know it seems like I understand everything that is going on, but really, I am still learning all the time. Air quality was something that I had never considered and just goes to show how much I still need to learn. I do try to minimize my mistakes...> I trailed off sadly, feeling like a bad dungeon.

Dani tried to shake me out of my melancholy, "Hey! Listen!"

<Huh?> For some reason, the way she said those words made me slightly upset. I tried to move past it.

"Mistakes happen, big guy. You are fixing it now, right? Then let's move on. What were you working on?"

Her sweet voice eased my tension, and I gratefully described my experiments with Essence. She listened raptly and offered some suggestions for my playtime. Um. Practicing.

"By the way," Dani mentioned as a thought crossed her mind, "has Minya brought all of the gemstones that you asked for?"

<She is having trouble finding infernal-grade opal. I have the rest, and if you follow the pathways, you'll find veins of them through the entire place. Matter of fact,> I was fully distracted at this point; nice work Dani, <I have them all connected to two distinct points if applicable. For instance, I have topaz connecting to the pane of celestial quartz as well as an oversized Core designed for corruption storage. To deal with infernal Essence, I have diamond mixed in for transportation, but I'll replace it as soon as I can.>

"Has that helped with your corruption cleaning efforts?" Dani was flying along, visually inspecting the plants now growing on this floor.

<I think so. Interesting tidbit, you know the Essence accumulation Rune I've been using?>

"Yeah?"

<Well, powering it with taint makes it draw in *corruption*! So what I've done is placed that Rune on the corruption-connected Cores, and it pulls corruption along the lines of gemstone, just like a human running Essence through meridians!>

I really enjoyed watching the process. It was fun to watch loose Essence stick to the wall before floating free, corruption removed. There was constant cycling and pretty coloration if you could see it.

"Wow! When did you make that? Why didn't you tell me? I hadn't noticed!" Dani went from elated to curious to slightly angry in the span of a single breath.

<Well, you took a nap yesterday, then I was done and started testing Essence...>

Dani made a small noise. "You actually forgot that you had made corruption collection devices?"

I gave her a mental shrug. <Memory is an imperfect storage device.>

"Ugh." Dani sounded disgusted. "Minya just had to talk to that mind-cleric here."

<I like learning,> I started as someone stumbled into the dungeon, bleeding heavily. I looked at the time; it was getting near midnight.

<That's odd. Normally, people *leave* here bleeding...>

"Something is happening out there, I'm gonna take a look," Dani informed me, flying out her specially-designed escape tunnel just as the ground began shaking.

DALE

"Dale. They're coming." Frank jogged up to the serious, young city Lord at a normal human speed.

Dale looked at the Guild leader in shock. "What?! They're way ahead of schedule! They shouldn't be here for another *day* at the earliest!"

"This part is non-human," Frank frankly revealed. "The infection is far worse than we assumed; it affects more than just humans—it also takes animals and magical Beasts. They're far faster than their two-legged counterparts, and we need to be ready to defend right *now*."

The alarm was sounded, just a guy with an Essence-enhanced voice. They had had to improvise, as no-one had expected an attack this early. Fighters began running the distance to the walls, and there was no formation or discipline to be seen amongst the cultivators—at first. As they moved, they slowly began to separate from a mob of people into small groups of five.

The wall was easily large enough to hold the entire defending population with just enough room that the line wasn't *too* thin in any spot. Melee fighters had a slightly disgruntled look, while archers and other various ranged attackers were flushed, excited to show off their ability.

A sound reached the ears of the defenders, a low rumble of feet pounding the ground, hooves clopping intermittently against stone. Above all, a wailing, anguished noise tickled their eardrums, creating a feeling of primal dread in more than one person.

The first of the things came into view, and what may have once been a regal or handsome animal now appeared as a fungus encrusted, diseased horror. It bleated. Had it been some type of goat?!

The eagerness and bloodlust were starting to fade as more and more infected specimens appeared. Herds of various cattle, forest creatures, packs of wolves... The disease had taken everything in its path. Towering, lumbering forms appeared, some massive type of Beast that was totally unrecognizable under the parasite.

The horde was moving quickly but without appearing to be violent. They were totally silent apart from the wailing and crying sounds they emitted. That was... until the first arrow *thunked* into the lead animal. Then the creatures stopped, actually going quiet before screaming, bleating, whinnying, or roaring with rage and charging the wall.

Arrows began to fall like rain, slicing through unprotected flesh. Dozens of the creatures died, then hundreds as the slaughter continued. Still, they came onward, throwing themselves at the wall, their blood painting it red, their cries shaking the very foundation. For now, the towering defense held. The stone crafting abilities of Dwarves were more than ready for this test.

A blast of fire from a defender charred a swath of beings below but prompted Frank to shout, "Hold your Essence! This is only the advance group, bare animals with a sprinkling of weak Beasts! Wait for the *dangerous* opponents!"

This had a sobering effect. People had been getting a bit exuberant, seeing the enemies fall so easily. The slaughter continued for hours, with the once-animals unable to overcome this barrier in their path. A few hours after dark, the creatures below started having a different shape to them, and the howls became disturbingly human.

Brianna, standing with her half-dozen Dark Elves, peered into the gloom below. "Those were definitely people recently."

The human monsters were slightly more intelligent than their bestial counterparts, using tools, weapons, and armor. They climbed the huge mound of bodies in their way, reaching the wall and starting to climb. A flicker of fire was seen before Frank shouted 'hold!' again. These humans were struggling up to the wall, slow and easily slain.

Amber pointed. "Frank, *Mages* approaching!"

A trail of light followed the form of a man sprinting at superhuman speeds. He blasted *through* the infected in his path; their flesh gave way, their bodies pulverized from the impact. Then a wave of gore shot in every direction as the glowing infected man sprinted directly *into* the piled dead in front of the wall. The effect would be best described as if a large rock were tossed into a shallow pool of water. He made it to the wall and impacted the shuddering blockade, beginning to pound away at it with sledgehammer-like blows. Chips flew at every strike, his punches enhanced with an earth-type Mana.

"Kill that bastard!" Beor the Dwarf was screaming. "He's breaking Cliff!"

Dale glanced at the furious Dwarf. "You named the wall? You named it '*Cliff*'? Won't that be confusing with all these cliffs around?"

"No! We didn't want the wall to feel out of place, so we're letting it think that it is a natural rock formation!"

"What are you...? I don't..." Dale paused, Dwarven logic didn't matter right now. Only one thing did. "Kill that bastard!"

Arrows and rocks fell on the man who was pounding on the wall, but though his clothes were destroyed, he took no damage.

"Damn Mages and their near-physical invulnerability," Hans grumbled. Amber stepped forward, opening her mouth and releasing an eye-drawing stream of multi-hued light. It seemed to flow into the infected man, and he dropped, blood pouring from his ruined ears. "What did you do to him?"

Amber shook her head, "I spoke to his brain and convinced it that it was dead. His physical state soon followed his mental one."

Dale shuddered, trying not to be disturbed. Mana was terrifying. He looked into the darkness, seeing lights begin to sprout amongst the people affected by this madness of the dungeon. "More Mages!"

"That Mana signature! That's–" The Spotter who was speaking gasped. "Those are three of the Mages from Spotterton!" He finished his statement as shimmering colors flew from the Mages, impacting the wall. The strike knocked dozens of people off their feet, and some fell off the wall entirely. Those who fell on the defended side of the wall were injured, but those who fell toward the infected were torn apart amidst howls of fury. Chunks of stone fell from the shaking wall, killing a few Beasts at the base, but the wall held firm.

Midnight was swiftly approaching when lesser cultivators appeared, those in the C-ranks and below. They moved faster than their counterparts and were able to begin scaling the wall using personal Essences. There were easily a thousand C-ranked or below Cultivators at the base of the wall, interspersed with a few Mages. They were scaling the wall like spiders when Frank suddenly took action.

He moved to the edge of the wall, Mana gathering around him like a thundercloud, dense and heavy. Dale had seen this before and tried to intercept him.

"*No*, Frank! Remember what happened with Father Richard!"

Frank either didn't hear him or didn't care. His Mana poured out of him, shaking the air with its power. "*STOP!*" he roared into the night.

Dale spun around, now facing toward the city center and his team. He reached deep inside himself and held a pattern with his mind. Forcing his Essence into the pattern, it burst past his aura, successfully activating for the first time. He took a step forward, moving with a speed he had never managed before as the earth itself tossed him away. He threw his arms out, catching his team in a half-collision, half bear-hug before jumping into the empty air behind the wall. They were moving at such high speeds that even with the added mass and air resistance, they were a dozen feet past the edge. Then what Dale had feared... occurred.

The rolling Mana from Frank washed over the horde, but the ones on or near the wall were the most affected. Their movements slowed, finally coming to a total stop as all of the kinetic energy was stripped from them. For a moment, they struggled. Then realizing they could not move or escape, the most affected group shattered their Centers.

The wall was blasted to rubble from the pressure wave as a thousand lower ranked and three Mage-ranked Centers shattered simultaneously. The wall bearing the brunt of the outpouring of energy was the only thing that saved Dale's group, though the blast pushed them further away from their looming landing point. The group was now thirty feet away and falling quickly.

They were pelted with searing hot chunks of stone and thrown further from their impact site when a secondary explosion happened, by happenstance changing their landing point to a thick snowdrift. Dale stood as quickly as he could, turning to look at the shimmering air behind them. The massive quantity of raw power was having a horrible effect on the environment, and clouds were already gathering and turning sickly colors from corrupted Essence lying thick upon the world.

Bodies and body parts were raining down around the group. Some were moaning, and some sprang to their feet immediately. Dale looked at the survivors closely. It seemed that all of the Mages had survived, but beyond his group, there were no other people below the C-ranks among the survivors from the wall. That meant, at a minimum, there were already five-hundred and fifty casualties. Not *all* of the C-ranked people had survived, so the death toll was actually higher than Dale could estimate. From *one*. *Simple*. *Mistake*.

"Dale." Brianna limped toward him. "We need cover. My people are going to go and protect the Silverwood tree. Your defenses are gone, and your hopes of keeping the remaining *things* out of the dungeon are crushed. I advise you to seek shelter within the dungeon, but it is your choice. Good luck." The Dark Elves gathered together, moving toward the entrance at a limping run.

Dale looked over at the wall of deadly Essence and Mana. The ground was poisoned; the air was blazing with fire and poisonous gasses. He could hear the horde weeping on the other side, only held back by the deadly barrier. He tried to focus his addled mind, looking around. Minya appeared in front of him and grabbed his chin, forcing him to look at her.

"Gather any survivors. We need to get to the third floor in the dungeon! It is the only defensible location remaining."

CHAPTER TWENTY-FOUR

<Now there are a *lot* of bleeding people entering. What's going on?> I muttered in consternation.

"Cal-Cal-*Cal.*" Dani shot down her personal tunnel. "Shut this behind me, *now!*" I filled the wall with stone behind her, all the way to the top.

Suddenly, I was fighting to keep the stone solid as it cracked and shattered along the weakened path.

<What is *happening* out there?!>

"Something horrible. There is an army of infected, and somehow, millions of them just *exploded!* They died and released all of their Essence and corruption in a single burst!" Dani was sobbing, terrified at her close brush with death.

<Dani, it is *okay!* Don't be sad! I'm not even sure I could have absorbed all of that at once.> She looked up at me, confused. <I mean, I would have given it my best shot, and I know it was a huge waste for *millions* of people all to die out there, but there is only so much I can do.>

She let out a weak chuckle. "Oh, *Cal.* Not everything is about you! Also, you should know by now that I exaggerate."

<Hmm?> I was casually inspecting at all the people pouring in but did a double take when I realized that a group of Elves had just entered the third floor via portal and were sprinting toward the Boss Room. I roused the Goblins, but the Elves simply avoided them and ran down the exit. Strange behavior. That was fine, the Cats hadn't had anything to do in days... oh feces. The Cats were all dead. I struggled to get some Mobs going on the floor, but the air quality was still so poor that they fell unconscious as soon as they came into being. <We have incoming, Dani. A group of Elves, headed straight for us.>

"No, I'm pretty sure those are the ones that have an unhealthy obsession with the Silverwood tree. I'll bet that they are coming to stand guard around us. Let them in!" Dani demanded, following this statement by flying out to meet them, something she had never done before.

<Dani! What are you doing?!> I bellowed as she zipped along the tunnels.

"Excuse me, Elves?" Dani moved to the side as a knife flashed through where she had been. "Well, *that's* rude."

"Hold!" Brianna directed, stopping the next attack. She looked at Dani, eyes wider than usual. "Are you a... Dungeon Wisp? You are supposed to be just a legend." Her voice was almost accusatory.

Dani laughed, the sound like tiny bells mixed with deadly threats. "I'm real enough to be here, aren't I? Why are you racing in?"

"The Silverwood tree..." Brianna shook herself. "We need to protect the tree."

Dani started drifting away. "Works for me, but you don't want to go that way. Traps."

<Dani!> I whined at her. She ignored me.

"I'll help you. If this horde wipes out the rest of you, there won't be anyone to lure in anymore. My own strength will wane. I'll make you a deal." Dani stopped, hovering near a trap. "I can stop the Mobs from attacking the adventurers, and I will even help them."

She paused, staring at them. "There *is* a catch. You will all need to swear an oath to me that you won't reveal any secrets you learn while you are here, at least those that pertain to the dungeon. Personal achievements, brag about whatever you want. You are also in damaged armor, and a few of you have broken weapons. I can replace those for now, but a part of your oath will be returning them to me before you leave here."

Brianna didn't answer right away. When she did, it was considering. "I want something else as well. The Silverwood tree is doing very well here, and I want to know what the difference is between your attempt and our attempts to grow one. Also, I want direct access to the tree via a portal if it is within your power. Do so, and I will swear not to take advantage of your trust, as will my people. We will follow the spirit of your words, not just the letter."

"Cal?" Dani spoke into the air.

<What, you can tell whoever you want about us, but I get yelled at for letting two humans into the loop?> I griped as I stared at the tasty, tasty Elves.

"Cal..."

<Fine, whatever, I'll make it happen.>

"Good." Dani paused. "Plus, think of all the people who are going to be dying in here even with your help *and* all the infected on their way that you get to eat!" She always knew how to make me see the silver lining in a situation.

Dani turned her attention back to the Elves. "I agree to these terms. If you will swear the oath, I swear I will uphold my portion of the deal."

Brianna and the others swore the oath, binding themselves to their word of their own free will. Dani nodded, telling them to place all of their armor and weapons on the ground. They stepped away and watched nervously as the scrap was absorbed. Dani started moving again, and they turned a corner to come face-to-stinger with two Assimilators, who were crackling with unreleased lightning. The Elves tried to scream, but before they could utter a sound, I allowed the Essence stored in the Assimilators to fade away.

"What was that, Cal?" Dani angrily berated me.

<Insurance. If they attacked you or didn't swear the oath, I would have killed them if at all possible.>

"While we walk, and since we will never be able to tell anyone else, could you satisfy my curiosity?" Brianna prodded as they got over their shock. Not literal shock, I didn't use lightning on them. The mental kind of shock. Anyway.

"I suppose... you can certainly ask?"

Brianna launched into full question mode, asking about the dungeon, the tree, and Dani. Dani answered as well as she could, and I filled in any gaps in her knowledge. Possibly the most horrified look I had ever seen on an Elf came when Dani explained that I was alive and intelligent. Well, wait. That isn't accurate. The most horrified look was when that one crazy Elf let herself be killed by my Bashers. Heh.

"All this time, even the most knowledgeable of us thought that the dungeons of the world were simply places where Essence would accumulate intensely, and this was what spawned the monsters that inhabited them." Brianna shook her head sadly. "People have always had wild theories... I guess not as wild as I had originally thought. Dungeon Wisps were supposed to be the guiding factor according to legends."

<Where does she think the loot comes from? It just grows on saplings?> I paused, struck by the thought. <Dani, I just had an idea... vines that grow arrows on them instead of thorns!>

"Not now, Cal. There are things to do right now. I can't let you go all introspective."

They made it to the center of the floor, bypassing a snoring Snowball. They walked up to the tree, gasping in shock at the items waiting for them. There was a full set of Mithril armor waiting for each of them, fully Inscribed. To ensure that they would be able to fight as well as possible, the Inscriptions were powered by fully-charged Cores. Reverently, the Elves put on the armor. There were no gaps in this protective gear after it was equipped; even their faces were covered by a fine mesh of woven Mithril!

"This, on top of our bodies' normal durability... we should be unstoppable." One of the Elves seemed about to break into song.

Dani spoke up, souring his mood a bit, "Don't get *too* attached. The gear comes back to us when this is all over."

<Dani, have them take their weapons. I think they are going to need them sooner than we had hoped.>

There was a scratching coming from the mouth of the tunnel the Goblins had created. I had covered it with stone but had not gotten the chance to reinforce it yet. In a few moments, the scratching turned into pounding, and cracks formed on the wall.

Dale

Hans stepped through the portal, the last of the wounded with him. "Dale, we have good timing. The barrier is failing, and a Mana storm is coming. A snowflake the size of the King's palace just drifted past. It caught on the *Pleasure House* and cut it in half." Hans shuddered. "At least it was drifting and not plummeting. I can't imagine how much that weighed."

"I'm assuming a Mana storm creates odd weather phenomenon?" Dale helped his teammate carry the wounded man into an empty fortification.

Hans agreed with a few reservations. "More than that, it creates... *things.* All of that Mana could just go up and up, then suddenly turn into a new moon! Who knows what could happen? Even if we survive the night, we may not survive the weather."

"Is this why shattering your Center is so illegal?" Dale wondered, hoping a solution could be found.

"Pretty much."

<Dale, you need to get ready. The first of the infected have begun coming into the dungeon. They are on the first and fourth floor, so look out for infected coming up the stairs as well. I'm going to be allowing the Mobs to fight at full strength, so avoid them and *don't attack them*. There is a new kind, a berserker, who attacks any threat,> I told him, lifting out Dani's Mithril armor.

She took over the Goblin Boss, getting ready to hold the stairs.

"*The fourth...? How?*" Dale demanded impatiently as he helped the wounded into a fort.

<What? You think I just *created* the concept for Goblins? Use your head! They tunneled in.> I was taking out my nervousness on him, but it couldn't be helped. <Seriously, this guy fights magical things all the time! You'd think he could assess a situation,> I muttered.

"*I heard that. Who has ever heard of Goblins tunneling?*"

<Don't care.>

Dale growled, then started giving orders. They were far too close to the fourth-floor exit. He finished explaining to one group, then moved to the next half-hex fort. He yelled for them to open the gate, but they just glared at him and told him to leave. It took Dale a moment to realize why he recognized the people on the wall. He snapped his fingers. "You are the Nobles that came a while back! Why are you still here?"

"Oh, I don't know." One of them spat at him. "Maybe because *someone* basically called everyone cowards and told them if they left they couldn't come back? The same person who killed *hundreds* of cultivators with that order? Sound *familiar?*"

Dale's gut twisted. He had been thinking along those same lines, but hearing someone else say it was *much* worse. He took a deep breath, reminding himself of the phrase he had been raised on. "Death is everywhere in the Phantom Mountains. By being here, everyone accepted those risks. They could have left, but their greed held them here. I accept no blame for wanting to protect my home!"

"Shut up, you common-born *filth!* You're just trying to get us all killed!"

Dale's vision flashed red. "If I wanted to kill you, I could order you to leave my land *right now!*" he bellowed at the man on the wall, who paled at the revelation. "Now, follow my orders and those of the council, or I *will* make you leave! Failing to assist in the defense of the dungeon kills us all, and doing it knowingly is punishable by *death.* Starting *now!*"

There was a pause as the people behind the wall went silent. Dale wasn't having it. "Move your blue-blooded asses!" There wasn't exactly a scramble for the door, but a slow shuffle of people made their way toward the midpoint of the floor. Dale had to take several deep breaths to calm himself. The Prince and Princess had been called back to their Kingdoms after the Nobles had been settled and the infection announced, and Dale missed them. He hadn't had to bother with the stubborn branch family members a single time after punishing the unruly Barons and sending them away. Their respective monarchs had kept their promise, forcing the Nobles to stay in line and under control.

Dale waited a minute after the last people had left. Just long enough to see a contingent of exceedingly well armed and armored Goblins walk into the fort. "Good," he thought. The rear would be defended. "*Cal, we need a bit more protection. Eight-foot walls aren't going to keep the infected out.*"

<I'm having my own problems, Dale. What do you want?> Contrary to my words, I was really enjoying how the infected didn't bother to dodge Raile's attacks. I had made five versions of him, and they were really fun to watch as they squashed bodies as a team.

"*I need these walls to connect to the ceiling. Can you make it happen?*" Dale begged the Essence-hungry dungeon, using his mind to speak so he could avoid odd glances from the stragglers.

<You know, Dale, sometimes you need to solve your own problems... but in this case, I *may* have something prepared. There was a fifteen person group that came through here once—you may have heard of them—and I made corrections to my defenses in case a large force attacked again.> I paused my speech, releasing a small block of stone above each hex fort that allowed granite fortress enhancements to slowly drop. When they were all the way down, there would only be small gaps for arrows and other projectiles to move through. I sure hoped people were claustrophobic and panicked as they saw the walls closing in on them. Heh.

"Is the ceiling falling?" Dale muttered aloud while he looked at the roof with serious concern. Now that he was alone, he was much more talkative.

<If I were you, I'd get into a fort before those came all the way down. I've never tested them. They might block off the entrance.> Dale started scrambling to get to his chosen fort. <Good luck! Kill a lot of things for me!>

"Yeah, yeah, Minya told me that killing things is how you get stronger. Don't remind me. I don't like to help you," Dale mentioned breezily, keeping his breathing even as he jogged.

<Don't judge me like that. You do the same thing!> My words almost made Dale stumble.

"I do not!"

<You are personally responsible for the death of one thousand four hundred thirty-two and a half Bashers. Forty-eight Goblins. A few human criminals. Finally, one human that was going to cut you out of the profits when you found me,> I informed him primly.

"That's diff..." Dale trailed off as he realized the extent of my memory.

<Go on. Keep telling yourself that I am the one of us that is evil and terrible. Everything I do, I do to survive and get stronger. People die here, but death is all around in the Phantom Mountains, isn't it, Dale?> I taunted him, expecting him to wither. Instead, he smiled.

"Why, yes it is, Cal. I'm so glad you *asked*." Dale laughed as he ran to safety.

<Oh, you brat!> I hated wasting my questions! Sneaky human!

Dale closed the door behind him, and soon, the walls met with the descending stone. A grinding noise was heard for a few moments as things settled, but all of the walls held. Just in time, too. Wailing and sobbing noises were echoing into the room as the infected stumbled down the stairs. Soon, the sound of battle joined the ruckus as Goblins in the forts were attacked. They showed their mettle, keeping the horde occupied for nearly a half hour as they fought to the death. Hundreds of lower-ranked infected cultivators died throwing themselves against the walls, but it was the Mages that ended their desperate defense.

The Mages blasted the walls into splinters with very little effort, and the Goblin defenders were soon overrun. Dani had done well holding the Boss area, but she wasn't ready for Mages yet. She hurried back to me as the Amazon finally fell.

The infected used Essence and Mana liberally, sparing nothing in an attempt to kill as quickly as possible. The Goblins' armor offered little protection against the globes of water that suddenly surrounded their heads, drowning them where they stood. Blasts of fire cooked them; gusts of wind tore them apart, blasting through gaps in armor. The snarls and screams of rage from the infected slowed, replaced by their sobs and wailing when they ran out of things to kill.

Dale looked around the packed little fort that his people were planning to defend, taking heart in the fact that there was no terror showing. Fear was present, but determination shone in people's glinting eyes and their firm stances. They may die here, but they would die *fighting*! Dale nodded, pleased at what he saw. He gave one last command, as softly as possible, "Everyone... first off, good luck. Let's try to stay as quiet as we can. It's possible that they may ignore us if we don't attract their attention."

He got some nods in return, and all conversation ceased. The infected started filing past, a trickle at first. The trickle quickly turned into a flood. The infected in front of the group moved along toward a noisier fortress, the ones behind them following like sheep. More people looked to Dale, nodding and giving him a thumbs up. The Guild cook was among them, and he patted Dale on the back.

"THAT WAS A GOOD PLAN, M'BOY!"

The people in the fort looked at the smiling cook in horror, and the smile slowly slid from the cook's face. "Dammit. I shoulda let that healer fix my ears."

A shriek of rage pierced through the walls, impacting their ears as the nearest infected turned toward them in a rage. They almost seemed more furious than usual, as if they knew they had been tricked. The mushroom encrusted beings charged the fort, bent on the destruction of all things living.

CHAPTER TWENTY-FIVE

<These Dark Elves are seriously interesting to watch! They've been fighting non-stop for at least two hours, and I don't think they've stopped moving and swinging their blades for a single second!> I cheered as one of the Elves landed a particularly tricky attack, removing an infected's head followed by slicing another in half without slowing.

"Nice one, Jason!" Brianna called, laughing right along with me. Somehow, she was able to keep these random people's names straight.

The labyrinth was stuffed full of infected beings. I had Bashers and Cats spawning constantly. Well, at least as fast as I could make them. The infected were expending Essence so frequently that I was easily able to continue production! As the fighting progressed, my Essence gain began to outpace my expenditure, filling me with joy... and Essence! I had Wither Cats hunting Mages because—while Mages were hard to damage—if a Wither Cat landed a successful attack, the Mage's access to Mana and Essence was heavily restricted. A short while later, the Mage would collapse. They were alive but unable to access their Centers. This kept them from exploding while taking them out of the fight. Win-win!

"Are you making sure to get all the spores, Cal?" Dani nagged me a bit.

<Yes, yes. We've been over this. I've got it!> When the infected died, they tended to release a cloud of spores, and I was making sure that I absorbed them as fast as possible. It wouldn't do to have my defenders join the attackers.

"You've got it today or sometime next week?"

<I'm a little busy here, Dani.>

"You'll be busier if we lose an Elf!"

<Gah! Here, I'll give them a reprieve!>

In two of the tunnels that connected to the Boss Room, I raised portal arches. They took a few minutes to become fully active, but there was so much loose Essence in the air that they soon began to shimmer and hum softly. Fully active at a speed I had not been able to achieve before, the deadly traps were ready!

The infected could still see through the boiling air and so had no idea that they were running into the backside of an active portal. In another tunnel, I placed a row of Assimilators along the ceiling and had them fire shards of stone and blasts of fire as continuously as possible. The hanging Assimilators went to work immediately, killing several infected that made their way into the tunnel.

The unending stream of infected began pouring into the shimmering space of the open portals, their deaths silent but for the spray of meat slapping against the nearest surfaces. The group as a whole moved faster into their impending death while the ones at the front struggled, trying to avoid the deadly light. Sadly for them, the infected in the rear were pushing the mass of bodies forward, noticing that there was room to move again.

<Fifty dead in two seconds! They're still coming, too!> I crowed. The Essence in their Centers was mingling with my own, bringing me ever closer to my next ranking. Hundreds of deaths were slapping against my senses every minute, and I grew more powerful by the moment.

"Are you doing okay, Cal?" Dani flew around me, staring at me as if she could tell with her vision if I were starting to go insane from the influx of power.

<I am doing *amazingly*,> I reassured her with a wide mental grin. Which, now that I think about it, may not have confirmed my sanity in her mind.

"I'm worried."

<What? Why?>

Dani paused, looking at the enormous death toll in the dungeon. "I think it is only a matter of time before a Mage dies in here. I have no idea what might happen in that case... will you move directly into the Mage rank? Will you only get their Essence? Will you die from the sudden gain? What if..."

<I have a plan, Dani.>

This seemed to throw her off. "You *do*? What?"

<I'm going to put the Mana into a bag and save it for later!> I told her cheerfully, and I suspected she began to question my sanity again. <Seriously! I made a dimensional bag, a 'pocket space' that is totally empty. There is nothing in it except for an exit, but that is a one-way door. *I* can make it two-way, letting it flow back to me, but I won't until I am ready!>

"And you are... *sure* it will work?" Dani asked in a skeptical tone.

I turned a bit red. <Well, it should work in theory. The transfer of energy, as long as I am not trying to make it stop existing, should allow for an unoccupied space to contain said energy. It will not dissipate nor will it move into an alternative form as it has nothing that can act upon it.>

"It's a what?" Dani spun in place, trying to understand what I was saying.

<Don't worry too much. It is a theory I heard about the Elven conservation of energy. The idea let me build the portals much more efficiently than I had thought I would be able to. Basically, in that space there is nothing, and so the energy—in this case Mana—will remain there, unchanging, until acted upon

by an outside force—which can *only* be me, since I'll bind it to myself.> I tried to tell her a bit more, but she cut me off and went to kill something. <What? What did I say?>

Snowball started moving in different attack patterns as Dani took over his movements. Dani went for weak points like throats and joints, whereas Snowball usually just mauled whoever got near him. It seemed she was not going to answer my question. Ah well.

I gauged the amount of Essence I was accumulating. So far, the majority of dying creatures were in the D-ranks. They did not give me much Essence overall, but a constant drop in a bucket will still fill it up eventually! I began devoting more attention to refining what Essence I was gaining. My cultivation pattern allowed me to passively and efficiently remove the corruption I was accumulating, but directly and actively removing it was even faster. I was moving through the C-ranks quickly, as I had already reached C-rank four!

A fort was breached on my third floor, and soon, the death toll began increasing yet again. Most of the attackers were too weak to do much damage, but their huge numbers allowed C-ranked and even B-ranked infected to attack without warning. When the first C-ranked defender died, it felt like a lightning bolt had struck me! Essence shot into my Core, swiftly swirling into the hole in my aura. My mind's construct of a galaxy of cultivation lit up with points of brilliant Essence appearing in the void!

The fighting above raged on while my Elven guards mercilessly slaughtered the few infected that made it into my room. The fighters on the third floor were holding up well, protected as they were by the forts. I was feeling very good about their chances of survival until a massive blast of Mana slammed into the mountaintop above my dungeon. It was strange, and I soon understood the issue; it was undirected Mana! When the Mages above had detonated their Centers, the freed Mana began reacting according to its nature. All Mana was accumulated by forcing Essence into a concept, a law of the world. The Mana above was attempting to re-shape the world in its image, causing catastrophic damage.

One of the types of Mana must have been a gravity derivative because everything above was being sucked into a gravity well and slammed against the ground with the force of a falling star. What was currently impacting the mountain and reducing it to rubble? Birds. Flying overhead, their mass in the gravity well was enough to dig ten-foot holes into the rock. The real issue arrived when a quagmire of Mana was sucked in, impacting the Celestial quartz and shattering the rock holding it in place with a huge outburst of power.

The quartz that had been directly Inscribed by the Runescript was nearly unaffected—Runes were *quite* durable when made properly—but the small portion of the quartz reinforced with celestial Essence that *did* break sent a shockwave of concentrated power outward, killing any infected within a dozen feet. The huge plate of minerals smashed forty feet to the dungeon floor, breaking off the activation sequence of the Inscription. The remaining Runes were intact but now useless because the bridge to their power was removed. That was the *good* news. The bad news was that there was now an opening the infected could pour into, increasing how many could enter the dungeon at a time.

<Well, Dale, it's been a pleasure, but I don't think you are gonna make it,> I cheerily thought my good-byes at the fragile human.

DALE

"You are way too happy about that," Dale muttered, getting an odd look from the people around him, who were all exceedingly somber.

"How are you so *clean*?" Hans glared jealously at his friend. "My clothes have poop on them, Dale. *Poop*. You don't even have *blood* on you!"

Dale laughed at his overly cleanly friend and demonstrated. He threw a punch into an infected person who got too close, blasting its face into meaty chunks. A bit of gore got on to him, but waving his battle gauntlet near it sent it zipping away to land on someone else. "Fluid repulsion Rune." Dale chuckled smugly at the angry look sent his way by the other—now slightly filthier—defenders. "Seriously, though, I have a feeling that things are about to get worse."

Hans made a face. "What tipped you off? The ground shaking or the underground thunder?"

"Definitely the ground shaking."

"Cheeky brat." Hans ducked a wild swing from a weak once-human, retaliating with a blow that removed the creature's head.

The number of attackers started to swell, increasing until they were literally crawling over each other in an attempt to fill the room with wriggling bodies. Dale was worried that they would be overrun—but soon had a bit more to be concerned about.

As the press of bodies became too intense, the weaker infected were pinned to the ground. After a few moments of being walked on, they gave up and shattered their Cores. Their suicidal assault blew holes in the attacking line. Chunks of stone began raining down as the walls and floor were damaged. Fire filled the air, and chaos reigned supreme!

"We need to make sure there aren't too many of them on the walls at one time!" Rose screamed over the hubbub. "If they pack in, they'll blow us all to the abyss!"

<There are Mages approaching your position. Best of luck!>

Dale was amazed at the amount of death that had followed the relatively weak cultivators shattering their Centers. In the confined space, the blasts had been far more effective at tearing apart bodies than anything he had been able to muster.

"Dale! Move!" Tom cried out, tackling Dale away from the wall as a form blasted a small section of it to bits.

Tom cried out in pain as his good arm was grabbed through the opening and he began to be drug out of the safe area.

"Tom!" Rose screamed, racing forward. The defenders moved together and began a painful tug-of-war using Tom's body as the rope. Tom screamed as the defenders won with a roar and a jerk, pulling off the arm of the creature that had been gripping him.

"Anyone need a hand?" Tom panted, then chuckled. "I... ha-ha... I got a spare arm now!"

There were chuckles all around as people went back to defending. Someone called out, "I wouldn't use that one; you have no idea where it might have been!"

"Looks like we don't need to give you a hand."

"Seems you have a good *hand*le on things!"

"Yikes, this fight is getting out of hand!"

Rose shuddered. "You all need to *stop*." Her statement was met with laughs. The laughing turned into loud cheering as

Tom used the scavenged arm to beat a creature to death while the Dwarves worked to fix the wall and reinforce it.

"There we go! I am at thirty-eight!" Tom called out with a grin on his face. "I'm doing better than all of you with one hand tied behind my... oh, right." He grinned as people laughed, wiggling his stump.

Dale was struck by inspiration. "A platinum bonus to whoever gets the most kills! And after this, drinks are on me for a *week*!" A roar of approval met his words, and the flagging spirits of the fighters were rejuvenated. Arrows, blades, darts from blowguns, and all sorts of artillery flew into the crowd, killing the bestial ex-sentients at a distance.

As the *things* closed in on the fort, the defenders activated dozens of different techniques. Blood rose from the ground and formed whirling blades that tore chunks of meat from anything they touched. Shards of stone zipped into the melee. Apparitions appeared and flew into the ranks, killing without leaving a mark. One Mage released some kind of gas that only moved among the enemy ranks, not doing anything until he snapped his fingers. Then the whole group it had engulfed seemed to turn to dust and scattered on the floor. A bleeding Frank whispered *stop* repeatedly, targeting individual combatants. They would slow, then stop, finally detonating and taking out groups around themselves.

"I'm counting *all* of those as mine," Frank stated calmly as some people jeered.

"Of *course* you are, Franky." Hans patted him on the back, leaving a bloody handprint. "We all know you need the *money*, right?" Frank glared at him and shrugged.

Even with the wholesale slaughter happening on the killing ground, the infected were still coming, even more dangerous now that the weakest of them were dying off.

"Oh, abyss no," Dale heard a soft voice say near him. He turned to see the swordsman Nez looking into the crowd. Nez pulled in a gasp of air. "Don't worry, I've got this one." He moved as close as he could to the wall, taking a defensive stance and breathing deeply. Just as he sharply inhaled, a thunderous boom began shaking the walls.

Dale had to blink rapidly to clear his vision, blinded by a massive, writhing column of lightning that had formed a continuous stream from an infected Mage. The path of it was still burning in the air as the Mage attempted to channel it into the defenders. At the halfway point, the path acquired a sharp turn, pulsating toward Nez. There was a beautiful Runescript in the air in front of him, spinning in place as the lightning accumulated on it like flies on feces. Nez was beginning to pant as sweat poured off of him. The wall—inches from his face—was glowing and melting from the plasma burning through it. Any infected that ran through the light had whatever bit of them that touched it lopped off and the wound cauterized even while the flowing electricity killed them.

Nez roared in triumph as the lightning stopped, then slammed his foot down and released the energy back into the crowd. The lightning shattered into individual bolts, arcing to and fro in the seething crowd. The chained lightning expended all of its fury upon the unsuspecting diseased people, killing hundreds in seconds as their hearts stopped. The wall of bodies was motionless for a long minute as Nez sank to the floor.

"Celestial..." Adam whispered. "How did you catch that?"

Nez wheezed in reply, "Lightning... cultivator." He took a sip of offered water. "*You* try cultivating in a thunderstorm without having a way to hold the lightning in place!"

A light seemed to dawn on the faces of the Mages around the small area. Dale felt uncomfortable as they exchanged glances. "What?"

"That Mage should have easily been able to return the favor, catching the lightning and returning it..." Chandra spoke up, trailing off. "They have no defenses in place! Defending against elemental attacks takes *focus* and... they don't *have* any! We have been using more powerful abilities than we needed to, thinking that they would have defenses in place that we would need to break through. With this knowledge, though... we can be *far* more effective."

Rose spoke over the resulting noise, "That didn't kill the Mages! They are getting to their feet out there!" She pointed at bodies that were being tossed to the side as the most powerful infected returned to their feet.

"A little thing like their heart stopping wouldn't stop a Mage!" The portal Mage Justin scoffed, bringing the group's attention to him. "Haven't you ever heard the description of a Mage's body? 'Near physical invulnerability' is not just a saying we use to scare off assassination attempts! Watch and learn." He raised his hands, and after a few seconds of intense concentration, the lightning Mage who had just seemed to come back from the dead dropped dead. Again.

"What did you just do?" Dale whispered in horror as blood leaked from the dead Mage's eyes.

<Oh *abyss* yes!> The next words from me were drowned out by the hubbub of noise that followed.

Justin, not catching the interplay, smugly announced, "I made a small portal in his head and transported his brain a few feet away." He got a few cheers and pats on the back as Dale waited for something horrible to happen.

CHAPTER TWENTY-SIX

<Oh *abyss* yes! Here it comes, Dani! Lightning based Mana, coming towards my Core! Rerouting, opening the holding container now... It's working! Dani. We're set here!> I grunted in pain as a huge mass of Essence from the man slammed into me. Luckily, my chi spiral was up to the task of holding all of it. My chi threads were currently bloated with power; the Essence of over a thousand people was trying to force its way into my Core simultaneously.

<Whew! Wasn't expecting that. I thought Mages only had Mana in them?> I queried Dani, disturbed by this development.

"They do, right until they die. Then a small portion of their Mana is reduced to Essence as their soul separates from their body," Dani explained to me, much to my relief.

<Thank you, my fantastical floating friend!>

She gave me a *look.* "That is far too long for a nickname, and I think you are trying too hard."

<I'll eventually find something you like,> I mumbled petulantly.

"Why not just call me by my name?!" Dani sounded a tad exasperated. "Whatever! Did all of the Mana get into that extradimensional space like you had planned? No leakage?"

<I am pretty sure it did.>

"*Pretty* sure?"

<Yeah, and I'm not exploding, so I think I am okay. I can't double check to see if the *storage* went as planned... if I reopen the space, at least *some* Mana will come out... but all of these deaths are driving me closer and closer toward the B-rankings! I think we need to come up with a plan of action for

making sure that happens smoothly.> My change of topic caught her off guard. She turned, considering what I had just said.

"Do you mean finding a concept to meditate on? Something compatible with your Essence type? That will be difficult. You have pure Essence, and I am not certain what kind of Mana you will be able to bind with..." Dani trailed off, both of us deep in thought.

<Hey, Dani?>

"Yeah, Cal?"

<After this little war, how about we take a vacation? Ignore the adventurers unless they get really close and just spend some quality time together?> She started turning pink as I spoke. <Realistically, most of what we have been doing has been fighting or learning. I've been learning concepts; you've been training to fight as every creature in here. I'd like to learn more about your past. Where you came from and so forth.> I almost felt embarrassed, but we were going to be together a long, *long* time.

Dani sounded a bit shy. "That sounds like a plan, Cal. The last few months have been rather stressful, huh?"

<They have. I know that I am usually focused on the things going on, but I know that I need to work on helping you as well. Maybe we can find a way for you to travel for a while?>

"I would like that! Not too long, of course!" Dani paused mid-chuckle. "Cal! I just realized! The concept you could bind your Essence to, the concept to bring you into the B-ranks!"

<What? What?!>

"Oh, this is just perfect." Dani started to vibrate, she was laughing so hard. "Cal, what is the difference between your Essence and *everyone* else's?"

<Um. It is really pure?>

"Right!" she shouted, startling a nearby Elf. "And as we know, as Essence becomes purer, it gets closer to its true state..." She trailed off leadingly.

<Are you saying that I should be a Quintessence Mage?> I paused, realizing the joke. <So I will transform my Essence into the... *concept* of Essence?>

"*Right?*" Dani could barely contain her glee. "*Right?* It would be totally unique! There has never been a Quintessence Mage before! Well, that I know of anyway!"

<Awesome! Dani, that is hilarious and brilliant!>

"Here is how to begin. Focus on the concept, in this case, Essence. Feel the Essence, meditate really hard on what Essence actually *is*. As you approach the B-ranks, if your affinity for Quintessence is high enough, you will begin to understand it in ways that are unexplainable to anyone else. In your mind, during your breakthrough, you will form a bond to Quintessence and learn its true potential."

<Do you think I have a high enough affinity?> I hesitantly questioned.

"I hope so. You are the only being that I can think of that could do it." Dani coughed. "Except Dale, at this point, I suppose."

<Would that be an issue?>

"Well, not really. It is just that... the more Mages of a certain type there are, the more likely that there will be someone to counter whatever you throw at them. Two Mages that follow the same cultivation path are basically at a stalemate against each other."

<Well, he is a long way away from the Mage ranks. I'm getting closer by the second!> I announced proudly. I *would* be the first Quintessence Mage. Dale might never find out that this was an option, so I may stay the *only* one.

"Well, hopefully everything is as it should be. The Mage trials are difficult, and if you aren't suited to the Mana type, it could break your mind..."

<...> I sighed, a completely unnecessary noise, as I didn't breathe. <You know, you could have just kept that tidbit to yourself.>

A scream reverberated down the tunnel, returning my attention to the battles raging. I frowned in concern as I realized that a few defenders had been affected by spores while my attention was elsewhere. They didn't know it yet, but if something weren't done soon, they would sink into madness.

<Dale.> I waited for a response.

"*A bit busy here,*" came the reply. "*You promised not to distract me in battle, remember?*"

<This is important. I need to talk to your alchemist about a cure or at least an antidote for the spores. I can provide materials and anything else he needs, but a few of the defenders have been infected,> I told him earnestly.

Dale imperceptibly paused in his fighting. "*Why are you offering to help?*"

<If you all die, I am doubtful that other people will feel secure coming here. Total self-interest here.> I blatantly ignored the fact that I was also in danger from these things.

"*Can't you bother Minya with this?*" Dale's thoughts were filled with frustration.

<I would, but she is killing things a lot more efficiently than you. Taking her from the front lines would leave a big hole in the defenses. Taking you... well, let's just say you won't be missed too much.> I looked at the people around him. <Except as a laundry service, perhaps.>

"*You are such an ass.*"

Dale told the people around him that he was moving back. Just as I predicted, there was almost no change in the quantity of dying infected. He moved to the rear where healers, the apothecary, and the alchemist were doing their best to get people patched up.

"I need to talk to you!" Dale called to the alchemist. The man in question glared and told Dale off for interrupting him. He stopped grumbling at Dale's next words. "I may have a way to formulate an antidote."

"Fine. You have five minutes to explain how *you*, an untrained, know-nothing, non-alchemist can help me find a cure for this before we all die. Also, without a lab or any kind of equipment." The man glared at Dale, seemingly ready to jump down his throat at the first mistake.

<Tell him we have all the equipment he needs if he can describe it accurately enough. Say you can also get him any material he needs if I know how to make it. I also have a *deep* understanding of the disease itself, as well as how it interacts with humans and animals at this point,> I instructed Dale.

He repeated verbatim what I said, and the alchemist—though skeptical—nodded and followed Dale to the back wall of the fort.

They pushed against the wall where I told them, opening the Goblin respawn room. The alchemist looked around in confusion.

"Why haven't we been using this room for the wounded? It is far more defensible!"

"I just found it," Dale told him honestly. He pointed at the jumble of alchemy equipment that I had whipped up. "What else do you need?"

The alchemist looked at the equipment. "First, I need to make sure that you can get me what you promised. Let's start with rare material. I need two strong-type Beast Cores, a pound of powdered aluminum, and an alembic."

<Have him describe the alembic and its function,> I told Dale. He did, and I was able to create what I hope would be close to what the man was talking about. I had Dale open the top of an oversized chest in the corner of the room. To get around the concentration of auras in the area, I had a chute attached to the back of the chest that I could drop things into. This setup also had given me a good idea for a new trap!

"Here you go!" Dale cheerfully told the incredulous alchemist, handing over the requested items.

The man looked at the gear in wonder. "We may actually have a chance to..." He rushed to start setting up his lab, calling out for various things. I have no idea why he wanted some of the things, but I was watching raptly. There was one point where he asked for Elves ear but had a disgusted look on his face as Dale handed over the dripping flesh.

"What?" Dale was taken aback at the look on the craftsman's face.

"Riiiiight..." He sighed. "I'll be more specific. Elves ear is an herb, not a *literal* ear. I've seen it upstairs. You may also call it 'mountain lavender'?"

<Oh, that's easier.> I dropped a bag of the herb down.

Next, there was an intense interview, where Dale was asked exceedingly detailed questions about the fungus. Dale had a delightfully confused look on his face as I answered through him. The poor lad really had no idea what he was saying, just repeating as best as he could.

"...and I soiled myself," Dale repeated, before turning red at the realization of what he had uttered.

"Oh. Um." The alchemist took a step back. "Well... battle isn't for everyone..."

"What the shit, Cal," Dale muttered, choosing poor phrasing in my opinion.

<Just trying to lighten the mood.> I chuckled at his embarrassment

"I need crushed topaz, but if you want to go clean yourself first..."

"I'm fine!" Dale snapped, grabbing a bag of topaz and nearly throwing it at the man. The alchemist looked at Dale, nodded, and began calling out ingredients whilst continuing his questioning.

Dani kept me up to date on the goings-on of the fight. After a small reminder from her, I returned to using a portion of my willpower focusing on collecting and eradicating any spores that the infected released. The battle was not going well for the defenders at this point. Though they were killing hundreds every few minutes, there were *thousands* more making their way down the tunnels.

An exhausting hour passed, the alchemist squeezing information out of me that I had no idea was relevant. Dale was hoarse from the constant stream of speaking and looked like he would rather be fighting mindless humans.

"Now we wait for the distillation to complete." The alchemist sat down with a heavy sigh. "I don't know how much this will make, but it *is* a start. We need someone to test it on as well."

"How sure are you about this?" Dale asked the first question in an hour that wasn't from me.

A slow shake of the head. "This will end up being one of two things. I am sure it will have an effect on those poor souls, but in what way? If it works as intended, it will be an antidote for the fungus, killing it without harming the host... I suppose it may

Page | 356

simply be an effective way to kill them quickly." I perked up at hearing this. "Otherwise... it will end up being a reagent."

"A reagent? What do you mean by that?" Dale looked at the fluid flowing slowly through glass pipes.

"When an Inscription is powered, certain things in the pattern can allow the Rune to have additional or more powerful effects. A reagent is added for a single-use 'effect', whereas a catalyst is used to reduce the Mana or Essence needed to power the Inscription." The alchemist took a deep, shuddering breath. "If this turns out to be a reagent, we will need a huge amount of celestial Essence—or a moderate amount of Mana—along with a compatible Rune for it to have any effect at all. The process will most likely kill anything with the aural signature of the disease."

"Let's hope it's an antidote which will simply be a cure then." Dale patted the man on the shoulder.

Another head shake. "Has our luck ever been that good?"

DALE

Dale left the alchemist to his fussing over heat levels, preferring to be in the thick of battle. He surveyed the dungeon, and it appeared that the only forts remaining were the one housing the Nobles and this one. He had to stop himself from sinking into depression at the thought that everyone had stayed on his command. He shuddered for a moment and inhaled sharply. The knowledge that your mistakes led to the death of others was the price of command, and he would do his duty by joining his vassals in combat. Falling apart would help no one except the dungeon.

Dale moved forward, replacing a much-relieved, exhausted man on the wall. His fighting style was simplistic with these beasts, draw back a fist, straight punch. Draw back a fist, punch. Pull, punch. The infected didn't bother to defend; they were one hundred percent attack. Dale chuckled at the thought that his combat instructor would actually approve; he had made Dale punch like this into a wooden post five hundred times to end every session. Constantly drilling the simplest moves was the best way to improve the foundation of your art, at least according to the crotchety old Moon Elf.

As he was putting down another rabid humanoid, Dale realized that he was seeing a dark haze of Essence in the air. It reacted to his cultivation, so he attempted to draw it in. For the first time in his life, he unwittingly cultivated infernal Essence. He stopped fighting in shock as the Essence did everything it could to be absorbed by him. When he started drawing it in, the dark power *poured* into his Center, attempting to overwhelm whatever else was there. Only the fact that the taint was drawn into a small Core to the side of his Center saved him from being overwhelmed by the tendril of corruption.

"Dale?" Hans was standing next to him. "Are you okay? It looks like there is infernal Essence being drawn into you. Did an affinity channel get forced open or something?"

Dale hesitated to respond, then realized that if he couldn't trust his teammate with his secrets, he shouldn't trust him with his life on a daily basis. "I actually think I have... all of them open?" he stated weakly.

Hans looked deeper into Dale, then gasped and took a step back in shock. "You're a *Beast*?"

"What? No!" Dale reached out to reassure his friend, patting him on the arm. "I do somehow have a Core embedded around my Center, though. I think it has something to do with the Beast we fought a while back. After that, all my affinity channels were open."

Hans inspected Dale's pure Essence. "How have you not been overwhelmed by corruption? If they are all open, you should be absolutely *sick*."

"Watch." Dale opened himself up to the infernal Essence in the room, and Hans watched as it sank into him and vanished.

"Wow! Some kind of... where did it go?" Hans was poking Dale in the chest, as though that would help explain the situation.

Dale smacked away the offending finger. "Stop that. It goes into a small Beast Core to the side of my Center."

"How have you been cultivating?" Hans waved away the answer. "Right, pure Essence in here. On the next rest rotation, I want you to open all of your affinity channels and suck in everything. Essence and corruption. We need to find your limits so that we can set up a training plan when this is all over."

Smiling at his friend, Dale nodded. "I'm loving the optimism."

"Better than planning to die!" Hans reached out and stabbed an infected man that was getting too close, punching his dagger through the man's forehead as easily as pushing a knife though unenchanted parchment. He chuckled. "I'm going to enjoy you having to purchase enough alcohol to make a Mage drunk."

Dale felt a shiver of apprehension at these words. How much booze would it take to make that happen? He looked up as he heard a now-familiar explosion; somewhere in the dungeon, an infected had ruptured its Center.

"Shards! Hit the floor!" a voice rang out, followed by shrapnel from damaged rock pinging off the defenses hard enough to gouge chunks of rock. The unlucky few who didn't respond fast enough fell screaming as holes were torn in their bodies. The Mages hit released a short grumble as their clothes were torn a bit more.

Dale waved at the man that had called out the warning. "A fifty silver bonus to you, sir! Teamwork is the only way we are getting out of here. Nice work!" His praise made the man swell with pride, and soon, warnings were ringing out across the fortification.

"The line is getting thin on the left wall! Get some archers up there!"

"Big-ass infected charging! Mage! Mage!" *Boom!* "Thank you, Mage!"

"We need some relief in the center! They haven't had a break in hours!"

"Who needs a break? We've got this!" A roar of agreement rose from the center of the line.

Hans threw an arm around Dale's neck. "Look at that. You're inspiring! Who would have guessed?"

"Rude," Dale responded, pushing Hans away and punching an infected that was scaling the wall.

"Oh, gods!" a man suddenly screamed. "I can feel it! I'm infected!"

Hans looked askance at Dale. "Erm. Want me to go check on that?"

"No, I'll do it. We needed a test subject for... a... thing." Dale looked at his nonplussed friend. "I'll go now, how about?"

"Sure?" Hans tried to suppress a grin. "Just so you know, people don't really like their liege-lord experimenting on them..."

"It's for a cure, I'm not exper... dang it, Hans," Dale sputtered as Hans started laughing at him. Dale hurried over after confirming that his team was holding up well. He walked up to the small group looking at the man who was slowly sprouting mushrooms. "Come with me, the alchemist has been working on a potential antidote."

The man looked up, fury beginning to build in his eyes. "*You!* I'm the leader of *The Collective*, and you ordered us around like *animals!* If I turn, I'm coming for you first!"

Dale was shocked by the anger directed at him but didn't let it show. "Nick, correct? If the cure works, then everything will be fine. Don't worry, if you turn too quickly, we'll put you down *before* you become a threat."

Nick's face drained of color as he realized he was being threatened. He was used to people of lower cultivation rankings cowering before him, and the look of total unconcern on Dale's face made him quail inside.

They moved over to where the alchemist was putting the finishing touches on his concoction. He looked up as they entered the room. "Ah! Do we have a volunteer?"

Dale hesitated a moment. "He was kinda volun-told."

"A death for research is better than a death by devolving into a ravenous creature. Hopefully, you will even survive!" The alchemist didn't seem to notice nor would he have cared about Nick's unhappy face.

A thick sludge streamed into a vial, and when it was full, the alchemist began to put it into a thin blade, similar to the style of injecting daggers that Hans used.

<Dale, get some of that before he uses it all! I can make a whole lot more than he can in a limited time frame!> Dale ducked as my words entered his mind; the others looked at him in startlement.

"Sorry, stress," Dale hurried to explain.

The alchemist leaned closer to Nick, whispering, "He made a mess earlier..."

"Stop that!" Dale commanded, face flushing. "I need a drop of that liquid. In the chest here, please."

"I can't just waste this potion!" came the indignant reply. "Who knows if we have enough time to make more?!"

"Sir," Dale interrupted the tirade. "Please don't fight this. I promise it is for a good reason. Have I let you down yet?" A grumble came, and a tiny droplet of the concentrated solution was dropped into the chest.

"Happy now?"

<Yes.>

"Yes, that should do it," Dale affirmed on my behalf.

The alchemist turned and jabbed the short dagger into the muscle tissue of Nick's thigh. Nick yelped and started to take a swing at the man but stopped himself as the potion hit his system. Nick went pale and dropped to the floor convulsing.

"Blast and damnation!" The alchemist stomped on the ground. "Hold his head, or he will damage himself!" No one made a move to touch the infected man writhing on the ground. "Oh, right, the disease. He should be fine, then."

"What went wrong?" Dale asked as the alchemist began mumbling about the quantity of potion remaining.

The man slumped and sighed. "This turned out to be a reagent. We will need to fill the lines of a Rune with this, then channel celestial Essence or Mana into it."

"We can do that!" Dale determinately turned, preparing to call the clerics and celestial Mages.

"No point." The alchemist shook his head. "We would need a massive Rune, an *Inscribed* Rune, and we just don't have that kind of time. An enchantment won't work. The reagent would be used up as it was applied instead of in a quick, evenly activated sequence."

<Can we use a smaller one?>

"Why couldn't we use a smaller one?" Dale questioned the reasoning presented to him.

"The area it affects would be too small to be of any real use. A few would be stopped, but an arrow or three can do *that*." The alchemist scoffed.

Silence reigned in the room, at least as much silence as could be garnered while the world seemed to be ending.

<Fine, I have had enough! Time to fix things. *Again*. Ugh.>

CHAPTER TWENTY-SEVEN

<Dale, ask him what kind of Rune it has to be,> I directed. Dale relayed my words, which had the alchemist rubbing his patchy beard.

"Well... I suppose really any Rune that is specifically anti-infernal. This fungicide should do the rest." He waved the small remaining amount of potion around.

Dale chimed in, "How much of that will we actually need in order to activate a Rune large enough to be effective?"

"Enough for at least an even coat," came the calculated reply.

Easy enough. I had been working on examining the pattern of the potion that had been put in the chest. At this point, I had almost... done! I fully understood the potion and how to make it. My method of creation was far less time intensive, and a *thud* announced the arrival of an oak cask in the treasure chest of the room.

"What was that?"

They lifted the lid and opened the cask, revealing a large jar of the precious fluid.

The alchemist looked around with bright eyes. "I never want to leave this room again," he muttered under his breath.

<That could be arranged,> I muttered in a completely non-threatening way. Dale still glared around the room.

"Could we test the potion with this?" Dale reached into his tattered, bloodstained shirt and withdrew an amulet. This amulet had the first Rune that I had ever learned, a celestial-attuned Inscription that would weaken the bonds of infernal influence when powered by Essence.

"I see no reason why not." They moved over to the weakly thrashing leader of The Collective and waited as the alchemist carefully poured an even coat of fluid along the lines. He started to lean down but, with a frown, looked around. "I don't suppose any of you are celestial cultivators?"

Head shakes all around.

"I'll go get someone." Dale took off at a run, grabbing Adam and sprinting back with a breathless explanation. Adam gingerly took the amulet from the alchemist and, with a quick prayer, thrust it against the spasming man's chest. Activating the Inscription with a burst of Essence, Adam was knocked back as a ripple of celestial Essence interacted with the reagent and expanded in a sphere from the Rune.

Nick screamed as the light flowed over him, and the visible mushrooms withered and died. They tore themselves out of their host, leaving gaping holes as the semi-intelligent parasite tried to save itself. The light seemed to hunt down every last bit, spearing even the smallest speck and converting it to ash.

Adam applied his Essence in a different way, working to heal Nick before he bled out on the floor. He looked around as he spoke, "That took a lot more Essence to activate than it ever has before. Did you say that you were planning to make a *larger* version?"

"Yes, the hope there was that we would be able to stop the infection by creating a cure, killing only the mushrooms." Dale glanced at the pool of blood around Nick. "It appears that this process will be a bit more... *fatal* than we had originally hoped."

Adam looked surprised. "You thought this could fix them without killing them?"

"I had hoped," Dale stated glumly. "That hope is gone now, though. Nick here was barely infected, and the *cure* nearly finished him off."

The alchemist chimed in. "This Rune was pretty much our only hope. The area it affects is too small to be of any use in combat, though. We will just have to do our best to survive."

<Did you not hear the determination in my voice, Dale? I think I have a solution for you.> I was getting a bit cross about them making decisions based on incomplete data.

"*Do tell*," Dale thought at me sarcastically.

<We have a few options. The first is that you clear a large area of anything not sworn to me, and I build a Rune on it. This includes people and the infected. Then your celestial Essence users would sacrifice their entire cultivation for the Runic activation,> I began, only to be cut off.

"*I don't see that happening. Most of them would seriously rather die than give up decades worth of Essence,*" Dale rebutted in frustration.

<Fine. Then you could have everyone here swear a binding oath to me, so I could ignore their auras and build the Rune here,> I offered hopefully. I could use some new material-gatherers.

"I *would rather die than give you that kind of access to people,*" Dale returned unhelpfully.

I snorted. <Well, that is just *mean*. Fine! The last option is to go collect the celestial quartz that was knocked into the Boss Room of the first floor. That is stuffed full of Essence and even has the appropriate Rune!>

Dale sighed in frustration. People were dying!

"*I don't know if you were listening, but the reagent has to go on an* inactive *Rune.*"

<Yes, exactly my point. There is a Mana storm raging outside, something hit the quartz hard enough to knock it loose from its stone setting, and it fell into the dungeon. The activation portion of the Rune broke off from the strike, so the Rune is sitting inert,> I spoke to him a *tad* condescendingly. He really needed to listen to me more.

Dale perked up, a bit shocked at the information I was freely giving him. He relayed my story to the others, and the alchemist agreed that it was their best shot. The man also danced a bit when we told him it was an option. They quickly gathered the leaders in the area, asking for help in gathering a group to get to the powerful Runescripted quartz.

Frank was not at all interested. "Why would we do that? We're holding the area, and they can't last forever! We have a defensible area, supplies, and enough people to survive the horde!"

Dale was taken aback at the Guild Leader's vehemence. The other Mages of the group agreed with Frank's words.

Adam boldly joined the conversation, doing his best not to stammer in the face of these powerful people, "That is inaccurate. While we *are* holding out for the time being, almost a quarter of our people have received serious injuries. We have been able to patch up most of them, but we are running out of potions and Essence to make this happen. The people injured are weakened, and they will be exhausted for at least a few days. That increases their chances of being re-injured significantly."

Frank waved his hand. "We can make it *just fine*. We've killed thousands. The end is in sight!"

"How many Mages were in Spotterton?" Dale had a flash of insight.

Amber glanced at him. "Dozens. Maybe as many as fifty?"

"And how many have we seen in this fight? Just the known ones from Spotterton?" Dale questioned leadingly.

Sometimes it was better to let powerful people think that they were the ones making the important decisions.

"Oh, abyss," Chandra cursed. "We've seen a bare handful."

Frank powered on, "Maybe they all were the ones to rupture their Centers up above!"

Dale sighed. "Frank, you are making good points, but we can't rely on 'I hope so' right now. We have a proven method of defeating this enemy, and I feel that we need to take this chance."

"Frank. You... you have something on your arm," Amber announced in a tremulous voice, pointing at his left arm.

"What are you...?" Frank swatted at his arm, wincing when he hit a small mushroom. "Oh no."

"You have seemed a bit more... aggressive." Chandra took a step away from him.

Frank looked at Dale, eyes wild. "You said something about a proven cure?"

"Better, I've *tested* it. The cure takes a large amount of celestial Essence, though. We can't continuously use the process on individual people," Adam spoke again.

Frank looked at his arm, deeply troubled.

"I'll go." Frank's voice cracked as another mushroom began to sprout from his elbow. "I can't order other people to go, though. It would not be right, and we still need defenders."

"I'll go as well," Dale stated, hushing the people that started to object. "I have access to information that you just... don't. I really cannot explain." His words had all of the Mages in the room *look* at him. Several did a double take, and a few gasped.

"You... you *Beast!* What did you do with Dale?" Chandra's hands and eyes lit up with Mana.

"I'm still me." Dale tried to remain calm, eyeing the deadly glow. "Also, if I understand my situation correctly, I am immune to the disease."

More gasping and a few suspicious looks were his reward for honesty.

<Well... not technically, but for all real purposes, I guess that works. If you don't mind me chopping bits off of you,> I slowly agreed.

"*I mind. But as long as you only do it to* infected *bits and you grow them back, I think it'll be fine,*" Dale agreed to my statement and also found the loophole I was trying to use.

<Darn, I was hoping you would agree to let me eat you when this was over.> I laughed as his face twisted.

"Immune... and there is a Core in your system. How did we not see this?" Frank muttered, still mistrustful of this new situation.

"I *really* can't say," Dale apologetically muttered.

"There is going to be some long talks when this is all over, Dale," Chandra threatened. "You'd better get your story straight by then."

"I'll see what we can do," Dale promised, then quickly tried to recant his slip of the tongue. "What *I* can do."

"Fine. You still need more people. You need to make it up the stairs, through the horde, and apply the reagent. That isn't a two-person job." Amber's voice was harsh and filled with frustration.

"I'll only take volunteers," Dale agreed with Frank on that particular subject. They went out and asked for people to brave the conditions, but the area stayed near-silent. Dale's group all stepped forward bravely, but no other Mages or regular cultivators offered their services. They had already agreed that the rest of the council would stay as a last line of defense.

<Wow. What brave people you have in your little city,> I told Dale sarcastically. <I'll bolster your ranks then. Clear your pet alchemist out of that room, and please don't kill your helpers.>

I set to work creating a full contingent of Goblins, not giving them Mithril but still filling their weapons and armor with powerful enchantments. That way, if they were killed when they stepped out, a human wouldn't make off with a nearly indestructible material.

Dani interrupted my concentration, "I'm going too, Cal. I don't trust these people to get the job done without some serious Goblin power."

<Dani, no...> She was already following her secret tunnels to the next floor. I sighed; I try so hard to keep her safe, and she just throws herself back into the fight. Oh well. <If you feel you must go, I am going to be setting your armor and weapons to the maximum.>

"Neat." she chimed, circling the spawn room as I formed the Goblin Amazon. I didn't bother to set her armor to the side; I formed a seamless set of aluminum around her towering form. Dani entered the huge Mob and took a deep breath as I flooded the aluminum armor with Essence, pleased as it darkened to a silvery-purple. Mithril. She prepared her weapons and nodded as I swung the door open.

There were a few shouts as a dozen Goblins and one Goblin Amazon entered the area, but they stayed right next to the door and didn't make any hostile moves, so the humans calmed down fairly quickly.

<Dale, I have a matching battle gauntlet for you. Actually, I am equipping your whole group. We are going through the tunnels to a different fort that didn't have the defenses lowered, so hurry up.> I was looking for the best place to move the group to, and I found one closer to the entrance of this floor that wasn't entirely flooded with infected. Just *mostly* flooded.

The group started moving hesitantly past the steel-clad Goblins and *very* cautiously past Dani's over-armored form.

"Wait!" a voice called. "I'm coming with you."

Dale and I looked at the speaker, watching as Nick strolled up to the group. Dale was quite a bit happier about the help than I was. "Alright, Nick! Thank you, any help is greatly appreciated! You'll be well rewarded for your services."

"Yes. I will be," Nick stated flatly.

Hans clapped him on the arm. "Ah, yes. Nothing like being a jackass to make people want to shower you in silver. Well, molten silver. How do you feel about being a statue?"

"Look, I am here to make that cure happen and get the hell out of this deathtrap," Nick growled. "I'm the leader of The Collective! All I was supposed to be doing was making money here, not playing nursemaid to a bunch of incompetents."

"I am coming as well."

"Me too!"

Dale looked back to see both Minya and Nez trying to stare the other down. "Yes, and abyss no. Nez, you're with Adam. Minya, go play with the infected."

"When are you going to let go of your anger toward the dungeon, Dale?" Minya asked scathingly. "The dungeon is just following its nature."

<I usually go by 'he' or Cal,> I stated blandly. <You know what? I suppose you're just trying to protect my identity. Carry on.>

"Minya, if I'm not here, you are the only one that can," he leaned in close and whispered, "talk to the dungeon and get a backup plan. You *need* to stay."

She scrutinized his face. "Is that really the reason you don't want me along?" She crossed her arms.

"No, but it works really well as a reason to *make* you stay," Dale answered, eliciting a squawk of rage from the Mage. She turned and stormed off, fuming.

"That was harsh, Dale." Rose shook her head at Dale's treatment of the lady. "We could have used her help."

"Trust me, we don't want it," Dale firmly stated. "Let's go."

They walked into the room and found a few presents.

I had made a matching battle gauntlet for Dale with a slight variation. Instead of a fluid repulsion Rune on it, I had placed an Essence gathering Rune combined with the draining portion of the demon summoning Rune I had, um, 'acquired' a while back. I was unsure if it would work as intended, but I had run Essence through a different version a while back, and it didn't explode. It was supposed to rip the Essence out of whatever Dale hit and store it in the Core hidden in the folds of fabric. It would drain infernal, water, and earth corruption from Dale to power itself, but that shouldn't be an issue with the taint gathering Cores around his Center.

For Tom, I had made a large chunk of armor. It was basically a greatshield that strapped on to his body. A person with two arms couldn't have worn it at all, so it was perfect for the one-armed barbarian. With this on, he could act as a mobile battering ram! I also made it enchanted so that he wouldn't need to use his personal reserves to use it correctly. I chuckled in merriment when his eyes lit up; he had gotten his warhammer back as well.

He roared in approval. "Today is a glorious day for battle! Perhaps I can fall in combat and join the ranks of the fallen warriors on the fields of heavenly war!"

"Or maybe you could try really hard to survive and keep *us* alive too?" Nick scathingly snarled. Dale started to have second thoughts about this man being on the team.

Rose acquired a bow with a force enhancement enchantment as well as reinforced arrows that wouldn't shatter when the bow fired them. A few arrows were tipped with small jars of explosive fluids, and there was a small collection that had sharpening enchantments for piercing armor.

Adam got a white robe with a fine mesh of Mithril throughout it, well hidden by the cloth. This would stop almost any stabbing weapons but didn't offer too much protection against direct force or blunt weapons. Dale explained to him in a whisper how amazing the robe was, keeping it a secret from the greedy leader of The Collective.

Hans got nothing.

"This is total... why doesn't your mysterious benefactor like me?" Hans whined as he simultaneously twirled four knives across his fingers.

"Shall we?" Dale looked around the nervous faces, ignoring Hans.

They set out, walking along the tunnel to the next fort, nervously listening to the sounds of fighting, wailing, and scraping through the thin stone walls. Periodic explosions transformed the wailing into snarls and screams of pain or fury, but the weeping would soon return to being a constant background noise.

"This is horrifying," Rose whispered, her eyes round with fright.

Dale made a motion at her as the ambient noise lessened a bit on the other side of the wall and querying sounds could be heard. Holding a finger to his lips, Dale pantomimed Rose closing her mouth. The noise picked up on the other side, and the group breathed a collective, silent sigh of relief. Treading carefully, they soon found themselves in a room identical to the one they had begun their journey in.

"It should be safe to quietly talk if you *really* need to." Dale looked around. No takers.

<Ahhh!> I screamed in his mind. Dale jumped, nearly falling and bashing into the wall next to him. Luckily, a huge hand caught and steadied him.

"*Cal? Must you be so... 'funny'?*" Dani thought at me in consternation as she patted Dale on the head.

<I just think Dale is being too serious about this. I believe in you, Dale!> I cheered him on in a falsetto.

"I hate this place," Dale muttered softly.

"It grows on you." Dani patted him on the head again and ruffled his hair. Her voice made the others all stare at her.

Hans asked the question they were all thinking, "You are an intelligent being? I thought you Mobs were mostly animals..."

"I'm smarter than you are, Hans." Dani walked forward to the exit.

Hans gave a panicked look to Dale. "It knows my *name*," he whispered harshly.

Dani threw open the door and charged into battle amidst howls of outrage from the infected. I watched as she plowed into them, a whirling cyclone of blades.

<I'm gonna lock the door behind you so the fort isn't overrun.>

She didn't answer, too caught up in the slaughter.

The remaining people charged into battle, doing their best to clear a route without stopping to try and set up a defensible area. They were surrounded, and their best chance was to charge the stairs. With the loss of only four Goblins, they reached the bottom of the upward spiral. A huge mass of bodies greeted them; this was the choke point of the entering abominations.

"How the abyss are we supposed to get through *that?*" Adam muttered anxiously.

"I'll take care of it," Dani informed them with a growl. "Cover me."

<Dani, I've been using the vents in this area to filter out nitrogen and other gasses from the homogeneous mixture of breathable content->

"Cal, all you told me was to start a really hot fire. Is that still the plan?" Dani rumbled ominously, cutting me off quite rudely.

<Well, yes, I just wanted to let you know *why* this->

Dani grunted and held forward her weapons. Crossing them, she released a gout of fire through a thin film of celestial Essence. Holy fire raged outward, reducing all in its reach to cinders. The fire suddenly roared higher as it reached my prepared area, and a concussive blast resounded, throwing Dani back like a ragdoll. Hans was suddenly in front of her, casually holding out one hand. In front of him was a wall of fire which curled back and away. The fire was only racing up the stairs. The high oxygen content in the area allowed the blaze to burn exponentially hotter than it ever could have under normal circumstances.

The celestial tinged fire moved quickly but consumed all the available air in the tunnel, burning out too quickly to superheat the stone stairs or wall. Dani bellowed, "Go! Go! Go!"

Fresh air was beginning to be pulled up the stair shaft, and they ran forward, propelled by an updraft.

The sentients raced up the stairs, slipping over meaty chunks of semi-seared flesh. I did my best to absorb all of the bodies before they got to them, trying to ease their passage. Scores of low-cultivation infected had died, but a few lived through the initial blast. Most of those were writhing on the floor, burned, blinded, and dying, but a few were standing up, trying to breathe the de-oxygenated air. Those few took swipes at the running group but were killed in passing, much to my delight.

I looked at where they were running and swore vigorously. <Dani, unfortunately, that blast cleared the way for a few Mages to wander to the Boss Room. Do you want me to open a Basher warren and hide you while they pass?>

Dani paused, causing those behind her to bounce off of her armored form with a curse. Her guttural voice uttered, "How many?"

<A good handful. They seem more confused than the low-level infected. They didn't sprint down the stairs right away or seem to focus on an area to target. I'm betting that if they noticed you, they would be much more active...>

"Open a passage, Cal," Dale chimed in, speaking aloud for his party's benefit. "We don't have the strength to fight a large group of Mages."

I gave a tiny mental nod, and the stairs in front of them slid open, revealing a few startled Impalers and a Glitterflit. Dani pushed past them and sat in the small room. The others joined her, though Tom began having trouble breathing when the walls closed around them.

"I do not like this at all," Tom whispered, earning a glare from the people hushing him.

<The Mages are beginning to descend. Oh crap, who pushed the Impaler out into the–>

A blast of Mana shook the stairway, vaporizing the Impaler and putting cracks in the stonework in all directions. The attacking Mage screamed, then began glowing and charged down the stairs. I thought that this was finally the end of the line for Dale's group, but the Mage ran right past them, never turning around.

<Huh. I guess he thinks there is more prey down there.> There was, so it was a fair assumption. The other Mages saw the first run off and chased him at high speed, eager to participate in some good ol' fashioned killin'. They raced down the stairs, pounding their feet in a deadly staccato. All of them passed the hiding place of the group except the last, whose feet burst through the stairs and tripped him. He bounced headfirst off the floor.

The Mage stood up slowly, growling... and continued down the stairs with a howl.

<The room is filling up again! Also, easily a dozen Mages just entered the dungeon. You are only going to have a short while until they reach the Boss Room. Move! Go now!> I barked instructions at Dale and Dani.

They nodded and started moving. Tom let out a sigh of relief as they left the enclosed area and rushed upwards.

<In case you wanted to know, the Mages that passed you have reached the floor and are starting to attack the fort. I need to concentrate down there for a bit. Good luck!>

"We need to hurry!" Dale told the others as they reached the top of the stairs. He ran into Dani's still form. "That isn't good," a nearly inaudible whimper left his lips.

CHAPTER TWENTY-EIGHT

The room, utterly filled with infected, went quiet for a moment, the collective sobbing of the crowd postponed before howls of rage filled the air. Reacting to the sound of prey being found, dozens of infected dropped through the opening in the ceiling. The weakest of them hit the ground and splattered gore across the room, dying upon impact. The remaining ones ran, limped, or crawled at their new targets.

"Screw this." Rose raised her bow and fired a jar of explosive oil into the crowd. It blasted a hole in the wall of infected, and the battle began.

Tom—laughing—charged into the infected, acting as a battering ram. He used his shield as a mobile wall, and Nick scoffed at what he thought was a suicidal charge. When a large group had gathered to attack him, Tom took a sharp step back and swung his warhammer with a mighty grunt. A wave of death followed the swing. The beings hit directly had large swaths of their bodies blasted into vapor, their bones flying from their still-twitching corpses to act as projectiles.

"*I! Have! Missed this!*" Tom roared, swinging his hammer ever faster.

Nick's eyes were bulging from their sockets.

"He's insane," Nick whispered.

The leader of The Collective looked to the side to see Dale pounding on infected with his—apparently—only cloth covered hands, leaving behind craters in the flesh. An arrow from Rose ripped through everything from her to the wall in a straight line, tearing through bodies and armor like paper. Hans was jauntily strolling along, poking enemies with casual grace and disregard for his own safety.

"They're *all* insane!" affirmed Adam.

Nick looked his way to see him ignoring several infected that appeared to be stabbing him with daggers. "If you don't mind, could you start clearing the area?" Nick shook himself, then threw his power hesitantly into the fight. Nez walked up to Adam and killed the infected near him with efficient strokes from his longsword.

Nez looked over Adam, noting his Mithril-lined robe and nodding. "Good, that'll make it a lot easier to protect you." He settled in, killing any infected that tried to close with Adam.

The Goblins got into a tight group and made their way to the center of the fallen quartz plate. They pushed the infected back, slowly clearing the savages away from the Rune. As soon as I had enough room to work, I began dissolving the bodies and any fluids left behind, leaving a sparklingly clear space for them to apply an even coat of the reagent. I would have done it myself, but the constant attacks from the infected kept throwing aural interference in the area, and I would hate to have to put down a half-formed version of the needed fluid.

Dani left the quartz and began walking toward the tunnel that connected to the room. Taking a deep breath, she forced Essence along her weapons. They began to glow slowly as she built up the Essence to levels that became visible to the naked eye. Her breathing increased in speed, and she laboriously held her form, forcing the Essence to the utmost compression.

With a tortured scream, she released a torrent of holy fire, and it surged down the tunnel. Released from their mortal coil, the infected in the tunnel simply died. They exploded into ash as the heat reached into the multiple *thousands* of degrees.

"Now, Cal! Drop the security door!" Dani wheezed as she collapsed.

I dropped the five-ton chunk of cursed-earth granite, cutting off the only tunnel into the Boss Room. Thank goodness! I had been unable to release the panic doors, cut off by the auras in the area. Infected still jumped down from above, but now there was only one direction for the enemy to appear. For now, at least. In the tunnel, infected were shattering their Centers as they raced into the molten tunnel and had their limbs melt off. Explosion after explosion rocked the corridor, and the rock began to crack.

Adam stepped on to the quartz plate and pulled the huge jar of reagent from his storage bag. With steady hands, he used the built-in nozzle to begin pouring the viscous fluid along the lines of the Inscription. He went at a measured pace, not only because he didn't want to make a mistake but also due to the fact that the fluid left the container oh so very slowly. He bent down to fill a deep portion of the Rune, and Dale used him as a springboard to punch a sprinting infected in the face.

"Done!" Adam shouted, several minutes later.

A ragged cheer reached his ears while he noticed that the Rune wasn't doing anything. "The activation sequence! Where is it?!"

A moment of frantic searching turned up the missing chunk of quartz, and Adam began filling its lines with the remaining fluid. They were moving toward the Rune to place the piece... when a familiar body landed next to the Rune, falling from above. Dozens more fell to the ground from on high.

The area seemed to go still, just for a moment. Dale saw the face contorted by rage and shuddered. The words that left his lips caused the fight to return to its previous intensity.

"Father Richard... no..."

CAL

I was looking in on my other pet, er, minion, uhh... Minya. She seemed to be doing well.

"Fear death not!" she intoned above the raging battle. "Our work empowers our dungeon, and with each death, we will increase our reward in the afterlife!" This was met with sideways glances and muttering,

"With each *enemy* slain, we increase our rewards in *this* life!"

That was the way to get the people motivated, it seemed. A constant flow of valuables. Well, if that was the case...

When a group of infected was cleared enough for me to create things, I rained down an explosion of shining gold coins. The defenders were quiet for a moment, and then all abyss broke out. They redoubled their efforts, and with every explosion of the elements, I followed it with a hail of coin. Chandra whooped at the suddenly vigorous group and spread her hands out over the crowd of flailing attackers.

"Hold on to something!" she screamed in delight.

Thousands of seeds left her outstretched palms, seemingly appearing from nowhere. Thick foliage and intertwined vines grew in front of their fort and the defenses holding the group of Nobles. I was disappointed at first, as she had been preparing to attack for almost half an hour! The infected were trying to attack the barrier but were having little effect on the dense vegetation. Then the *attack* portion of her incantation went off! Thousands of thorny vines sprouted from the seeds in the air, wrapping around anything moving. The infected in the area were suddenly all pinned to something. The floor, each other, themselves. They struggled to escape for a moment, then collectively relaxed, shattering their Centers.

The room shuddered, and the explosion was so loud that any non-Mage was instantly deafened. Chandra laughed as the elemental storm broke against her barrier of flora, then sat down to enjoy the fireworks. I worked overtime to collect all of the Essence that was suddenly in the air and within my grasp. The corruption gathering gemstones threaded throughout my body began sucking at the air, desperately trying to bring the dungeon system back to homeostasis.

The corruption gathered into a thick sludge that, surprisingly, started moving. A *slime* Mob? No. Nope, I want no part in that. Not again. Again? What? I shuddered at the memory of a night a while back, forgotten for some reason. I would think about that later. If I remembered. Um. Remembered what? Huh. That was strange...

A Rune that I had never noticed before shimmered into view and... whatever was on the floor vanished with a plop and bubble as it jiggled and wiggled. Bizarre.

Oh! Right! A huge amount of creatures had just died! I looked at the fort where all the defenders were waiting with bated breath and staring at the now open space. I made a small mental shrug, then created a sheet of gold coins across the entire room! The people cheered with happiness and greed as the coins rattled and clinked. The hailstorm of ringing metal *almost* drowned them out.

Then I noticed that there was a new group entering the room. Even before the cheering died down, one of the infected Mages raised a hand and *squeezed*. The stone wall the defenders were attacking from shattered, spilling people into the open area. On the plus side, they had access to a sea of shimmering gold.

Conversely... well, there was nothing between them and the Mages.

The Mages started forward, moving at high speeds. One allowed himself to fall flat, an inch of space between him and the ground. A gust of wind propelled him forward, and a ringing *boom* trailed his passage, echoing tremendously in the dungeon.

<Interesting! It is possible to move fast enough that you temporarily shatter the air around you?> I was taking meticulous mental notes as the Mages moved since all of them were activating some kind of ability. The humans were not having as fun of a time with this since they were dying. That tended to ruin the mood.

I spoke at Dale and Dani, <In case you wanted to know, the Mages that passed you have reached the third floor and are starting to attack the fort. I need to concentrate down there for a moment.>

Two of the Mages were tearing open small holes in reality, and birdlike creatures—possibly giant, wasp-like creatures, depending on if birds can have stingers—were pouring out of the rippling portals. I was *very* excited by this until one of them was killed and turned out to be merely a Mana construct. No new Mobs for me... I still examined the tears hanging in the air. They had similar qualities to my dimensional bag. These required a bit of Mana constantly, unlike a magical item. Good to know it was possible to create temporary effects without needing an item! I memorized the pattern and watched the fight.

A wave of light passed from one of the infected, the particles amalgamating into a spear of luminous metal. A holy weapon Mage? The spear flew forward, then shattered into thousands of miniature fléchettes, shredding screaming people as they were continuously fired into the fortified area. As the shards of spear struck, they shattered further, and those shards hung in the air, daring anyone to breathe them in. Anyone breathing in the dust-like metal clutched their neck, gasping as blood poured out of their orifices.

The Mage zipping around low to the ground had invisible blades made of air surrounding him. He didn't bother to move his arms or give any signs of attack, simply ramming through bodies. Literally through them. About a foot from where his body touched them, the people would just be violently blended by whirling air. When his flying form impacted the newly-ground corpses, they splattered apart, chunks of bodies falling to the ground.

In the first few seconds, at least forty people died. Then my pet Mages retaliated! Chandra stepped forward, face twisted in a rictus of pure, pissed-off fury. She began chanting, firing thorns that intercepted the fléchettes with ease. Her focus shifted as she devoted a minimal amount of attention to keeping the attack going. Chandra was a terrifyingly powerful Mage, the only currently known A-rank nine cultivator in the Phoenix Kingdom. Splitting her focus was never an issue; Chandra was a master multitasker!

While her specialty was plants, she had powerful earth and water magic to augment her abilities. She popped open a water skin and drew out all of the moisture, compressing the water and infusing it with Mana. With a poke of her finger, the water moved in a thin stream at unimaginable speeds.

The rock wall behind the Mage split in a perfectly straight line. The Mage himself stumbled, then fell into two halves with a grotesque, slapping *splurt* as his entrails slipped out of him. I was watching with fascination. *Water* could cut through not only a body but *stone*? I'm sure that the infusion of Mana helped, but was that something water could do naturally at high compression? This had already been a banner day for information, and the fight was just starting! I remembered at the last second to redirect the Mana into my dimensional storage space. I shuddered; that had been too close!

Amber was speaking in a conversational tone, her words subtly making the air thrum. One of the Mages that was summoning wasp-constructs slumped, and his creatures turned on him. They tore him apart a small chunk at a time, his naturally durable body resisting their efforts. Someone glanced at her, and she shrugged, "I convinced his mind that he was his own worst enemy. He was already programmed to attack his enemies, so..."

Minya was going toe-to-toe with the wind-powered Mage, and she was losing pretty badly. She specialized in elemental magic, and blasts of fire, stone, and water rained down upon the infected Mage. His whirling wind—infused with unhealthy amounts of Mana—redirected even her most well-timed attacks. Minya was working to counteract the wind with her own ability, but the highly specialized wind Mage was able to ignore the majority of her blows as he counterattacked.

Minya's skin began to tear as she was assaulted by atmospheric-speed winds. She tried to leap away, but the wind caught and blasted her into the stone, imprinting her into the solid granite. She began to scream, but even that was torn away as the air rushed into her.

DALE

"Father Richard..." Dale whispered as he slowly raised his fists.

The priest turned bloodshot eyes on the young man. "...Dale. *Runnn*," he moaned, tears forming as a sob ripped out of him. Surprise showed in his eyes as his body moved without his consent, a glowing fist soaring at Dale.

Dale yelped and ducked, pushing up instinctively with his hands. He caught Father Richard's arm at the elbow, surprising himself. Trying to stay ahead of a devastating blow, he gripped the unyielding muscle and twisted. To Dale's surprise, the priest went flying, landing heavily several feet away. The man got back to his feet, totally unaffected.

Father Richard stumbled toward Dale, uncoordinated as he tried to fight the invasive parasite controlling his actions. He threw another wild punch, which Dale dodged again, following up with a one-two combo before putting some distance between them.

"Are you in there, old man?" Dale called at the slightly glowing priest.

The only response was a stumbling charge. Father Richard suddenly stopped, shuddered, and looked at Dale with clouded eyes. His steps now were smoother, and his speed increased dramatically. "Oh, shi–"

Tangg-g-g! Father Richard was now flying backward and impacted the wall hard enough that he stopped moving for a moment as dust rose in a cloud away from the stone. Dale looked in wonder at Tom who had landed a full-power blow on the priest as he was running.

Tom was hopping up and down, shaking his hand. "Ow! Ow!"

"Thanks for the rescue, Tom!" Dale called. He hurried to find a better defended position before Father Richard started moving again.

"**Sonder,**" was all Dale heard before flying into Tom.

"What?!" Dale yelled at Tom to let him go, but no matter how much they tried, they were stuck together.

"I'll distract him!" Hans shouted as they were futilely struggling. He was going full out, a glowing line of plasmatic fire highlighting the edge of his weapons. Every movement was smooth, although it seemed that the wind was favoring him by enhancing his movements to triple their normal speed. Hans reached Father Richard, and his body became a blur.

StabStabStabStabStabStabStabStab.

The priest howled with vexation as his clothes ignited. He took a few swings at Hans, which were easily avoided. Hans kept moving, poking his blade at every weak point possible. During Richard's howl, a blade poked the back of his esophagus, his gums, and the uvula twice. There was no effect. Richard's body was too empowered by the Mana flowing through him.

Richard locked red-stained eyes on Hans and whispered a word that could only be understood as, **"Sonder."** Hans started to be pulled away, so he landed a double kick to Richard's groin. Again, no effect.

"*Really?*" Hans yelped as he was also stuck to Dale. "I've always wanted to know if Mana took care of that issue, but this *isn't* how I wanted to find out."

Tom looked at the two men he was stuck to. "I am uncertain how his magic works. Is there a weakness?"

Hans sighed as he gained his footing, lifting the other two as easily as a backpack. "He has a weird Mana base. Celestial and infernal users often find odd concepts to bind to." He shook his head, rattling Tom a bit. "His magic is based on the bonds between people and how they all interact." He jumped, avoiding a hurled stone slab. "I had no idea he could use it to *physically* bond people together."

"Whatever you say, Hans!" Dale was trying not to get sick as his perspective changed and death missed him by inches. "Just keep going!"

"*Sonder!*"

Hans slammed to the ground, bound by an irresistible force.

"Apparently," Hans wheezed, "he can bind us to more than... just... each other!" He vomited as the pressure affected his inner ear, splattering bile across the two bound to him.

"This is a terrible way to go." Dale snarled, shifting his position as much as he could. He was trying ridiculously hard to keep his face out of the growing puddle of partially digested food as Father Richard stalked toward them.

Whap! An oversized arrow hit Richard, knocking him back a foot. Another hit his face, exploding into flames that blocked the priest's view for a moment. Arrow after arrow impacted, but none had any more effect than simply yelling at him would have. He raised his hand, and Rose flew to him, her forehead binding with his palm. She smacked into it with enough force to cause her a moment of blackout.

Rose came around just as Father Richard raised his hand to strike her. His glowing hand began to descend as Hans screamed.

The priest paused, and Rose went limp. Between them was a glowing ball of Essence. Neither of them could look away, and both were locked in position as the ball of glowing light began to dissipate.

"Chaos Essence!" Hans whooped as he felt a rush of pride for her. Then he only felt terror as Richard began to shake off the effects. Just as the powerful Mage began moving again...

"Done!" Adam screamed, giving the activation Rune a final twist.

CHAPTER TWENTY-NINE

The world seemed to end in a wave of light as a thunderclap of celestial Essence imbued with a special-purpose reagent tore through reality. The light formed a perfect sphere, ignoring any physical material that got in its way. At ground zero, Dale's group was blasted to the wall, damaged and healed almost simultaneously. They remained pressed against the wall as the pressure of flowing Essence stripped away layers of skin. They may have screamed, but there was no sound.

There was no time.

The cure was worse than the disease for the infected, tearing large chunks out of them as the parasite tried to abandon them and flee. Again, there was no time. Thousands of bodies caught in the wave of power simply died, and only a fraction of them was within the dungeon's sphere of influence.

The Mages fighting on the third floor were slammed to the ground, and the deeply ingrained infection nearly tore their bodies to bits. Some of the defenders cried out as unknown sores and spores were eradicated from their system.

As the bodies were forced on to the ground, the light vanished as if it were simply a figment of the imagination. People looked around, their adrenalin pumping as they searched for the next enemy to fight. Almost a full minute passed in silence before a ragged cheer was struck up and joined by nearly all the survivors! Then there was a general scrabbling and rioting as I made another wave of gold wash over the dungeon floor.

I reward those that serve me, even if they do so inadvertently.

My mind turned upon the first floor, watching as Dale and the others, including the remaining Goblins, eased themselves off the ground and stood on shaking legs. They looked around at the destruction that was already beginning to fix itself in amazement. They had survived!

Adam was unconscious. Rose was checking on him as Hans rolled over Father Richard, searching for signs of life.

"He's breathing!"

Dale ran over, seeing the huge tracts of flesh that were torn out of the Mage's body. The wounds seemed to be sealing themselves, and Father Richard glowed with internal celestial light. "Will he make it?!"

Hans shrugged. "Anything that doesn't outright kill a Mage... well, probably won't. He should have a good chance of coming back from this. It may take a while, but he *should* be okay."

Dale whooped, shouting and pumping his fist in the air. Hans smiled at his exuberance. They made Father Richard as comfortable as possible and went to check on Adam.

There was a grim outlook for their friend, though it seemed that Adam was waking up. His eyes fluttered open, and they recoiled when they saw his eyes. What had been the whites were now a shining, corrupted celestial gold. "Huh...? Whazzat?" Adam muttered painfully, tongue swollen in his mouth.

"His affinity channel for celestial Essence..." Hans whispered in awe. "It's *beyond* open. He has a *higher* than one hundred percent affinity for it... His infernal affinity channel was ripped out! Replaced!" Hans looked sick. "I... I don't know what this means for you, Adam. I do know that you are corrupted beyond anyone I have ever seen with celestial Essence."

Nez extracted himself from a crater in the floor. It closed behind him as I noticed the unsightly blemish in my pretty granite. "Ugh..." he moaned as he stretched his back and cracked his neck.

"What? What happened to you?" Hans looked at the man judgmentally.

"He pulled me back down to earth," Adam breathed heavily. "The blast started directly under me. I went through the hole and was continuing up at a speed I didn't know was possible. He appeared and wrapped me in static, which drew me back down safely while he took my momentum. He set about saving me at the cost of doubling the force of his own impact."

"You were conscious for that?" Nez coughed out some rock dust. "It didn't look like you were."

Adam looked at him, puzzled. "I was just repeating you. No one was listening to what you were saying for some reason...?" He looked around, trailing off as the others looked at him oddly.

"You read a piece of his recent history off of his aura." Hans was looking at Adam's eyes with great interest now. "This could be a very useful ability..."

"You could see the truth in a situation!" Rose babbled, patting Adam on the back and helping him up. "You could save hundreds of people who are wrongly convicted or..."

"How do you feel about card games?" Hans interrupted her by swinging an arm around Adam.

Rose glared at Hans. "He has a new ability that he gained by sacrificing his body and saving all of us, and you want to use said ability to *cheat at card games?*"

"No!" Hans indignantly took a step away. "I want *him* to cheat at card games for the both of us!"

Rose looked ready to explode, but Adam put a calming hand out to her. "This is how he tries to come down after a battle, joking in tough situations." He took a shuddering breath. "I'm ruined for cultivation. There is no way I could rank higher than I am with this level of taint. He is trying to keep me calm."

"Then again, this ability may be super *annoying* instead," Hans grumped as he looked around. "Where's the Nick guy?"

<Pff. He ran back to the Basher warren and never left after he saw you all start to fight Father Richard,> I told Dale, whose face darkened.

Nick came out of the stairway just then, grinning broadly and cheering. "You are all amazing!"

"Go downstairs and tell the defenders that it is over," Dale got out through grinding teeth. "You can at least be useful as a *messenger.*"

Nick's face turned red and furious. With shaking hands, he turned around and marched downward.

"Wow, Dale. Where did that come from? That was harsh and uncalled for." Rose crossed her arms and glared at Dale. The others didn't try to defend him either. "What if he had just been blasted into the tunnel? I saw him fighting at the start..."

"No." Dale shook his head. "When he saw Father Richard show up, he slipped away and hid in the Basher warren. He left us to die. I feel no pity for him, and I refuse to rescind my words or apologize."

The others were awkwardly silent as Dale busied himself by picking up Father Richard. They started their trek down to the third floor with the few remaining Goblins trailing along.

CAL

<Oh, come on, Dani! I need you down here to translate for these Elves! They won't leave me alone and keep caressing

the Silverwood tree in a creepy, sexual way.> I shuddered as Jason tickled Brianna with a leaf. <So odd.>

"*Cal, you want me to just drop out of the Amazon and leave this huge amount of Mithril laying around?*" Dani retorted tiredly.

<Well. No, but...>

"*I'll get down to the spawn room and come straight to you,*" Dani assured me. "*I'm sure the Elves will leave soon if no enemies show up.*"

<Fine, but if they try to take the armor...>

"*Their Mana will force them to leave it there before they leave the dungeon.*"

<Well... I just miss you. Hurry down!> I finally admitted to her.

A smile tinged her tired voice. "I'll be there soon," she said aloud.

The group limped into the third floor to see scores of people crawling around on all fours. "What the...?"

"The floor is *gold*, Dale!" Hans shrieked like a teen girl and dove at the floor.

<Well, there are coins all over it.> I was starting to feel embarrassed by that and was making the coins that hadn't been collected vanish slowly.

The group collected coins for half an hour while Dani waited patiently to be let into the fort. <Hey. I'm really close to reaching the B-rankings, and I just had a bit of inspiration! I'm gonna be thinking about foundational effects of primordial energy and how matter and energy are actually the same thing and...>

"Go ahead!" Dani sounded a bit panicked for some reason. "I'll be right down. Then I'm sleeping for a week."

The fort gate opened, and Dale's group—now in more dignified positions—entered. The gold had been cleaned up so I sank into my contemplations, waiting for everyone to leave so that I could repair all the damage.

DALE

Entering the fort, Dale's group was met by cheering, hugs, and sobbing. Rose was intently inspected by Chandra before giving her the okay to go *anywhere* again. Hans and Dale left Father Richard with the healers and joined the gathering. There was to be a small meeting of the council, but all they decided was that they needed to take a few days to recuperate.

Dale looked over to see the Goblins entering the small spawn room and decided to go and thank them before they became enemies again. He walked over, spotting the Amazon removing her helmet. He opened his mouth to offer his gratitude when a spray of blood splashed wetly across his face.

Confused, Dale looked down. He wasn't injured...? He looked up to see the Amazon Goblin slumping as her head rolled away.

"What the abyss are you *doing*?!"

Nick glanced at Dale and scoffed. "What, you expect me to believe that I'm going to have a warm reception here? With *you* in charge?" He ducked down and collected the Mithril helmet. "Do you have any idea what this is *worth*? I won't need to *bother* coming back."

Dale was furious that Nick had killed a Goblin instrumental in their survival. "How are you planning to leave? Did you forget that the portal is closed? You going to walk?"

"No need for that." Nick turned with a sickly grin. He held up a small, enchanted vial. "Emergency portal access. Lets me get where I need to go, as long as I can make it to the portal arch." His eyes flickered past Dale, and an awestruck look crossed his face. He shot forward, and Dale yelled, ducking into a defensive position.

Looking at where the man was currently standing, Dale gasped to see a shining, pink orb trapped in bands of Mana.

"What are you *doing*?" he repeated the words again in the span of a few seconds.

"It's a real Dungeon Wisp!" Nick whispered. "I thought I had imagined it, looking down into the Boss Room weeks ago."

"A Dungeon Wisp?" Dale looked at the orb of swirling light. "Wait. Minya told me that dungeons go insane if they lose their Wisp! You can't take that!"

Nick looked at Dale, sneering mightily. "Like. I. Care." His eyes shone with greed. "The bounty for a Dungeon Wisp... I'll never need to–"

"*Get off my–*" Dale bellowed, all he could get out before a fist impacted his throat.

"Can't be having that now, can we?" Nick *tsked* at him. "Who knows, I may need to come back some day."

"I'm Dani!" a tiny, chiming voice sounded. "Tell Cal that I *will* find a way back! I prom–"

A heavy fist impacted Dale's face, and the world went dark.

CHAPTER THIRTY

Dale woke up with a start. Someone was waving a vile-smelling vial under his olfactory organ. "Gah! No! Never that!"

"Dale," Chandra's calm voice reached him through his sputtering, "what happened?"

"What?" Dale looked around; they were in what remained of the church. A bitterly cold wind was blowing in through the holes in the walls and roof.

Amber stepped forward, eyes flashing. "Do you know who the *abyss* used a *highly* illegal portal jump? People are *dead* from this, and trust in the Portal Guild has plummeted!"

Realization was slowly dawning in Dale's mind, and he threw off his blanket, trying to run out of the room. He was stopped by Frank, who was just entering the room.

"Wow, where is the fire, young man?" Frank queried him, holding him with his unbandaged arm. "Shouldn't you be in bed? You had a nasty head wound."

Dale stopped, knowing that they needed explanations. "The person who used the portal was Nick, leader of The Collective." He started to sink into despair as it dawned on him that he was too late. "Where did he go?" he asked weakly, already sinking into depression.

"We don't know," Amber stated grimly. "That is one of the reasons they are so illegal. That and also if someone is *using* the portal and it is intercepted, they get *cut in half.*"

"That is horrible, but–" Dale was interrupted.

"Damn, right it is!" Amber was about to go on a full tirade when Dale held up a hand.

"I'm sorry, but I have more bad news." He took a breath. "The dungeon's Wisp was taken."

The group looked at him, nonplussed. Chandra broke the silence, "So a collector took a Mob? That isn't uncommon, Dale."

Minya strode into the room, eyes fixed on Dale. "Are you sure?"

Dale nodded. "I was there. That's why he attacked me."

"What is the big deal?" Frank's voice had high notes of nervousness creeping in.

Minya sighed. "This is why my lore is so important, but no one bothers to read it... Frank, when a dungeon loses its bonded Wisp—its Dungeon Wisp—it goes insane. Its influence spreads wildly, and corruption becomes rampant. That is usually when a crusade is called to kill a dungeon."

"The... like the Kantor incident?" Frank shook, gripping the wall for balance. "Is *that* what caused the disaster?"

Minya nodded grimly. Chandra leaned her head against the wall. "This is bad. Should we take preemptive action and kill the dungeon now?"

"We have time, and that needs to be a last resort," Minya hurriedly stated. "If the dungeon dies... so does Dale and so do I."

Amber looked at Dale. "I think it is time we all had that chat we've been looking forward to."

"I think so." Dale nodded and began his story.

CAL

<I think I've got it, Dani! I know *exactly* what I need to do to enter the Mage rankings!> I smiled brilliantly, looking around for my partner. She always had the best reactions to good news!

<Dani?> I cast my mind about, but she wasn't in here. She must be out flying around...? Something felt different. I ached. How strange...? I examined myself and found the issue. There was a rip in my aura! I tried to fix it, but it resisted my tampering. I looked closer. It wasn't so much a tear as a horrendous stretch, extending so far away from me that Essence was leaving but was unable to cycle back to me.

If I remembered correctly, that was the part of my aura bound to... to Dani? <Dani!> I shouted frantically. Maybe she just couldn't hear me? <*Dani!*> I shouted. No response. I flooded my aura with an amount of Essence that I would normally be horrified about wasting.

<*DANI! DANI!!*> I screamed from the bottom of my soul, Essence flooding the world around me.

Weaker beings went through a short period of rapid growth as the massive surge of power flooded their affinity channels, forcing natural evolutions upon their bodies. Those that survived would have interesting changes that even just *yesterday* I would have loved to study. Today, I was a broken soul.

<Dani! Dani...> I broke off, sobbing. <...Dani...>

"Cal," a pained voice broke through my weeping.

<Dale! Dale, Dani is missing! You need to help me!> I latched on to his voice like a lifeline. Dale had legs! He could go find her! <She must have flown too far away and gotten trapped. She's likely weak from loss of Essence, you have to->

"*Cal*," Dale called firmly, cutting off my babbling. "I'm *so* sorry. I'm going to do everything that I possibly can to get her back for you."

My dread shifted into suspicion. <Dale. What do you know?>

"Cal, we are–"

<*What do you know?*> I screamed at him, and the room jumped ten degrees as fire Essence flooded the room.

He paused, stunned by my anger directly assaulting his brain. "Cal... Dani was taken. By Nick, the leader of The Collective. He ran and teleported away before we could stop him. She talked to me. She said she would find a way back to you, no matter what."

I stared at him, and even though I didn't have actual eyes, I could project a mental image of myself into his mind. <She was taken? You didn't *stop him?*>

"Cal, I tried, he..." Dale petered off as the air began to fill with corruption. The light shifted from a soft blue to an undulating, patterned red.

My voice was the barest of whispers as I turned to my work, <I. Am going. To kill. You. All.> I had so much to do. There was no time.

No time like the present.

I shifted my attention away just as someone else entered the dungeon.

"How did it go?"

Dale let out a heavy sigh and a few tears. He gulped, trying to clear his voice. "You were right, Minya. He... he's already drifting into Dungeon Madness."

EPILOGUE

Nick swallowed dryly as he was led into the musty castle. He would have been feeling far more confident if his escort hadn't been an infernal-Essence-radiating demon. Nick yelped as the creature spoke, its terror-inducing voice echoing. "The Master approaches. I would offer you a seat, but I would *highly* recommend kneeling."

Nick had to resist scoffing at the demon. He turned as it spoke, realizing it was gone. "Kneeling? Pah." He shivered as an aura of dread washed over him, far greater than the feeling had been from the demon. He turned and had to resist a scream as he saw a person standing near a wall. There were no doors nearby, so Nick had no idea where he had come from.

"Is a little *respect* too much to ask for?" a melodious yet rasping voice buzzed in his ear. Nick swatted at his head; the sensation was maddening.

"N-not at all, m-my Lord." Nick genuflected a bit late but deeply. "Demons... have a reputation for misleading information."

"Hmm." The dark figure strode forward, and Nick's skin began to itch horribly. "I am told you are here to claim the bounty that I was offering. Is this so? If so, you will certainly get what is coming to you."

Nick reached into his bag, pulling out a glowing ball of Essence wrapped in bands of undulating power. His cocky attitude began to return to him as he realized he had something the 'Master' wanted. "Right here. It's all yours... if you have the funds, of course."

A burning stare made his attitude wither again. The Master made a motion, and they were surrounded by a sphere of smothering darkness. Somehow, Nick could still see perfectly without any natural light.

"Release the creature. If it is what you promised, you will get your reward."

Nick wanted to refuse, but he got a little too close to the wall of darkness and had bits of his skin flake off. "If it gets away, I'm still claiming my..." He found himself unable to finish his sentence and so instead broke the bands of power, allowing the ball of light to shoot away at high speeds. Nick gave a hoarse cry, but the ball of light impacted the darkness and fell, catching itself just before reaching the floor.

"Ow! Let me go, you *assholes*!" Dani screamed at the pair. "You have no idea what is going to happen if you don't!"

Nick's face twisted into a snarl, but the Master smiled. The smile was a terrifying expression that seemed to have no place on his face. "Ahhh, finally! Hello, little Wisp."

"Let me go!"

The Master gave a slow shake of the head. "I am truly sorry, little one, but I have need of your services. Also, you are mistaken. I know *exactly* what is about to happen."

Dani vanished in a burst of shadows.

"Satisfied?" Nick had his arms crossed and a grin on his face. "Now, about that bounty? I'd like to go retire."

"You *certainly* deserve your reward." The Master turned away. "Enjoy your retirement." He turned around and threw something at Nick, impacting him in the chest.

Nick's hands flew up, grabbing at the object. He gasped, looking down as he sank to his knees. "I... this..." He made a throaty noise.

Nick looked up at the Master for the last time. "This is even more than was promised! Thank you!" He turned and scurried away, clutching the dimensional bag stuffed with gold, platinum, and silver. "I'm buying an island!"

The Master nodded as the man left. "Those who serve shall be duly rewarded."

Afterword

Thank you for reading! I hope you enjoyed Dungeon Madness! Since reviews are the lifeblood of indie publishing, I'd love it if you could leave a positive review on Amazon! Please use this link to go to the Divine Dungeon: Dungeon Madness Amazon product page to leave your review: geni.us/DungeonMadness.

As always, thank you for your support! You are the reason I'm able to bring these stories to life.

The Divine Dungeon Universe

The Divine Dungeon

Dungeon Born (Book 1)

Dungeon Madness (Book 2)

Dungeon Calamity (Book 3)

Dungeon Desolation (Book 4)

Dungeon Eternium (Book 5)

The Completionist Chronicles

Ritualist (Book 1)

Regicide (Book 2)

Rexus (Book 2.5)

Raze (Book 3)

ABOUT DAKOTA KROUT

I live in a 'pretty much Canada' Minnesota city with my wife and daughter. I started writing The Divine Dungeon series because I enjoy reading and wanted to create a world all my own. To my surprise and great pleasure, I found like-minded people who enjoy the contents of my mind. Publishing my stories has been an incredible blessing thus far, and I hope to keep you entertained for years to come!

Connect with Dakota:
Patreon.com/DakotaKrout
Facebook.com/TheDivineDungeon
Twitter.com/DakotaKrout

ABOUT MOUNTAINDALE PRESS

Dakota and Danielle Krout, a husband and wife team, strive to create as well as publish excellent fantasy and science fiction novels. Self-publishing *The Divine Dungeon: Dungeon Born* in 2016 transformed their careers from Dakota's military and programming background and Danielle's Ph.D. in pharmacology to President and CEO, respectively, of a small press. Their goal is to share their success with other authors and provide captivating fiction to readers with the purpose of solidifying Mountaindale Press as the place 'Where Fantasy Transforms Reality'.

Connect with Mountaindale Press:
MountaindalePress.com
Facebook.com/MountaindalePress
Twitter.com/_Mountaindale
Instagram.com/MountaindalePress
Krout@MountaindalePress.com

MOUNTAINDALE PRESS TITLES

GAMELIT AND LITRPG

The Completionist Chronicles Series
By: DAKOTA KROUT

A Touch of Power Series
By: JAY BOYCE

Red Mage: Advent
By: XANDER BOYCE

Ether Collapse: Equalize
By: RYAN DEBRUYN

Axe Druid Series
By: CHRISTOPHER JOHNS

Skeleton in Space: Histaff
By: ANDRIES LOUWS

Pixel Dust: Party Hard
By: DAVID PETRIE

APPENDIX

Adam – A mid-D-ranked cleric who joined Dale's group. He was corrupted by a massive influx of celestial Essence, which may have given him powerful abilities.

Adventurers' Guild – A group from every nonhostile race that actively seeks treasure and cultivates to become stronger. They act as a mercenary group for Kingdoms that come under attack from monsters and other non-kingdom forces.

Affinity – A person's affinity denotes what element they need to cultivate Essence from. If they have multiple affinities, they need to cultivate all of those elements at the same time.

Affinity Channel – The pathway along the meridians that Essence flows through. Having multiple major affinities will open more pathways, allowing more Essence to flow into a person's center at one time.

Amber – The Mage in charge of the portal-making group near the dungeon. She is in the upper A rankings, which allows her to tap vast amounts of Mana.

Artificer – A person who devotes himself to creating powerful artifacts, either by enchanting or Inscribing them.
Assassin – A stealthy killer who tries to make kills without being detected by his victim.

Assimilator – A cross between a jellyfish and a Wisp, the Assimilator can float around and collect vast amounts of Essence.

It releases this Essence as powerful elemental bursts. A pseudo-Mage, if you will.

Aura – The flows of Essence generated by living creatures which surround them and hold their pattern.

Bane – An F-ranked Boss Mob that is a giant mushroom. He can fire thorns and pull victims toward him with vines made of moss.

Basher – An evolved rabbit that attacks by head-butting enemies. Each has a small horn on its head that it can use to bash enemies.

Beast Core – A small gem that contains the Essence of Beasts.

> Flawed: An extremely weak crystallization of Essence that barely allows a Beast to cultivate, comparable to low F-rank.

> Weak: A weak crystallization of Essence that allows a Beast to cultivate, comparable to an upper F-rank.

> Standard: A crystallization of Essence that allows a Beast to cultivate well, comparable to the D-rankings.

> Strong: A crystallization of Essence that allows a Beast to cultivate very well, comparable to the lower C-rankings.

> Beastly: A crystallization of Essence that allows a Beast to cultivate exceedingly well, comparable to the upper C-rankings.

Immaculate: An amalgamation of crystallized of Essence and Mana that allows a Beast to cultivate exceedingly well. Any Beast in the B-rankings or A-rankings will have this Core.

Luminous: A Core of pure spiritual Essence that is indestructible by normal means. A Beast with this core will be in at least the S-rankings and up to SSS-rank.

Radiant: A Core of Heavenly or Godly energies. A Beast with this Core is able to adjust reality on a whim.

Brianna – A Dark Elf princess that intends to build a city around the dungeon. She is a member of the council and knows that the dungeon is alive and sentient.

Cal – The heart of the Dungeon, Cal was a human murdered by Necromancers. After being forced into a soul gem, his identity was stripped as time passed. Now accompanied by Dani, he works to become stronger without attracting too much attention to himself. This may soon change.

Cats, Dungeon – There are several types:

Snowball: A Boss Mob, Snowball uses steam Essence to fuel his devastating attacks.

Cloud Cat: A Mob that glides along the air, attacking from positions of stealth.

Coiled Cat: A heavy Cat that uses metal Essence. It has a reinforced skeleton and can launch itself forward at high speeds.

Flesh Cat: This Cat uses flesh Essence to tear apart tissue from a short distance. The abilities of this Cat only work on flesh and veins and will not affect bone or harder materials.

Wither Cat: A Cat full of infernal Essence, the Wither Cat can induce a restriction of Essence flow with its attacks. Cutting off the flow of Essence or Mana will quickly leave the victim in a helpless state. The process is *quite* painful.

Catalyst – An item that allows an Inscription to be powered with less Essence.

Celestial – The Essence of Heaven, the embodiment of life and *considered* the ultimate good.

Center – The very center of a person's soul. This is the area Essence accumulates (in creatures that do not have a Core) before it binds to the lifeforce.

Chandra – Owner of an extremely well-appointed restaurant, this A-ranked Mage is the grandmother of Rose. She also spent a decade training the current Guild Master, Frank.

Chi spiral – A person's Chi spiral is a vast amount of intricately knotted Essence. The more complex and complete the pattern woven into it, the more Essence it can hold and the finer the Essence would be refined.

Cleric – A Cultivator of celestial Essence, a cleric tends to be support for a group, rarely fighting directly. Their main purpose in the lower rankings is to heal and comfort others.

Corruption – Corruption is the remnant of the matter that pure Essence was formed into. It taints Essence but allows beings to absorb it through open affinity channels. This taint has been argued about for centuries; is it the source of life or a nasty side effect?

Craig – A powerful C-ranked monk, Craig has dedicated his life to finding the secrets of Essence and passing on knowledge.

Currency values:
    Copper: one hundred copper coins are worth a silver coin
    Silver: one hundred silver coins are worth a gold coin
    Gold: one hundred gold coins were worth a platinum coin
    Platinum: the highest coin currency in the human kingdoms

Cultivate – Cultivating is the process of refining Essence by removing corruption, then cycling the purified Essence into the center of the soul.

Cultivator – A cultivator is one who cultivates. See above. Seriously, it is the entry right before this one. I'm being all alphabetical here. Mostly.

Dale – Owner of the mountain the dungeon was found on, Dale is now a cultivator who attempts to not die on a regular basis. As a dungeon born person, he has a connection to the dungeon that he can never be rid of.

Dani – A *pink* Dungeon Wisp—is that important?—Dani is the soulbound companion of Dale and acts as his moral compass and helper. She is also an integral portion of his psyche, and losing her would drive Cal into madness.

Dire – A prefix to a title that means "Way stronger than a normal version of this monster". Roughly. Kind of paraphrasing.

Distortion Cat – An upper C-ranked Beast that can bend light and create artificial darkness. In its home territory, it is attacked and bound by tentacle-like parasites that form a symbiotic relationship with it.

Dungeon Born – Being dungeon born means that the Dungeon did not create the creature but gave it life. This gives the creature the ability to function autonomously, without fear that the dungeon will be able to take direct control of its mind. The dungeon can "ride along" in a dungeon born creature's mind from any distance and may be able to influence the creature if it remains of a lower cultivation rank than the Dungeon.

Dwarves – Stocky humanoids that like to work with stone, metal, and alcohol. Good miners.

Elves – A race of willowy humanoids with pointy ears. There are five main types:

High Elves: The largest nation of Elvenkind, they spend most of their time as merchants, artists, or thinkers. Rich beyond any need to actually work, their King is an S-ranked expert, and their cities shine with light and wealth. They like to think of themselves as 'above' other Elves, thus 'High' Elves.

Wood Elves: Wood Elves live more simply than High-Elves, but have a greater connection to the earth and the elements. They are ruled by a council of S-ranked elders and rarely leave their woods. Though seen less often, they have great power. They grow and collect food and animal products for themselves and other Elven nations.

Wild: Wild Elves are the outcasts of their societies. Basically feral, they scorn society and civilization and the rules of others. They have the worst reputation of any of the races of Elves, practicing dark arts and infernal summoning. They have no homeland, living only where they can get away with their dark deeds.

Dark: The Drow are known as Dark Elves. No one knows where they live, only where they can go to get in contact with them. Dark Elves also have a dark reputation as assassins and mercenaries for the other races. The worst of their lot are 'Moon-Elves', the best-known assassins of any race. These are the Elves that Dale made a deal with for land and protection.

Sea: The Sea Elves live on boats their entire lives. They facilitate trade between all the races of Elves and man, trying not to take sides in conflicts. They work for themselves and are considered rather mysterious.

Enchantment – A *temporary* pattern made of Essence that creates an effect on the universe. Try not to get the pattern wrong, as it could have... unintended consequences.

Essence – Essence is the fundamental energy of the universe, the pure power of heavens and earth that is used by the basic elements to become all forms of matter.

Father Richard – An A-ranked cleric that has made his living hunting demons and heretics. Tends to play fast and loose with rules and money.

Fighter – A generic archetype of a being who uses melee weapons to fight.

Frank – Guild Leader of the Adventurers' Guild. He has his Mana bound to the concept of kinetic energy and can **stop** the use of it, slowing or stopping others in place.

Glade – A Mini-Boss mushroom that uses tentacles and thorns to kill its prey.

Glitterflit – A Basher upgraded with celestial Essence, it has the ability to *mend* almost any non-fatal wound.

Hans – A cheeky assassin that has been with Dale since he began cultivating. He was a thief in his youth but changed lifestyles after his street guild was wiped out. He is deadly with a knife and is Dale's best friend.

Incantation – Essentially a spell, an incantation is created from words and gestures. It releases all of the power of an enchantment in a single burst.

Infected – A person or creature that has been infected with a rage-inducing mushroom growth. These people have no control of their bodies and attack any non-infected on sight.

Infernal – The Essence of death and demonic beings, *considered* to be always evil.

Inscription – A *permanent* pattern made of Essence that creates an effect on the universe. Try not to get the pattern wrong, as it could have... unintended consequences. This is another name for an incomplete or unknown Rune.

James – An uppity portal Mage who may have learned the error of his ways. We shall see.

Josh – A massive shield wielding human, Josh is very strong and sturdy. He is always there to protect his friends as best he is able.

Mages' Guild – A secretive sub-sect of the Adventurers' Guild only Mage level cultivators are allowed to join.

Mana – A higher stage of Essence only able to be cultivated by those who have broken into at least the B-rankings and found the true name of something in the universe.

Meridians – Meridians are energy channels that transport life energy (Chi/Essence) throughout the body.

Mob – A shortened version of "dungeon monster".

Necromancer – An infernal Essence cultivator who can raise and control the dead and demons.

Nick – Leader of 'The Collective', Nick is a C-ranked human that is only interested in gaining money at any cost.

Noble rankings:

> King/Queen – Ruler of their country. (Addressed as 'Your Majesty')
>
> Crown Prince/Princess – Next in line to the throne, has the same political power as a Grand Duke. (Addressed as 'Your Royal Highness')
>
> Prince/Princess – Child of the King/Queen, has the same political power as a Duke. (Addressed as 'Your Highness')
>
> Grand Duke – Ruler of a grand duchy and is senior to a Duke. (Addressed as "Your Grace")
>
> Duke – Senior to a Marquis or Marquess. (Addressed as "Your Grace")
>
> Marquis (or marquess) – Senior to an Earl and has at least three Earls in their domain. (Addressed as 'Honorable')

Earl – Senior to a Baron. Each Earl has three barons under their power. (Addressed as 'My Lord/Lady')

Baron – Senior to knights, they control a minimum of ten knights and, therefore, their land. (Addressed as 'My Lord/Lady')

Knights – Sub-rulers of plots of land and peasants. (Addressed as 'Sir')

Oppressor — A Basher upgraded with wind Essence, it has the ability to compress air and send it forward in an arc that slices unprotected flesh like a blade.

Pattern – A pattern is the intricate design that makes everything in the universe. An inanimate object has a far less complex pattern that a living being.

Raile – A massive, granite covered Boss Basher that attacks by ramming and attempting to squish its opponents.

Ranger – Typically an adventurer archetype that is able to attack from long range, usually with a bow.

Ranking System – The ranking system is a way to classify how powerful a creature has become through fighting and cultivation.

G – At the lowest ranking is mostly non-organic matter, such as rocks and ash. Mid-G contains small plants such as moss and mushrooms, while the upper ranks form most of the other flora in the world.

F – The F-ranks are where beings are becoming actually sentient, able to gather their own food and make short-term plans. The mid-F ranks are where most humans reach, before adulthood, without cultivating. This is known as the fishy or "failure" rank.

E – The E-rank is known as the "echo" rank, and is used to prepare a body for intense cultivation.

D– This is the rank where a cultivator starts to become actually dangerous. A D-ranked individual can usually fight off ten F-ranked beings without issue. They are characterized by a "fractal" in their Chi spiral.

C – The highest-ranked Essence cultivators, those in the C-rank usually have opened all of their meridians. A C-ranked cultivator can usually fight off ten D-ranked and one hundred F-ranked beings without being overwhelmed.

B – This is the first rank of Mana cultivators, known as Mages. They convert Essence into Mana through a nuanced refining process and release it through a true name of the universe.

A – Usually several hundred years are needed to attain this rank, known as High Mage or High Magous. They are the most powerful rank of Mages.

S – Very mysterious spiritual Essence cultivators. Not much is known about the requirements for this rank or those above it.

SS – Not much is known about the requirements for this rank or those above it.

SSS – Not much is known about the requirements for this rank or those above it.

Heavenly – Not much is known about the requirements for this rank or those above it.

Godly – Not much is known about the requirements for this rank or those above it.

Reagent – An item or potion that creates a specific effect when added to an inactive Inscription.

Rose – A Half-Elf ranger that joined Dale's team. She has opposing affinities for celestial and infernal Essence, making her a chaos cultivator.

Rune – A *permanent* pattern made of Essence that creates an effect on the universe. Try not to get the pattern wrong, as it could have... unintended consequences. This is another name for a completed Inscription.

Impaler – A Basher upgraded with Infernal Essence, it has a sharpened horn on its head. At higher rankings, it gains the ability to coat that horn with hellfire.

Shroomish – A mushroom that has been evolved into a barely dangerous Mob. Really, only being completely unaware of them would pose danger to a person.

Silverwood tree – A mysterious tree that has silver wood and leaves. Some say that it helps cultivators move into the B-rankings.

Smasher — A Basher upgraded with earth Essence, it has no special abilities but is coated with thick armor made from stone. While the armor slows it, it also makes the Smasher a deadly battering ram.

Soul Stone – A *highly* refined Beast Core that is capable of containing a human soul.

Steve – A ranger that uses his bow as either a staff or a ranged weapon. Rather quiet chap.

Tank – An adventurer archetype that is built to defend his team from the worst of the attacks that come their way. Heavily armored and usually carrying a large shield, these powerful people are needed if a group plans on surviving more than one attack.

Tom – A huge, red-haired barbarian prince from the northern wastes, he wields a powerful warhammer and has joined Dale's team. He is only half as handy to have around right now.

Made in United States
Troutdale, OR
08/15/2023

12107269R00257